Jean Weso is a child of the sixties. He was born after an encounter between a Swedish woman and a Danish man. He grew up in Copenhagen and Paris with his identical twin brother Christian. After many years working as an editor and journalist, he has turned to crime almost full time. Since 2009 he has lived in amazing Amsterdam with his Capetonian wife Ingrid, who happens to have an identical twin sister.

Author website:	jeanweso.com
Social media:	jeanweso
Cover design:	Jens Sorensen

Also by Jean Weso

Amsterdam Sniper
Amsterdam Strangler
Amsterdam Stalker

LUST, LIES, LIQUOR & LOVE

JEAN WESO

First published in 2022 by JAWS MEDIA

Visit the author website at www.jeanweso.com
Follow the author on facebook.com/jeanweso and twitter.com/jeanweso

Cover design by Jens Sorensen

Typeset in Adobe Garamond Pro
Printed by Books & Catalogues Ltd
First Printing: July 2022

ISBN 978-94-92962-11-9 (Paperback)
ISBN 978-94-92962-12-6 (Kindle)

We'll always have Paris

In memory of my father, Flemming Sorensen

1931 - 2020

Acknowledgement

A special thanks to Jerry Fielder, Andrew Smock, and Johan de Villiers for their patient guidance, enthusiastic encouragement, and helpful critique.

I give a thumbs-up to my editor Sally Stone for her commitment to make some sense of it all and to dot the i's and cross the t's.

I humbly thank my fellow writers for inspiring me with their books and everyone else for their personal and professional guidance and advice.

I kneel in gratitude before God for giving me a bit of talent, the confidence to believe in my passion, and the courage to pursue my dreams.

And last, but by no means least, I bow my semi-bald head in gratitude to my wife Ingrid for her love and constant support.

AMSTERDAM
1974

1

THE DOORBELL'S persistent ring woke him. It took him a few seconds to realise that he was in his living room. He cursed and rolled off the couch, where he'd spent the night fully dressed. He retrieved his Dr Martens from under the coffee table. The bell gave another hostile ring as he laced them up.

Heading for the tiny hallway, he rubbed a hand over his chin and ran his fingers through his thick brown hair. A razor and a comb would have a field day. Looking through the tinted pane of glass in the door to the staircase, he saw the contours of a woman. He tucked his rumpled shirt into his trousers and adjusted his tie.

She tormented his bell for a third time.

"Take it easy, sister," he said under his breath and pulled the door open a little more aggressively than he'd intended.

In front of him stood a clone of Raquel Welch, with a bit of Jacqueline Bisset and Jane Seymour thrown in for good measure.

He wanted to say something, but only managed to pant, as he drowned in her big, innocent, emerald eyes.

"Are you Lex Spijker?" she asked in a deep and resonant voice.

BEING DRAGGED out of bed (or in this case off the couch) with a hangover the size of a zeppelin, he wasn't in the mood or condition to receive visitors, let alone any potential clients (drop-dead gorgeous or otherwise). Lex blamed his disposition this Sunday morning in mid-June on several factors. The previous evening, he'd gone to his local watering hole to watch Holland play the first game in the 1974 FIFA World Cup. He'd promised himself to go easy on the liquor, not only for his well-being but also for the welfare of his impoverished wallet.

When Bart, the bartender, announced that he'd reduce the price of drinks by half with every Dutch goal, Lex's feeble backbone wasn't helped much, although his wallet was. To acknowledge Bart's generosity, J.C. (Johan Cruijff, not Jesus Christ) and his apostles scored the first goal seven minutes into the game. Then they added another one early in the second-half. With the price of booze reduced by 75 percent, Lex's original plans for a reasonably sober night had as much chance of survival as a white mouse in a snake terrarium. Bart showed him the door at around two-thirty, and Lex crawled home. Fortunately, he lived in the same building as his local pub, the Café de Monico on Rembrandtplein, and only had to make it up the stairs to the second floor.

LEX MADE a mental note of her alluring figure, well-formed buttocks, and long dark hair as he led her into the small office. She carried herself with a certain haughtiness and her tight, short, backless, red dress triggered his sordid and booze-impaired imagination.

"Have a seat, Mrs ...?" he said and pointed towards an old brown Chesterfield chair (inherited from his father) in the corner.

"Didn't I give you my name?" She lowered a red and white plaid handbag to the worn wooden floor, then delicately placed her shapely posterior in the chair. She kept her suntanned knees glued together. "When I'm nervous, I seem to forget my manners."

"Are you? Do you?"

"My name is Lure de Lang."

"How can I be of service, Mrs de Lang?" *What can be urgent enough to disturb me on a Sunday morning?* Lex thought.

"It's Miss, and my friends call me Lure."

"Are we friends, Miss de Lang?" Lex walked past her to his desk and dumped his tired body into the office chair (another leftover from his old man). He tilted it backwards, but stopped himself from putting his feet on the desk. "How do you know about me?"

"I saw your advertisement in *de Telegraaf.* The one that says: 'If you need to know, contact Private Detective Lex Spijker'."

"And what is that?"

"I'm sorry, Mr Spijker. You seem to talk in ..."

"I mean, what is it that you need to know?"

"It's a bit delicate, so first, I need to know if I can trust you," she said, suddenly sounding as strung up as an archer's bow. To Lex, it seemed a bit contrived. He offered her a cigarette from his pack of Player's Navy Cut to ease the tension (if that's what it was). She fished one out with her long, manicured fingers. The blood-red nail polish looked freshly applied.

Lex lit the cigarette for her with a hand as steady as a kite in a gale and wished she'd given him time to repair last night's damage. He pushed the overflowing ashtray towards her. "Can I offer you something to drink?"

"Coffee is always nice."

"Will Nescafé do?"

"Fine, but not too strong."

Heading to the tiny kitchen adjacent to the office, Lex thought of asking her if she wanted it spiked with his friend Johnnie Walker. Being uncertain if she was that kind of gal, he didn't.

Lex put the kettle on the stove. As he waited for the water to boil, he dumped a level teaspoonful of Nescafé into one mug and two into another. "Milk or sugar?" he shouted through the open door to the office.

"Black is fine, thanks," she responded.

Good answer, he thought, as he had neither. Lex filled her mug and stirred, then filled his own, leaving enough room for the medicine. He grabbed the whisky bottle from the cupboard, unscrewed the top as quietly as possible, and then added a healthy dose—Johnnie to the rescue.

When he returned, she was standing by the window, showing off her gorgeous long mane and her well-shaped *derrière*. She made no effort to turn around as he squeezed past her towards the desk chair. She smelled like the Keukenhof gardens with the tulips in full bloom—an exotic fragrance.

He put the mugs on the desk.

"Can I also have some whisky in mine?" she asked as she turned towards him. An indulgent smile played on her pretty face as she flashed a perfect set of teeth.

She's a perceptive one, he thought. Lex opened the bottom drawer of the desk and took out his backup bottle. "Why not? If you take a sip of the coffee, I can accommodate you."

She pursed her luscious red lips, blew on the hot liquid, and followed his instructions. She held the mug towards him as Lex held up the bottle.

"Say when."

"When," she said almost immediately.

He returned the bottle to the drawer, pushed it closed with his foot, and they both sat down. As she took another sip, he studied her pretty face again.

She had the most attractive slim nose with a protruding tip at the end and a dent in the nose bridge. Her cheekbones sat nice and high, and she seemed to have a tiny scar under her perfectly rounded chin, which somehow enhanced her beauty.

Lex wondered why beautiful girls, apart from making him tense, always made him believe in angels and the good of humankind.

"I've decided to trust you," she said.

"How gracious. I'm all ears." Lex took a notepad and a pen from the top drawer of the desk, lit a cigarette, and then looked into her big, innocent, almond-shaped eyes. The emerald had become sapphire.

Stalling for time, or maybe for courage, she took a sip of her spiked coffee. Then another. She put the mug on the desk and stubbed out the cigarette in the ashtray.

"I'm still here," Lex said, letting his impatience show.

"It's a delicate matter," she said for the second time.

"Look, Miss de Lang ..."

"Lure," she insisted.

"Pretend I'm a priest, psychologist, or bartender."

"A man is stalking me." The revelation left her mouth slightly ajar. The tip of her tongue travelled along her lower lip.

He felt disappointed, as he'd expected something a little juicier. "Someone, you know?"

"No."

"Have you any idea why?"

"No."

"Could it be a scorned lover or someone you're trying to get away from?"

"No."

"You sound mighty certain."

"Because I am," she said as she caressed the scar under her chin with the tip of her right-hand index finger.

"In what way are you being stalked?"

"He calls me on the telephone."

"What does he say?"

"I have no wish to repeat it, but it's all of a sexual nature."

"Hardcore?"

"It's not for children."

"How about changing your number?"

"I did consider it, but the calls are no longer what bothers me."

Lex waited for her to talk it out.

"The last week or so, I've noticed a man watching my house from across the street."

"When?"

"Most evenings."

"So, you know what he looks like?"

"More or less. The guy hides in the shadows. But I can see that he's medium height, clean-shaven, and has short, light brown hair."

"How do you know if it's the same guy?"

"I'm not sure I know what you mean?"

"How do you know if it's the same guy calling on the telephone?"

"I assumed so. I do hope there's only one."

"Have you confronted him?"

"No. I'm too scared. That's why I've come to you."

"Where do you live?"

"Utrechtsedwarsstraat."

He wrote it down. "What is the house number?"

"69."

He wrote that down too. "Have you reported it to the police?"

"They're not interested in protecting women from being harassed. There are too many male pigs among them."

"Uh-huh."

"That's why I've come to you," she repeated. "Could you come to my home this evening and confront him if he turns up?" she said. Again she caressed the scar under her chin, and Lex wondered if it was something she did when feeling nervous or not telling the truth.

Lex hesitated. A voice in the back of his hungover skull told him not to get involved. Somehow, the story seemed too constructed, too calculated. Miss de Lang seemed oddly detached, as if she was talking about someone else. It could be a way of protecting herself, but he doubted it.

She probably sensed him second-guessing her and his hesitation as she repeated her plea.

"I'm not right for the job. There are better agencies for dealing with protection," Lex said.

"I'll pay you handsomely. Name your price."

"My fixed price for a day's work is 100 guilders plus 25 guilders to cover expenses. But that would be a waste of my time and your money."

Her cheeks flushed, and he sensed that she was not used to being turned down.

"I'm disappointed in you, Mr Spijker, but I'm not going to beg," she said, displaying some genuine emotion for the first time. She grabbed her bag, stood up, and headed for the door. "There's no need to show me out."

Lex didn't move as this gorgeous creature disappeared from his insignificant life. Or at least, so he thought.

2

LEX HAD a single girl in his single bed. Although her face was a blank canvas, her long dark hair, small firm breasts, and gorgeous body were the hallmarks of Miss Lure de Lang. He slid a hand between her suntanned legs, and it felt as though he had dipped it in a bucket of lukewarm water. He withdrew the hand and held it up. It was soaked in blood.

His scream woke him, and he opened his eyes. The early summer morning light_streamed towards him through the Venetian blinds. There was no girl and no blood—only Lex drenched in sweat. According to the Bosch Flip alarm clock on the floor, it was five minutes to five.

Lex rolled out of bed and walked through the hall (the size of a phone booth) to the toilet (the size of a closet). He relieved himself and then headed to the kitchen to put the kettle on. While waiting for the water to boil, Lex fetched his cigarettes from the living room. He lit one and returned to the kitchen to make a cup of instant coffee. He avoided calling upon the healing powers of Johnnie Walker—his backbone might be feeble, but his parents did raise him with certain standards.

Lex carried the mug to the office. It was self-evident from the distressing dream that his encounter with Lure de Lang had gotten to him. After she had walked out of his office the previous day, he had tried hard to forget about her. *It shouldn't be that difficult*, he thought. After all, he knew hardly anything about her, and they'd only shared a common space for about half an hour.

It hardly surprised him that her delicate and captivating beauty had physically drawn him, but what seemed to be an irrational intoxication didn't make sense. Although she was gorgeous, she wasn't the first lovely female creature he'd run into. Lex wondered if her resemblance to his deceased fiancée had triggered something deeper. He also wondered if he'd dismissed her plea for help too easily. Turning down potential work was a luxury he could ill afford, and paying the rent and the salary of his part-time secretary should have provided enough motivation to accept almost any paid assignment that came his way.

After some consideration, he decided to get on his Vespa scooter and ride, like a knight in shining armour, to her rescue. As if to confirm his decision, he spotted the notepad in front of him with her address.

HE PUT on a clean white shirt and the same black trousers he'd worn the day before. He found his thin black tie tossed over the back of a chair in the living room. Lex put it on as he walked into the office. Within a couple of minutes, he heard a key in the front door and then a creak as it opened. He checked the time on his Omega Seamaster—it was almost nine.

"Lex, are you in?" said the affectionate voice of his part-time secretary.

He'd met Roos Mertens in the autumn of the previous year when he'd located a missing girl in the Red Light District. The girl (mostly to spite her parents) had wasted her talent, youth, and beauty on horny buggers. Her *souteneur* was reluctant to see his prime earner leave the fold, but they found a compromise with help from the experienced Roos, a seasoned worker in de Wallen (as the district is known locally). It had put Roos in a tight spot, but being almost fifty, she was ready for new challenges. Since Lex wanted to hire a part-time secretary, they had come to an arrangement.

They saw eye to eye when she was in her boots and Lex in his socks. She was a bottle blond with a big nose and a big bust. Too many late nights in the hustler business had challenged her once-good looks, but an engaging smile, which she gave away freely and abundantly, made up for it.

In general, she didn't talk much about her past, and early on, she made it clear that Lex could keep his investigations to his clients. He did know that she was a real Amsterdammer, that she'd never taken vows of marriage or added to Mother Earth's population.

Lex heard the sound of eager paws on the old wooden floor. Roos' pug Hercules darted into the office and bounded towards him. Lex pushed the chair away from the desk and bent down to pet his small head. The dog snorted happily and presented the tip of his rosy tongue, while his stump of a tail wagged his whole body.

"Attaboy!" Lex said. It wasn't very original, but it seemed the best thing Hercules had ever heard.

"Hope you didn't work too hard this weekend." A pair of red boots appeared in the doorway.

Lex raised his head, and his gaze followed a pair of long legs in tight jeans towards a colourful blouse with a red floral design. He returned the smile Roos sent him.

"I guess you, as usual, forgot about breakfast," she said, pushing a white Hartog's Volkoren paper bag towards him. The aroma of fresh bread reminded him that he had indeed skipped breakfast.

LEX WATCHED Roos take another bite of her cheese sandwich. She was in an uncharacteristically chatty mood this Monday morning. Usually, he had to drag any word not related to work out of her. Her full red lips and big mouth worked overtime as she alternately chewed her bread and cheese and told him about her weekend. A couple of years back, she'd taken up gardening and had bought a small plot in a community garden in the northern part of the city.

"You should have seen Hercules helping me with the digging," she said, looking lovingly at the little creature curled up beside her on the couch. "Here I am doing all the talking," she said as her rosy cheeks flushed. "How did your weekend go? You must have enjoyed Saturday's game."

It surprised Lex to hear her taking an interest in football. On a few occasions, he'd seen her shake her head, baffled by his obsession with Ajax Amsterdam, Johan Cruijff, and the formidable Dutch national team, now playing in the World Cup. "Did you watch it?" he said in disbelief.

"Hell no. But you'd have to be both blind and deaf not to be reminded. You can't go to any bar without being harassed or to any supermarket without being offered world cupcakes with orange icing," she said.

"World cupcakes! Nice one," Lex said, which seemed to please her. "You can hardly blame the nation for going bananas when the tournament is being played just across the border," Lex offered.

"They'd go bananas if it was being played on the moon."

"I guess you're right. Apart from the Dutch games, I don't pay much attention to the other matches. I prefer club soccer."

"Are you still trying to get a ticket for a game?" she asked.

"Not anymore. The chance of getting my hands on a ticket through any official channel is as likely as Haiti becoming world champions. I'm not crazy enough about our national team to pay some outrageous price for a ticket on the black market and risk it being counterfeit."

"Yes, the racketeers—organised or otherwise—are having a field day."

"Field day, ha!" Lex said with a giggle. "You're on a roll."

Her rosy cheeks once again reddened.

"But my weekend wasn't all hebetude," Lex added.

"Hebiwhat?"

"Idleness. Yesterday morning, a lady woke me up."

"Now, where have I heard that one before? Please, spare me the details."

"It wasn't like that," Lex said. It was his turn to redden. "The lady came to my door at an ungodly hour for a Sunday morning and would not let up until I answered the doorbell."

Lex told Roos about Lure de Lang's visit and her request to be protected from a stalker. Lex left out the details about her extreme beauty. He couldn't explain why, since Roos knew a thing or two about the effect good looking girls could have on a relatively young man.

"Isn't that a case for the authorities?"

"I guess, but she didn't trust the police, and I didn't put much trust in her story. Something just didn't sound right, so I decided not to take her on."

"Pity. We could do with some more work."

"However, sleeping on it has given me second thoughts."

Roos didn't say anything. She was probably getting used to seeing him sitting on the fence.

"I've decided to pay her a visit before lunch."

"I guess it won't do any harm to check it out," Roos said as they both stood up. Famous last words.

LEX GRABBED his leather jacket and pork pie hat from the coat rack in the corner of the office.

"See you in a couple of hours," he shouted as he crossed the hall. Energised by a decent breakfast and the prospect of going somewhere with a purpose, he pulled the door open and darted down the stairs. As he stepped outside, a light summer breeze, as soft and warm as a cat's paw, embraced him.

Bartender Bart stood at the door of the Café de Monico. The buttons on his dirty white shirt hung on for dear life, trying to contain his beer belly, and his ginger goatee did its best to cover his throat sack. He looked like an orangutan (the agreeable kind). "Ready for the next game on Wednesday?" he shouted, cupping his relatively small hands around his mouth to be heard above the noise from the traffic.

"I'll be there," Lex said, although he doubted Bart had heard, as he turned without a response to go back inside.

Lex made it across Rembrandtplein and narrowly escaped being hit by a white Peugeot 403 Cabriolet. Not that he was big on car brands, but this specific model he knew from *Columbo*—a new American crime-fiction television series. The middle-aged man behind the wheel shook his bald head disparagingly at Lex for gambling with his life in front of his car.

Lex headed for a sky-blue Vespa Sprint, parked on the pavement near the hedge surrounding the park famous for its statue of Rembrandt van Rijn. Lex found it ironic that while Rembrandt himself had been laid to rest as a pauper man in an unknown grave in the Westerkerk, the giant iron statue of the famous painter was condemned from its pedestal to forever overlook the vault-like building of the Algemene Bank Nederland headquarters.

Lex unlocked the scooter, pushed it off the kickstand, and navigated through the usual chaos of parked bicycles and mopeds on the broad pavement. He ignited the two-stroke engine, jumped on, and joined the traffic. With its sharp Italian design and a top speed of around 100 kph, the Vespa gave him plenty of riding satisfaction. On a beautiful June day, it was perfect for getting around in a city with narrow, congested streets dominated by an ever-increasing number of cars and trucks.

Swinging onto Utrechtsestraat, Lex remembered (for once) to give a signal with his right arm (since his 1970 model lacked turn signals). The scooter quickly gained speed, and as he passed a yellow tram, he glimpsed a reflection of himself in its windows. He looked like a modern-day Zorro with his hat, Ray-Ban shades, and leather jacket flying out behind him like a cape.

He felt a sudden wave of optimism and gratitude for being alive. He didn't have a religious bone in his body, and with the death of his parents and his fiancée, he'd dismissed whatever concept of God he had; however, on several occasions lately, he had felt something bigger than himself lifting his spirits.

Lex reached the location where Lure de Lang claimed to live. He killed the engine and freewheeled into the narrow street. As he parked, a young mother pushing a carriage came out of the bakery on the corner. Her little boy was engrossed in eating a bun. *I must be going crazy*, Lex thought. *I see Lure de Lang in every slender woman with long hair.*

He crossed the street to a concrete staircase at the side of the red-tiled bakery and looked up to a green door with a brass mail slot. For no apparent reason, he counted the nine steps as he ascended. The door had no nameplate, but a '69' in small white numerals told him he'd reached his destination. Lex pressed the doorbell and heard it ring somewhere inside. He waited, then pressed it again. Either Miss de Lang wasn't there or was pretending not to be. As Lex turned to leave, he heard a noise behind the door. Instinctively, he pushed the handle, and the door squeaked open.

"Miss de Lang, are you home?" he called out. There was no response, and he took two steps into the hallway. A door on the left was ajar, and through the crack, he could see into the living room. He pushed the door open with his foot. "Anybody home? It's Lex Spijker." He paused for a reply, and as none came, he stepped into the room. He nervously looked behind the door. Calm down, he told himself. There's no need to get worked up.

On its daily journey from east to west, the sun cast a bright light into the room through two narrow windows which faced onto the street. Below windows stood a dark blue velvet love seat and a glass coffee table decorated with a ceramic bowl full of oranges. Opposite, was a small wooden dining table and three wooden chairs. One of the chairs was pulled out, and on the table stood a bowl filled with what looked like cold tomato soup and a half-empty glass of red wine with traces of lipstick on the rim. You didn't have to be a private detective to detect that someone—most likely Lure de Lang—had left in a hurry.

To the right, Lex saw a closed door, and as he didn't know if he was alone in the apartment, he said with a booming and firm voice, "If there's anybody here, you'd better show yourself." For effect, he added, "I'm warning you, I'm armed," knowing he hadn't handled a firearm since his days as a police sergeant. Lex waited in silence to ensure that the only noises he could hear were coming from the street. He crossed the room and swiftly pulled open the door. It led into a dark hallway, but in the light from the living room, he could see two closed doors and in the corner, a small table holding a red rotary telephone. There were too many closed doors for his liking. He preferred open ones—it's much easier to see what's going on behind them.

Lex discovered that the nearest one, straight ahead, concealed a small restroom. He took three steps towards the door to the left, opened it slowly, and if it hadn't been for the body on the floor, it could have been any rundown Amsterdam kitchen.

The man lay with his arms spread out like Jesus Christ on the cross; only his hair was too light and too short for Jesus. He was lying in a pool of blood, presumably his own. A kitchen knife, or the handle of one, was sticking out of his chest.

Lex walked into the room, staying clear of the blood on the floor. He kneeled down to get a better look. Judging by the stiffness of the body and the colour of the blood, Lex figured the victim hadn't been dead for long. Death wasn't new to him, but he'd never seen an eyes-wide-open corpse before. This one had dead blue eyes that stared vacantly towards some imaginary spot on the kitchen ceiling or perhaps towards heaven. Lex wondered if the man was Lure de Lang's stalker. The feeble description she'd given could fit, but it matched plenty of men in Amsterdam.

Lex stood up, feeling only slightly queasy. He assumed that some fresh air would do him good, but first, he needed to call his old nemesis at police HQ. He didn't want to, but he had no choice with a corpse on his hands. Lex headed for the phone in the hall. By now, sweat was running down his cheeks, and the back of his shirt was soaked.

Lex lifted the receiver and dialled.

"Sergeant Schenk, Amsterdam Crime Unit," said a familiar voice.

"I have work for you, Wouter." Before Lex could say another word, he felt something like an explosion go off in his head. The receiver slid out of his hand, and he journeyed through the twilight and landed on the old wooden floor. Then total darkness took over.

3

TWO FACES came into focus despite Lex's blurred vision. One with a substantial double chin, a narrow moustache, and thinning hair. The other face was long, clean-shaven and sported a crew cut. Lex shifted his head and immediately regretted it. The pain made yesterday's hangover seem like a long-lost friend.

"Glad you could join us, Alexander," said Fat Face. "Or is it Lex these days?"

"Yes, awfully glad," Long Face chipped in.

"You have some explaining to do," Fat Face stressed.

"Yes, awfully much," Long Face emphasised.

"But how do you explain two men lying unconscious in an apartment? One of them so unconscious that he's dead," Fat Face said, as his beefy hand stroked his thin moustache.

"What's your theory, Sherlock?" Long Face asked.

"Elementary, my dear Watson. Man number one gets stabbed in the chest by man number two. Man number one, now with a knife in his chest, hits man number two with a... say... rolling pin. Man number two drops back into the hall and falls unconscious. Man number one, still with a knife in his chest, drops dead on the kitchen floor."

"Interesting theory. I have another."

"Let's have it," Fat Face said with encouragement.

"Man number two stabs man number one in the chest. Man number one drops dead on the kitchen floor. Man number two hits himself over the head with a ... say ... rolling pin, falls backwards into the hall and ..."

The double chin belonged to Inspector Roy Holst, at least thirty kilos overweight and around fifty years old. The long face belonged to Inspector Wouter Schenk, as lean as his colleague was broad, a head shorter, and about ten years younger.

Lex wished Laurel and Hardy (as they were referred to at HQ, for obvious reasons) would stop acting like second-rate stand-up comedians. In his present state, with his back resting against the wall and a bump on his head the size of a baseball, he didn't find the situation remotely funny.

It did nothing to lift his mood to know that they, for various reasons, hated his guts. Lex wanted to protest his innocence, but with his stomach in his throat, he was trying to focus on not being sick.

"Alexander, you'd better come with us to the station," Holst said. They dragged Lex to his feet, through the apartment, out the front door, down the stairs, and across the street to a Volkswagen Beetle. Schenk opened the door and tilted the seat forward to allow Holst to toss Lex onto the back seat. The short trip to the car had not improved his dizziness, and Lex tilted to the side to stop the world from spinning.

"You have a good rest, Alexander. You're going to need it," Holst said, as he pushed the seat back into place. The car shook as he slumped into the passenger seat. "Let's go, Wouter. We've seen enough. The forensics team will wrap it up." The doors slammed shut, and Lex felt the car set in motion. He doubted they would object if he took a nap.

LEX CAME around as the Beetle made its way down Leidsestraat towards the police station on Leidseplein. Lex winced as he tried to sit up.

"You don't look all that hot," said Schenk watching him in the rear-view mirror.

"I might have concussion, and I need to see a doctor."

"Not possible," Holst replied without turning. Lex doubted he could, even if he wanted to. The view of the man's neck spilling over his collar only nauseated Lex further.

"You can't prevent me from getting medical attention," he protested.

"I wouldn't dare. I meant that you couldn't possibly have concussion, as you'd need a brain for that," quipped Holst. The two policemen laughed.

WITH LAUREL and Hardy as chaperones, Lex made it up the few stone steps and into the Leidseplein police station, where he'd worked for more than five years. After graduating from the Police Academy in 1967, he had joined the crime unit at the police headquarters in Amsterdam. At first, Lex enjoyed the job as a young sergeant under the supervision of the middle-aged Inspector Grijpstra. Unfortunately, he and the other superiors were not keen to address the high level of corruption in the police force. It wasn't that Lex was whiter than snow, although his parents, who generally didn't know much about bringing up their only child, had managed to give him some principles of right and wrong and standards of behaviour. Most likely, his upbringing had contributed to him wanting to become a policeman in the first place. Once on the force, Lex's unwillingness to take bribes had made his colleagues suspicious, and his position became impossible after he reported a fellow officer who openly helped himself to a substantial commission from money confiscated in a drugs bust. The colleague in question was Roy Holst. Not surprisingly, his dislike for Lex had turned into something more sinister. Although no disciplinary action was taken against Holst, he'd hated Lex's guts ever since. After Lex left the force, he and his sidekick Wouter Schenk had resolved to make his life as a private detective as tricky as possible.

The two policemen escorted Lex down the stairs to the detention cells in the basement.

"We have a important guest for you," Holst said to the young officer in charge, who seemed fresh out of the academy.

"Please sign him in, Reint. His name is Alexander Felix Spijker," Schenk said.

"Nice to meet you, Mr Spijker. Your reputation precedes you," Constable Reint said, sounding as if he was trying to impress the two seasoned cops from the crime squad.

"You're kidding me," Lex murmured through gritted teeth. "The only crime I've committed is being in the wrong place at the wrong time."

"Yes, that's an unfortunate habit of yours. As responsible and incorruptible cops, we naturally want to make sure you've had no part in a murder," Holst said.

Constable Reint opened one of the eight wooden cell doors. Holst put a foot in front of Lex and pushed him forcefully in the back. Lex stumbled forward and crashed into the wall. The pain brought tears to his eyes.

"Holst, you're a jackass, and couldn't get laid in a brothel, even if you could locate your dick," Lex barked, as he turned onto his back.

Holst came at him like a raging bull and directed a solid leather shoe towards his kidneys. Lex rolled into a foetal position to absorb the impact, glad that he was still wearing his leather jacket. When Holst's foot caught Lex in the stomach, he grabbed hold of the fat man's leg.

"Is that all you've got, you wimp?" Lex groaned as he gasped for air.

Holst shook his foot free and prepared for another kick, but Schenk stepped in front of him. Holst could have removed his colleague without much effort, but he didn't.

"That's enough, Roy. We don't want the doctor to ask awkward questions, do we now?"

"You're right, Wouter. He's not worth it anyway."

They both turned on their heels and walked out. Before the cell door closed, Lex heard Schenk telling the young constable to get the doctor. He picked himself up off the stone floor and sat on the narrow wooden bench with its thin mattress. Strangely enough, for the first time since someone had decided to use his head as a punch-bag, Lex felt like he might survive. Even though his stomach had recently received a kick, he suddenly felt hungry. Lex glanced at his watch to see it was twenty to three in the afternoon.

"Could I have a look at the menu?" he called out, not expecting any reaction. "This is a lousy joint with bad service." *No surprise—it's Leidseplein after all,* he thought, as he stretched out on the bench.

Apart from the muted sounds from the Leidesplein of people getting on with their lives, nothing interfered with the questions in his sore head. *What had happened to Lure de Lang? Was she dead or captive somewhere? Who was the dead guy on the kitchen floor, and who had killed him? Did Lure de Lang kill him? Was she on the run? What if he'd accepted the assignment and gone with her yesterday? Would the man still be alive, and would Lure de Lang not have vanished?* Lex wondered if he would ever see her again. With the vision of her attractive face and her gorgeous, seductive body, he once again drifted off.

AT SIX o'clock, or about three hours after the doctor had told him that his hat had saved him from any severe head injury, Lex heard a key in the door. He stood as it opened. The uniform looked the same; however, the young constable had grown a beard and had turned into a middle-aged man.

"Has the kid been given his cocoa and put to bed, Guus?" Lex asked.

"I wouldn't know, but they do seem to get younger and younger," he laughed. "Mind you, Alexander, you can't be more than thirty-five?"

"Try twenty-nine. You've caught me on a bad day."

"I've no idea why you're spending a beautiful summer afternoon locked up here, and I don't think I want to know."

"Don't worry; I'm not going to bore you with the details."

"Laurel and Hardy have asked me to take you to interrogation room number one. I think you know it well. Regrettably, I'll have to put you on the wrong side of the table."

"Guus, could you get me some water, a sandwich, and a cup of coffee?"

"I'll see what I can do," he said.

"Much appreciated." Lex followed him up the stairs. "They took my cigarettes, and I'm dying for one."

"Can't help you there. I've given up smoking." He unlocked the door to the interrogation room. "Go in and take a seat, and I'll see if I can get you a bite to eat."

Good old Guus! Agents like him had helped the Amsterdam police retain some decency in times of severe corruption, and when their reputation was in tatters for playing hardball with a younger generation who spoke their minds.

Lex looked around the room where he'd spent many hours interrogating suspects. Like the rest of the police station, it badly needed a facelift. The tattered wallpaper was the colour of a baby's used nappy, and the ceiling bore an indefinable greyish-brown coloration produced by the fumes of too many cigarettes. Lex put a hand on the old wooden table, stained with ring marks from a thousand cups and glasses. To his surprise, it felt clean.

Lex heard a key in the door and stood up. Laurel and Hardy sailed in. He couldn't say that it pleased him to see either of them, but it did please him to see Schenk carrying a glass of water and a decent looking cheese sandwich on a plate. He put it on the table in front of Lex, who sat back down. One more ring mark for the collection.

"I hope you'll enjoy Guus' dinner," Holst remarked.

"Tell him I'm forever grateful."

"Do it yourself," Holst replied with his usual condescending sneer. He remained standing as Schenk took a seat opposite Lex, who emptied the glass of water in one gulp, tucked into the sandwich with gusto, and finished it within a couple of minutes.

Schenk lit a cigarette and offered Lex one.

"Bless you, Wouter," he said as he took it. The policeman lit it, and Lex inhaled greedily.

"Is it too much to ask for a cup of coffee?"

"Where do you think you are? Café Hoppe?" Holst said as he sunk onto the old wooden chair beside his colleague. It creaked under his weight, and Lex expected it to collapse.

"Let him have a coffee, Roy. For old times' sake."

"Okay, but I'm not going to get it."

Schenk left the room, and Holst did his best to ignore Lex.

"I need to go to the toilet."

"And I need you to stop making demands. You'll have to wait until Wouter returns with your damn coffee."

After a couple of minutes, Schenk returned with a mug. The coffee smelled like it had spent the entire afternoon on a hotplate. One taste confirmed it.

"Okay, let's get started," Schenk said and sat down.

"His Lordship needs to use the restroom," Holst said, imitating an English butler.

His colleague let out a long sigh of frustration as he got to his feet. "For Christ's sake, Alexander, you could have asked Guus to take you."

"When you gotta go, you gotta go," Lex said defensively.

"Come on then, but spare us the clichés."

They walked to the lavatory, and Lex stepped inside. He could hear Schenk humming softly to himself outside the door as Lex did the business. Schenk took hold of his arm when he came out, guided him back to the interrogation room, and steered him onto the chair across from his colleague.

Holst dragged his double chin up from the folder in front of him. "I don't like you, Alexander."

"I'm shocked to hear it," Lex rejoindered ironically. "You may dislike me enough to keep me in detention, but I doubt it's enough to hang a murder on me."

"Why don't you explain what you were doing in that apartment?" Schenk said.

"Tell us why you stabbed the guy. It will make you feel better," Holst added.

"Fuck off, Roy! You know I didn't do it. I've had enough of being pushed around. Like any other miserable sod, I'm just trying to get by. If that's a crime, feel free to lock me up."

"You should be locked up for being a private detective who gets knocked unconscious, just like a cliché in a pulp fiction novel. That's a crime in itself," Holst said.

"Roy, let Alexander tell his side of the story," Schenk reasoned.

WITHOUT PILING on too many details, Lex told them about Lure de Lang's visit to his office the day before and how, after a restless night, he came to regret not helping her. "That's why I went to that address."

"How did you get in?" Holst asked.

"Through the unlocked door. Unfortunately, I stumbled upon a man with a knife in his chest."

"And that's when you called me?" Schenk said.

"Yes, but I didn't get far before someone knocked me out cold."

"With a rolling pin," Holst said, with a hint of glee in his voice.

"You must be joking?" Lex touched the bump on the back of his head.

"I never joke when innocent people get assaulted."

"Who's the dead guy?" Lex asked.

"You tell us," Holst said, as he leaned his broad frame towards Lex, whose arms were resting on the table. Holst grabbed both of them and pulled before Lex could withdraw. His face was an inch from Lex's, and he could smell stale cigarette smoke and sour jenever on his breath.

"You're a fucking liar, Alexander! Why don't you tell us the truth for a change?" he bellowed, as he tightened his grip.

"Stop it, Roy! You're hurting me."

"Let him go, Roy," his colleague said.

"Miss Lure de Lang is a figment of his imagination, I tell you, Wouter." He pulled Lex's arms once more, then let go as he resisted. Lex tilted backwards, almost falling over. Holst gave a sardonic laugh.

"But you found a body in her apartment," Lex protested.

"No, we didn't," Holst said, raising his bushy eyebrows.

"I don't understand."

"The apartment belongs to a lady called Amanda Artz," Schenk said.

"Maybe Miss de Lang was using a false name when she came to see me," Lex suggested.

"Is Lure de Lang blond and middle-aged?" Holst asked.

"Have you talked to her?"

"Lure de Lang?" Holst said, playing dumb.

Lex had had enough of this fragmented conversation. His head and body ached, and he needed a shower, fresh clothing, and a decent meal. Most of all he needed a good night's sleep in a proper bed, preferably his own. "For Christ's sake, cut to the chase and tell me what you know," he uttered through gritted teeth. "Or at least answer my questions."

Holst ignored him, but Schenk responded. "We haven't tracked down Amanda Artz. Or Lure de Lang."

"*Cherchez la femme*," Holst interrupted. Nobody laughed.

"But we know that Amanda Artz is a blonde lady in her late forties. The woman from the bakery next door, a cornucopia of information, mostly gossip, told us that Amanda Artz, who buys bread in the bakery now and then, is a blond lady in her late forties. She also told us that Mrs Artz is the quiet type, who lives alone and frequently changes her boyfriend," Schenk said. "The woman from the bakery insisted she's no gossip and then informed us that Amanda Artz is a 'loose woman'."

"Two missing women and a dead man. Another normal day at the office," Holst sighed. "If you're withholding information that can assist us in our investigation, now is the time to tell us. I'm only going to ask you once, before Guus takes you back downstairs," he added.

"You have no right to keep me here!" Lex protested, looking at good-cop Schenk, hoping for him to intervene. He avoided eye contact.

"We have every right. As you damn well know, we can hold you for forty-eight hours without charge," Holst stressed with a smirk.

4

CONSTABLE GUUS brought Lex a cup of coffee at six.

"Morning, Alexander. Did you sleep well?"

"What terrible accommodation! Where can I complain? And don't get me started on the noisy neighbours. I might as well have slept in the middle of the Leidseplein."

"It wasn't my idea to keep you here overnight."

"A few cigarettes would have made it more tolerable."

"No smoking in detention cells. Station policy, as you know."

"Are Laurel and Hardy here?"

"Most likely at home in their PJs."

"I can visualize it—not a pretty picture."

"Drink your coffee. Then you can go home."

"No offence, Guus, but the coffee here is terrible," Lex said, then took another sip.

"You ungrateful sod," Guus laughed.

Lex liked that the middle-aged constable didn't take himself too seriously. Not like the bloated Roy Holst and his sidekick Wouter Schenk. It would give Lex great pleasure to see those two crooked, incompetent cops kicked off the force.

LEX DRAGGED greedily on his cigarette as he walked down the Leidsestraat as the city came to life. After satisfying the nicotine beast, he was ready for decent coffee, fried eggs, aged cheese, and freshly baked bread. Fortunately, an *eetcafé* on the corner of Kerkstraat was open.

As Lex entered, three men dressed in hard-wearing denim trousers looked up from a table near the door. He raised a hand to his pork pie hat, but they ignored him and continued with their breakfast. He couldn't blame them—his unshaven face and baggy eyes made him look like an escaped convict.

A small Turkish man with a bushy moustache approached and handed Lex a menu. He took it and ordered bacon, eggs, buttered toast, and aged cheese without studying it.

"Tea or coffee?"

"Strong, black coffee. Lots of it."

"No offence, sir, but you look like you need it."

"More than you know."

Lex hung his leather jacket over the back of a chair on the other side of the table and dropped his hat on the seat. He was grateful that the neighbouring tables were empty, since his odour seemed out of place in a breakfast room. He helped himself to *de Telegraaf* from a newspaper rack by the door and found what he was looking for on page seven. Under the heading 'Man stabbed to death', the one-column article read: *Monday morning, the police found the body of a man stabbed to death in an apartment on Utrechtsedwarsstraat. The deceased is yet to be identified. The police have detained a suspect but declined to give further information.*

The released suspect looked up from his newspaper as the Turk approached with a tray. Lex studied his face to see if his body odour would put his nose out of joint, but the man showed no reaction as he arranged the breakfast on the table.

"The orange juice is on the house. *Eet smakelijk!*" he said, turned around and trotted away.

Lex tucked into the food with gusto, and it tasted like the finest breakfast in all of Amsterdam.

Lex pushed the plate away ten minutes later, lit a cigarette, and turned his attention to the newspaper's sports section. Since no games had been played in the World Cup the previous day, the paper ran an interview with the national hero, Johan Cruijff. Lex usually wouldn't neglect reading about one of the best footballers in the world, but after a sleepless night, he found it hard to concentrate on the star's words of wisdom. Lex finished the coffee, stubbed out the cigarette, and put on his jacket and hat.

"What's the damage?" he called out. The waiter brought the bill, and Lex noticed the orange juice was listed, but he was too tired to bring it to the man's attention.

Total fatigue hit Lex as he stepped out into the busy street, so he abandoned his original plan to retrieve the scooter from outside the crime scene. In a daze, he headed towards Koningsplein, swerving to avoid the fellow pedestrians on the narrow pavement. Lex turned down the flower market, then upped his pace, as his apartment was just a few hundred metres away.

Bart, the bartender, stood in the doorway of his café where Lex had left him almost twenty-four hours earlier.

"You look like shit, Lex," he said with a broad, nicotine-stained grin.

And you still look like an orangutan, Lex thought.

"Do you party every night?"

"Do you always work?" Lex said sourly, before stepping onto the staircase to begin the climb. He unlocked the front door and crawled over the threshold. With some effort, he managed to hang his jacket and hat on the coat rack. He took a notebook and a pen from the desk.

"Tuesday, 18 June at 8:05," Lex wrote on top of the page and then, *Hi Roos, I've had a rough night. Please do not disturb me, and I'll explain later. Feel free to take the day off.*

Lex put the note on her desk in the living room and headed for the bedroom. He drew the curtains and stripped to his boxer shorts. Lex should have washed before crawling into bed but couldn't be bothered. He fell asleep before his head touched the pillow.

LEX WOKE drenched in sweat and filled with dread. The alarm clock on the floor beside the bed informed him that he'd slept for more than seven hours. The small room smelled like the boys' locker room after a game of football. He rolled out of bed, put on a jogging suit, and headed for the public bathhouse on Amstelstraat, about a hundred metres from the apartment.

Half an hour later, Lex returned, feeling and looking like a new man. He exchanged the jogging suit for a fresh white shirt and a pair of clean black trousers, then made himself a cup of instant coffee. Lex opened the cupboard to check on Johnnie Walker, but decided whisky wouldn't contribute to his well-being —not at that moment, anyway. He walked to the office and took a seat behind the desk.

Lex put down the mug and saw a note from Roos. It read: *Hope you had a good sleep. We'll talk tomorrow. Hugs from Roos and Hercules.* Lex crumpled it up, tossed it, and missed the wastebasket by some distance.

He took a telephone directory from behind him. Lure de Lang wasn't in it, but Amanda Artz was and listed at the Utrechtsedwarsstraat address. Lex lifted the receiver to dial the number but then decided it would be a waste of time. He finished the coffee, put on his jacket and hat, and went to fetch his scooter.

LEX ENTERED Café de Monico, and the television screen in the corner above the bar drew his attention. On it, Scotland's captain, Billy Bremner, had just floored the Brazilian captain, Wilson Piazza, with a rugby tackle. *So much for exchanging handshakes and pennants a few minutes ago*, he thought.

"*Taigh nam gasta ort!*" bellowed a stout youngster at the bar. He wore a white Leeds United football shirt and a tartan kilt.

"Fuck off ref! That was never a free kick," corroborated his buddy, who wore a red T-shirt and shorts.

Bart reached for the whisky bottle, but Lex stopped him and asked for a pint of Heineken. In English, he added, "and whatever our two Scottish friends are drinking."

They turned their heads towards him. "That's kind of you, sir," said the man in shorts. "I'm Alistair, and this is Clyde."

"The same again, gentlemen?" Bart interrupted, pointing to their almost empty pint glasses.

"Please," Clyde said.

They toasted. "May you have a successful World Cup," Lex said.

"We don't have high expectations. We're Scottish after all," Alistair laughed.

"Somehow, we managed to put two past Zaire on Friday night. Peter Lorimer and Joe Jordan scored," Clyde said with pride.

"My mate is a Leeds United fan, in case you haven't noticed," Alistair said.

"I see that, and may I congratulate you and your team on winning the championship." Lex put the lit cigarette between his lips and extended a hand to Clyde.

He shook it. "Thank you, sir."

"Leeds have five players in the squad," Alistair said. Apparently, he was their spokesperson.

"I suppose you support Ajax, sir?" Clyde said.

"You bet. We have six players in the Dutch squad."

"Holland has the best team in the tournament, and I'd be surprised if you don't win it," Alistair offered.

"Long way to go," Lex said. "Shouldn't you be in West Germany?"

"It's a long story," Clyde offered.

"Do tell."

Not surprisingly, Alistair took over. "We had tickets for tonight's game, but en route to Frankfurt, we decided to watch the Zaire game in Amsterdam and let our hair down at the weekend. And we did. Maybe too much, as we somehow lost the tickets and our passports."

"Some bastard nicked them," Clyde snarled.

"Fortunately, I was in charge of our traveller's cheques," Alistair said. "Mislaid or stolen, we're now stuck in Amsterdam until we can get our emergency passports."

"It could be worse! We could be stuck in Dundee!" Clyde said, and roared with laughter.

They turned their attention back to the game. Lex looked around Bart's establishment, since it was a dull affair for those who weren't taking sides in the match. The café was empty apart from two lovebirds, lost in each other's eyes, sitting by the big window overlooking Rembrandtplein.

"Not much going on tonight, Bart."

"The lull before the storm. Come early tomorrow if you want your regular seat," he said, knowing that the place would be packed for Holland's game against Sweden.

"Are you going to cut the drink prices by half again every time Holland scores a goal?"

"Same procedure as last time, Lex. Same procedure as every time. Don't you worry."

"But that's what worries me," Lex said, and finished the beer.

"Another? Or a whisky?" Bart, the perfect host, asked.

Lex declined, stubbed out his cigarette, and told him goodnight. He wished his two new Scottish friends the best of luck with their team and getting their passports.

A GARBAGE truck rolled down Rembrandtplein and woke Lex at twenty-past six. Lure de Lang had walked in and out of his dreams all night. He wished that she hadn't, but had no say in the matter in his unconscious state. Now that he was awake, Lex ordered himself to let go of the whole damn business, forget about the dead man and the two missing women. Laurel and Hardy didn't need his help to mess up the investigation.

Lex boiled water on the stove and then poured it into the kitchen sink. He added cold water from the faucet to make it the right temperature. He washed, shaved, and dressed, then popped downstairs to buy a cheese sandwich and a newspaper.

Lex returned to the apartment and ate his breakfast at the coffee table. He grabbed the newspaper and read the sports pages first. The game between Scotland and Brazil had ended without goals. The match between Yugoslavia and Zaire didn't—the African nation conceding nine times without scoring. In another group, West Germany beat Australia 3-0, and East Germany and Chile drew one-all.

Lex lit the first cigarette of the day, turned to the culture section, and read a review of *All the President's Men*, Woodward and Bernstein's book about the Watergate scandal, released the previous Saturday. Lex found it fascinating that the American Congress had considered impeaching President Richard Nixon. He flipped through the rest of the pages, but found no mention of the murder on Utrechtsedwarsstraat.

Lex made another cup of coffee before relocating to the office. He wanted to look busy when his secretary arrived, although, apart from an insurance fraud investigation, she knew his schedule was as clean as a hound's tooth.

Within a few minutes, Lex heard the front door open, and Roos appeared on the threshold of the office. She was all smiles, and even Hercules in her arms seemed happy to see him. She lowered the dog to the floor, and he bounded towards Lex, who lifted him up to watch the creature dance excitedly on his lap while he petted him.

"Good to see you looking well. It worried me slightly when you didn't return on Monday," she said.

"Only slightly?" he laughed.

"You may be solid, but I wouldn't call you dependable."

"It comes from only reporting to myself. However, some unpleasant business did prevent me from coming back."

"I'm eager to hear about it, but let me first put the kettle on."

ROOS SIPPED her coffee and gazed at Lex over the mug, her big blue eyes filled with concern. He told her about the dead man on the kitchen floor, being knocked unconscious, the run-in with his old colleagues from HQ, the two missing women, and the night in detention.

"Are you going to investigate any further?"

"I've had enough, and I don't want trouble to come looking for me, so I'm keeping a low profile."

"That's probably a good idea."

"It doesn't change the fact that the woman has somehow cast a spell on me."

"Is she beautiful?"

"Captivatingly gorgeous," Lex said.

"When the little head gets hard, the big go soft."

"Never heard that one before! I'm reluctant to admit it, but I guess you nailed it," Lex said.

LEX RETURNED from enjoying a primarily liquid lunch. He took off his shoes, loosened his tie, dropped into the Chesterfield chair, leaned back, and put his feet on the desk. He closed his eyes and rested his neck on the cold leather. It didn't take long for him to doze off.

The ring of the doorbell woke him.

Annoyed, he got up, walked in stockinged feet to the hall and pulled the front door open.

"Good afternoon, Alexander. You look disappointed. Expecting someone else? May we come in?" Wouter Schenk said.

"What do you want, gentlemen? I'm busy."

"We're all busy, and we won't take too much of your precious time," Roy Holst said.

"We need to clear up a few things," Schenk said.

"Don't tell me I'm still a suspect?"

"Let's say you're helping us with the inquiry," Holst said.

Lex invited them in (as if he had any choice).

"Hope you don't mind if we keep our shoes on?" said Holst as he glanced down.

Lex ignored him and showed them into the office. He picked up his shoes from the floor, walked round the desk, and sat down.

Schenk slumped into the Chesterfield, and Holst slid his substantial backside onto the edge of the desk.

Thank God it's made of solid oak, Lex thought. "I would offer you coffee, but I gave the maid the afternoon off."

"Never mind. Let's get to the point," Holst said.

"Have you heard from Lure de Lang?" Schenk asked.

"Your lady friend is a murder suspect," Holst said.

"She's not my lady friend. I've no idea of her whereabouts, and I don't want to know."

"We would," Schenk said.

"As a model citizen, you'll tell us if she contacts you?" Holst said.

"You'll be the first to know. You are probably incapable of finding Miss de Lang without my help."

"Are you calling us incompetent?" Holst said, as he leaned towards Lex, who did his best to ignore him. "Any news about the dead man or Amanda Artz?" Lex asked, helping himself to a cigarette.

Holst snatched the cigarette from Lex's lips as he was about to light up, squashed it in his fist and scattered the tobacco over Lex's head. "Put this in your pipe and smoke it," he laughed.

"I don't know what I detest the most: your constant use of clichés or that you insist on behaving like an asshole."

"As it happens, we've identified the deceased," Schenk interrupted.

"Shall we tell him the name?" Holst said.

"I think he's entitled to know. He found the poor bastard after all," Schenk said. "His name is Jan Berger. Or was, I should say."

"A small-time hustler with a sheet long enough to choke a horse," Holst said.

"Still didn't deserve to end up with a knife in his chest," Schenk said.

"Life's unfair," Holst said.

"Never heard of him," Lex said to stop them from sliding into their Laurel and Hardy routine. "What about Amanda Artz?"

"Still missing. The dear Mrs Artz could be fucked, and it wouldn't surprise me if your lady friend is fucked too," Holst said.

Lex felt the anger taking hold of him.

"You outstayed your welcome before you came, gentlemen. Please leave."

Schenk raised himself.

"Don't call us; we'll call you," Holst said, as he slid off the desk.

Lex followed them out. Holst turned and seemed about to make a departing wisecrack, but Lex slammed the door in his face. He heard them talking as they descended the staircase. Lex went to the kitchen to make a generously spiked coffee. He deserved it more than ever. He put the kettle on, opened the cupboard, and saw that good old Johnnie Walker was ready for a stroll.

TWENTY MINUTES into the game, and the drinks were still at the regular price. Lex ordered another whisky anyway. The Dutch were wasteful, and the Swedes defended well. His attention wavered until an increase in the noise level in the packed, smoke-filled room made him look up at the television.

The screen showed the Dutch captain, Johan Cruijff, take a long pass out of the air. He was immediately tightly guarded by a Swedish defender, and although he had control of the ball in his attacking position, it looked like the move had come to nothing. But JC had other plans. He feinted a kick with his right foot, then dragged the ball behind his standing leg, turning 180 degrees. He accelerated away and left the Swedish defender glued to the spot. It was a move of pure poetry, and that the delivery across the penalty area found none of his teammates was a detail no one cared much about.

"Did you see that turn, Bart?" Lex shouted spontaneously. Even if Bart had heard, he seemed too busy to reply.

As another Dutch attack came to nothing, Lex's attention drifted again, and he turned to look towards the street. To his surprise, he spotted Lure de Lang gazing in through the open door. Her dress and beauty remained unchanged since the last time he'd seen her, but Lex detected a hunted expression on her face.

"Lure!" he shouted, trying to make himself heard above the noise.

A big man blocked his view. Lex jumped off the bar stool, pushed past him, navigated through the crowd, and rushed out the door onto the Rembrandtplein. He looked up and down, but the girl had vanished. Lex cursed and returned to the café.

"What happened to you?" Bart asked.

"I thought I spotted a friend," he said, then paid up.

"See you Sunday for the next game."

Lex nodded to confirm, turned, and headed for the door. He suddenly felt a hundred years old and was grateful that a bed was waiting for him two flights up.

5

"DO YOU need help with that?" Lex asked.

"Thanks, but I can manage."

"Not according to your disability insurance, Mr Vink."

"How do you know my name?" He lifted the second bag of lawn fertilizer from a cart and shoved it into the back of a white Renault 6. He turned his bulky frame towards the private detective. His facial expression revealed that he knew the game was up.

"Your description and name were given to me by your insurance company. They also disclosed the information that you claimed you couldn't lift anything heavier than a cup of coffee."

"What's it to you?" he said, pulling off his garden gloves.

"It's nothing personal. I'm just doing what your insurance company hired me to do."

"How did you know I was going to the garden centre today?"

"Call it luck."

"Have you been following me for long?"

"On and off for a couple of weeks. Mostly off."

"What happens now?"

"I'll report it to the insurance company, and then I'm sure you'll hear from them."

A NOTE from Roos asked Lex to return a call from a Mr Hans Dulfer. *A blast from the past*, he thought. But first, Lex had to make another call. He lifted the receiver and dialled.

"United Insurance, how can we help?"

"Lex Spijker for Mr Isaak."

"Hold the line Mr Spijker." While waiting, he took a sip of his spiked coffee and lit a cigarette.

"Nice to hear from you, Mr Spijker. I guess you've made some progress?"

"Indeed. I caught Mr Vink at the garden centre today, lifting a few bags of soil. They looked heavy."

"Brilliant."

"My secretary will send you the report tomorrow and the invoice."

"Good work, Mr Spijker. Undoubtedly, you'll hear from us again."

LEX'S FEW friends had come with his fiancée, and when she died, he had stopped seeing them, or perhaps it was the other way round. It would have been too painful to keep in touch anyway. So the last thing Lex expected was a call from Hans Dulfer. He hadn't talked to him since the funeral a few years back; however, his brilliant career as a saxophonist was something Lex followed in the mainstream media. When Lex first met his future fiancée, Hans Dulfer was like an older brother to her. Although only a few years older, he'd also become like an older brother to Lex.

Lex dialled the number Roos had written on the notepad.

"Thanks for returning my call, Alexander. How are you?"

"Holding up."

"I understand you've quit the force and are working as a private investigator."

"Private detective."

"What's the difference?"

"None that I know. But I prefer 'detective'."

"Still a stickler for detail."

"I guess."

"I have to be honest with you; it's not entirely a social call. I need your help. Or do you call it services?"

"Help will do."

"Can we meet?"

"Sure. Is today good? Do you have my address?"

"Listen! I'm playing with my band tonight at the Paradiso. If I leave a ticket for you at the door, would you come to the show? We can have a chat afterwards."

Lex had nothing planned for the evening, so it didn't take him long to make up his mind. A bit of jazz would do him good.

"What time?"

"Come at nine."

"What are you and your band playing these days?"

"It's a mix of cross-over jazz and jazz fusion. I'm sure you'll like it. Most young people do," he said with a laugh.

THE PHONE kept ringing, dragging Lex out of a deep sleep. He stumbled out of bed into the office and lifted the receiver. "Yes, who is it?" he said with a voice that exuded irritation, not to mention the effect of too many cigarettes and too much booze the night before.

"I'm sorry if I woke you."

The voice of Lure de Lang commanded his full attention. Lex looked at his wristwatch: almost ten o'clock. He'd returned home from the concert and his talk with Hans Dulfer around four. Since Roos didn't come in on Fridays, he had an excuse to sleep late.

"I expected your call yesterday."

"Did you?" She sounded relieved.

"I spotted you outside my café on Wednesday evening."

"I lost my nerve."

"I have a bone to pick with you. It's been a bit of a rough ride since your visit on Sunday."

"I never meant to get you into trouble. Unfortunately, things have taken a turn for the worse."

"Murder can be distressing."

"So you know about that. Can we meet?"

Lex was of two minds. Although she'd never really left his thoughts, and her predicament had aroused his curiosity, he'd decided not to get involved. He was well aware that he often acted spontaneously and that his judgment was sometimes poor.

"Are you there?" she asked.

"Still here."

"I promise to tell you the truth," she insisted.

"You know where to find me," Lex said, "but give me an hour."

"I'm not sure it will be safe to come to your office."

"Whatever you say. Tell me where I should meet you."

"Can you come to the Artis?"

"The zoo is a big place."

"Meet me at the new elephant enclosure."

"Okay. I'll be there at eleven."

She hung up, and Lex replaced the receiver.

AT FIVE to eleven, Lex parked the Vespa opposite the main entrance to the zoo. He crossed the Plantage Kerklaan and joined two families with kids waiting in line to buy tickets. A poster announced that Prince Bernard would officially open the new elephant enclosure on 4 June. The announcement was outdated, but not as much as Lex's last visit to the zoo on a school outing more than twenty years ago.

Lex paid and entered. It seemed like a quiet day, with the animals outnumbering the people. He followed the signs until he spotted an elephant in the distance. He turned past a hedge surrounding a patch of grass and saw a row of benches across from the enclosure. Lure de Lang sat alone on the second bench. She looked gorgeous in her tight, black bell-bottoms, black turtleneck, and chunky heel sandals.

"Miss de Lang," Lex said, as he approached. He touched her shoulder, and she jumped.

"Oh, it's you."

Lex wondered if she'd been expecting someone else. Again her beauty struck him, although her face looked tired, and her emerald eyes were anxious. She moved her red and white plaid handbag to make room for him to sit beside her. Lex sat down, and the pleasant fragrance of her perfume entered his nostrils.

"Sorry, I was far away. I haven't slept much lately." She was nearly in tears. "I've made a big mistake, and I'm fucked."

The rough language coming from her red lips confused him. When she'd visited him on Sunday, she'd sounded posh. Was she a well-bred lady trying to sound common, or was it the other way around? He suspected the latter. Her natural beauty clouded his judgment, and it didn't help that whatever she wore made every other woman look dowdy.

"Why don't you take a deep breath and tell me what's bothering you? And this time, no lies. I warn you—if I sense you're not telling the truth, I'll walk away."

"You'll probably do that anyway, when you hear that you're helping a criminal."

"Are we talking about murder?"

"That wasn't me," she said. Lex noticed she was caressing the scar under her chin with the tip of her right-hand index finger, and again he wondered if it indicated she wasn't telling the truth. *At least she's admitted to knowing about the dead guy on the kitchen floor*, Lex thought. He offered her a cigarette, and her hand trembled as she took one. He lit it for her, then helped himself to one. "Let me hear your story," Lex offered.

"On the first Sunday of this month, I met a guy in the bar of the Grand Hotel Krasnapolsky. I was there to celebrate my birthday." She blew out a puff of smoke and turned to look at him.

"Alone?"

"A friend stood me up. Anyhow, as I said, I met a guy. I couldn't have missed him if I wanted to. No one could. He behaved like he owned the place, insisting on buying drinks left, right, and centre. I was sitting at the bar drinking white wine, minding my own business when he snuggled up to me. He asked me why such a beautiful girl was drinking alone. I told him I was celebrating my birthday, and he insisted on ordering a bottle of Taittinger.

"It didn't take us long to get through the bottle. He was getting quite drunk, and I wasn't exactly sober myself. I suggested that we continue the evening either at my place or his. As it turned out, he was staying at the hotel, so I helped him upstairs. He was all over me in the elevator, and I didn't do much to discourage him. As soon as we entered his suite, he disappeared into the bathroom. I undressed and jumped into the king-size bed. I expected him to join me, but within a few minutes, I heard him snoring.

"I found him unconscious, fully clothed, in the bathtub. I decided to let him sleep it off. I tucked him in with a pillow and a blanket from the bed to make him more comfortable. I switched off the bathroom light, closed the door, and dressed. I was about to leave when my curiosity got the better of me. He'd never introduced himself, and I was curious to know his name. I looked for some ID. I didn't find it; instead, I stumbled on a Pan Am cabinet duffle bag. Opening it gave me a shock. I'd never seen so many 100-guilder notes in one place. I'm not proud to admit it, but it didn't take me long to decide that I was not leaving without the bag. It was too tempting for a girl who likes a bit of the high life, but continually struggles to make ends meet.

"I told myself he probably wouldn't remember much about the evening and that the chances of him finding me were slim. I'd visited the Krasnapolsky bar only a couple of times, and I'd never made any real contact with anyone. I left the hotel with the bag."

"Didn't you consider that the money could belong to someone in organised crime and that if a sum like that went missing, the owners wouldn't rest until they recovered the money? Amsterdam is a small city."

"Perhaps, but my greed took over."

"Do you still have the money?"

"Most of it."

Lex studied her profile as she stared straight ahead. A few people stood along the fence looking into the enclosure, and the benches filled up in the sunshine. Lure looked around nervously.

"Don't worry. I'm here to protect you," Lex said in a confident voice.

She put her hand on Lex's arm, looked into his eyes, and smiled at him full of tenderness. It unnerved him slightly the way her touch and the attention aroused him.

"Tell me what happened after you stole the money."

"I went home to count it. With twenty-five bundles of 100-guilder notes with a hundred notes in each, it didn't take long."

"250,000 guilders is not bad for one night's work," Lex blurted out.

"Only I wasn't working. You're wrong if you think I was there to pick up potential customers." Her temper flared, and her face flushed.

"I wasn't thinking that at all."

"Sorry, but I'm exhausted."

"I understand, and I'll do ..." Over his left shoulder and through the hedge, Lex saw the massive frame of a man approaching. He was heading straight towards them, and Lex doubted he was there to admire the new elephant enclosure. Lex cursed.

"What's the matter?"

"Do you know anyone built like a tank?"

"I've no idea what you're talking about."

"If I'm not mistaken, he's looking for you—probably with a few buddies."

"I ..."

"We're leaving." Lex got to his feet, but kept low to stay out of sight. He grabbed Lure's arm and pulled her up. "Keep your head down, or he'll see you." She wanted to say something, but Lex silenced her with a finger to her lips. "Stay right behind me," he whispered.

They crab-walked along the hedge in the opposite direction from where the man was coming. Lex assumed they'd escaped unnoticed until someone shouted, "Over here, Boris! They're heading south!"

The whistle-blower stood about twenty metres away. He was a stout, middle-aged man, bald as a coot and half the size of his big friend. He wore a Hawaiian shirt and stretched out his arms to block the path. Fortunately, he held an ice cream cone instead of a weapon. "You're trapped," he shouted with a self-satisfied smirk.

Lex turned his head, looked over Lure's shoulder, and saw Boris approaching like a Sherman tank. "Full steam ahead!" he shouted, and they darted towards Bald Head, who jumped towards them with his legs apart. Lex kicked him in the groin, and his ice cream went flying.

"Bastard," he squealed and dropped to his knees, grabbing his crotch.

A woman screamed and pulled her child out of the way as Lex and Lure flew past them.

"Move it, Boris, let me pass!" came a shout from behind.

Lex looked over his shoulder and saw a third accomplice squeezing himself past Boris. Tall, lean, and dressed in a white suit and a white Panama hat, he reminded Lex of the American author Tom Wolfe.

Lure de Lang was a good runner and much fitter than Lex (which, in all honesty, didn't say much).

"We need to get out of here! The main entrance is no doubt guarded. Is there another exit?" he shouted.

"There's one onto the Plantage Middenlaan," she replied and took the lead. "Move it," she shouted to a couple walking hand in hand in front of them. By that point, Lex believed his lungs would explode. Only the threat from behind and Lure's lithe body in front kept him going.

"We're almost there!" she called out.

Lex looked back nervously as he followed her past the penguin enclosure. They'd lost their tail.

An older couple stood in front of the turnstile which led to the street.

"Hold it," Lure shouted, and they stepped aside.

"We're in a hurry," Lex explained.

Exiting onto the street, they had a stroke of good fortune. A demonstration was taking place on the broad Plantage Middenlaan, and they pushed their way towards the centre of the crowd.

"Keep your head down," Lex said, as he struggled for breath.

Lex was dripping with sweat, but Lure showed no signs of discomfort from running through the Artis with a few gangsters in close pursuit. He expected she was braver than she let on. None of the hippie types around them wore hats, so Lex removed his pork pie to look less conspicuous.

'NUCLEAR-FREE HOLLAND' was painted in big, reversed letters on a white fabric banner up ahead. Lex looked through the crowd and spotted the Tom Wolfe wannabe leaving the zoo through the turnstile.

Boris joined him on the pavement almost immediately, but there was no sign of Bald Head. He was in all likelihood still recovering from getting his nuts kicked, or perhaps he'd bought himself another ice cream cone. Judging by the interest they were showing in the mass of people moving steadily towards the intersection, it was apparent that they'd figured out that their prey had joined the demonstration.

"If we can get to my scooter, we'll have a chance," Lex said.

"Where is it?"

"It's parked around the corner, across from the main entrance to the zoo."

Lex saw Boris and his friend join the row of people around twenty metres behind them and assumed they were working their way through the crowd. Staying put and out of sight was only a short-term solution.

Lex felt Lure's warm hand in his—an intimate moment intensified by the duress.

"Stay in line, man!" complained someone loudly. The towering figure of Boris pushed a few demonstrators out of the way. Lex squeezed Lure's hand to get her attention. "They're right behind us, so we'll have to run for it," he said into her ear.

She nodded. Lex guided her to the edge of the crowd. The intersection was about a hundred metres ahead, and the Vespa another hundred metres further on.

"Run!" Lex shouted, as he let go of her hand and sprinted towards the corner. It probably didn't take more than twenty seconds, but it felt like an eternity.

Lex saw the pursuers coming out of the crowd, but he lost sight of them as he turned the corner.

As Lex reached the scooter, he heard Lure curse. She'd tripped over a curb stone, and he turned just in time to act as a buffer to her fall. The force catapulted them both backwards. Landing on the pavement, they missed the Vespa by inches.

"Are you alright?" Lex said, as she crawled off him.

"Slightly shaken up, but no broken bones." She stood up.

The guy in the white suit rounded the corner and headed towards them. As Lex got to his feet, he saw Bald Head crossing the street. Lex assumed that he'd come out of Artis' main entrance. The opportunity to escape on the scooter was gone. As Boris joined the party, Lex tried to guess their next move. Lure had dropped her bag as she'd tumbled over, and Lex picked it up and handed it to her.

The Tom Wolfe wannabe approached. "I know who you are, but we have no score to settle with you. But the lady has something that belongs to us. All you need to do is hand her over, and we'll be on our way," he said.

"It's not for me to hand anyone over. Why don't you ask her if she wants to come with you?"

"You can ask as much as you like, but I'm otherwise engaged," Lure told him.

Boris took a step towards them. Lure put her right hand into the bag, and when it reappeared, it held a pistol. Lex was no expert on handguns, but it looked like a Baby Browning and was almost small enough to be concealed by her hand. Lex doubted a bullet fired from it would have much more effect on Boris than a mosquito bite, but it made him stop. *Maybe he's a softie*, Lex thought.

"Lex, get your scooter fired up. We're leaving," Lure said, waving the gun in the direction of the three men. "Come any closer," she said, "and I'll reward you with a bullet in your balls. I'm not kidding! I'm a decent shot."

What happened to the girl crying on my shoulder half an hour ago? Lex wondered. Miss Lure de Lang certainly switched between personalities. One minute she was swanky, and the next, classless. One minute a frail girl, and the next, a ruthless woman. One minute she seemed genuine, and the next, bogus. But this was hardly the time for him to try to fathom the mental state of this gorgeous creature.

"What are you waiting for, Lex?"

It was a good question, to which he had no answer, and she probably didn't expect one. He unlocked the Vespa, inserted the key into the ignition, and pushed it off the stand. He rolled it past Boris and his two pals. None of them looked pleased with the development. Lex couldn't blame them for being disappointed. Close, but no cigar.

Lex jumped onto the scooter, and Lure jumped on behind him.

"Hold on tight."

"We'll meet again, bitch!" yelled the man in the white suit as they pulled away.

6

LURE PUT her arms around Lex and rested her head against his back. It felt good to have a beautiful girl clinging on, and he caught a glimpse of them in the reflection of a shop window—her long dark mane blowing in the warm breeze.

Riding west along the Prins Hendrikkade gave Lex a moment to let his tired mind reflect on the wretched state of affairs. It upset him that Lure carried a weapon, although it had saved their bacon. Lex needed to take charge and find answers to the many questions piling up: *What's her story? Is Lure her real name? Can she be trusted? Did she kill Jan Berger? If not, who did and why? Was he the guy she robbed? And if so, where did he get the money? What happened to Amanda Artz, and what's her involvement? Who knocked him out cold? Who were the men chasing them in Artis, and how did they know that Lure and Lex were meeting there?*

Lex didn't know how many answers Lure could, or would, provide, but he intended to find out. First, they needed a quiet and safe place to get a bite to eat, something to drink, and plan the next move. Lex decided to ride to a bar in the Jordaan, where he knew the owner.

THE OLD café was empty, and Lex guided Lure past the billiard table to the back.

"Anybody here?" he called.

Immediately, a door next to the long wooden bar swung open. "The café is closed until two," came the reply.

"The door was unlocked," Lex explained.

Tom de Wit pressed his vast body through the narrow door. He owned and ran Café Chris together with his third and much younger wife. It was a traditional brown café and, as he once proudly told Lex, "the oldest operating bar in the Jordaan." According to legend, Rembrandt had enjoyed his jenever at the café back in the day. Tom (who had been a school friend of Lex's deceased father) was in his late fifties, and as far as Lex knew, he'd lived in the Jordaan all his life. Lex didn't know him well, but a few years back, when still on the force, he'd gotten him out of paying protection money to a crooked colleague of his. It made him a friend for life, but it was another nail in the coffin regarding Lex's police career.

"Alexander, you old bandit!" Tom bellowed. "What brings you to my humble establishment?"

"Thirst, hunger, and to ask for a favour."

"For drinking and eating, you've come to the right place. About the favour, we'll have to see."

"It's not too complicated, and it should be within your reach."

"How about first introducing me to your beautiful girlfriend?" Tom said, scratching his thick beard with one hand and resting the other on his substantial beer gut. His hairy chest was showing through his unbuttoned white shirt.

"This is Lure. She's a client of mine."

Tom took her extended hand and kissed it gallantly.

"I apologize, but the way you looked at the young lady, I believed you were lovers." His booming laughter echoed around the engraved, dark wooden beams above their heads.

Lex blushed. "Can I talk to you somewhere privately?"

"Sure. Come into the kitchen."

"Could I have a drink first?" Lure said.

"Of course," Lex said.

"I was just about to suggest it. What can I get you?" Tom said.

"Have you got any dry white wine?"

"Is Pinot blanc d'Alsace dry enough for you?"

"Sounds good. Can I also have some mineral water —sparkling?"

"Coming up. What can I get you, Alexander?"

"I'll wait until after our little chat."

"As you wish," Tom said, and returned to the bar.

"Do you have a plan?" Lure asked.

"Calling it a plan is too grand. I have a few ideas in mind, but I need to talk to Tom first before discussing them with you. I hope you're okay with that?"

"You're in charge. That's what I pay you for."

"Show me the money," Lex said with a wink.

Tom returned with the refreshments.

Lex offered Lure a cigarette and then lit it for her. "It will only take a few minutes," he said.

"Take your time. I have no immediate plans."

Lex followed Tom through the swinging door into the kitchen.

"You still drink whisky?"

"Is the pope a Catholic?"

Tom took a bottle of Jameson from the shelf above the sink and two water glasses from a drying rack next to it. He poured two fingers of whisky into each glass. They clinked and drank.

"Too much of anything is bad, but too much good whisky is barely enough," Lex said.

"Oscar Wilde?"

"Mark Twain."

Tom took a cigar from his breast pocket and offered it to Lex, who declined and lit a cigarette. Lex watched as Tom lit a match and rotated the cigar's tip over the flame.

"What can I do for you, Alexander?" Tom said and puffed on the cigar, then blew a cloud of smoke.

"Do you still have the cottage?"

"Yes, but we're hardly using it."

"Can my client stay there for a few days?"

"Sure. I have someone coming this weekend to do the garden, but I'll tell him not to come."

"No need for that."

"Okay, then I'll let him know that someone is staying in the house. May I ask why? I suppose it's not only for a love nest?" He roared with laughter.

"Whatever gives you that idea?" Lex said, as he felt his cheeks redden.

The music of Wings and the voice of Paul McCartney singing "*Band on the run, band on the run, and the jailer man and sailor Sam*" filtered through from the jukebox in the café.

"Your music is up to date. I'm impressed," Lex said, to change the subject.

"Yes, thanks to Erna. She's young enough to keep up with that dreadful pop music. But I still insist on a good collection of *levensliedjes*. We're in the Jordaan, after all."

"I'm not immune to a good pop tune, but I prefer jazz," Lex said, "but perhaps we should get together some other time to discuss our tastes in music?"

Tom topped up the glasses as Lex filled him in on the events that made it necessary for Lure to keep a low profile.

"I'm glad to help, but it's not going to solve your problem," said Tom.

"I agree, but first, I'll need to know what I'm dealing with."

"Let me know if you need a bit of muscle. Some of my … associates … are fairly handy when it comes to the rough stuff."

"For now, a quiet and safe place will do."

"You go and join your gorgeous girlfriend—I mean, your 'client'—and I'll make you one of my famous farmer's omelettes. Do help yourself to drinks from the bar."

TWO HOURS later, Lex was driving through an underpass of the recently opened A4. He turned right onto Riekerweg to get to Tom's cottage in the Tuinpark Ons Buiten community garden. Lex was reasonably familiar with its location since visiting with his parents. He recalled the occasion, which must have been the summer of 1959 or 1960, as a blissful afternoon with his parents, a good friend of his father, and what must have been Tom's second wife.

"How far to go? My backside is getting sore," Lure said, and Lex felt her warm breath against his ear. He couldn't blame her for being eager to get off, as the Vespa was a single-seater, and she was sitting on the luggage rack.

"A couple of minutes."

Lex slowed down as he drove onto the narrow dirt path leading into the park. They passed a small convenience store, and about two hundred metres further on, Lex spotted the cottage on the left. It was a spacious, white, one-story house with big windows and a black gabled roof. The front lawn, the size of two tennis courts, had been recently mowed, and the low beech hedge surrounding the plot was nicely trimmed.

Lure jumped off the Vespa to open the iron gate. Lex drove in and killed the engine. He pushed the scooter up the garden path to the back of the house. He had no intention of hanging around for too long, but he didn't want to call attention to their presence.

"Nice house," Lure said.

Lex pulled out the key and unlocked the door. "Ladies first."

The front door led to a spacious living room that featured a picture window. The dining area was open to the kitchen and had a sliding glass door opening up to a wooden deck at the back. A door at the far end led into a narrow hallway, and on the right was a spacious bedroom with a king-size bed. Lex lifted the covers— the bed was already made.

Lure opened the door on the opposite side of the hallway to a fully renovated bathroom. "Look at that nice big bathtub," Lure said, sounding like she'd stumbled upon a treasure chest. "Would you mind if I take a bath?"

"Why should I mind?"

"Maybe I can get you to scrub my back?"

Lex envisioned it with delight. "You have a bath, and I'll get us something for supper."

"IS THAT you, Lex?" she called out.

"Who else would it be?" Lex said under his breath. He left the shopping bag in the open plan kitchen and walked into the hallway. The bathroom door was ajar, and he saw Lure submerged in the soapy water. Her alluring breasts floated on the surface like twin volcanic islands.

"This is paradise. I haven't felt this relaxed for ages."

"I'm glad."

"You know what would make it perfect?"

"A good book?"

"No, a drink, dumb-ass."

"What would you like?"

"What's on offer?"

"Name it," Lex said, having checked the stock before going to the convenience store. "This is the property of a man who runs a bar, remember?"

"A glass of dry white wine would be heaven."

"I'll see what I can do, Your Majesty."

LEX ENTERED the bathroom carrying a glass of wine and a whisky tumbler.

Lure took the wine and said, "Here's to my knight and saviour."

"Here's to the magic of a hidden handgun," Lex replied.

They drank.

"Are you cross with me?"

"Who am I to be cross with anyone? Your little trick did save us, but I'm not much for those kinds of surprises. Introducing weapons always raises the stakes."

"If not for the interruption, I would have told you I carried a small gun."

"Never mind. But as soon as you're out of the bath, we need a good talk. There are plenty of unanswered questions."

"Fine, but I'm not getting out before you've scrubbed my back," she said. "You promised."

Lex was sure he'd done no such thing, but subconsciously, he had hoped she would suggest it. Her right arm appeared from under the water, and her

hand held a sponge. Lex drained the tumbler, and as
he put the glass on the sink, he caught a glimpse of his
clean-shaven face in the mirror. Most girls found him
attractive with his square jaw, brown eyes, Roman
nose, and thick dark hair kept short at the back and
long in the front. If it hadn't been for his eyes being set
a little too close together, they might even have found
him dishy.

Lex took the sponge and slid behind her to sit on
the tub's edge. He dipped the sponge in the water and
caressed the top of her back with it.

"Do it properly!" she protested.

Lex scrubbed harder.

"That's better," she said.

He hovered over her with a clear view of her firm
breasts and erect nipples. They were on the small side
(if you liked bosomy women). For a back door man,
they seemed just the right size.

"Whoops."

"What's the matter?"

"I got my sleeve soaked."

"Why don't you take your shirt off? It's hardly fair
that you're dressed when I'm naked."

"If you insist," Lex said, trying not to sound too
eager. He stood, tossed the sponge into the tub, and
removed his tie and shirt. He could see Lure admiring
his hairy chest (or maybe it was the tattoo of the Greek
hero Ajax on his left shoulder).

"Why don't you join me in the bathtub?" She put a
hand on his crotch. "I think your friend could use an
airing."

"And a cold wash," Lex said, slightly embarrassed.

"If you jump in, I'm sure we can find a satisfying solution to the swelling."

By that point, Lex needed no more encouragement. Under her watchful eye, he removed his trousers, boxer shorts, and socks. Facing her, he lowered himself into the hot soapy water, leaned back, and put his legs on her hips. His erection surfaced like a periscope.

"Hello there." Lure took hold of it with her right hand and stroked it, while the tip of her tongue played lustfully between her inviting red lips. Lex moaned as her left hand gently washed his testicles. He lifted her foot and kissed her toes.

"Why don't we relocate to the bedroom?" she said.

IN BETWEEN short spells of sleep, they yelled, moaned, groaned, screamed, howled, wrestled, grappled, and scuffled. Around ten, tired and satisfied, Lure was already asleep when Lex dozed off.

Someone pulling his arm was the next thing he recalled.

"Lex, are you asleep?"

"Not anymore." He turned towards her and opened his eyes.

"Nothing like good sex to make you hungry." She switched on the bedside lamp.

"How about cheese, bread and red wine."

"Sounds like heaven," she said and kissed him. "I'll take a shower while you set it up. How's that?"

Lex grabbed for her as she jumped out of bed, but she brushed him off. She picked up his shirt from a chair and put it on. Lustfully, Lex stared at her naked buttocks peeking out from under the hem as she crossed the hall to the bathroom. He heard the closing of the door and then the splash of the water.

Lex rolled out of bed, found his boxer shorts on a chair and slipped them on. Since Lure was wearing his shirt, he opened the wardrobe to see if Tom could help with one. A stack of neatly folded polo shirts presented itself. He opted for a blue one and slipped it on. It was big enough for two of him. Lex headed for the kitchen to get the food and drinks ready.

BEFORE GOING to the community garden, Lex had been eager to get some more answers from Lure about the mess she'd landed herself in, so he could get back home and attempt to do something about it. After taking a bite of the forbidden fruit, he was in less of a hurry.

"Tell me about yourself?" Lex said.

"There's not much to tell."

"When and where were you born?"

"In Amsterdam in the summer of 1950. My birthday is on 2 June. I'm afraid I haven't done anything significant in my twenty-four years on this planet."

"Is Lure your real name?"

"Laura Louise de Lang is the name on my birth certificate. I had a teacher in school who often joked: 'Here comes the lure of beauty.' Hence, my classmates started calling me Lure."

"What about your parents?"

"I never knew my father. I grew up as the only child of an alcoholic mother. She died when I was fifteen, and I lived with my aunt. Offered a modelling contract when I was seventeen, I quit school and moved away from my aunt." Lure became lost in thought, and Lex waited for her to continue.

"My first modelling contract turned out to be a front for erotica, and I did take part in a few movies. It was all softcore and paid good money. I met a man twenty years older who wanted to take care of me. We married in 1969."

"Any kids?"

"Thank God, no. I never loved him, and we divorced after two years of marriage. Since then, I've drifted from one unhealthy relationship to another. It's sometimes a curse to be beautiful. That's all men want from you, and it's all you give."

Lex wondered if her beauty was all he wanted from her.

"How do you support yourself?" he asked.

"I've done a bit of modelling, and otherwise lived on the meagre divorce settlement. I've been hard up for the past few years, and as I've already told you, I didn't think twice when I laid my hands on such a vast sum of money."

Lex refilled her glass with red wine and offered her a cigarette. She took it, and Lex lit it. She inhaled deeply, exhaled, and looked past him.

At that moment, Lex felt very drawn to her. The feeling awoke memories of his late girlfriend, also a stunner, but without Lure's captivating beauty. He'd loved her with every fibre of his being, until a freak accident took her life. Since her death, he'd stayed clear of any genuine emotional involvement. It always seemed to be head over heels when he did fall for someone.

Lex was in two minds about getting too mentally and physically attached to Lure. First of all, she was supposed to be a client, and he had to stay objective and clear-headed. Secondly, Lex still needed answers to several difficult questions and had no idea if he could believe a word she'd said. Admittingly she'd grabbed hold of his heart, and there wasn't much he could (or wanted to) do about it. He was a man, after all. He convinced himself that when a gorgeous creature like Lure gave herself entirely and passionately to him, it was foolish not to enjoy it.

Lure cleared her throat, and Lex expected her to continue her story. Instead, she demanded Lex say something about himself. "Let's keep some balance in the proceedings," she said.

"Fair enough. But first, we need another drink."

7

"ARE YOU from Amsterdam?" Lure asked.

"I was born on a spring Saturday afternoon in 1945, at the Sint Lucas Andreas Hospital in Haarlem. Coincidently, it was on the same day that the Nazis finally capitulated."

"Are your parents still alive?"

"Both dead—killed about four years ago in a plane crash."

"That's dreadful. Do you mind talking about it?"

"It's okay. I've talked about it so many times. They died in the attack by the Palestinian terror group PFLP. You probably remember the incident. My parents were on the Swissair flight from Zürich to Hong Kong, with a planned stopover in Tel Aviv. The plane blew up in mid-air.

"How old were they?"

"My father was fifty-four, and my mother, forty-seven."

"What were their names?"

"Adam and Julienne. They were devoted to each other. And to me." Lex wondered why she was taking so much interest in his parents, but concluded that she had never really had any of her own.

"Tell me about them."

"They met in Amsterdam shortly before the war. My mother was an exchange student from Paris, and my father was studying economics. At the outbreak of World War II, my mother, who was Jewish, remained in Amsterdam. In 1942, when the Nazis rounded up the Jews in Holland, my father's family in Haarlem hid her. They got married secretly on my mother's twenty-first birthday in 1943. Most of my mother's family didn't survive the war, and both my grandparents died in Auschwitz."

"What did your father do for a living?"

"After the war, he worked for IBM. In 1950, when I was five, he landed a new role at the company's European headquarters in Paris, and so we relocated from Haarlem to the city where my mother was born and raised. When I turned thirteen, we moved back to Amsterdam.

"*Parlez-vous Francais?*" she asked.

"*Évidemment.*"

"I'm better at doing it," she said with an inviting smile.

"Amen to that."

She surprised Lex by getting up and walking round to his side of the table. He pushed out his chair, and she sat on his lap. She kissed him passionately, and the feeling of her tongue against his gave him an erection.

"I guess the rest of your story will have to wait," she said.

"THUMP! THUMP! Thump!" At first, Lex couldn't place or define the noise that woke him. Then he realised that it was a fist banging against a wooden door. He opened his eyes. The curtains kept most of the daylight out of the room. Lex turned his head and saw Lure asleep next to him, oblivious to the noise. He looked at his watch. It was almost two o'clock.

"Thump! Thump! Thump!" Lex rolled out of bed, then slipped on his black trousers and the oversized polo shirt. Lure still didn't move as he headed for the front door. Lex turned the lock, pulled the door ajar, and peeped through the gap to see a dirty white baseball cap with the bill turned upwards and a Peugeot logo emblazoned on the front.

"Good afternoon, young man. I'm sorry if I woke you." The suntanned face, with a bushy white beard, looked more annoyed than remorseful for dragging him out of bed on a Saturday afternoon.

"Can I help you, sir?" Lex said, opening the door fully.

"I doubt it, unless you want to assist me in the garden."

"Ah, you're the gardener."

"I was about to let myself in, but then I saw the scooter in front of the shed."

Tom must have forgotten to inform him, Lex thought. "I'm a friend of Mr de Wit, and he's lent me the house for a few days."

"I can come back another time if it's inconvenient."

"Not at all. You go right ahead, Mr ...?"

"Name is Bram."

"I'm Alexander. Can I offer you coffee?"

"If it's not too much trouble."

"I'm about to have a cup myself."

"Then I accept. No sugar, but a few drops of milk would be nice."

"No milk, I'm afraid. I can offer you a few drops of whisky."

"Too early for me. Black will do," Bram said and took a pipe from his pocket. He put it between his lips but did not attempt to light it.

"I would invite you in, but my ... girlfriend is still asleep."

"No problem," he said, looking past Lex, his eyes burning with curiosity. He refocused on Lex and said, "All I need is the key to the shed from the top left kitchen drawer."

Lex fetched the key and handed it to him.

"Tell you what," Bram said, looking as though he were about to reveal a great secret. "I'll attend to the lawn and then leave you and your girlfriend to enjoy your Saturday. How is that?"

He would hear no argument from Lex, who was planning to interrogate Lure and could do without a nosy gardener lurking in the bushes. "I'll leave your mug of coffee on the doorstep," Lex told him.

"That's kind of you. I'll leave the key to the shed there when I'm finished. I would hate to disturb you two lovebirds more than I have to." Again, he looked past Lex and into the house.

"Much appreciated."

"Do you mind if I move your scooter to the side as it's blocking the door to the shed?"

"Please do," Lex said and closed the door.

THE GARDENER left after an hour. Lex and Lure had a snack before moving out onto the deck at the back of the house. It was a hot and sunny day. Lure wore her tight, black bell-bottoms and a white, sleeveless top she had found in the bedroom wardrobe. She'd pulled her long black hair back into a bun, which allowed Lex to admire her beautiful neck. Lex had to stop thinking about their night together in order to concentrate on getting some answers.

"Why did you lie to me about the apartment of Amanda Artz being yours?"

Judging by her reaction, the question and his unyielding tone surprised her. "It was only half a lie," she responded. "The apartment may not have been mine, but I did stay there."

"How do you know Amanda Artz?"

"She's my aunt. I'm looking after her place while she's on vacation in Italy."

"When did she leave for Italy?"

"On a Wednesday, so that must have been"—she counted on her fingers—"ten days ago."

"Was the dead guy the one you met at Hotel Krasnapolsky?"

"Yes."

"And you didn't know his name?"

"As I've already told you, he never introduced himself. When I searched for his ID, I found the money."

"And that's all you found?"

"What else would there be?" Her tone was tense.

"Does the name Jan Berger ring a bell?"

She appeared to be searching her memory, but to Lex, it seemed she was stalling for time.

"I've never heard the name before."

"You're doing it again," Lex said.

"What?"

"From time to time, you seem to caress what might be a tiny scar under your chin, and to me, it looks like you only do it when you feel nervous or tell porkies."

"I'm not aware of it, and I'm not telling porkies, as you put it," she said and put her hand in her lap.

"Anyhow, according to the police, Jan Berger was the deceased's name. He was a small-time hustler, so it makes you wonder why he had a bag stuffed with 100-guilder notes in his possession."

"Do the police know about me?"

"I'm afraid so. You're a murder suspect, and they are anxious to hear from you."

"Damn."

"I think that's the least of your worries."

"Why did you tell them about me?" Her nostrils flared, and her cheeks burned.

"Because you gave me no choice." Lex told her how he'd regretted rejecting her plea for help; how he'd gone to see her, only to find a dead man; how someone had knocked him out cold and how he'd spent a night in detention. "Your fantasy put me in a tight spot, and I had to give a reason for being in the wrong place at the wrong time."

"I don't see any need to raise your voice."

"There's every need. I don't know if I can believe anything you tell me. Is Lure de Lang your real name?"

"It is."

"Show me some ID."

She fetched her handbag and took out a wallet. Lex saw a small stack of 100-guilder notes when she opened it. She handed him a card with her name on it.

"It's a library card. That doesn't prove anything. How about something with a photo? A driver's license or a passport."

"I don't drive, and someone stole my passport."

"How convenient."

"If you don't even believe that I'm telling you my real name, why are you still here?"

"Isn't it obvious after our night together?"

She paused, and Lex waited her out.

"Will you stay another night?" she asked.

The question surprised Lex, but perhaps she wanted to divert him from his 'interrogation'.

"Would you like me to?"

"Oh, yes."

"I might, but first, I need you to tell me what happened after you left me that Sunday."

"I felt upset when you refused to help and didn't want to go home. I visited a friend in the north of Amsterdam and stayed with her all day. We had dinner in town, and then I returned to my aunt's apartment. I could hardly stand on my feet and went straight to bed. I slept like a log. You can imagine my shock the next morning when I found the guy whose money I'd stolen dead on the kitchen floor. As if Monday mornings weren't bad enough already!"

"Why didn't you report it?"

"Isn't that obvious? How could I explain a dead man on my kitchen floor without implicating myself?"

"With the available alternatives, I would have taken my chance."

"All I could think of was to get away as fast as possible."

"Did you lock the front door?"

"I made damn well sure I did. Why?"

"Because when I came a little later, it was unlocked."

"I can't explain it."

"Where did you go?"

"Back to my place in Amsterdam West."

"Nice of you to leave a parting gift in the form of a dead man for your aunt. According to my information, she would prefer a live one."

"I don't understand?"

"The lady in the bakery next door told the police that your aunt is fond of male company."

"I can't see the relevance."

"The relevance is that the lady, a cornucopia of gossip, seems to know a lot about your aunt, but not that she went on vacation to Italy."

"How should I know why that is?"

"Have you been in touch with her?"

"The lady in the bakery?"

"As you damn well know, I mean your aunt."

"How could I? She's travelling around Italy, and I've been hidden away in a hotel most of the past week."

"Tell me about it."

Lure told Lex that she'd been too upset to stay at home in her apartment. She'd wandered around the city until about eleven o'clock that evening. When she returned home, another shock awaited her. Someone had broken into her apartment and turned it upside down. That's when her passport had disappeared.

"And you believed that the only person who knew about you stealing the money lay dead in your aunt's apartment. That must indeed have freaked you out," Lex said unsympathetically.

"I don't think I care much for your tone," she said.

"Tell me, did the intruders find the money?"

"I may be naive, but I'm not stupid. The money is safe."

"And where is that?"

"If you're a good boy, I might tell you later."

"I'm dying to hear what happened next."

"I packed a bag and left."

"Where did you go?"

"To a small hotel in the city centre. I stayed in my room most of the time. By Wednesday, I couldn't take it anymore. The uncertainty was driving me crazy, and I needed to do something."

"The newspaper mentioned the murder."

"I didn't read any papers."

"If you had, you would have seen that the police had a suspect."

"Did they? Do they?"

"Not anymore, as far as I know. And the suspect was probably me."

"I felt alone and didn't know where to turn. As you were never far from my mind, I decided the best option was to see you and come clean about the whole damn mess. I went to your place, but you weren't at home. I spotted you in the downstairs bar, but I lost my nerve."

Lex looked at her pretty, anxiety-ridden face. He watched her delicate hands nervously playing with the silver locket around her neck. He reached over the table and offered her his hand. She took it, and the warmth of her touch felt nice.

"I'm glad you called me yesterday, and I want to help you. But I can't do that unless you're honest with me."

"I've told you exactly how it happened."

"I used to be a cop, and I've interviewed enough suspects to realise when someone is not being honest with me. I don't mind a few loose ends, but too many make me suspicious."

Lure withdrew her hand.

"Do you want to hear my version of the events?" Lex asked.

"Not especially, but you'll tell me anyway."

"After visiting me Sunday morning," he began, "you went home. Or should I say, you went to your aunt's apartment, if that's what it is? At some time on Sunday afternoon, Jan Berger rang the doorbell. I doubt we'll ever know how he managed to track you down, but that's not important right now. I guess you were expecting his visit, since you knew he was on to you, and that's why you'd asked for my help in the first place. Luckily, you'd stolen money from a small-time wimp suffering from big-shot-ism. No doubt, Jan Berger was pissed off, but he was not a violent man by nature. All he wanted was for you to give him back the money. How am I doing so far?"

"You should write a crime novel."

"You believe that what was once his money is now your money, and you're reluctant to part with it. But that's not what you tell him. Instead, you put on your vulnerable-little-girl act, and as he's not immune to your beauty, he's caught off guard. At some opportune moment, you plant a kitchen knife in his chest."

"That's insane. I could never do that."

"Okay, let's say that he confronted you physically, and you knifed him in self-defence. Same outcome, and you'd upgraded yourself from thief to murderer," Lex said hard-heartedly.

Tears of self-pity rolled down her cheeks, but Lex forced himself to stay unmoved.

"Bear with me while I finish the narrative. After killing Jan Berger, you decided to leave the apartment for greener pastures. But it's not that simple. It never is. Jan Berger himself was under observation by the people he stole the money from in the first place. When you came out of the apartment without him, the person or persons who were tailing him decided to check you out. Of course, they had no idea of your involvement. But when they found him dead without the money, they were not prepared to let two plus two make five."

"I think you need to rewrite that last part. It's a lousy plot."

"Maybe. The rest of the story could be the truth."

Lure stared off into the distance with gloom painted on her face. After a moment, she pushed her chair back, stood up, and walked into the house. Lex followed her.

She began collecting her few personal items.

"What are you doing?"

"I'm leaving."

"Don't be so melodramatic."

"Either you leave, or I do."

"I'm sorry if you don't appreciate me being blunt, but I'm just trying to get to the truth."

"You're repeating yourself, and somehow it's getting tedious."

"Perhaps, but we're not playing some silly game. There's a gang out there that we—or at least I—know absolutely nothing about and who are looking for you and whatever belongs to them. After the lucky escape at the Artis yesterday and the stunt with the gun, I doubt they will handle you with kid gloves."

"It's one thing to be straightforward, but why do you have to be cruel about it? We made love all night long. That must for sure mean something to you?"

Oh, Lure! What are you doing to me? Lex thought. He was a bag of mixed emotions. He longed for more sex with the gorgeous creature standing before him, even if he had to compromise to get it. His desire blinded him.

"It wasn't my intention to be cruel, and for that, I'm sorry." Lex sensed she was about to cry again. "Come over here," he pleaded. "Please."

She walked over to him, and he gazed into her teary eyes, and his mouth sought hers. They kissed; her tongue on his felt silky smooth like a mature whisky.

She kneeled in front of him, and pulled down his fly. Lex felt the warmth of her mouth and tongue, giving him the kind of gratification for which most men would do a deal with the devil.

8

THE HANGOVER woke Lex around five-thirty Sunday morning. *Plus ça change*, he thought. He turned his sore head and expected to see Lure sleeping beside him. She wasn't, and he felt a surge of anxiety.

"Lure?" No reply. Lex rose with some effort and headed to the bathroom. He knocked on the closed door. "Lure, are you in there?" He pushed the door open, hoping to see her in the tub. The bathroom and tub were empty. Lex walked through to the living area, relieved to see her bag on the couch. He looked out the glass door to the deserted deck at the back of the house —empty. Lex pulled the front door open and almost tripped over her as he rushed out. Lure sat on the steps, resting her head in her hands. He sat beside her.

"Are you okay?"

She turned to look at him. "Never felt better," she said with little conviction.

"That's wonderful. I can't imagine how you would feel without the police and some gang searching for you."

"Thanks for bringing it up. I'd almost forgotten."

"Do you have any idea who the gangsters might be?"

"Do we need to go over this again?"

"I'm only trying to help."

"I don't see how you can."

"Let me worry about that for the moment. All you need to do is stay out of the way for a few days."

"I don't know how long I can stay here alone without freaking out."

"Pretend you're on vacation and work on your tan. Get some supplies from the convenience store. Drink some wine and read a book in the garden. You can also go for some walks if you don't leave the community garden area."

"I'll need some fresh clothes and makeup. Could you get some stuff from my apartment?"

"It's not a good idea to go there myself, but I can ask my secretary. Write down what you need, the address, and give me the key before I leave."

"When can you bring it?"

"Tomorrow after breakfast."

LEX TOOK a copy of *de Volkskrant* and put it on the counter. Behind it stood a young guy with shoulder-length blond hair. An orange national team jersey covered his skinny torso. Lex couldn't remember if he'd seen him before.

"Nice hat, sir."

"Thanks. It's a Stetson Pork Pie."

"That's funny."

"You mean funny peculiar, or ...."

"Huh?"

"Forget it. Where's Wim?"

"He's on vacation."

"I thought he hated vacations?"

"Well, he's on one now. He's visiting his sister down south and will be back on Friday."

"No need to go to extremes."

"I'm not sure I follow?"

"Never mind. I see you're ready for the game this afternoon?"

"You bet. All we need is a draw to progress to the next group stage. The Bulgarians have already drawn twice, so it should be no problem. And with Johan Cruijff showing ...."

"And a pack of Player's Navy Cut," Lex interrupted the football lecture.

The young man grabbed a pack from the shelf behind and put it on the newspaper. Lex tossed a 25-guilder note on top of it all.

"Do you have something smaller, sir? I've just opened."

"I can come back later to get my change."

"No need for that. I'll give you credit until next time. As long as it's before the boss returns."

"Thanks," Lex said, picking up the 25-guilder note, the cigarettes, and the newspaper. "Enjoy the game."

Lex walked round the corner to the apartment. Rembrandtplein was more or less deserted, and it reminded him how much he loved the tranquillity of early Sunday mornings in Amsterdam (perfect for his usual hangover).

No time for regrets, he thought. Although the circumstances were far from ideal, he wouldn't have been without the two days cooped up with Lure in Tom's cottage. She'd made him feel alive again, and he smiled at the thought of her divine body and what she'd done with it to please him. Lex wanted more from this gorgeous creature. Like an addict, he was hooked and longed for the next hit.

"You look happy this morning." Bart stood in the doorway to his café.

"Sorry, Bart. I didn't see you there. Does your ugly face have to greet me every damn time I come home? Surely there must be other places for you to hang out?" Lex said with a chuckle.

"Feel free to stay away this afternoon if my ugly face is too much for you."

"Behind that bar of yours, it transforms into an object of beauty, especially when your mouth announces reduced prices."

Lex walked up the stairs, unlocked the door, entered the apartment, and opened the window in the office to air out the room. He put the kettle on, and while waiting for it to boil, he changed his clothing. Lex made coffee, walked to the office, sat behind the desk, and lit a cigarette. He absentmindedly skimmed the paper until a mug shot caught his attention. At the bottom of the page, the sombre portrait of the deceased Jan Berger stared up at him. According to the short accompanying article, the police were asking the public for information, especially about the victim's whereabouts before his death.

The photo gave Lex an idea. He stubbed out the cigarette, took a pair of scissors from the desk drawer, and cut it out. Then he lifted the receiver and dialled a number. It rang twice.

"Morning, Roos. Sorry to disturb you on a sacred Sunday morning."

"If it were so sacred, I would be in church," she said with a snicker.

"Have you got any plans for this afternoon?"

"Nothing apart from doing a bit of work in my community garden."

"Could you do me a favour?"

"Name it."

Lex told her about meeting Lure at the zoo, their lucky escape, and that he'd put her up in a cottage in the Tuinpark Ons Buiten. "She needs some stuff from her apartment in Amsterdam West. I don't want to go there myself in case the place is under observation. Would you mind going?"

"Not at all. Shall I come over?"

"I'm going to the Grand Hotel Krasnapolsky in a couple of hours. I'll stop by your place with the key, the list, and the address if it's convenient."

"That's fine." Lex ended the call.

AT PRECISELY 11:45, LEX rang the bell to Roos' fourth-floor apartment in de Wallen. He climbed the steep, narrow staircase. Roos' welcoming smile and Hercules' wagging tail rewarded his efforts as he reached the top landing. Lex found it odd to see Roos barefooted and in a dress.

"Do you have time for coffee?"

"Thanks." Lex removed his hat.

He'd visited her at home only once before. The size of her apartment made the spaciousness of his own seem lavish. What her place lacked in square metres, it made up for with its cosy, lived-in feeling; to say it was homey would be an understatement. Lex complimented her on how nicely she'd decorated the room.

"It ain't much, but it's mine," Roos said. She pointed him to one of two *bergères* in front of the small windows facing the street. "Make sure you don't bump your head against the ceiling."

Before taking off his jacket, he took Lure's key, the list, a packet of cigarettes and a lighter from his pocket. Lex sat down, and Hercules spun a few circles before making himself comfortable at his feet.

Roos brought two mugs of coffee and put them on the small, square wooden coffee table between the chairs.

"I have whisky if you want it spiked."

"That's tempting, but I'd better not. I'm going to the pub this afternoon. The boys are playing."

"Yes, of course—the nation will hold its breath at 4 p.m. I doubt I'll hold mine."

"That's what I thought."

"Do you want me to take the things to her this afternoon?" asked Roos. "I'm curious to meet the new mysterious woman in your life."

Lex took a sip of the coffee to conceal his blushes. "It's better you don't know where she is staying. Just bring her things to the office tomorrow morning."

"I understand."

Lex offered her a cigarette; she took one; he lit it and then lit one for himself.

"Here is the key to Lure's home and the list of stuff she needs. Her address is on the paper. As you can see, she lives near Westerpark."

Roos studied the list.

"While you're in her apartment, could you have a good look around? I'm interested in anything that might look odd. Also, see if you can find anything with her name on it. She claims someone stole her passport."

"I'll do what I can."

"But be sure to stay away from the windows."

"Will do."

"One last thing. Could you discreetly look around to see if anyone seems to be watching the place?"

"I'll disguise myself as a middle-aged woman walking her dog," she said with a wink.

THE GRAND Café Krasnapolsky is indeed grand. And so are the prices, Lex discovered soon enough. The spotlights shining from the high, white ceiling competed with the natural light coming through a huge window facing Dam Square. It made the place brighter than a college professor.

Lex walked across the white carpet with embarrassment for not taking off his shoes. He headed for the long mahogany bar with its white marble top and its row of light brown leather bar stools. They were all empty, and he slid onto one. The softness of the seat felt awkward to someone accustomed to spending a considerable amount of time on an old wooden bar stool at the Café de Monico.

A middle-aged bartender in a crisp white shirt and a black bow tie approached. He gave Lex a smile to show how happy he was to see him.

"I'll have a Heineken, please."

"Would you care for some snacks, sir?"

"Can the chef make me a cheese omelette?"

"That's our speciality, sir," he said. He pulled out the beer from somewhere under the counter. He opened the bottle, took a glass, and filled it halfway. "Anything else I can do for you, sir?"

"Yes, there is one thing." Lex took the newspaper clipping from his wallet and unfolded it. "Have you seen this man before?"

The bartender raised his bushy eyebrows for a moment, then shrugged. "Are you from the police?"

"I'm a private detective."

He studied the picture. "It's from the newspaper," he pointed out as he looked at the back of the clipping. "Who is he?"

"A small-time crook when he was still alive."

"I'm proud of my ability to remember faces, but I can't recall seeing his. Although the bar is fairly calm now, I see several hundred faces every week. It's impossible to remember them all."

"Does the name Jan Berger mean anything to you?"

"Should it?"

"You tell me."

"It doesn't."

"Were you behind the bar on Sunday, 2 June?"

"I'm here every Sunday from noon to midnight and on my poor feet most of the time."

"According to a witness of mine, he was behaving like he owned the place, insisting on buying drinks left, right, and centre. Then he hit on a beautiful woman sitting at the bar, before ordering a bottle of Taittinger. The two of them eventually left together."

"It didn't happen on my watch."

"Are you sure?"

"I might forget a face, but I never forget when someone orders a bottle of Taittinger. Especially on a Sunday evening. Maybe your witness is mistaken about the day?"

"Could be. Do you remember selling any bottles of Taittinger at the beginning of June?"

"Let me check the register." He disappeared through a door on his right. He returned about ten minutes later with the cheese omelette and a bread basket containing two small slices of bread. "I'm afraid we didn't sell any full bottles of Taittinger at the beginning of June. Too bad."

Lex couldn't have agreed more as he saw dark clouds ahead, with Lure having more explaining to do.

IT LOOKED like the opposition were moving in slow motion from the kick-off, and within five minutes, the Dutch inflicted the first damage. Johan

Cruijff (who else?) waltzed into the 18-yard box, and the opposing Bulgarian defender, moving at half speed, had no option but to bring him down.

"Penalty!" announced the television commentator enthusiastically, as a packed Café de Monico erupted.

"Can I reorder my drink in a minute?" Lex shouted to Bart, who pretended not to hear. He took a sip of whisky as he watched the other Johan (with the surname Neeskens) step up and release a rocket of a shot to the goalie's right.

"Unstoppable! One-nil Holland!" boomed the television.

The man standing behind Lex (whom he didn't know from Adam) gave him a bear hug, while he kept his eyes on the screen above the bar. "What the fuck is the referee playing at?" he shouted into Lex's ear.

Lex didn't enjoy it and pushed him away. He didn't seem to notice.

The man with the whistle ordered Johan Neeskens to retake the penalty. He stepped up once again: same shot, place, and result. This time, the Australian referee had no choice but to let the goal stand. For Neeskens, it didn't matter much. He could have done it over and over again with the same outcome.

Conceding the goal seemed to energise the Bulgarians slightly. But tempo is nothing without precision, and you would have had to be Bulgarian or believe in miracles to think the team would pull one back.

Lex ordered another whisky—this time at half-price. He had to admire Bart. The place was packed, and people were pushing to get served, but Bart went about his business in his usual, systematic way to satisfy every customer.

Lex desperately needed to pee, but decided to wait for the referee to blow the whistle for half-time. He watched Johan Cruijff pick up the ball near the Dutch penalty area and run half the length of the pitch with it before passing it with precision into the path of Wim Jansen. One-on-one with the goalie, the Bulgarian defender clipped him. A second penalty was awarded (or a third if you count the disallowed one). Again, Johan Neeskens stepped up—same shot, same place, same result. The score was two-nil to Holland at half-time. Lex asked his bear-hugging friend to keep his seat warm while he went to relieve himself.

He duly vacated the seat upon Lex's return, so he offered to buy him a drink.

"That's kind of you, mate," he said, "but with the prices down to a quarter, I'd rather have the pleasure myself of paying next to nothing."

"Fair enough," Lex replied, then turned to get Bart's attention. Paying next to nothing, as the man put it, was also something Lex enjoyed. He eventually caught Bart's eye. "Make it four fingers," he shouted.

Holland scored another two goals in the second-half. By then, the Dutch defender Rudd Kroll was feeling sorry for the Bulgarian team and scored an own goal. The game ended four-one to Holland and with a safe passage to the second group stage.

The match in Dortmund had shown a Dutch team at the absolute peak of its powers: total football at its finest. The team had set an unfair benchmark for all the other contenders in the World Cup, and a lesser standard would no longer satisfy. And yet, Lex's heart wasn't in it. He knew from previous experience that the only thing to compete with his love for the beautiful game was his love for beautiful women.

Lex's heart ached, and he longed to be with Lure. He thought about driving to her straight away, but as he slid off the bar stool, he found it challenging to walk straight. He blamed it on Bart and the Dutch team. They were in it together—too many Dutch goals and too many cheap drinks.

"No driving for you, buddy," Lex mumbled to himself as he headed upstairs to his single bed.

9

CONSIDERING THE level of intoxication the night before, Lex felt remarkably clear-headed. He took a stand-up bath in the kitchen and ran an electric razor over his face. Roos arrived as he was making coffee. She had Hercules in her arms and a Pan Am cabinet duffle bag over her shoulder. She lowered the pug dog to the floor and handed Lex the bag.

"You look like you've seen a ghost," she said.

"It's the bag."

"The only one I could find."

"When Lure stole the money from Jan Berger, she specifically mentioned it was in a Pan Am cabinet duffle bag. Why would she take the money out and then keep the empty bag in her apartment as evidence?"

"Maybe she lied?"

"Or perhaps she felt that she needed to name the bag to make the story sound true. She had a Pan Am bag at home, and that was the one that came to mind."

"Could be."

"Well, now you've seen her apartment, what do you make of it?"

"Two sparsely furnished rooms. An armoire, a wardrobe, and a double bed in one; and a love seat and dining table with two chairs in the other. No television or telephone. There was nothing on the walls, no photos, and hardly any knick-knacks."

"Any personal documents?"

"Nothing. Not even a name on the door. If it hadn't been for the key fitting in the lock, I wouldn't have known it was the right apartment."

Lex unzipped the bag and looked inside to find a couple of dresses, a black turtleneck, a pair of jeans, some underwear, and some toiletries. "Apart from the jeans, it's her style," he said.

"That's another strange thing. From what you've told me about the girl, I expected there would be more to choose from in the wardrobe."

"What are you saying?"

"The apartment doesn't look much like a home. It looks more like a place to crash for a night or two."

"Hopefully, she can explain it when I see her later."

THE DOORBELL rang as Lex was about to leave. He heard the click of Roos' heels on the old wooden floor as she walked into the hallway to answer it. "Gentlemen, you can't push your way in like that," he heard her say.

Lex stood and walked to the front of his desk.

"Get out of the way, lady, or you might get hurt."

Lex took a step into the hallway, and a hand as big as a medium-sized stingray covered his chest and pushed him back into the office. The hand belonged to a man with his shoulders and face chiselled from a single block of stone. His massive bald head hovered at least fifteen centimetres above Lex. Boris wasn't hard to recognise.

"We don't want any trouble, Mr Spijker," someone behind Boris said.

The giant slid his hand off Lex's chest and did his best to step aside in the small office—like an elephant trying to turn around in a phone booth. His eagerness to make way for the man behind him made it clear who was the boss.

"Why don't you go and sit behind the desk, Mr Spijker?"

Lex followed the suggestion as the man moved to the old brown Chesterfield in the corner, while Boris attempted to make himself scarce by filling the doorway.

"Take the weight off your feet, Mr Spijker. Or may I call you Alexander?"

"You can call me anything but late to dinner," Lex said, as he studied the middle-aged man with a receding, grey hairline and a ducktail beard. He wore a brown single-breasted jacket over a white shirt and held a fedora with a narrow brim. He reminded Lex of the Frog One character in *The French Connection*.

"Very amusing, Mr Spijker," he said, adjusting an immaculate red tie. He took a brown leather cigar holder from the inside right pocket of his jacket. "You mind if I smoke?" he said, eyeing the full ashtray on the desk.

"It's your health," Lex said.

He lit the cigar, and his ruddy complexion vanished for a second behind a cloud of thick smoke, and the heavy aroma filled the little room. The cigar smelled expensive.

"How can I be of service? Not to make any premature assumptions, but you look like you can afford my competitive rates." Lex lit a cigarette to calm his nerves and to contribute to the contamination of the indoor air.

"We're not here to hire you. Nor are we here to waste your time, so don't waste ours."

"Then, you'll excuse me for not offering you coffee."

"We have no bones to pick with you. All I need from you is to give me a satisfying answer to one question. If I don't like it, I may ask my friend Boris to shake or squeeze another one out of you." He pointed the cigar at Lex as if it was the barrel of a smoking gun.

"Try me."

"We're looking for a woman. A specific one. A specifically beautiful one."

"I do know a woman. But not of the specifically beautiful kind."

"Rumour has it you were spotted at the zoo on Friday with the woman I have in mind."

"I don't care much for rumours."

"Several eyewitnesses back it up."

"They must have seen my twin brother. I haven't been to the Artis since I was a kid."

"Are you familiar with the word 'mythomania'?"

"I must have missed class that day."

"It's the pathological tendency to exaggerate or tell lies."

"Happy to report it's a disposition I suffer only mildly from."

"Let me give you an easier word: 'nymphomania'."

"What is this? A lesson in linguistics?"

"Combine 'mythomania' and 'nymphomania', and what do you get?"

"Mythonymphomania," Lex suggested, not to disappoint the teacher.

"You're a real comedian. But you're mistaken. What you get is trouble on two pretty legs, Mr Spijker."

"Don't look at me."

"Trouble personified in the flesh of a goddess. I've no idea what name she gave you, but a fairly reliable source, while still alive, informed me that she called herself 'Lure'. However, an associate of mine, one you met on Friday at the zoo, tells me she was the spitting image of a girl I once met called Linda."

"The ideal has many names, and beauty is but one of them," Lex said, quoting Somerset Maugham.

"Yes, I'm sure she charmed you with her beauty. Did you nail her?" he said and laughed.

Boris grunted in the doorway.

"Speak for yourself, mister ...."

"Are you calling me a dirty old man?" he said.

"I wouldn't dare to call you old."

"That's enough, Mr Spijker. Tell us where you're hiding her, and we'll be on our way," he said heatedly.

Lex mirrored his anger. "What is it you don't understand? Let me spell it out for you: I haven't the faintest idea where she is, and I don't want to know."

"I don't buy it."

"I don't give a damn what you buy. The conversation is over, and I'd like you to leave. Take Boris the Bear with you on the way out."

"Shake him, Boris." Frog One waved his cigar towards the big man, who wrestled free of the doorway and stepped into the room. Lex, deciding offence would be the best defence, jumped from his seat, and swiftly walked round the table. Frog One blocked him with his legs, but Lex pushed them aside. Before Boris could take another step, Lex directed his right Dr Martens towards his groin. The kick would have made Bruce Lee proud, and Lex expected the giant to go down, at least onto his knees. One knee would have sufficed. Any ordinary man would have dropped to the floor after a kick in the balls, but Boris the Bear either didn't have any, or they were made of steel.

It would be an understatement to say he didn't flinch, but he showed no pain as he grabbed Lex under the arms with his enormous hands, lifted him from the floor, and shook him like a rag doll. Lex feared his head would part from his neck and tumble to the floor like a bowling ball.

He punched the giant in the face with his right hand, then went for his eye with his left, forcing him to lower Lex to the floor. It didn't matter much. He wrapped his massive arms around Lex and began to squeeze. The horrible sound of Lex's ribcage cracking didn't seem to bother him. It bothered Lex, and he prepared himself to end up like a crushed car in a scrapyard.

"That's enough!" called Roos in a firm voice from the door. "I rang the cops as soon as you arrived, and they should be here any minute."

"Let him go, Boris," Frog One said.

The giant tossed Lex towards the desk as if he was throwing a steak onto the barbecue. He slid across the top, landed headfirst on his chair, and then tumbled to the floor. He grabbed hold of the edge of the desk to pull himself up, but the pain in his chest stopped him.

"It's all a misunderstanding," Lex heard Frog One say to Roos. "We came here to hire your boss to locate a missing person for us. Suddenly he decided to attack my poor associate. It's no way to treat potential clients."

"Yes, your associate looks like a real victim," Roos said sarcastically. "I overheard my boss asking you to leave, and I think it's an excellent idea," she added.

"Come, Boris, let's take our business somewhere else. Before we leave, I'd like to give your boss some free advice. If he wants to live a long and prosperous life, he should stay clear of the Lure-Linda woman. She's not ...."

"I asked you to leave," Roos interrupted.

"Adieu, Mr Spijker and my fair lady. Don't call us; we'll call you."

Roos slammed the door behind them and then returned to the office.

Lex had finally managed to pull himself up onto the chair. "Did you call my friends at HQ?"

"Nope. I bluffed. I know you don't want to spend too much time with them."

"It worked like a charm. I think you saved my life."

"By the look of you, it was just in time. Are you alright, Lex?"

"I've felt better. I'm having trouble breathing. I think the brute cracked a few of my ribs. The pain is almost unbearable."

"I think we need to get you to the emergency room."

"Don't be silly. All I need is to rest for a few hours." An attempt to get to his feet made him cough, and the pain almost made him faint. Lex put a clenched fist to his mouth.

"My God, Lex!" Roos said. "You're coughing up blood!"

Lex opened his hand and saw that it was indeed covered in blood.

"That does it! I'm calling an ambulance," Roos said.

10

FOR A couple of days, Lex suffered from confusion, light-headedness, and dizziness. The pain in his abdomen was dulled only by the torment of the simple act of breathing. When he'd finally gotten through the emergency room trauma, the doctor gave the verdict: a couple of fractured ribs, a ruptured spleen, and a punctured lung. The doctor at Sint Lucas Hospital told Lex surgery could be avoided if he stayed immobile in a hospital bed for a few days. Painkillers helped him get through the day, and sleeping tablets, through the night.

After being hospitalised, he'd no other choice but to ask Roos to take Lure her stuff and let her know about his run-in with the two gangsters. Lex stressed that she should tell Lure not to worry, that he would survive and come to see her later in the week.

On Wednesday morning, Lex felt well enough to insist on being discharged. The young nurse informed him, with a disarming smile, that it was up to the doctor to make that decision.

Waiting for the doctor to make his rounds, Lex dozed off. He thought it was a dream when he heard Roos' voice. He opened his eyes to see her beat-up face. Her black eye and split lip made him forget his own pain.

"What happened to you?" Lex gasped.

"The two shady characters from Monday returned to have another chat, and I'm afraid they have no respect for women."

"I'll kill them," Lex said through gritted teeth. "It's all my fucking fault."

"I'll live," she said, putting on a brave face. "They forced me to tell them where Lure de Lang is staying."

"Have you warned her?" Lex exclaimed.

"How could I? I've no telephone number for the cottage, and somehow I didn't feel like going there for another encounter with the gangsters. You don't pay me well enough to risk my life twice in one day."

"I'm sorry for being so inconsiderate."

"And I'm sorry for revealing her whereabouts. It wasn't the beating. I could take that. I broke down when the gorilla held Hercules out of the window and threatened to drop him if I didn't give them the information." Tears filled her eyes. "Fortunately, Hercules is okay."

"The bastards!" Lex exclaimed, with a sinking feeling. Lure was probably done for, and if she'd tried to defend herself with her Baby Browning, she could be dead, although Lex doubted they would kill her without first finding out where she had hidden the stolen money.

"I must go to the cottage."

"You're not well enough," Roos protested, "and what can you do? It will be too late by the time you get there. Don't you think this woman has caused you enough trouble already? Since her ...."

"Maybe, but ...."

"Please don't interrupt me, Lex!" Roos snapped. Her nostrils flared, and she took a step towards the bed. "That woman has been nothing but trouble since her first visit ten days ago. I get that her beauty has cast a spell on you and that spending last weekend in her arms did nothing to dampen your, in my eyes, irrational intoxication with her."

"It's hard for me to explain, but I have my reasons, which I don't expect you to understand. Anyhow, it's no longer only about Lure. They've attacked me, and now you. It has become personal, and that demands a response."

"You don't need to play the gallant hero on my behalf." Roos put her hand on his arm. Her anger had evaporated as quickly as it had flared.

"Let me check out the cottage, and then we'll take it from there. How's that?"

"It's your call, Lex."

Ignoring the pain, Lex slid out of bed and headed for the wardrobe in the corner of the room. The nurse entered as he was opening the door to take out his clothing. "What do you think you're doing?" she said.

"What does it look like?"

"Like you're planning to get dressed."

"I'm afraid some urgent business has come up, and I have to leave immediately. Please give my regards to the doctor."

She protested, but Lex ignored her as he headed for the bathroom to get dressed.

THIRTY MINUTES later, the taxi was driving through the A4 underpass and turning right onto Riekerweg. Lex told the driver where to enter the Tuinpark Ons Buiten community garden, and he slowed down, navigating the Mercedes along the narrow dirt path.

"What time did you leave Rembrandtplein?" Lex asked Roos, who was sitting next to him. He wanted her to go home and rest, but she had insisted on coming along.

"Around half-past ten."

Lex looked at his watch. If the gang had gone directly to Tom's cottage, they had a head start of more than an hour.

They reached the convenience store, and Lex told the driver to stop. Driving straight up to the house would be foolish, although he expected they were long gone. Lex didn't have much of a plan for his approach, unless 'sneak-up-on' could be called one.

"Roos, you stay in the car. If I'm not back in fifteen minutes, you can call the police from the payphone in the store." Lex wrote down a number and gave her a few coins.

"I wish you'd called them already." Lex heard no reproach in her voice, only concern.

Lex caught a glimpse of the driver's inquisitive, plump, rosy face in the rear-view mirror.

"Don't do anything foolish, Lex. I don't want to have to go back to the hospital," Roos said as he got out of the car.

Seeing her damaged face and feeling the pain from his own fractured ribs, Lex needed no encouragement to be careful. He walked the two hundred metres to Tom's white, one-story, black gabled house as quickly as possible and kept low to hide behind the beech hedge. He reached the black iron gate and peeked towards the house and the big window. The place was as quiet as a prayer meeting. To approach the house from the rear would be sensible, but that meant climbing over a few fences, which his injury prevented.

Lex took a deep breath, felt the pain from his punctured lung, and headed up the garden path towards the front door. Slowly he pushed down the handle to discover a locked door. He moved to the big window and cupped his hands around his eyes. He saw no one nor anything to cause alarm, so he walked around to the back of the house. Closed curtains prevented him from looking into the bedroom.

Lex walked across the wooden deck at the back and pulled the sliding door, which, to his surprise, slid open. He entered the cottage and walked through the living room towards the bedroom. He pushed the door open, hoping to see Lure asleep in the bed. She wasn't. Lex opened the door to the bathroom, hoping to see her taking a bath. She wasn't.

He returned to the living room, and it was as though she'd never been in the house. He could find no clues to what had happened to her. If she'd gone for a walk, there would be traces of her. Had she packed up and left of her own free will, or had someone taken her by force? Lex would expect her to have defended herself with the handgun if cornered. Maybe she was asleep or had decided to go along without resistance? Perhaps ….?

Lex had to decide if he wanted to walk away from the whole damn mess. As Roos had pointed out, it was the sensible thing to do, but he was still reluctant.

He'd failed to keep Lure safe. With an approach to the truth as lean as her beautiful body, she'd undoubtedly contributed to the situation. It could be justified to leave her to stew in her own juice, but they'd been lovers, and she was, in a sense, still his client. He was also reluctant to let the gang get away with it. Lex had to stay positive, although the all too familiar feelings of hopelessness and inadequacy told him his 'black dog' was in the neighbourhood. Lex checked his watch. The fifteen minutes were almost up, and he must get back to Roos before she alerted the police. The last thing Lex needed was the interference of Laurel and Hardy. He left the way he had come.

LEX OPENED the door to Café de Monico. Half an hour until kick-off, and the pub was filling up. He took his usual seat at the bar. Bart stood at the cash register with his back turned. Lex was sober, but he wouldn't be by the end of the game—goals or no goals. His mood was foul, and tonight he needed alcohol to dim the physical and mental pain. Lex lit a cigarette, the first since getting injured. It was a terrible idea. The doctor was right; smoking with a punctured lung was stupid, dangerous, and unpleasant. He stubbed out the cigarette in the ashtray in front of him.

Bart finally paid him some attention. "What happened to you? You don't look too good."

"I feel worse than I look, but you don't want to know."

"Whisky?"

"Make it four fingers."

"As your local bartender, I suggest you pace yourself."

"I don't need any instructions on how to get intoxicated. And certainly not from my bartender."

"Just saying."

"Let's keep it simple. I order, you serve, and I pay." Bart poured the drink for Lex, who downed it in one gulp to emphasise that he meant what he said. "Hit me again."

"I'm warning you, Lex. If you make any trouble, I'll kick you out."

Lex wanted to tell him he couldn't promise anything, but instead, he told Bart not to worry. "Like everyone else, I'm just here to enjoy the Clockwork Orange team torment the boys from the pampas."

TO SAY that Holland tormented the Argentinians was putting it mildly. Within the first thirty minutes, the team in orange had at least five chances to score.

Perhaps out of pity, Johan Cruijff and his teammates settled for a couple of goals.

Lex didn't pay much attention to the game. He wanted to, as it's not every day you got the chance to watch a game played with such finesse. His state of mind made it hard to concentrate, and the noise level was deafening. With his reduced lung capacity, Lex struggled to breathe in the smoke-filled room. He did pay enough attention to notice that by the time Holland had scored a third goal, midway through the second-half, the price of the whisky (which he ordered whenever he managed to attract Bart's attention) was extraordinarily agreeable. Johan Cruijff's decision to add a fourth goal in injury time had no bearing on Bart's generous arrangement. The Scottish referee's last whistle of the game must have come as a relief for Argentina and their compatriots. It certainly did for Lex. He was beat. And drunk.

Just as he was sliding off the bar stool to leave, someone pushed him hard in the back, and he stumbled on his drunken feet. He cursed from the pain in his fractured ribs, whirled round, and stayed upright by grabbing hold of a guy standing in front of him. He may have been noticeably shorter than Lex, but the muscles rippled beneath his tanned skin. He forcefully removed Lex's hands.

"What's your problem, man?" Lex slurred.

"The problem is that you've been all over my girlfriend for the last hour," he said, and reached up to place a firm, possessive hand on the shoulder of a blonde girl standing next to him.

Lex didn't recall having 'been all over her' as he put it. Lex was in no condition to take the man on in his drunken state, but he didn't care. "Piss off! Come back when you're tall enough to look over the counter."

The guy took up a boxing posture, flexing his biceps for his girlfriend and Lex to admire.

"Stop it right there, gentlemen! There'll be no fights in my humble establishment. What's the matter with you two, anyway? How hard can it be to show each other some brotherly love and respect after what our team has done?" Somehow Bart managed to look twice the size, and the orangutan had transformed into a grizzly bear. "The door is there, gentlemen," he said, pointing in the direction of the Rembrandtplein. "You both have the red card for the next game on Sunday."

11

LEX WOKE on the couch, almost fully dressed. He'd managed to take off his hat, leather jacket, tie, and shoes. It was hardly an achievement to celebrate. He couldn't decide what troubled him more: the sore head and aching body or the qualms over his drunken behaviour.

Lex sat up and looked at his watch: ten to eleven. Thankfully, he'd told Roos to take a few days off to let her black eye and bruised lip heal. He didn't want her to see him like this, and Hercules would not have approved of the big 'black dog' that had moved in overnight. The black dog answered to the name 'Depression' and fed on isolation, booze, and self-pity.

Lex closed the curtains in the living room, the bedroom, and the office to keep the outside world at a safe distance. He checked the stock of whisky—with a half-full bottle in the desk drawer and an almost full bottle in the kitchen cupboard, he decided it was enough to spike the coffee for at least twenty-four hours.

Lex's hands shook as he dumped two teaspoonfuls of instant coffee into an Ajax Amsterdam mug, filled it half full with boiling water and topped it up with whisky. He stirred it carefully, before carrying it to the living room.

Lex made himself as comfortable as possible on the couch. He took a healthy gulp of the magic potion, then another and leaned back and waited for the healing effects. He stared up at the ceiling, which needed a coat of paint, and he knew that's what he should be doing instead of cultivating his self-pity.

Lex let random thoughts of dread roam around inside his head for about half an hour, while emptying the mug sip by sip. He lit a cigarette and inhaled softly to test if his lungs could endure the pain. The odds stacked against him, he gave up after another drag and stubbed it out in the ashtray.

It was time for a refill, and Lex walked to the kitchen and fired up the kettle. As he waited for the water to boil, he fetched a photo album from the bookshelf in the office.

Flipping through the album was a favourite pastime when letting the black dog out of its cage. Lex tormented himself with memories from happier times, when everyone was still alive and when he believed that some of God's grace still shone upon him. While Lex blamed Him for putting his parents on that fateful flight, he only blamed himself for the death of his fiancée.

Lex made the coffee, poured in the whisky, and walked back to the living room with the mug in one hand, the bottle of whisky in the other, and the album tucked under his arm. He put the coffee and the bottle on the coffee table, and lowered himself onto the couch. He opened the album and found the page he usually sought. Lex studied the black and white photo closely. Not that he needed to, as he'd seen it enough times for it to be imprinted on his memory. The happiness shining from her eyes reflected in her smile. Her long dark hair blew in the wind, and her gorgeous, young body leaned up against his as they stood in front of the rented Fiat 124 Sport Coupe.

After a few rainy days, they had enjoyed a beautiful sunny day without a cloud to disturb the blue sky. They'd made love in the morning and eaten a sumptuous breakfast on the hotel terrace before hitting the road to Palermo. One minute she was sitting beside him, full of life, talking about their upcoming wedding, and the next, she was gone.

It was the stupidest of accidents and could easily have been avoided. The traffic on the road was moderate, and so was the car's speed. She told him she needed her sunglasses from the back seat, unfastened her seatbelt, turned around, and leaned over the seat. The sight of her well-curved bum in tight shorts distracted him, and he failed to react in time to a truck, which came to a complete and sudden halt about ten metres in front of them. He slammed into its back, and the impact catapulted his fiancée into the dashboard. She died instantly from a broken neck.

If this wasn't devastating enough, the autopsy showed that she was six weeks pregnant.

During the investigation, Lex was reprimanded for not ensuring that his passenger was wearing a seatbelt. That was as close as anyone came to blaming him for her death. Lex was traumatised, remorseful, and ashamed, especially since he had walked away with only whiplash and a sore shoulder.

As soon as Lex returned to Amsterdam, he sold his car and bought a Vespa scooter, promising himself he was done with driving and falling in love.

The death of his fiancée was also the last straw when it came to his job at the Amsterdam police. He could no longer live with the department's indifference to corruption and the increasing intimidation from his colleagues. Lex handed in his resignation two weeks after the accident, and no one protested.

He closed the photo album and emptied his mug. The sensible thing would be to eat something, but all bets were off with regards to common sense. He grabbed the whisky bottle, took a pull and then another. He curled up, closed his eyes, and waited for the sleep of the unconscious. Thankfully, he didn't have to wait long.

LEX WOKE with a sense of foreboding and a feeling of discomfort. Without switching on the light, he walked through the apartment to the window in the office. There was a small hole in the curtain, and he peeked through it. Darkness had descended upon Amsterdam and the Rembrandtplein crowd. Their ever-increasing weekend disturbances began every Thursday evening. It seemed as though they were intent on ensuring that nobody with their bedroom windows facing the square should get any sleep (unless they were intoxicated, deaf, or wearing earplugs).

Seeing the café and restaurant lights made him realise he hadn't eaten in more than twenty-four hours. Not sure what he would find, he opened the cupboard. To his delight, there was a can of sweet corn and a package of sliced white bread. Perfect. He heated the corn and toasted two slices of bread. He spread the bread with mustard and then piled the hot corn on top. He took a beer from the fridge and carried the plate to the living room. It tasted like the best meal he'd ever had. The beer also hit the spot.

Lex finished his dinner, pushed the plate away, lit a cigarette, and immediately felt the sting from his punctured lung. He went for a pee, dropped the cigarette into the toilet, and flushed. He made himself another spiked coffee and returned to the living room.

He took a random paperback from the bookcase. It was a *Tanner* novel by Lawrence Block, and after a couple of pages, having read the same sentences repeatedly, he gave up. It wasn't the story that was out of focus, but his mind. Images of his fiancée and Lure kept popping up. One was dead, and the other could either be dead or in serious trouble. Lex should be out there looking for her, but in his present state, he preferred to drink, feel sorry for himself, curl up on the couch, and sleep. So that's what he did.

HE FELT someone gently shaking his arm.

"Lex, wake up!" He opened his eyes and saw Roos hovering over him.

She wore a colourful blouse and tight jeans, and her perfume stood in stark contrast to the apartment's foul odour. A worried look had replaced her usual smile. "I've called you a few times."

Lex rubbed a hand over his three-day stubble beard. "What day is it?" he asked, to emphasise the state of affairs.

"It's Saturday."

"What's the time?"

"Around 10:30."

Lex felt embarrassed for letting his secretary find him like this. It was his living room, but it was also her office. Not knowing what to say, he blurted out, "You look better."

"You don't."

"I'm just taking a time-out."

"Sure, but it looks more like you've given up."

"I've had better days."

"Are you just going to wallow in self-pity when there is someone that needs you? I don't get it, Lex. A couple of days ago, you were all fired up to find your lady friend and go after the gang, even though I advised against it. What happened?"

"I let the black dog in," he mumbled.

"You did what?"

"I lost hope. What can I do, anyway?" he said tearfully.

"For a starter, you can stop drinking and feeling sorry for yourself. Then you can start using those detective skills of yours. You do call yourself one, don't you? It's your choice, Lex, but if you want to piss away your life like this, I'm afraid you'll have to look for a new secretary. Although a psychologist would probably do you more good."

She drew the curtains and opened the windows. The breeze felt good.

"Time to get cleaned up, and the same goes for the apartment." She took a couple of dirty plates from the coffee table and carried them to the kitchen.

Lex sat for a moment, battling his demons.

Roos returned to the living room. "What will it be?"

"I think I'll head for the public baths."

"Good idea. While you do that, I'll clean up."

"Thanks, Roos, I'm grateful," he said and managed a timid smile.

"You can show it by getting your act together. You're a better man than this, Lex."

12

A NEW day. A fresh start. That's how it felt, waking up without a hangover on that Sunday morning. After Roos had rescued Lex from the black dog the previous day, he'd promised her and himself to go easy on the booze for a few days and eat properly.

It was a blessing in disguise that Bart had banned Lex from watching the Sunday afternoon game at Café de Monico. Instead, he would listen to the commentary on the radio, while enjoying a nice cup of coffee without milk, sugar, or the comfort of Johnnie Walker.

The afternoon before, he'd cleaned up, feasted on Roos' excellent chilli con carne, then spent a couple of hours making a plan of action for the coming days. It was in no sense rigid, since Lex had no idea what would happen when he set the ball rolling.

Lex put on a clean white shirt, a black tie, and black trousers. After having coffee and toast, he went out immediately. He rode on his Vespa down the Rokin, past Dam Square, along the Damrak, turned left at

Prins Hendrikkade and headed west towards Café Chris in the Jordaan. It was overcast, with a mild breeze, and he enjoyed speeding along the almost empty streets—one of the free pleasures of driving in Amsterdam on Sundays.

Lex parked across from Café Chris and checked the time on his watch. Tom immediately spotted him across the narrow street. "Alexander, you old bandit!" he bellowed. "I've been expecting your visit."

"I thought you would." Lex walked towards him, and since they never hugged or shook hands, Lex tipped his hat.

"Bram told me you'd vacated the cottage. When he came to work in the garden on Thursday, the sliding door to the terrace was open, and I suspected you'd forgotten to lock it. It got me slightly worried, and I've called you a few times."

"I've been out of circulation for a few days." Lex followed Tom into the café. He walked behind the bar as Lex slid onto a stool.

"Would you care for a cup of coffee? It's freshly made."

"Sounds good."

"Spiked?"

"I'm off the booze for a few days. My account of events will make it clear why."

Tom poured two mugs of coffee and put one in front of Lex. "I'm all ears, but you'll have to accept a few interruptions as I deal with my customers."

"No problem. Maybe I should get started while we're still alone."

Lex filled Tom in for the next couple of hours, over several cups of coffee and in between a few regulars coming and going.

He told him how he'd stayed with Lure at the cottage for a few days. Lex saw from Tom's expression that he needn't go into detail about his crush on the girl. Lex told him about her predicament, the first visit from the gang that put him in hospital, and their second visit forcing Roos to reveal Lure's whereabouts.

"Walking away is not an option, is it?" Tom said.

"Not anymore. I almost gave up, but I've made my decision. That's also why I'm here and why I'd like to ask you for another favour."

"You know I'll do anything to help, Alexander. Well, almost."

"You still have connections in the Amsterdam underworld?"

"What do you think?" he said, grinning.

"Could you dig up any information about the gang?"

"Are they Dutch?"

"Absolutely, and they may even be Amsterdammers." Lex described Frog One, Boris the Bear, and the Tom Wolf wannabe.

"I'll see what I can do."

"Much appreciated."

"They sound like a mean bunch, and I think you could use some assistance," Tom said as he excused himself, serving a couple seated at a table at the back of the room. He returned, refilled Lex's mug with coffee, and said, "I'll put you in touch with one of my friends.

He's a former boxer, and at the risk of insulting the profession, I'll say that not only is he as strong as an ox, but he's also got brains. His name is Alwin Smit, but he's known as 'Big Al' among his friends. He's the most loyal friend you can wish for, but if you get into his hair, he can be, if you pardon my French, a mean motherfucker."

"If I can have him as my friend, I wouldn't mind. What will he want in return?"

"You leave that to me, and if it works out, we can call it even."

LEX STOPPED for lunch at the Grand Café in Amsterdam Central Station on his way home. After a few days, cooped up in the pigsty with the black dog as his only companion, a bit of stylish ambience, and some decent food in a lively atmosphere would do him good.

Lex entered the spacious waiting room of yesteryear and admired the high rosewood wall panels. Most of the oak tables and leather chairs were occupied. Orange shirts and hats dominated the room and served as a reminder to anyone who should be so careless as to forget about the afternoon game.

A waiter dressed in a white shirt, black waistcoat, and bow tie showed Lex to a table for two near the panorama window overlooking platform one. Lex took off his jacket and hat and hung them on a nearby coat rack. As he sat down, the waiter handed him a menu and asked what he wanted to drink. To keep his alcohol-free promise, Lex ordered a Coke. Half a minute later, the waiter returned carrying a tray holding a highball glass with ice cubes, a bottle of Coke, and a thimble-sized glass bowl of peanuts. He poured the drink, and Lex ordered the 'Home-made American Hamburger with Iceberg Lettuce, Tomato, Cheddar Cheese, Bacon, and Fried Onion'. Reading the description on the menu made his mouth water.

"Can I have some fries with that?"

"All our burgers come with fries, sir."

Fortunately, Lex didn't have to wait too long for the food. He'd only taken a few bites when a different waiter approached the table, with a stout man on his tail.

"Would you mind sharing your table, sir?

"Be my guest," Lex said with a welcoming motion.

His new lunch companion squeezed his corpulent backside into the seat while his paunch pushed against the table. Lex was immediately put off by his chubby, flushed face.

The man ordered a pint of beer.

"Anything to eat, sir?"

"I'll have what he's having," the man said and pointed to Lex's plate. "Looks like a decent burger."

To avoid making conversation, Lex took a bite of his burger. It was, indeed, decent.

"Do you mind?" the man said and helped himself to a few of Lex's fries. "I'll pay you back as soon as my food arrives."

The waiter brought his pint.

"Cheers, mate." He lifted the glass, and as Lex didn't want to appear rude, he raised his glass, and they clicked.

"Is that a Cuba Libre?"

"Plain Coke."

Within a few seconds, the man had almost emptied his pint.

"Warming up for the game this afternoon?" Lex said, feeling the craving for a nice, cold beer.

"Whatever makes you think I'm following the football?" He roared with laughter and helped himself to some more of Lex's fries.

"Maybe the fact that you're wearing an orange football shirt."

"You've got me there, Mr Holmes," he said with a chuckle. "I'm meeting my buddies at a pub in de Wallen at three. You're welcome to join us. The more, the merrier."

It took Lex two seconds to consider his offer. "That's kind of you. Unfortunately, I have another appointment."

The waiter brought the burger and fries, and the man emptied his pint and ordered another. He didn't offer Lex any of his fries to 'pay him back'. He took a large bite of the burger, but it didn't stop him from talking. "A win against East Germany today and against Brazil on Wednesday, and we're in the final."

"Let's not get ahead of ourselves," Lex suggested.

"It's a formality," he insisted. "The others have no chance. We're too good. Did you watch the game against Argentina?"

"I did."

"That was brilliant. Almost divine. I must admit it's the best I've seen. I tell you what, our team is better than the Brazilian team that won four years ago."

"That's a big statement."

"Maybe, but I'm right. One more week, and we'll be champions of the world."

"Cheers to that," Lex said, and lifted his empty glass.

The waiter must have thought that Lex had signalled him, as he approached the table. "Another drink, sir?"

Had he been alone at the table, he would have ordered a cup of coffee. "Let me have the bill, thanks."

"Let me get this one."

"That's not necessary."

"I ate half of your lunch."

"Nonsense. You had a few of my fries."

"And a seat at your table."

"Hardly mine."

"I insist."

"What will it be, gentlemen?" the waiter said impatiently.

Lex's dining companion settled it by handing the waiter a 50-guilder note.

"Much appreciated. Thanks," Lex said and stood up. He took his hat and jacket from the coat rack and put them on. "I wish you a good game and a pleasant afternoon with your friends." Lex tipped his hat as a parting salute, and the man waved as Lex walked out onto platform one.

A FEW years earlier, Lex had been a regular listener to football commentary on the radio. Due to the increasing number of televised games since the previous World Cup in 1970, he'd fallen out of practice. Lex tried his hardest to stay focused on the game, but his mind kept drifting. Not knowing Lure's fate, he told himself he should be out looking for her. On the other hand, roaming the streets of Amsterdam on a Sunday afternoon would serve no purpose, no matter how much Lex longed for her.

The first goal of the game (scored after seven minutes by the ever-dependable Johan Neeskens) stopped him from speculating. Lex didn't need the radio to tell him that Holland had scored. The collective roar from a city in lockdown, carried by the summer breeze through his open windows, made it abundantly clear.

Rob Rensenbrink's goal at the hour mark put the game out of reach for East Germany, and the game ended with no more goals. According to the commentator, nearly 70,000 people in the Parkstadion in Gelsenkirchen, the entire nation, and millions worldwide had witnessed another masterful performance from the team in orange. With their unique brand of total football, the Dutch team had once again ripped up the rule book and created their own.

Maybe the optimistic guy Lex had shared a table with at the Grand Café was right: one more week, and Holland would be world champions. By then, Lex hoped that he'd have confronted the gang, found Lure, made her take responsibility for her part in the mess, and determined whether they had a future together.

13

TO SAY that Lex slept like a baby would be going a bit too far, but it was the best night in a long time. There's nothing like a decent sleep to give optimism and self-confidence.

When Roos and Hercules arrived around nine, he looked sharp at his desk. Roos' broad smile showed how pleased she was to see him restored to his old self, and Hercules seemed none the wiser about the visit of the black dog.

"I have a job for you this morning." *It sounds good saying it*, he thought. "It's out of the office."

"As long as it doesn't involve gangsters," she said, pointing to her bruised face.

"I pray never to put you in danger again, Roos."

"Never mind. I survived, and so did Hercules."

"The task does involve gangsters, but should have no risk whatsoever. That is, as long as you keep your voice down."

"I guess it's either the morgue or the library."

"I would never send a pretty lady to the morgue."

"That's reassuring. What's the task?"

"It's a long shot, but from now on, we'll leave no stone unturned. Could you browse through the papers, say from three months back, and look for any news on crimes committed by a gang or a syndicate? I've no evidence whatsoever. It's just a hunch, but it could have something to do with ticket racketeering. You could also keep an eye out for any news about the murder of Jan Berger."

"I'll get right to it," she looked at her watch, "as soon as they open in about forty minutes."

"Great. I will make a few calls, and then I'll also be out and about."

"That gives us time for coffee. Would you like a cup?"

"You know me. I'm always ready for a nice fresh brew—spiked or not."

"Let's make it not, shall we?"

"Is that non-negotiable?" Lex said with a twinge.

AS SOON as Roos had left for the library, Lex called Wouter Schenk's direct number at the Leidseplein station. He let the phone ring a few times and was about to give up when someone answered.

"Is that you, Wouter?"

"He's not here. Can I take a message?"

Lex recognized the voice. "Good morning, young Constable Reint. Remember me?"

"Should I?"

"You were kind enough to put me up for a night a couple of weeks ago."

"Oh, it's you."

"Please tell Wouter to call me."

"Give me your number."

"He's got it already."

Ten minutes later, Wouter returned the call. He skipped any small talk and cut straight to the chase. "What can you tell me about your *femme fatale*?"

"You mean Lure de Lang?"

"Who else?"

"I've had no contact with her," Lex lied.

"Why the hell are you wasting my time then?"

"Because I hoped you had some news you might want to share with an old colleague."

"You should hear yourself, Alexander. Did you drink your breakfast this morning?"

"I'm as dry as the Sahara."

"Then I don't know what excuse you have for wasting my time. If you have nothing for me, I have nothing for you."

"I think a gang may have murdered Jan Berger."

"Why would you say that?"

"Because he stole from them. I think it's something you should investigate."

"Who says we're not already doing so? Did Lure de Lang tell you it could be a gang?"

"Maybe you didn't hear me the first time—I haven't had any contact with her."

"Amanda Artz has resurfaced—unharmed. She was on vacation in Italy and had nothing to do with the murder. Did you know she's the aunt of Lure de Lang?"

"How would I know that?"

"Mrs Artz calls her Laura and tells us that her niece is a compulsive liar and not to be trusted."

"What else did she say?"

"Listen, Lex, I've already told you more than I should." He hung up.

Lex made another cup of coffee and smoked a cigarette. He considered calling Amanda Artz but decided to go and see her instead.

LEX PARKED the Vespa and trotted up the stone steps to the green front door of number 69. He rang the bell, but no one came to the door.

On his way back to the office, he stopped at Café Krom on the corner of Kerkstraat to have a drink. He needed it. The brown café, with its art deco interior and classic jukebox, had been a favourite watering hole of his for a few years. He ordered two fingers of Glenfiddich—a cut or two above his usual brand.

"Does Jaap van der Beek still work here?" Lex asked the bartender.

"Not exactly."

"Meaning?" Lex said and lit a cigarette.

"He died from lung cancer about four years ago," said the bartender in a flat and cold voice as he pushed an ashtray towards Lex.

"I'm sorry to hear it. Jaap was a good man."

"Were you close?" the bartender said acidly, as an arrogant smirk played on his long, thin face.

"Not exactly."

Lex decided to have lunch somewhere else. Somehow he didn't feel as welcome as he used to. He finished the drink and tossed a fiver onto the counter. "Keep the change."

"Come back soon, sir."

LEX ENTERED the apartment, and Hercules ran towards him. He followed Lex into the living room, which was also used as Roos' office. She sat behind her desk.

"Please pet him. You're his favourite uncle."

Lex leaned down and with a "attaboy," stroked his little head. The dog snorted happily.

"How was your visit to the library?"

"Interesting and informative."

"Sounds encouraging."

"Where have you been?" Roos asked.

"Amanda Artz has returned from a vacation in Italy, and I went to see her. But she wasn't at home."

"Are you ready for my briefing?" Roos said eagerly.

"I need to go to the toilet first. Would you mind making us some coffee?"

"Okay."

"Let's meet in my office in five?"

"Aye aye, Captain."

A FEW minutes later, Lex sat at his desk with Roos sitting on the Chesterfield across from him. She held a cup of instant coffee in her right hand, a pen in her left, and rested a notepad and a Xerox on her lap. The early afternoon sun bathed her and the room in bright light.

"Nice shirt," Lex said, admiring her colourful and stylish tunic.

"Thanks," Roos said with a smile.

"So, what have you got?"

"I've found something to point us in the right direction," Roos said. She unfolded the Xerox and handed it to him across the desk. It was a copy of an announcement in the *NRC Handelsblad*. It was dated 1 May, 1974, and showed several small pictures, mainly of men in suits. The copy wasn't especially good, so it didn't tell him anything immediately.

"What am I looking at?"

"If you study the faces on row two closely, I'm sure you'll see it."

Lex ran his eye along the row of faces and then spotted a vaguely familiar one.

"This guy bears a good resemblance to the man who paid us a visit with his enforcer last week," Lex said, pointing.

"That's what I thought."

Lex read the caption: 'Mr Allard Kuipers Celebrates 25th Anniversary at KNVB'.

"What kind of gangster works at the Dutch Football Association?"

"The corrupt kind," Roos suggested. "He's probably not the only one."

"Well done. How did you spot our friend?"

"I guess it's my lucky day. I flipped through all the mainstream papers as you instructed when suddenly my eyes fell on the portrait. That distinguished ducktail beard sets his face apart from all the others."

"I would have missed it," Lex confessed.

"I wonder if he still works at the KNVB or now spends all his time insulting innocent part-time secretaries and their pets?"

"Only one way to find out." Lex took the telephone directory from the shelf behind him and found the number for the KNVB Amsterdam office. He dialled, and a woman answered almost immediately.

"Thank you for calling KNVB. How can I help?"

"Please connect me with Allard Kuipers."

"Mr Kuipers is in a meeting, sir. I'll be happy to take a message."

"No need. I'll call back later." Lex hung up. "He still works at KNVB," he told Roos.

"What do we do now?"

"We need to plan it carefully, but I have an idea."

14

WATCHING HIS massive body block out the light from the staircase was like seeing an eclipse. The big man was dead on time, and Lex recalled what Tom had said about him: "He's as big as a house and as strong as an ox. But it's not all muscle. He's loyal and almost as smart as Muhammed Ali. He can keep a cool head, but try wasting his time by being late if you want to upset him. And believe me, you don't want to piss him off."

"I'm Alwin Smit," he said and offered Lex a hand. He shook it, feeling grateful he'd not come to hurt him. "My friends call me Al."

Lex stepped back a pace to let him enter the hallway, which seemed even smaller than usual. He somehow made it into the office without getting stuck. Lex walked round the desk to his chair and offered Al a seat on the Chesterfield. He squeezed into it and rested his big hands on his knees.

Roos appeared at the door, and Lex made the introductions.

"Delighted, ma'am," Al said.

"Coffee, gentlemen?"

"If it's not too much trouble, I would prefer a cup of tea. No sugar, but a little milk would be nice." For a man of his size, his voice was surprisingly high-pitched.

"No trouble at all," she said and turned away. She needed no reply from Lex, who could drink coffee anytime. He looked at the big man while he studied the office. He guessed his age to be in the late forties, and his weight more than double that (in kilos). His muscular arms and chest stretched his blue T-shirt to its limit. He kept his thick, dark brown hair short and his horseshoe-shaped moustache well-groomed. The colour of his moustache matched his hair, and Lex suspected it came from the same jar.

"Tom sends his greetings."

"I'm grateful to him for putting me in contact with you and that you could see me at such short notice."

"Any friend of Tom's is a friend of mine. He did tell me it was urgent, and hopefully, I can be of assistance, Mr Spijker."

"Please call me Lex."

"Only if you call me Al."

One look at his flattened snout implied he'd been in a few fights.

"You used to do a bit of boxing, is that right?"

"Yes, now and then," he emphasised with a chuckle. "I was the Dutch amateur champion in 1950, 1951, and 1954. I won most of my fights on KOs. I was kind of famous as Big Al 'Axe Man' Smit in my heyday.

You're too young to have heard of me." He sounded proud. "I was voted sportsman ...."

Roos arrived with the refreshments, and he stopped talking. Lex guessed that he was too modest to boast in front of a lady.

"Do you follow the World Cup?"

"Football is for sissies." He gave Lex another chuckle, "but please don't quote me on that one. Especially not when our boys only need to beat Brazil to reach the final. The city and country are in a frenzy."

"For someone not following the tournament, you are well informed."

"Yes, but that's because everyone insists on talking about it."

The mug disappeared into his hand as he sipped the tea.

Lex offered him a cigarette, which he declined. He lit one for himself.

"I hope you don't mind me smoking."

"Did I roll my eyes? I tend to do that when I disapprove of something. Don't take any notice."

"How much has Tom told you?"

"Apart from time not being on your side, he told me nothing."

"I hope you won't object if you have to abduct someone."

"It depends. Count me out if it's a child or if it's for ransom."

"It's a corrupt official from the Dutch Football Association. He has some information that could save the life of someone I care about if we're not too late."

"Then, I'm in."

"We might have to lean hard on him to get the information."

"Do I look like a boy scout?" There was that chuckle again.

"Before we begin, we need to discuss your fee."

"You'll have to talk to Tom about that. My arrangement is with him, and we like to keep paperwork to a minimum."

Knowing Tom's generosity, it did not surprise Lex that he'd already taken care of the financial aspects. But this one would have to be on Lex, even if he had to wash dishes in his establishment.

"The name of the official is Allard Kuipers, and I might also refer to him as Frog One."

"You sound like you have a personal grudge against him. Or maybe you don't like the French?"

"I think there's more French blood in me than in him."

"A grudge then?"

"I'll get to that." Lex showed Big Al the picture from the newspaper.

He took the clipping. "Huh, I see why you call him Frog One."

"You've seen *The French Connection*?"

"Indeed. I saw it recently at Filmtheater de Uitkijk."

Lex envisioned Al squeezing himself into one of the old theatre seats and the reaction of the poor people sitting beside and behind him.

"As I mentioned, he works for the Dutch Football Association or the KNVB. I've established that he has an office at their headquarters on Weesperstraat. I guess he comes and goes as he likes during the day, but we'll have to check it out."

"Obviously."

"But first, I need to explain why he's a man of interest."

A COUPLE of hours later, Al and Lex were walking in the sunshine along Utrechtsestraat. The KNVB headquarters was less than a kilometre from Rembrandtplein, so they decided to cover the distance on foot. Big Al's wide shoulders and broad hips filled the narrow pavement, so Lex either walked behind him or hobbled in the gutter beside him. He was a fast walker, and Lex had to put his best foot forward to keep up. Al politely stepped into the street whenever they encountered a pedestrian coming towards them. Lex thought that the big man could easily be mistaken for a gentle giant.

They reached Kerkstraat and turned left. Al said, "Have you considered putting a tail on the guy? He might lead us to the woman and or to his associates."

"I've given it some thought. I'm sure Mr Kuipers is extraordinarily alert, so I feel it's too risky. If he sees us or suspects anything, it could jeopardise everything."

"But is it riskier than abducting someone in broad daylight?"

"If we plan it properly, the element of surprise will minimise the risk."

"Surely, his friends will suspect something if he suddenly disappears."

"That's why it's important that we urgently persuade him to give us the information we need."

"But what if he doesn't want to talk?"

"You'll scare the shit out of him."

"Thanks for your confidence."

"I also sense that without the protection of his enforcers, he won't be so cocky."

"Hopefully, you're right."

"You think it's a bad plan?"

"Not at all. Don't get me wrong; you're the boss. It's just that someone has to play the role of devil's advocate."

"Let's check out the location before deciding on any definite strategy."

As they crossed the Magere Bridge over the Amstel river, a bicycle headed straight towards Al. He didn't flinch. He just stood there, forcing the young cyclist to swerve, missing him by inches. The cyclist looked back angrily. His mouth hung open, but nothing came out. He probably realised that he should be relieved.

I'd rather ride into a brick wall. At least it would only hit you once, Lex thought.

"Do you know the story about the Magere Bridge?" Lex asked.

"No! But I feel you're going to tell me," Al said with the familiar chuckle.

"The two Mager sisters lived on either side of the river and wanted an easy way to visit each other. So they had a bridge built."

"Fortunately for Amsterdam tourism, the sisters didn't decide to buy a couple of rowboats."

"Or swim," Lex suggested.

Al chuckled some more, which made him seem quite endearing for a mean son of a gun.

Lex heard the bells of the nearby Moses and Aaron church strike noon, and as they passed Eetcafé de Magere Brug, his stomach reminded him that he had only had coffee for breakfast.

"Let's have some lunch," Lex said eagerly and headed somewhat urgently towards the entrance of the café.

IN THE brown café, they each had an *uitsmijter* and washed it down with beer. They didn't talk much, but Lex managed to drag a bit of personal information out of Al in exchange for something about himself. Alwin was born in 1925 in Amsterdam, where he'd lived all his life. He'd always been a big boy, and beginning in elementary school, he used his size to his advantage. After finishing his studies, he'd always worked as 'muscle' in some capacity.

"It's not that I specifically enjoy hurting people. Like in boxing, I need to be sure it serves a purpose, and it helps when I have to inflict pain on some scuzzball."

"I can guarantee that whatever pain you'll have to inflict during this job, it will serve a purpose and will be on the bad guys."

"Cheers to that." Al lifted his glass of beer, and they toasted.

Lex noticed the ring on his finger. "Are you married?"

"I've been divorced for almost twenty years."

"Kids?"

"Thank God, no."

"Any hobbies?"

Lex expected him to say it was none of his business, but apparently, he decided to let Lex be his confidante.

"Don't tell anyone, but I'm an avid reader when I'm not working. I prefer the classics, and my library contains several first editions." He sounded as proud as when he'd talked about being a boxing champion.

"You're full of surprises, Al," Lex said amiably. The big man was growing on him.

"You ain't seen nothing yet," he chuckled.

COMPARED TO the narrow side street they had come from, Weesperstraat was luxuriously broad. The Dutch Football Association's office was located straight ahead in the modern six-story Metropool complex building. The ground floor, clad in glass with concrete columns, was high enough to allow Nieuwe Kerkstraat to continue its eastward journey through an underpass. The remaining five floors were covered with a grid of rectangular windows. What made the building distinctive were the three groups of cubes, set at an angle and perched on the edge of the flat roof. It made Lex think of the bridge on a ship, which could have been the architect's intention. Lex generally disapproved of modern architecture, but this wasn't too bad.

The reflection of the afternoon sun against the glass and chrome made Lex squint. On which floor and behind which rectangular window (or windows) Mr Allard Kuipers was hiding, they did not yet know. Nor if he was in the building or standing by a window, looking out into the street. The brim of Lex's hat prevented his face from being seen from above, but he didn't want to stand out in the open for too long.

"Let's cross over to the underpass," Lex said.

The constant traffic flow in both directions on the six automobile and two bicycle lanes made it easier said than done. Al floated across like a butterfly. *Muhammad Ali would be impressed*, Lex thought. Finally, he also made it safely across. Standing at the corner of the underpass, they had a clear view of the main entrance to the building. The white neon 'Metropool' sign above the sliding glass doors did its best to draw attention to itself in the sunlight.

"Nice broad pavement if you want to park a car or a van," Al said.

"What are you thinking?

"If you insist on abducting the poor fellow, we need to get him off the street as quickly as possible. One way of doing that is to force him into a car or a van."

"The problem is that it will look suspicious if we park on the pavement for too long," Lex said.

"We need to lure him out," Al suggested.

As if right on cue, the doors slid open, and Frog One walked out of the building. He was talking loudly to a woman half his age and didn't seem to care much about his surroundings. Lex couldn't believe his eyes and nudged Al.

Allard Kuipers tipped his fedora to the young woman, and they parted ways. She headed towards Lex and Al and passed nearby as she turned the corner, hurrying through the underpass and down the street. He crossed the pavement and the bicycle lane to a row of cars parked along the curb. He stopped at a white Jaguar MK II, unlocked the door to the driver's seat, and tossed in his leather portfolio. Before getting into the car, he looked around as though making sure that no one was watching him.

Lex stepped backwards to hide behind a column, and when he heard the smooth and powerful sound of the Jaguar engine warming up, he risked looking towards the car again. It pulled out onto the street and drove in the direction of the city centre.

"We now know which car he drives," Lex said, pleased.

"And if we do a stakeout in a vehicle, we'll be able to follow him. Then there's a chance he'll lead us to your woman."

"But there's no guarantee, and I still think it's too risky. If he gets a clue that he's being followed, we might not get a second chance."

"Abduction in broad daylight will have to do then," said Al.

"Yes, and I have an idea of how we can make it work."

15

LEX WAS grateful that Roos wasn't there to mother him, as he refilled the whisky glasses.

"Your plan is excellent," Al said and toasted Lex.

"Hardly," Lex said, lapping it up.

"But you'll have to do the driving."

"That's the snag in the plan," Lex exclaimed.

"What's that supposed to mean?"

Lex waited him out.

"Don't tell me you can't drive?" Al said.

Lex thought of lying about having his driving licence suspended or not having one at all, but in his semi-drunken state, self-pity had already made his eyes damp.

"Are you alright, Lex? Did I say something wrong?"

"Not at all. The drink brings out bad memories."

"Something to do with driving, I suppose?"

"I promised myself never to drive a car again."

"For whatever reason? It's essential to the plan."

"My fiancée died in an accident, and I was driving the car."

"That's tough. Was it long ago?"

"A few years back. It was the stupidest of accidents."

"Most accidents are."

"We were en route to Palermo in a Fiat 124 Sport Coupe. One minute she was beside me full of life, and the next, she was gone." Lex took a healthy sip of whisky and lit a cigarette before telling Al about the accident, omitting her six-week pregnancy.

They sat in silence for a while, listening to the noises coming from the Rembrandtplein through the open windows.

Life goes on, Lex thought. "If you get the car, I'll drive," he finally said.

"I'll get a van! How's that?" he said with a chuckle, which miraculously broke the spell.

"Cheers to that," Lex said and refilled their glasses.

"Not to spoil the party, Lex, but let this be our last drink. I doubt it will be a walk in the park tomorrow."

LEX AVOIDED, thanks to Al, waking up with a hangover the following day. He had a decent sleep and was eager to get the day started for a change. Lex wanted to wrap matters up before Holland's World Cup semi-final against Brazil that evening. It was not a game he wanted to miss, a sentiment he undoubtedly shared with the corrupt representative of the Dutch Football Association and millions of fans of the beautiful game worldwide. If all went according to plan, Mr Allard Kuipers would be cooped up in a basement in the Jordaan before kick-off.

Unfortunately, the accommodation had no radio and no television.

Lex washed in the kitchen, shaved, and dressed in his usual black trousers, white shirt, and thin black tie. He needed to look sharp and confident.

Lex headed downstairs to get a newspaper and some bread, and as he stepped outside, a light summer breeze greeted him, and Bart was unsurprisingly standing in the doorway to his café. He, too, wore his usual uniform of a dirty white shirt stretched over his beer gut.

"Hope to see you for the game this evening," he said with a smile, stroking his ginger goatee. His throat sack bounced up and down as he spoke. It pleased Lex to see him back in his good-natured orangutan mood.

"I thought you'd banned me," Lex said, playing hard to get.

"It was for one game, and it's water under the bridge. It's not the same without you."

"If you put it like that, I'll do my utmost to be there."

"Mind you, I expect your behaviour to mirror our brilliant team."

"I shall put my best foot forward. That's a promise."

Lex went round the corner and entered the shop. He took a copy of *de Volkskrant* and put it on the counter. "Welcome back, Wim. How was your visit to your sister?"

"Very long."

"Wasn't it only for five days?"

"It felt longer. I do love my dear sister, but I doubt there's any love strong enough to endure almost a week."

"And it's not because you hate being away?"

"No comment," he laughed. "Anything else?"

"Is your bread fresh?"

"Baked this morning. You can ask Hartog's Volkoren."

"Okay, let me risk two *tijgerbolletjes*."

"Cigarettes?"

"Please."

He took a pack of Player's Navy Cut from the rack behind him.

"Make that two."

He grabbed another pack. "Is that all?"

"I owe you for a newspaper and a pack of cigarettes from my last visit. Your assistant had no change for a 25-guilder note."

"He's my nephew."

"How convenient to have him steer the ship while you visited his mother."

"It's my brother's son, and the convenience depends largely on how many other customers he gave credit to without telling me."

Lex paid and wished him a good day.

Ascending the stairs, he heard the phone ringing and rushed inside.

"Hello?"

"It's your new best friend. The dungeon is ready."

"Great, Al, and so am I."

"As agreed, I'll pick you up at ten."

"See you then." Lex hung up. Time for breakfast.

A FEW seconds past ten, a white, four-door, windowless Ford E-Series cargo van pulled up onto the pavement across from the flea market at Waterlooplein. Lex opened the door to the passenger seat and jumped in.

"Good day to you, Al. Nice wheels."

"Stolen last night," he said, as he turned off the engine.

"Is that wise?"

"We needed a van, didn't we? And don't worry, I changed the plates. In a few hours, it will be cleaned up and parked without plates in another part of town."

"I guess you know what you're doing."

"Sure. Are you ready to take the wheel?"

"You want me to drive there?"

"You make it sound like a trip to the south pole. It's less than half a kilometre away, and this is your only chance to get acquainted with this model and warm up after your self-imposed driving ban." He swung the door open, got out, and walked round the front of the van.

Lex slid across to the driver's seat, grabbed hold of the steering wheel with both hands and looked straight ahead, visualising himself driving.

The van tilted slightly from Al's weight as he pulled himself onto the passenger seat and slammed the door shut.

"You'd better get the motor going before you begin to make engine sounds," Al said.

Lex turned the key in the ignition, and the powerful motor came to life.

LEX FELT okay to drive again, maybe because it was a van and not a car. Or maybe, enough time had passed since the accident. Or perhaps, Lex's focus was on the upcoming abduction. A few butterflies were flapping their wings in his stomach, but the presence of Al's sturdy, muscular physique and calm manner reassured him that it would all go to plan.

With the morning rush hour over, traffic was moderate. Driving down Weesperstraat, Lex caught a view of the distinctive cubes on top of the Metropool complex, and as they drove past the building, he was relieved to see the white Jaguar MK II parked in the same spot as the day before. On the bridge across Nieuwe Prinsengracht, Lex made a U-turn, pulled to the side, and parked next to the green telephone booth essential to the plan. Lex put on a pair of Ray-Ban sunglasses.

"With that hat and those sunglasses, you look like a saxophone player in a jazz band."

"Glad you like my disguise."

"Being disguised as a delivery man would be better."

"I could be a saxophone player with a day job."

Al opened the door and squeezed himself out.

"Do we need to go over the plan again?" Lex said.

"No need, but I still suspect that he might smell a rat."

"Perhaps, but the odour of his vanity will take over. I know the type."

"It's your gig."

"I'll flash the brake lights twice when I want you to make the call," Lex said, feeling nervous.

"I think I've got it by now. You can go."

At the first break in traffic, Lex pulled out. Looking into the rear-view mirror, he saw Big Al open the telephone booth door. He did not step into it but merely leaned in. Like many other things, it wasn't designed to accommodate someone his size.

Lex approached the main entrance of the Metropool complex and slowed down as if making a delivery. The Jaguar MK II was parked parallel to the bicycle lane in front of a brown Renault 16. Lex hoped the passers-by would mind their own business as he steered the van past the Renault and into the Jaguar's rear bumper. He didn't hit it hard enough to draw unwanted attention, as he merely wanted to make it look like a collision (when viewed from somewhere above). Lex flashed the brake lights twice. *Over to you, Al*, he thought.

Lex saw Al's reflection in the passenger's side mirror a minute later as he unlatched the sliding door to get ready. Then he stood next to the Renault and looked at the bumper of the Jaguar, pretending to survey the damage while scratching his head. Lex stayed put in the driver's seat.

They didn't have to wait long before Allard Kuipers came rushing out of the building. "What have you done to my car?" he shouted.

Lex looked into the side mirror again and saw Kuipers join Big Al in the tight space between the van and the Renault. Al pretended to make room for

Kuipers to get through. When Frog One indignantly tried to squeeze past him, Al slid the van door open with his right hand. They both disappeared from Lex's view, and he felt a tremor as they fell into the van. Lex heard the sliding door shut and turned to look through the small window to the cargo area. Al was on top of the poor man.

Lex backed up half a metre onto the street, and someone behind honked loudly. He put the van into gear and sped away from the abduction scene. Lex heard no sound from Allard Kuipers, so he guessed that Al had covered his mouth. Lex congratulated himself (or rather, themselves). The plan had worked to a tee.

LEX PARKED the van outside Café Chris on Bloemstraat and switched off the engine. He got out and walked to the green wooden door, and knocked on the glass. Almost immediately, the door opened, revealing Tom's broad, bearded, smiling face.

"Alexander, you old bandit! I'm pleased to see you this morning."

"The feeling is mutual. We have a delivery."

"Can you put it in the cellar?" Tom said with a wink.

Lex slid the van's side door open. Al sat with his back towards the cab, and Allard Kuipers lay motionless on his back next to him.

"Is he alright?" Lex said, concerned.

"Don't worry. I've injected the guy with a mild sedative, and he's just taking a nap."

Al had taken off the man's tie and his leather shoes. Lex suspected that the dapper Mr Kuipers would not appreciate them seeing the hole in his sock. Al shifted the limp body closer to the door, like a child moving a teddy bear.

Lex spotted a female cyclist riding towards them. "Hold it!" he whispered. She passed without showing any interest.

"Okay, let's get him inside." Lex took hold of the man's legs while Al grabbed his arms.

"Hold him while I get my feet to the ground," Al said.

"Tom, can you take his tie and shoes? And slide the door shut," Lex said.

Lex and Al carried the limp body inside, and a moment later, Tom followed. "Straight ahead, past the billiard table and down the stairs."

The staircase was a few hundred years old and not designed with Big Al in mind. Perhaps in reaction to the expression of doubt on Lex's face, Al said, "No worries. I'll pull my six-pack in." He chuckled, then continued, "I already made it up and down a few times this morning." Al lowered his head, backed through the narrow doorway, and walked down the steps. There wasn't enough space for a sheet of paper, but they managed to carry Allard Kuipers down.

"It's the room straight ahead," Al said. The information didn't help Lex much, since it was impossible to see past Al in the narrow hallway. All Lex could do was follow him as they dragged the body along and into a rectangular room with a large mattress at one end. The room was windowless, and the walls were covered with Rockwool insulation to make it soundproof. The only light came from a naked bulb hanging from the ceiling. They tossed Allard Kuipers next to the pillow and blanket on the mattress. He moaned.

"He picked the perfect time to join the party. The sedative has probably made his mouth as dry as a nun's gusset. Could you get him some water?" Al said.

Lex walked up the stairs and into the café. By that point, he was sweating profusely, so he took off his hat and leather jacket. Tom stood in the middle of the room, examining the prisoner's shoes. The tie hung over a chair.

"His shoes are hand-sewn," Tom said, scratching the top of his hairy chest with his free hand.

"It looks like our guest is coming around. Could I have a glass of water for him? And one for me? Thanks."

Tom put the shoes on the table and walked behind the bar.

"My mother used to say: 'Shoes on the table mean a death in the family.' Hand-sewn or otherwise," Lex said and dumped them on the floor.

Tom handed him two glasses of water. Lex emptied one of them with a long gulp. "You can't imagine how much this means to me."

"A glass of water?"

"That as well. But mostly letting me borrow your cottage, putting me in contact with Al, making a guest room ready, and ...."

"It's my pleasure."

"But I insist on paying Big Al's fee."

"Let's discuss that later. I think you have more urgent business."

Lex returned to the cellar, where the prisoner was sitting on a wooden chair in the middle of the room. His hands were tied behind his back and his eyes were closed.

Lex handed the glass to Al, who held it to the man's mouth.

"Drink," he ordered.

Allard Kuipers drank.

Al moved out of the way, and Lex took his place.

"So we meet again, Mr Kuipers."

Hearing Lex's voice, the man opened his eyes. The sharp light from the naked bulb made him blink. "Who are you? I've never seen you before."

"Let me jog your memory. The last time we met, your sidekick of a hoodlum put me into hospital."

"I have no idea what you're talking about."

"Don't worry; I didn't take it personally at the time. However, that changed when you returned a few days later, again with your hoodlum, and tormented my secretary and her dog into revealing the location of Lure de Lang's hideout."

"I have no idea what you are talking about. It must be a case of mistaken identity. The person you're talking about sounds like a gangster, and I'm a law-abiding official representing the Dutch Football Association. I have no contact with 'hoodlums', as you put it. I demand to know why you've abducted me."

"The list is long, but I've already given you the main reason. You came to me for some information, and in the end, got it by using force. Now the tables are turned, and I'm asking you for the same information. If you're not willing to supply it, my friend here is ready to convince you that it's in your best interest to do so."

"A little pain never hurt anybody," Al said with a chuckle. This one had a devilish edge to it.

"Fuck off. I know nothing."

"I don't want to be unreasonable. You can have until tomorrow to think it over."

"You can't keep me here. I'm hosting a VIP event tonight at the KNVB. A couple of important government officials will be in attendance."

"I had the impression they were all in West Germany," Lex remarked.

"They'll wonder what has happened to me, and the police will be looking for me." Even though he sounded desperate, he looked like he didn't believe his spiel.

"Good luck with that. I'm afraid you'll be missing tonight's game."

Al untied him, grabbed his arm, and pushed him onto the mattress.

"You can't do this," Kuipers protested. "At least let me have a radio," he begged.

"See you tomorrow," Lex said, ignoring his pleas, although the part of him that loved the beautiful game had some sympathy. He'd be missing out on the most crucial game in the history of the KNVB. And that as an official of the organization.

Al shut the door. Kuipers' barely audible cries of protest seeped through. The torment had begun.

16

"WHO IS it?" said a deep, throaty, mature female voice on the other end of the line. The voice sounded not at all unpleasant.

"Is this Amanda Artz?"

"Who wants to know?"

"My name is Lex Spijker, and ...."

"Are you a reporter?"

"I'm a private detective, and your niece is my client."

"Which one?"

"I think you know."

"What do you want?"

"I would like to meet you to clarify a few things."

"Why should I talk to you?"

"Because I found a dead man in your kitchen and because I have news about Lure."

"I prefer to call her Laura, and I haven't heard from her in more than a month. I returned from my vacation in Italy three days ago. There was a note for me to call the police. You can imagine my distress when they told me about discovering a dead man in my kitchen and that my niece might be involved. Not knowing where she is and what has happened to her is keeping me awake at night. I'm distraught."

"If you talk to me, I might be able to help."

"We're talking."

"Not over the phone. Can I come to see you?"

"When?" she said.

"As soon as possible."

"Okay. When can you be here?"

Lex looked at his watch. "Will four o'clock be alright?"

LEX PRESSED the doorbell and heard it ring inside. Someone wearing high heels approached the door, and it opened. How an aunt ought to look, Lex couldn't say, but the person at the door seemed far different from what he'd expected. If Amanda Artz was in her late forties (as Schenk had told him), she was a well-preserved specimen. Her dyed blonde hair hung in soft, loose curls almost to her shoulders, and her blue eyes were large and well-spaced. She was dressed conservatively in a classic white blouse and a navy blue sheath skirt. Her skin was fair, and her makeup seemed fitting. She was an attractive aunt. *Beauty runs in the family*, Lex thought, although she bore no obvious resemblance to her niece.

"Amanda Artz," she said and held out her hand. Her fingers were long, and her nails manicured. Her handshake was firm and confident. If she was distraught, she hid it well. "Do come in, Mr Spijker."

Lex followed her into the apartment. She pointed to the love seat below the windows he'd seen before. Lex took off his hat and jacket.

"Can I offer you coffee? Or something stronger?"

"Coffee would be nice. No milk and no sugar."

She turned and headed for the kitchen. Lex heard her high heels tapping on the kitchen floor. She must have prepared ahead of time because she returned within a couple of minutes carrying a tray. She set it on the coffee table.

"Please do the plunger," she said, pointing to the French press. "It needs a bit of muscle."

With minimal effort, and Lex wasn't strong, he pushed the plunger to the bottom of the cafetiere. "Shall I pour?" he said, without waiting for an answer.

"Please leave enough space for my milk," she said and lowered herself into a light brown upholstered armchair opposite the love seat.

Lex poured, and she leaned forward to take the demitasse cup. He noticed her hand tremble slightly—perhaps she wasn't as cool, calm, and collected as she first appeared.

"Do have a *cantuccini*. My own import from Italy."

Lex helped himself to an almond biscuit and took a bite.

"The Italians dip them in their coffee," she told him.

He took a sip. "Nice coffee and cookies."

"You told me you had some news about Laura."

"I do, but I'm not sure it's what you want to hear."

"Is she safe? Laura is my older sister's only child. Her mother died when she was fifteen, and as I'm a widow without children, I took a special interest in her. Unfortunately, we've drifted apart over the past few years, and we no longer have regular contact. As I told you, I haven't seen her for more than a month."

"I understand."

"Can I be frank with you, Mr Spijker?"

"Lex, please."

"Laura has a rebellious soul. After my sister died, she moved in with me. I love her as my daughter, but it was challenging to have a teenager in the house, even at the best of times. Do you have kids, Lex?"

"Not yet," he said as the emotions got the better of him, thinking about his fiancée being killed while carrying their child in her womb.

"Are you alright, Mr Spijker?"

"I'm fine. Someone just danced on my grave."

"Anyhow, Laura came and went as she pleased. She teamed up with the wrong crowd. Hippies, you know," she said with scorn.

"Did she take drugs?"

"It depends on what you mean. She smoked cannabis."

"Did you confront her about it?"

"We talked about it. Laura called me *petit-bourgeois* and reminded me that I was not her mother. The strain of living together became too much. Through a contact of mine, I found a small apartment for her. She was only seventeen, but I had no choice."

"Do you regret it?"

"I wish it could have been different, but it drove me crazy thinking about her and her hippie friends alone in the apartment while I was working."

"Did she get married?"

"No. Why?"

"Because your niece told me that she did."

"Impossible. I would know about something like that."

"She also told me she got divorced."

"That makes it even more implausible. What else did Laura tell you?"

"That she met her husband while working as a model."

"I'm afraid she has been less than honest with you."

"What do you do?" Lex asked.

"You mean professionally?"

"Yes."

"I'm a cosmetologist, working at a beauty parlour on Spuistraat."

"But not today?"

"I'm working on Saturday and therefore have today off."

"Do you have a male friend?"

"Are you interrogating me, Mr Spijker? I thought you were here to shed some light on Laura's whereabouts. Honestly, I'm struggling to see what my private life has to do with any of this? Unless you're accusing me of being involved in Laura's disappearance or having murdered someone by telepathy while in the south of Italy."

"Did your niece know you were on vacation?"

"I didn't specifically tell her, but she knows that I travel around Italy every summer."

"Does she have a key to your apartment?"

"She did, but after my return, and for obvious reasons, I've had my locks changed."

"Can I ask what the police told you?"

"You can, but first, you must tell me what you know about Laura."

"Do you have a photo of her?"

"Sure. Why?"

"I need to be certain that my Lure is your Laura. Or vice versa."

LEX HEARD the tap of high heels on the floor above and, a moment later, on the staircase. Amanda Artz entered the room and handed him a photo.

"Taken at a family picnic a few years ago. She keeps her hair a bit longer these days, but the likeness is still good."

A younger version of Amanda Artz smiled at Lex, and if the colours in the photo had been a bit more faded, it could have been of herself in her early twenties. The likeness was good, but it was not the woman Lex knew as Lure. The attractive body in the picture could have been hers, but the pretty face belonged to someone else.

"Is there a problem?" Amanda Artz must have noticed Lex's raised eyebrows.

"I'm afraid I've never met your niece."

"But I thought …?"

"So did I. Unfortunately, it appears as though someone is impersonating her."

"I don't understand. Who would do such a thing? And why?"

"I wish I had the answer."

"I can't get my head around it."

"I'm as baffled as you are. I didn't see this coming."

"But you must have some idea. You met the girl pretending to be my niece, and she gave you my address as though it were her own."

"It's all speculation and not very helpful at this stage."

"I'd like to hear it anyway."

"I appreciate you're looking for answers, and I hope to give you some soon."

"Am I in danger?"

"I don't think you need to worry."

"A man is murdered in my home, someone pretends to be my niece, and I have no idea what has happened to my Laura. How can you tell me not to worry?"

"I only meant you don't need to worry about your safety. You were never the target."

"I don't understand. Target for what, and from whom?"

"It seems a gang or syndicate is involved. The person pretending to be your niece stole something from them."

Lex didn't want to go into specifics, as he only knew what Lure had told him, and since she had even lied about her identity, he had no intention of passing on any other information that had come from her.

"I don't blame you for doing your job, and I'm sure it's not your fault that someone lured you into this mess."

You're mistaken, lady, he thought. *I'm to blame for not walking away in time and getting physically and emotionally involved.*

"Do you know if your niece is involved in any criminal activity?"

"I wouldn't put it past her. As I already told you, we haven't been close for a while, so I have no idea what she is up to."

"What's the address of her apartment?"

Amanda Artz told him.

"That squares with the address I know."

"Did that woman give it to you?"

"Yes."

They sat in silence for a moment.

"I don't think I can take much more right now," she said.

"Can I keep the photo?"

"Be my guest."

"One last thing—if the police contact you again, please do not mention my visit."

"Why should I keep it a secret?"

"It's a long story, but it could cause me trouble. Also, I believe I stand a better chance of getting to the bottom of this mystery without their interference."

"Okay, but on the condition that you keep me informed."

"That's fair."

THE REMBRANDTPLEIN was a sea of orange. The city and the nation held their breath. Most football fans Lex talked to told him the brilliant Dutch team was unbeatable. He wanted to convince himself it was so, but truly believing that the team could beat the formidable Brazilians was another matter. A newspaper told its readers that the defending champions (and three-time winners of the trophy) hadn't lost a game yet, but also that Brazil had drawn twice and scored only half as many goals as the Dutch. Not to mention that Johan Cruijff played for Holland and not for Brazil.

The unsettling pre-match nervousness (which any bona fide football fan feels before a big game) made Lex restless. He rechecked his watch: still more than two hours to kick-off. With no food in the house, he left the apartment and crossed the Rembrandtplein to have dinner at Indrapura.

The Indonesian restaurant had so many tables that it could always accommodate someone without a reservation. Lex wouldn't call himself a regular, but he'd eaten there enough times for the slender, middle-aged, Asian head waiter to recognise his face.

"How are we doing today, sir?" he said in perfect Dutch at the top of his voice to drown out the noise from the packed restaurant.

"Great. Even better if you can find me a seat."

"Go up the stairs to the first floor, and my colleague will seat you."

As soon as he had made it to the top of the stairs, a younger waiter in the same outfit approached. The room was decorated in a similar colonial style to the downstairs and was only about two-thirds full. He took Lex to a table by the window, which gave him a good view of the statue of Rembrandt van Rijn, Café de Monico, and his humble apartment.

"Let me have the *ayam balado* and a Bintang beer," Lex said, ignoring the menu the waiter offered in order to feel like a regular.

LEX FINISHED the fried chicken filet in red pepper sauce and lit a cigarette. As he smoked, he studied the people and the traffic on the Rembrandtplein. He looked towards the Café de Monico and his apartment on the third floor. It didn't register immediately, but he suddenly thought he could see movement in his office. Maybe the spices had gone to his head. He leaned closer to the window. There was at least one intruder in his apartment. It may have been an opportunistic thief, but Lex suspected something else.

Lex got up, pulled his jacket from the back of the chair, and grabbed his hat. Knowing someone had entered his home uninvited made his blood boil, and his first inclination was to rush home to confront the bastard.

Lex was halfway down the stairs, pushing past an elderly couple taking their time, when it occurred to him that the intruder or intruders might be there to confront him.

The head waiter was standing by the door when Lex reached the ground floor. "Was everything to your satisfaction, sir?"

"Have you got a telephone I can use?"

"Downstairs, sir."

Lex looked towards the staircase and felt somewhat silly when he spotted a large 'Toilets and Telephone' sign with an arrow pointing downwards. "Thanks," he said, rushing past the waiter and down the stairs.

A young lady in a red blouse and blue jeans was using the payphone. Lex moved up close to her as she turned her back to him. "I know," she said into the telephone. Lex took a 10-guilder note from his pocket and tapped her shoulder. "I need the phone. It's an emergency."

"Hold it, Liza. There's some idiot here." She gave him a cold stare. "What the...." She stopped when she saw the money.

"As I said, it's an emergency. Say goodbye to Liza and go buy yourself a drink."

"I'll call you later, Liza. There's an emergency, and someone needs the phone." She slammed the handset down onto the hook, snatched the note from his hand, and pushed past him. Lex pulled a piece of paper out of his pocket, put a coin in the slot, and dialled the number written on it. He listened impatiently to it ringing.

"The master of the house," a man finally answered. Lex was relieved to hear Al's voice, followed by his distinctive chuckle.

FIFTEEN MINUTES later, Lex was pacing the pavement nervously outside Indrapura. Big Al appeared from round the corner. Lex had known the big man for less than forty-eight hours, but seeing him felt like the homecoming of a long-lost older brother. He wore a grey sports jacket over a green polo shirt, and Lex spotted the bulge of a pistol in an underarm holster. Whether the piece was legal or not was none of his business.

Al shook Lex's hand. "Nasty surprise," he said. "Could it be that you were just imagining things?"

"I saw someone."

"Did you see them again after you called me?"

"I can't be sure. Also, I think I saw only one person."

"If they are there to confront you, there'll be more than one."

"How do we play this one?"

"I'll handle it," Al said.

"No way!" Lex protested.

"Listen! They'll be watching for you to come home. They haven't seen me before, which gives me the upper hand."

"You must be careful. They're a mean bunch."

"And I'm a mean son of a gun. They'll soon realise there's a new sheriff in town," he said. "Give me about ten minutes to check it out. Then dial your telephone number and pray that I answer."

Lex watched his massive back as he crossed the street into the small park at the base of the Rembrandt van Rijn statue. Al looked like a tank heading into battle.

TWELVE MINUTES later, Lex was back in the basement of Indrapura. This time the handset was on the hook. As he lifted it and dropped a coin in the slot, the door to the men's room opened. Lex waited until the man had passed and was halfway up the stairs before dialling. With his nerves on edge, he put the receiver to his ear.

"Come on, Al! Pick up!" Lex murmured to himself as it rang the third time. He was about to give up and go over to the flat when someone answered. To his relief, he heard Big Al's calm voice.

"Mister Spijker's residence. Whom may I announce?"

"What kept you?"

"Why didn't you tell me you keep the phone in a drawer?"

"I don't."

"Strange. But that's where the ringing eventually led me."

"Have you killed them all?" Lex said jokingly.

"Only two of them."

"You must be kidding."

"Don't worry. We don't have to dispose of any bodies tonight."

"What happened?"

"Come home, and I'll tell you."

With a sense of purpose in his step, Lex crossed the Rembrandtplein. He tensely scanned his surroundings, somehow expecting to run into Boris the Bear, or the Tom Wolfe wannabe, or both. He looked up to the apartment and saw Al keeping an eye on him from the bedroom window. Maybe he was also expecting them.

Lex rushed up the stairs and swung the door open.

Al was blocking the small hallway. "May I suggest you get a better lock. A baby could pick this one. With a wet nappy."

"Is that how you got in?"

"I didn't have a lock pick with me or a wet nappy, for that matter. But your visitors saved me the trouble. The door was open."

"Are you going to let me in?"

"Be my guest," he said and backed up. Lex followed him into the office, and Al took a seat in the Chesterfield. Lex looked around. The phone was back on the desk, and nothing seemed to be out of order.

Lex walked into the living room, and as far as he could tell, nothing had been taken or displaced. He returned to the office and looked at his watch: Twenty-five minutes to kick-off.

"You've just had your apartment broken into, and you're probably thinking about the damn game?"

"Can I offer you a drink at Café de Monico?" Lex said eagerly.

"To be honest, that doesn't sound very interesting. I'd prefer a drink here."

"Sorry, but I'm afraid nothing can keep me from watching the game."

"I've decided not to let you out of my sight until we've resolved this situation, so I have no choice but to join you downstairs. I hope there's room for little me?"

Lex expected a chuckle from him, but nothing came.

"The more, the merrier."

"Another cliché from you, and I'll change my mind."

17

WHEN TOTAL FOOTBALL meets Joga Bonito, you're allowed to expect something out of the ordinary. The first goalless forty-five minutes provided just that. But it was also something extraordinarily violent. Lex couldn't remember having watched anything like it before. Knee-high tackles were flying left, right, and centre. Ten men in white shirts determined to stop ten men in blue shirts by any means necessary, and vice versa. One man in black determined to let them get away with it. A meagre four yellow cards were an insult to the rules of the game.

"I owe you an apology," Big Al said.

"For what?"

"For claiming football is for sissies. I didn't know a group of youngsters with long hair and tight shorts could inflict so much pain on each other without even flinching. And that with millions watching! They're like modern gladiators. Well done, I say. Suddenly I'm looking forward to the next forty-five minutes of the scuffle."

"I'm glad you're feeling entertained."

"What's the gloomy face for?"

"While you seem to applaud this behaviour, I'm shocked."

"You're scared the Dutch team will lose the fight. You can't bear the thought of your heroes not reaching the final. If they were leading, you'd be all smiles. If they win, you'll tell me it was the best game ever."

Lex looked at Bart, operating behind the bar. He'd made a killing and most likely hoped that Holland would score only in the last minute of the game, thereby minimising his loss on half-price drinks. Even though his drinks were still at the regular price, Lex decided to support his business once again. "Another drink?" he offered Al.

"Thanks. I'll have a whisky this time."

"Two or four fingers?" Al held up four, and Lex held up a 25-guilder note to get Bart's attention. Bart insisted on cash upfront on football nights like these when he had a full house. Lex tried not to take it personally, although Bart ought to let him run a tab since he treated the bar as a second home.

"Same thing again?" Bart said, pointing to the whisky glass and Al's pint glass.

"Make it two whiskies," Lex yelled. The second-half had kicked off, and the noise was almost deafening. Lex held up four fingers. Bart got the message and nodded with encouragement.

Lex suspected most of the liquor Bart shifted over the counter came without a revenue stamp. But what did he care? He didn't work for the taxman.

The whisky arrived, and Lex focused on the television above the bar. Attempting to get a cigarette, he dropped the pack on the floor. Cursing, he slid off the stool and bent down to fetch it. That's when the room erupted. Lex got up to see the ball in the back of the net and the Dutch players hugging each other. It inspired a guy to his left to hug him and for Lex to thump Al's shoulder. Lex suspected that Al would not appreciate it if he threw himself around his neck in ecstasy, although the big man did seem as delighted as everyone else in the smoke-filled room. Lex was grateful for the replay, which showed an unmarked Johan Cruijff receiving the ball on the right. He ran to the level of the Brazilian penalty area, then passed it into the path of Johan Neeskens, who, with a perfectly timed slide, hit the ball with his right foot. It was pure poetry in motion when it rose in a perfect arc over the Brazilian goalkeeper and into the net. It was a brilliant move and a great goal. It had taken fifty minutes for the fight to turn into a game.

Although, as expected, Bart announced that drinks were now half-price, Lex decided to have just one more drink before bedtime. Apart from interrogating Allard Kuipers, Lex had no idea what the next day would bring. Depending on the information they could squeeze out of the man, it might be long and challenging. Having an important task the following day didn't usually prevent Lex from getting hammered on football night, but he wasn't working alone for the first time since the 'good-old-cop' days. His provisional partner and bodyguard was pacing himself; besides that, the effect of alcohol on Al seemed like water off a duck's back. Lex owed it to him to be at his best.

With half an hour remaining, the Dutch sealed Brazil's fate. Ruud Krol (with his rock-star good looks) flew down the left wing. With his opposing player, Luís Pereira, about to add to the tally of knee-high tackles, Krol delivered a pinpoint pass across the face of the goal. Johan Cruijff, as usual, in the right place at the right time, put his right foot to the ball. Two-nil Holland and no way back for Brazil.

Café de Monico went mental, and so did Bart, who announced that drinks would be free for the remaining thirty minutes of the game. *If there's something we Dutch can genuinely appreciate (even those of us who are half French), it's getting something for nothing,* Lex thought.

Lex immediately bid for another four-fingered whisky, the one he'd promised himself to be the last of the evening. As the area around the bar became like Central Station at rush hour, Lex soon gave up trying to attract Bart's attention. Al gave a despairing shrug. He'd probably been planning a peaceful evening in the company of one of his first editions before Lex had called him from the restaurant.

"The minute the game is over, we'll head upstairs," Lex said. Al nodded patiently, and Lex turned his focus back to the game.

The Brazilians huffed and puffed, but the Dutch defence was as steadfast as the Berlin Wall. Frustrated, Luís Pereira decided that knee-high tackles were no longer fashionable and floored Johan Neeskens with a kung fu kick to make Bruce Lee proud. On his way to an early shower, he strolled up to the fence, singled out a particularly vocal group of Dutch supporters, and held up three fingers. It could have indicated he'd received two yellow cards and a red, but Lex doubted it. More likely, it was a reference to the three times the Brazilian team had previously won the World Cup. They were not going to win this one, although Holland might. The team did seem invincible. Lex suspected that West Germany had other ideas, having qualified for the final by beating Poland earlier in the day.

LEX OFFERED Big Al the couch to sleep on, but he insisted on sitting in the Chesterfield chair in the office. Around half-past eleven, Lex closed the bedroom door, stripped down to his underwear, and crawled into bed. The noise from the crowd celebrating on Rembrandtplein kept him awake for about ten minutes before he drifted off.

A full bladder woke Lex at twenty-two minutes past two, and he heard Al snoring next door. Lex opened the bedroom door as quietly as possible, but as soon as he stepped into the hallway, one of the old wooden floorboards creaked and woke his friend.

"How's it going?" Lex said.

"All quiet on the western front."

"Do you have that Hemingway novel in a first edition?"

"No, because it's not him."

"What?"

"Hemingway didn't write it. Erich Maria Remarque did."

"Are you sure? Well, you're the expert," Lex said and yawned. "You can tell me all about it in the morning. I'm going to the toilet and then back to sleep."

LEX'S DREAM ended with someone knocking persistently on the bedroom door. He opened his eyes.

"Time to get up, Lex."

He turned his head to look at the alarm clock. It was precisely eight o'clock. The feeling of dread slowly gave way to relief for having made it through the night without trouble.

"Coffee is ready," said Al.

"Sounds good. I'll be right out."

Lex got out of bed, took an old Ajax Amsterdam shirt from the wardrobe, put it on, and opened the door to the hallway. Al stood in the kitchen with his back to the door. There was just enough room for him to turn and present two mugs of coffee.

"Let's drink it in the living room," Lex said.

Al followed him, put the mugs on the coffee table, and plunked himself down on the couch. Lex grabbed one of the mugs and took a seat on the edge of Roos' desk. "Did you manage to get enough sleep?"

"Under the circumstances, I can't complain."

"I did offer you the couch to sleep on."

"It wouldn't have made any difference. Look at it." Al made the three-person couch look like a slightly overgrown armchair.

"How do you want to play it today?" Al asked.

"First, I want to call Roos and tell her to stay home until further notice."

"I was going to suggest it," Al said, running a hand through his short, dark brown hair before stroking his moustache.

"Then, obviously, we'll have our chat with the man from the Dutch Football Association."

"Do you have any idea what he might be involved in?" Al said.

"I'm fairly confident that Lure stole the money from him and his associates. Where it came from in the first place is a good question. Maybe ticket racketeering."

"Surely, there must be more to it than that. No doubt selling fake tickets is lucrative, but it's time-limited," Al said.

"What do you suggest? Drugs? With the two young girls missing, it could be trafficking?"

"Let's first get Allard Kuipers to tell us where your lady friend is."

"If she's still alive?"

"If you're into trafficking, you don't kill an asset like her."

"But then she might be out of the country?"

"There's no need to speculate. Let's first see what we can squeeze out of Frog One."

"If anything."

"He'll be as dry as a dead dingo's donger after our chat. I promise you," Big Al said confidently.

18

LEX AND Al walked through the flower market on the Singel with a sense of urgency. As they reached the Koningsplein, it began raining hard, but fortunately, a yellow tram arrived at the same time.

Exiting the tram ten minutes later at the Westermarkt, the rain had become a drizzle. They crossed the Engelschman Bridge over the Prinsengracht and turned right. Lex looked towards the opposite side of the canal—come rain or shine, the line of visitors outside the Anne Frank house seemed to be a constant. The Nazis had killed her shortly before Lex was born in 1945, and as his Jewish mother had also been in hiding, this gave Lex a sense of kinship with the girl in the secret annexe.

Seeing the step gabled facade of Café Chris up ahead on the right, Lex felt a knot in his stomach at the prospect of tormenting Allard Kuipers. He'd hardly done Lex any favours. Maybe it would have been easier if he'd looked less like a distinguished uncle. Hopefully, a night in the cellar had worn off some of the gloss and made him less reluctant to talk. Lex was glad to have Big Al inflict whatever pain was necessary to make the crook reveal his dirty little secrets.

They reached Café Chris, and Lex knocked on the glass pane in the door. It opened almost immediately.

"Welcome, gentlemen." Tom de Wit looked weary.

"Late night?" Lex asked.

"It got a bit out of hand after the game."

"I thought you hated football and refused to show it in your café?" Lex said.

"Hate is a strong word. Let's say I'm indifferent. You'll never find a television in my humble establishment. Owning the oldest operating bar in the Jordaan comes with certain obligations. But I'll never stand in the way of people celebrating a glorious victory, especially when they do it in my bar and buy me so many drinks."

"But do you have to drink them all?" Al said with a chuckle.

"I only drank about half of them."

"May we come in?" Lex said.

"Of course. I'm sorry. I'm operating in low gear today. Hopefully, so will most of my regulars."

"How is our guest?"

"I was just about to bring him some water and coffee when you arrived. Last night, I took him to the toilet and gave him a sandwich."

"And rightly so," Lex said. "We're not barbarians."

"Did he say anything?" Al asked.

"He went into a rant about how important he was and that we had no idea who we were messing with. He also said he was expected at an important event and that people would be looking for him all over town. I tried not to engage with him."

"I can imagine the torment it must be for him working for the Dutch Football Association and missing the most important game in their history," Lex said.

"And not knowing if the team made it to the final," Al said.

"If he did, he would also dread missing the final," Lex added.

"But he doesn't know, and I suggest we keep it that way. All in all, it gives us another bargaining chip," Al said.

LEX SWITCHED on the light, unlocked the door, and swung it open. Frog One lay on the mattress. He looked startled by the bright light and by the appearance of his tormenters.

"Good day, Mr Kuipers. It's confession time," Lex said and entered the room.

"Fuck off. How dare you keep me here like an animal? I'm a respected pillar of society and a high ranking KNVB officer." With some difficulty, he raised himself. His white shirt was crumpled and untucked. Without a belt, his black trousers began sliding down as he stood up.

Big Al entered the room carrying a chair, which he put under the naked light bulb in the centre. "Sit down, Mr Kuipers," he commanded. "I won't tie you up unless you misbehave."

Allard Kuipers sat down, folded his arms, and crossed his legs.

"Would you like some coffee?" Lex said. "Milk? Sugar?"

He looked suspiciously at Lex. "I'll have some coffee with a little milk. Can I also have some water?"

"Sure."

"And a cigar would be nice."

"Forget it. No cigar," Al said.

"You can have a cigarette," Lex offered and held his pack of Player's Navy Cut towards him. Allard Kuipers' hand shook as he took one. Lex lit it for him, and he inhaled greedily.

"I need to go to the toilet."

"I'll take him while you get the coffee," Al said.

Lex ascended the narrow staircase. Tom de Wit stood behind the bar, stocking the drinks cooler.

"A coffee with milk and a glass of water," Lex said, studying the collection of whisky bottles. "Can I have…"

"A whisky?" Tom suggested, seeing Lex eyeing the booze.

"I was going to ask for a glass of water."

He filled a glass from the tap and handed it to Lex.

"Cheers," Tom said.

Lex emptied the glass and put it on the counter. Tom replaced it with a mug of coffee and another glass of water.

"I expect Al to hurt the poor man, so please keep the door closed. I'm opening soon, and there's no need to advertise the fact that I'm running a torture chamber in the basement."

Lex descended the stairs, entered the room, and closed the door.

"Can I have the water first?" Allard Kuipers took a drag of the half-smoked cigarette, exhaled, and then drained the glass. Lex exchanged it for the mug. Allard Kuipers took a sip. "Dreadful. Please remind me to order champagne next time."

"That's enough," Al said and removed the mug from his hand.

"Could you tell me last night's score? Did we win?"

"Was there a match last night? Do you know anything about that, Lex?"

"I've no idea what the man is talking about."

"You bastards."

"If you give us the information we need, we might be able to find out about the match."

"That would be nice. I have a personal interest, but it's mostly professional, as I'm sure you can appreciate. However, I doubt I have anything for you in exchange."

Lex couldn't help laughing.

"Have I said something amusing?"

"I was thinking of the last time we met. You came to my office and told me that you had no bones to pick with me. All you wanted was a satisfying answer to one question, and if you didn't like the answer, you would ask your friend Boris to squeeze another one out of me. And boy did he try to do just that—enough to put me in hospital."

"I've no idea what you're talking about."

"Now it's my turn to say that I have no bones to pick with you. All I need from you is to give me a satisfying answer to one question. If I don't like the answer, I may ask my friend to shake or squeeze another one out of you."

"I'd rather beat it out of him. It's more my style," Al emphasised.

"And what is your question?" Allard Kuipers sounded less confident.

"I'm looking for a particular girl—the same one you asked me about."

"Does she have a name?"

"You call her Linda, and I call her Lure."

"Never heard of her."

"Did I mention she's gorgeous?"

"I know many beautiful girls, but I do not recall any by the name of Lure or Linda. Maybe you can describe her?"

Without warning, Al struck the man across the face with the back of his right hand, and a few drops of blood appeared on his lower lip. He wiped it off with his hand—seeing the blood set off a tirade of abuse. Big Al lifted his hand again, and Mr Kuipers held his left arm up to protect himself.

Lex stepped between them. "Hold it."

"It's not a fucking skull session," Al hissed. "You're in a cellar, not in the corridors of power."

Allard Kuipers scowled defiantly but was sensible enough to keep quiet.

"No more war of words. Let's cut to the chase. We need you to tell us what happened to the woman you and your associates abducted from a cottage in Tuinpark Ons Buiten on Wednesday last week," Lex said.

"You can hurt me all you like. I've no idea what you're talking about."

"Maybe a few more hours alone in the dark will jog your memory."

"We'll return after lunch. Let me warn you that I normally work out on my punch-bag in the afternoon," Al said. He lifted Allard Kuipers off the chair and tossed him onto the mattress.

"Heeelp me!" he shouted in desperation as Lex was about to open the door.

"Do you want to be gagged?" Al said.

Allard Kuipers shut up. Lex opened the door, and they walked out, Al carrying the chair and Lex, the mug and glass. Lex shut the door and switched off the light.

"ONE DOWN, nine to go," Big Al declared blankly. Hearing Allard Kuipers' howl of pain was almost unbearable. The scream would have alerted the entire neighbourhood had it not been for the soundproofed walls. Allard Kuipers looked in horror at the back of his right hand and saw his middle finger pointing back towards him. Al grabbed his shoulder to prevent him from sliding off the chair. Lex couldn't blame Allard Kuipers for feeling faint. The sound of a finger snapping like a twig was enough for Lex to feel weak at the knees. He pulled himself together.

"As long as you keep refusing to give us some answers, my friend here will break one of your fingers every five minutes." Lex looked at his watch. "You have four minutes before we'll test how far backwards your index finger can go before it breaks."

They hadn't discussed which finger should go next, as Al had never mentioned the finger breaking business as a ploy to make the prisoner talk, and Lex sincerely hoped Allard Kuipers would come to his senses.

Lex looked pointedly at his watch. "Two minutes and ten seconds."

"I'll make sure you'll suffer for what you're doing to me," the man murmured.

"Speak up," Al said. "We can't hear you."

"I'll put a fucking bullet in your head," he hissed.

"That may be, but unless you start talking, it's going to be a long time before you'll be able to pull a trigger," Al pointed out.

"Fifty-five seconds and counting," Lex said.

Al grabbed Allard Kuipers' right wrist and held up his hand. It looked grotesque with the middle finger pointing the wrong way.

"You wanted the index finger? Is that right?"

"That will do very nicely," Lex said, trying to sound brave and not look away.

"Talk to me, Mr Kuipers, or feel the pain," Al warned.

"Go fuck yourself."

The shriek was deafening. Allard Kuipers fell unconscious, and once again, Al held him up to keep him from sliding off the chair. A moment later, he lifted his head.

If looks could kill? Lex thought. He had to give it to him. He was a brave man, but Lex doubted he could take much more.

"Which finger do you want next, Lex? Maybe one on the other hand?"

"I've heard that breaking the pinkie is the most painful," Lex said.

"Mr Pinkie, it is." Al took hold of his wrist and grazed Kuipers' two broken fingers.

"Ouch! Dammit!" Allard Kuipers yowled.

"You have a couple of minutes to prevent my friend from adding to your anguish," Lex said.

He watched the man sitting there, two fingers down yet unwavering. *He's no idiot,* Lex thought. He must realise where this is heading.

"Thirty seconds."

Allard Kuipers' little finger disappeared into Al's right hand. "One little finger, one little finger! Tap tap tap! Point your finger up, point your finger down, point your finger backwards," Al hummed softly to himself.

"Hold it," Lex said. "I'll give the signal."

"I'll talk on one condition," Allard Kuipers said in a barely audible voice.

"Come again?" Al said.

"I'll talk if you tell me last night's score," he said, resigned.

19

LEX KNEW that the Amsterdam harbour covered a large area, but he hadn't expected the vast wilderness, which revealed itself through the early morning mist as they drove along the Westhavenweg.

"It's hard to believe we're only a few miles from the city centre."

"It looks very different when it's not misty," Al said.

Lex presumed that he was referring to his reconnaissance visit the previous day.

Al sat behind the wheel of a dark blue Volvo Amazon station wagon. Lex didn't ask him where the car had come from.

Al's crew cut brushed against the ceiling as he glanced over his shoulder to check on the passenger slumbering on the back seat. Allard Kuipers had his left wrist tied to the door handle and his mouth covered with duct tape. Al had used Tom's first-aid kit to wrap up his right hand and had injected him with a sedative before transferring him from the cellar to the car. Al claimed to know something about broken fingers from his days as a boxing champion, and watching his handiwork both as a breaker and a mender, it was easy to believe. Lex did take the liberty of mentioning that it might be a good idea for a doctor to attend to Allard Kuipers' hand (sooner rather than later) if he planned to play the piano in the future.

Al turned left onto a narrow path and parked behind some wild shrubs.

"We'll walk from here," he said as he opened the door. Al exited the car, and so did Lex. They both wore black T-shirts and black trousers. Al walked to the back of the car, opened the boot, and took out a blanket. He opened the side door, covered the unconscious Allard Kuipers, and then closed the door again.

Al looked at his watch. "Ten past five. He should be out for another hour, maybe longer."

"Hopefully, it will all be over by then," Lex offered.

"Are you in a hurry? Haste makes waste," Al said with a low chuckle, as he took two small, black backpacks from the boot. He handed one to Lex, who opened it and found a roll of duct tape, some rope, a ski mask, and a pistol. Lex lifted the semi-automatic out of the bag.

"It's a Ruger Standard Model."

"I know what it is."

"You have a full magazine."

"That should do it," Lex said.

"For sure, and it's not a shooting party."

"Do I look like a trigger happy kid looking for vengeance?"

"No, just a kid. I'm aware you have a bone to pick with that guy Boris, but I think he needs to play with someone his own size."

"Whatever you say. And I don't hold Boris personally responsible for putting me in hospital. He only acted on orders."

Lex and Al walked down the road for about two hundred metres, and through the mist they saw a white wooden house with a slate gabled roof, perched between the gravel road and the elevated railway tracks. Old newspapers covered three of the house's four windows, and curtains covered the other. As far as Lex could judge, there was no light behind any of them. Wild heather and unkept heath grass covered the broad plot of land in front of the building. There seemed to be no visible path up to the house.

"Get your ski mask and your pistol," Al said.

Lex opened the backpack, took out the ski mask, and put it on. He grabbed the pistol, closed the bag, and slid it back on.

Al waved his pistol, what to Lex looked like a semi-automatic Colt M1911, towards the house entrance, and they hurriedly crossed the wilderness and made it up the grass-covered slope to the front door.

"Wait here while I check out the back of the house," Al whispered. He returned twenty seconds later. "Nothing to report."

He bent down to check the lock on the old wooden door. "I wonder why they bother locking it," he murmured. He slid the backpack off his broad shoulders and took a torsion wrench from a side pocket. He opened the lock within ten seconds to prove his point.

According to the defeated Allard Kuipers, two men and Lure (locked up in the basement) occupied the house. The men were Boris the Bear, and someone called Hans, whose description matched the Tom Wolfe wannabe Lex had seen at the zoo. After he'd finally given up and decided to talk, Allard Kuipers had made some effort to tell them that Boris slept in the first room on the right and Hans slept in the second room on the left. Kuipers' sudden verbal diarrhoea might have been disguising the fact that he was telling tales, but Lex doubted it. He'd experienced it many times as a cop: first pig-headed refusal and denial, and then when the boil was finally lanced, a yearning to lay the cards on the table.

Al mouthed, "Let's go." The ends of his horseshoe-shaped moustache stuck out through the opening of the ski mask, making him look even meaner.

He pushed the door with his foot, and it creaked open. Lex looked past Al as he paused for a second to listen. Lex saw a corridor with seven closed doors in the dim dawn light—three on each side and one at the end.

Al moved forward and stopped at the first door on the right. Lex squeezed past the big man and stopped at the second door on the left. Al gave the go-ahead, and Lex burst through the door.

There was enough light to see the empty twin-size bed against the wall and the pushed aside bedding, as if someone had jumped up in a hurry. Lex had hoped to see the contours of the guy called Hans underneath it.

He felt the presence of someone behind him and turned, only to see Boris and feel his enormous hands around his neck. He lifted Lex off the ground with the ease of a kid handling an Action Man.

Lex thumped a clenched fist into his solar plexus and slammed the pistol barrel against his left temple. It did little, if anything, to stop Boris from strangling him. Lex felt himself losing consciousness.

In a last-ditch effort to save his life, he pointed the pistol towards the man's head. The bang was deafening, and Lex dropped the weapon to the floor.

A look of surprise came over Boris' face after the bullet penetrated his thick skull. His hands refused to let go, but then his eyes went blank, and his grip loosened.

Lex tumbled to the floor, landing on the backpack and the pistol. Remarkably, Boris remained upright, with a fountain of blood pouring from his temple. Eventually, he realised that he was a dead man standing and fell on top of Lex. The impact of his more than one hundred kilos dead weight almost suffocated Lex.

"Help me move him, or you'll also get a bullet," Lex heard Al command. He felt someone lift the weight, and Lex rolled away from under Boris' limp body. Lex managed to sit up against the wall using the last of his energy.

Like a beached whale, Boris lay face down on the floor. Next to him stood Al with his pistol pointed at a man wearing boxer shorts and a T-shirt. Lex didn't need to see him in his white suit to know he was the Tom Wolfe wannabe.

"Why did you have to kill him?" Hans asked with a sigh.

"It was the big man or me. He had his hands around my throat and wouldn't let go, so I had no choice."

"He was unarmed."

"And wouldn't hurt a fly," Lex snarled as he struggled to his feet. *If it hadn't been for the firearm, I would be lying there dead.* Lex slid off the backpack, dropped it onto the floor, and picked up the pistol.

"Are you well enough to keep an eye on this guy while I make sure no one else is here?" Al asked.

Lex nodded and raised the pistol.

"There's no one else," the man said.

Al ignored him and walked out the door.

Lex wasn't comfortable with the man standing, so he ordered him to sit on the bed.

"I don't know why you bother to wear a mask. I know who you are."

"Who am I?"

"You're Lex Spijker, a private detective."

It didn't take Lex long to decide to remove the mask, especially as it made his head boil and his skin itch. He pulled it off with his left hand and dropped it onto the backpack.

"Did you break into my apartment the other night?"

"Would it make any difference if I deny it?"

"I doubt it. You're fucked either way."

"But I'm not telling you why."

"I already know why," Lex said. Hans looked at him with raised eyebrows, but Lex refrained from elaborating. "Mr Allard Kuipers has told us some interesting stuff."

"Who?"

"Kuipers."

"Don't know anyone by that name."

"Who do you think told us about this place?"

"I can't imagine. Who is this guy anyway?"

"He's an official from the football association, and he's working with your syndicate on a bit of World Cup ticket racketeering."

"I don't know anything about a syndicate or tickets for the World Cup."

Big Al returned and gestured towards Lex's face, but didn't comment.

"As I was just about to tell your mate, you're barking up the ...."

"What's in the basement?" Al interrupted.

"There's nothing."

"Someone told us Lure de Lang is locked up there," Lex said.

"Lure de who?"

"Never mind. We'll check it ourselves," Al said.

"Be my guest, you big, fat motherfucker."

Al walked over to him, grabbed his arm, and pulled him up from the bed.

"I'm sorry to disappoint you, but we're not here to gather information. We don't give a damn about your criminal activities. We'll leave that to the cops. They're bound to visit you later today, so don't make any plans. Great chatting to you, but it's time for you to get back to bed." Al dragged him out of the room.

Lex secured the pistol and tucked it into his waistband, then picked up the ski mask and backpack from the floor. He stepped over the dead man, walked out the door, and crossed the hallway to the other room. Hans lay on his back with his hands tied to the headboard of a twin-size, black iron bed and his mouth covered by tape. The drawn curtains caught the light of the early morning sun. Lex pulled open the door of an armoire and saw Hans' white suit and his Panama hat. Al finished tying up the man and tossed the roll of duct tape and the rest of the rope into his backpack. He headed for the door, and Lex followed. Al closed it behind them and pulled off his ski mask.

"Was it wise to show the man your face?"

"He knows what I look like and even my name."

"You've met him before?"

"He was at the zoo."

"Huh?"

"And most likely in my apartment the other night."

"Did you ask him about it?"

"I did. He all but confirmed it, but didn't want to tell me why. I think they panicked when Allard Kuipers suddenly disappeared off the radar. Not knowing what to do, they felt they had to act. So they came to my place to confront me or look for clues. What do I know?"

"It's no longer important," Al said and shrugged.

He opened the door at the end of the corridor. A wooden table with three chairs was on the right-hand side of the room. A newspaper, a pack of Marlboros, an ashtray, a couple of dirty coffee cups, and a black rotary telephone were on the table. In the far-left corner, a spiral staircase led to the basement.

Lex pulled open the drawer of the table and saw a keyring with five skeleton keys. "They've made it easy for us," Lex said and headed for the staircase.

"Let me go first, Lex."

"Why?"

"That's what you pay me for."

The iron staircase creaked under his weight. Lex guessed that Boris had been up and down a few times, so he wasn't too worried it would collapse. Lex followed as Al switched on a light, illuminating another hallway. This one had only five closed doors—two on each side and one at the end.

"Let's start with the door at the end," Al suggested. "If you unlock it, I'll open it. It's better to be safe than sorry," he emphasised.

Lex nodded, squeezed past him, pushed on the handle, and found the door locked. The keys looked identical, so Lex tried them one by one. He succeeded on the third attempt.

Al pulled the door open with his pistol raised, entered the room, and switched on the light. Metal shelves lined the walls of a reasonably large room, and you didn't have to be a dealer or a pusher to realise that cannabis, hashish, amphetamine, and cocaine stocked the shelves. A wooden table without chairs occupied the centre of the room.

"Ticket racketeering, my ass! Don't make me laugh," Al said.

"It sounds rather tame compared to dealing in drugs, but I wouldn't exclude it just yet. Racketeering is highly lucrative during the World Cup, and due to the success of the Dutch team and the tournament being played in West Germany, demand has gone through the roof. Tickets sell for exorbitant amounts."

"I wonder why Allard Kuipers mentioned only the ticket business? He must have known that we would eventually find this if he led us here," Al said.

"I think he hoped that his associates would stop us from getting this far."

Lex flipped open a notebook on the table to find rows of names and numbers. "Man, to be the investigating officer on this one," he said spontaneously. "I think we'll let your old colleagues deal with it."

"Indeed. Laurel and Hardy will most likely help themselves to a generous commission."

"No longer your problem. Let's get what we came for."

LURE DE LANG was one of three girls being held captive in the cellar. Unfortunately, Amanda Artz's niece Laura was not one of them. Or when Lex thought of it, maybe it was fortunate. Officially, she wasn't missing or mixed up in any of this. Just because Lure was using her name did not mean that something had happened to her.

Ticket racketeering, drug dealing, and human trafficking—nothing seemed out of bounds for this syndicate. Lex was sure more bad apples would eventually fall from the tree, but as Al pointed out, this was police business.

Al fetched the Volvo Amazon from down the road. He moved Allard Kuipers from the back seat of the car to the bedroom, where Boris lay dead on the floor. Al strapped him down on the bed. Kuipers looked shocked to see the dead man on the floor, but the gag prevented him from chewing them out.

Lure was drugged and did not seem to notice when Al picked her up and carried her to the car. He carefully laid her on the back seat and covered her with a blanket.

Before leaving the house, Al made an anonymous call to the Leidseplein police station to let them know about the den of thieves on Westhavenweg. Lex hoped they would rise to the bait. If getting a place full of drugs, women under lock and key, and a few gangsters dead or alive served up on a platter couldn't get Laurel and Hardy out of bed, Lex wondered what would.

Al parked on a side road nearby and waited for the police to arrive. To Lex's relief, Schenk and Holst passed in their Volkswagen Beetle thirty minutes later, tailed by a dark grey Mercedes-Benz van from the Mobile Unit.

As soon as the cavalry had passed, Al fired up the motor, put the car into gear, and headed towards the city centre. Lex looked at Lure sleeping in the back and wondered what drugs they'd given her. Did she need to see a doctor? And where should they take her to recover?

"Shall I drive you home?" Al asked as if reading his mind.

"Give me a few minutes to think about it." Lex looked at his watch and yawned loudly. "Sorry, but I'm not used to getting up at four."

"Will it help if I turn on the radio?"

"It won't hurt unless they play 'Twinkle, Twinkle Little Star'."

Al switched on a talk show, and Lex immediately searched for some music. As he turned the dial to Radio Luxembourg, 'The Ballad of John and Yoko' filled the air. They listened to the catchy tune for a couple of minutes.

"I have a suggestion," Al said. "Let's put your female friend up at the Amsterdam Hilton."

"I doubt they'll let us check in this early, and I don't fancy any of our names in the register. I can imagine them asking if we have any luggage and answering, 'Only this young lady. You can bring her up to my room!'"

"As it happens, I know the main man at the reception, and I also know from dealing with him previously that he can be a master of discretion."

"You're an absolute peach. I don't know what I would have done without you."

"Can I have that in writing?" Al said with a chuckle.

#

AFTER TUCKING Lure in at the Amsterdam Hilton, Al drove them to Lex's apartment on Rembrandtplein, where they stayed long enough for him to pack a weekend bag. Al had offered to let Lex sleep on his sofa for a day or two.

Lex envisioned the virtuousness on Allard Kuipers' face when he tried to convince Holst and Schenk of his innocence and to tell them how he'd ended up in the house on Westhavenweg. He'd hold up his hand with tears in his blue eyes and show them the damage done to his poor fingers. Whether they'd believe him or would be able to gather enough evidence to keep him in custody beyond the weekend was nothing Lex needed to worry about right now.

He did need to worry about Laurel and Hardy looking for him and wanting to lock him up to spoil his weekend. It might not have made a world of difference to him or anyone else, but right now, Lex had several good reasons for staying as far away from Leidseplein as possible. Until Monday, at least. The most important reasons were a heart-to-heart talk with Lure de Lang and the small matter of a World Cup final between a brilliant Dutch team and the host nation. Two attractive, as well as daunting, prospects.

LEX CALLED after dinner. She picked up almost immediately.

"Amanda Artz speaking."

"Private Detective Lex Spijker."

"I'm relieved to hear your voice. I've been trying to get hold of you."

"I haven't been in much, nor has my secretary."

"I've heard from my niece," she said without hesitation.

"That's a relief. Did you talk to her?"

"She sent me a postcard from Goa in India. It's dated 20 June."

"More than two weeks ago. What does it say?"

"Not much."

"Please read it to me."

"Hold the line while I find it." Amanda Artz returned within fifteen seconds and read, "Dear Aunty, I've gone to India to find my soul. I'm having a great time, and I don't know when I'll be back. Don't worry about me."

"Are you sure it's from her?"

"Why wouldn't it be?"

"You tell me."

"As far as I can see, it's her handwriting. It's also totally in her character to do a thing like that."

"Like what?"

"Going off somewhere on the spur of the moment without telling anyone."

"Have you informed the police?"

"How could I without letting them know about our conversation the other day? A promise is a promise."

"You're right. Thanks."

"I don't think they know I suspected she was missing, and I doubt they know that someone else has been using her name."

"Uh-huh."

"Have you found the young lady?"

"Yes."

"That's a relief. It seems things are falling into place. Have you heard anything about who killed the poor man on my kitchen floor?"

"I don't know anything more about it than the last time we spoke," Lex lied.

"Nor do I."

"I have a sense the police will contact you soon."

"Do I still need to keep your name out of it?"

"That won't be necessary anymore. I'm sure they are looking for me as we speak, but I'm staying in the shadows for a few days."

"Will you get in touch again?"

"I can't promise," Lex said and ended the call.

Al was out taking care of some other business, and Lex walked to the kitchen to make some coffee and check if his travel companion Johnnie Walker needed some company.

20

LEX KNOCKED on the door to room 702.

"Who is it?"

"Room service."

"I haven't ordered anything," said a voice on the other side of the door.

"It's me, Lex."

The door opened. Lure still looked slightly pale, but that only added to her beauty. Lex walked past her. For a hotel room, it was spacious. A queen-size bed stood in front of a panorama window draped in sheer curtains that framed a beautiful view of the city. Lex opened the door to the balcony.

"You mind? It's a bit stuffy in here."

"Be my guest."

"How do you feel?"

"Better, thanks, although I still feel a bit drowsy." She wore a white bathrobe with a gold Hilton logo. "I just had a nice hot bath."

It made Lex think of their bath together at Tom's cottage and the great sex it had led to. He shrugged it off.

"When I said room service, I meant it." Lex put two bags on the bed and took out a selection of sandwiches, a bottle of white wine, and a bottle of Scotch from one of them. He arranged them on the coffee table nearby and fetched two wine glasses from a tray on top of a chest of drawers. Lex opened the wine bottle and poured Lure a generous measure. He then broke open the whisky and gave himself an equally generous amount. "Cheers," he said, and they clinked.

"What's in the other bag?" Lure asked.

"A present for you."

"Can I have a look?"

"Go ahead."

Lure emptied the contents of the bag onto the bed and held up first one dress and then another.

"I'm impressed. Do you usually buy pretty dresses for girls in distress?"

"It's a first, and I hope they fit and do justice to your beautiful body," Lex said, feeling aroused as he said it.

"They look about my size, and I'll try them on after lunch."

They ate in silence. Lure lounged on the bed, and Lex sat in a club chair with the coffee table between them. The midday sun shone through the sheer curtains and lit the room with a pleasant, mellow light.

"I think it's about time you told me your real name."

"What if I insist it's Lure?"

"That won't work. It's your word against the woman you claim is your aunt and a man called Allard Kuipers."

She sat up straight. "You've been a busy boy, I see."

"What do you expect? How do you think I located the house on Westhavenweg to save you yesterday?"

"So, that's where I was locked up."

"Let me give you a bit of friendly advice. Be very careful what you tell me and how you answer my questions. I have enough pieces of the puzzle to see almost the whole picture and could probably tell you what happened. It might not be entirely accurate, but it will be close. I'd rather hear it from you. It's your choice."

"What if I tell you to get lost?"

"I'll hand you over to the police."

"Do I have any guarantee you won't do that anyway?"

"I can't make any promises."

"It's not much of a choice."

"Why so afraid? Don't you know I care about you and want everything to turn out for the best? What's the harm in telling me the truth? You could start by giving me your real name." Lex refilled her glass, and she drank half of it.

"My name is Linda Vogel," she said, in a voice as remote as her gaze. "I'm twenty-four years old and was born in Diemen. I moved to Amsterdam in the summer of '67. I'd just turned seventeen and was desperate to get away from the boredom of suburban hell and the bourgeois lifestyle of my parents. After a few years of living on the bare minimum and doing odd, underpaid jobs, I realised that freedom isn't much fun without money.

"By that point, I was twenty-one, and since people kept praising me for my good looks, I thought that I might as well benefit from it. I tried modelling, but it didn't work out. Instead, I joined an agency providing high-class girls to exclusive customers. That's how I ran into Allard Kuipers."

It pleased Lex to notice that she wasn't caressing the scar under her chin with the tip of her finger. Perhaps this time, she was telling the truth.

Linda, formerly Lure, took a sip of wine. "I need to go to the bathroom. Do you mind?"

Lex went out onto the balcony to give her some privacy. He looked over the railing and saw his scooter seven floors down in the parking lot. Lex immediately felt giddy and turned away to go back inside. He lay down on his back on the bed to stop the room from spinning.

He heard the door to the bathroom open and felt Lure, or rather Linda, slide onto the bed next to him. She put her right hand on his stomach. Lex felt the warmth from her palm and her moist lips against his ear.

"Make love to me, Lex," she whispered, as her hand undid the button on his trousers. She pulled down his fly.

Lex knew it was a bad idea and that he should have removed her hand. Instead, he pushed her onto her back and untied the belt of her bathrobe. She wore no panties, and he knelt on the floor and put his head between her suntanned legs. She moaned, and Lex felt her fingers playing with his hair. After a couple of minutes, she lifted his head. "Do it to me," she pleaded, as she spread her legs to let him inside.

After the climax, they lay close together and dozed off. Lex woke first, got out of bed, picked up his pants and boxer shorts, and went to the bathroom. Looking in the mirror, Lex blamed himself for being weak and letting his desire interrupt her story. He turned on the cold tap and splashed water onto his face. "Get on with it, Lex," he said to himself.

"WHERE WAS I before you interrupted me?" Linda said as she returned from the bathroom. She wore the black and white sheath dress Lex had bought her, and it fitted her like a glove. She slid onto the bed.

"You were about to tell me how you met Allard Kuipers."

"I was one of a group of four girls invited to entertain at a cocktail party in the Metropool complex. Before we arrived, I had no idea it was the headquarters of the KNVB. Allard Kuipers, who did not introduce himself at the time, welcomed us at the door. He told us to give him and his important guests a good time. To get us into the groove, we were offered booze and cocaine. Allard Kuipers decided I should be his girl for the night and took me to his office. It was very spacious and equipped with a couch. Although he acted like a man of the world, he seemed oddly shy and inexperienced when it came to intimacy between a man and a woman. Afterwards, he acted as though I'd done him a great favour and insisted on giving me a tip. Like in a gangster movie, he had a wall safe behind a painting. Before he handed me a small bundle of notes, I saw stacks of money inside the safe."

"So, you decided to steal it?"

"That was later."

"When you met Jan Berger?"

"You have done your homework," she said.

"But, you didn't meet him at the Grand Hotel Krasnapolsky."

"Does it matter where it was? He was a small-time hustler with grandiose behaviour and an inflated self-opinion, who was pleased to have a pretty girl on his arm. He boasted how he could open any lock or safe, so I challenged him to open the one in Allard Kuipers' office. I promised him half of the money for his efforts."

"And he believed you. I'm sure he was under your spell."

"I do seem to have that effect on most men."

"Uh-huh."

"Anyhow, Jan Berger stole the money and brought it to me."

"And you took it all, as you never intended to share it. Conveniently, he believed your real name was Lure and that he knew where you lived. But the apartment belonged to your friend Laura, who'd gone to India. So you decided to relocate."

"I'd gone with Laura to her aunt's apartment after she went to Italy and knew where she kept the spare key. I told myself that Jan Berger would never find me there."

"But then you saw him sniffing around in your new neighbourhood, and you panicked. After seeing my advertisement in *de Telegraaf*, you came to visit me. Unfortunately, your charms didn't work immediately on me. Then Jan Berger tracked you down and confronted you in Amanda Artz's kitchen. Was that Monday morning?"

"It was."

"The lock must have been child's play for him, and he must have been fairly pissed off."

"He said he wanted to kill me."

"But Jan Berger was not a violent man per se, and he needed you to tell him where you were keeping the money. Being under your spell, he'd let his guard down, and you knifed him."

"It was self-defence."

"Maybe it was, but it's still manslaughter or murder."

"I didn't mean to."

"Now you had a dead guy on a kitchen floor that wasn't your floor in the first place. Time to relocate again. Where did you go?"

"I went to a small hotel in the Red Light District."

"You called a taxi to take you there."

"How do you know that?"

"You were seen. Allow me to backtrack. When Jan Berger stole the money from the safe, some video surveillance equipment recorded him entering the building. It was only a matter of time before Allard Kuipers and his associates discovered Jan Berger's identity and where he lived. What Jan Berger didn't tell you was that he'd upped the stakes by helping himself to a package of cocaine. The gangsters gained access to his apartment, where they found the drugs, but not the money.

"They had no intention of hurting or killing him, at least not before he'd returned the money. He told them a girl called Lure de Lang had taken the loot and that he would get it back. We'll probably never know how he persuaded them that it would be better if they waited outside Amada Artz's apartment as he confronted you."

"So they saw me when I came out of the apartment and got into the taxi?"

"Right. To be more precise, a guy in a white suit and a white Panama hat saw you."

"Him! He was at the Artis and one of the two men who abducted me from the cottage in the community garden."

"He must have wondered what had happened to Jan Berger when he saw you rushing out the door and into a taxi. He gained access to the apartment and, instead of finding the money, found Jan Berger on the kitchen floor with a knife in his chest. You must excuse me if you think you've heard it before, but there have been a few additions and alterations to the narrative."

"I don't like it any better this time," she said.

"Picture this: A private detective comes to Amanda Artz's apartment to help a beautiful girl in distress. She's no longer there, but he finds the door open. Now it's his turn to discover the body in the kitchen. The private detective may be a man with a drink problem, a feeble backbone, and poor judgment, but he's also a former cop. So when he stumbles on a corpse, he calls his old police mates. Unfortunately, someone else in the apartment thinks it's a bad idea. Down goes the private detective. You couldn't make it up, unless you were writing pulp fiction."

"I regret getting you involved."

"So you keep telling me. I wonder why you bothered contacting me in the first place. Why didn't you just relocate again when you saw Jan Berger sniffing around?"

"I can't explain. Maybe I was tired of running."

"And why contact me again after Jan Berger was dead? I presume you still had the money."

"After a few days alone in the hotel, I couldn't take much more. I guess paranoia got the better of me. I'd never stolen that kind of money or killed anyone before, and I was certain the cops were hot on my heels."

"By contacting me again and arranging to meet, you opened up a can of worms. What none of us knew at the time was that the guy who knocked me out cold at Amanda Artz's apartment had checked my ID. Since they couldn't locate you, they decided to keep me under surveillance. That was a smart move, since I unwittingly led them to you."

"So, that's why they confronted us at the Artis?"

"Indeed, but the gang didn't expect you to be armed."

"How did they find me at the cottage?"

"They persuaded my secretary to reveal the location by dangling her little dog out of a third-floor window."

"Bastards. Is the dog okay?"

"Still wagging his little tail."

"Thank God."

"Tell me what happened at the community garden." Lex poured himself another whisky and held up the bottle of white wine, but she declined.

"I was asleep, so I didn't have a chance. Maybe I should have been more alert, but I didn't expect a visit. They tied me up and drugged me, and when I woke, I was in a cellar somewhere."

"Did you see Allard Kuipers again?"

"Once to tell me that he regretted treating me like a lady, when he should have known I was a lowlife hooker with good looks. He said it was an insult to his intelligence to have anything to do with women of my kind, and that his associates would deal with me."

"That's rich. Did you give up the money?"

"I had to."

"Where was it?"

"In a locker at Central Station. I had the key in my bag, so it wasn't difficult for them to do the maths."

"Did you think they would let you go when they'd recovered the money?"

"I pleaded with them. I said I didn't know who they were, and I didn't care."

"You knew Allard Kuipers."

"So what. It would be my word against a respectable official from the KNVB."

"Not for long. Especially if you would be willing to testify about his involvement."

"No, thank you."

"Did you know they were into the trafficking of young girls?"

"I figured as much when they told me how valuable I was." Tears welled up in her eyes, and she got off the bed. She walked over to the window and gazed out. Lex waited her out. She turned and came over to him, lowered herself onto his lap and folded her arms around his neck. "You saved me from a horrible fate."

"Maybe."

"Are you going to tell the police about me?"

"Maybe."

"Please sleep on it."

"Maybe."

"Here with me," she said, as her mouth covered his.

LEX WOKE around nine o'clock with a hangover. It was Sunday morning, after all. It didn't do him any good to see the almost empty whisky bottle on the coffee table. Lex turned his head and saw the alluring curves of Linda's shoulders and back. Her steady breathing showed she was sleeping.

Lex's indecision about what to do had kept him awake half the night. Doubt raged in his mind: *Should he let her off the hook or give her up? One minute he told himself they could have a normal relationship, that he could trust her, that Jan Berger had it coming, and that Allard Kuipers deserved to have his dirty money stolen and his fingers broken. The next minute Lex believed she was suffering from mythomania, that theft was theft, murder was murder, and that she must take the consequences for her actions.* Around six, he'd finally made a decision.

Lex slid out of bed quietly, walked the few metres to the bathroom, switched on the light, closed the door, and relieved himself. He washed his hands and caught a glimpse of his craggy face in the mirror.

He exited the bathroom to find Linda sitting in bed in her bathrobe, her head turned towards the panorama window.

"I hate rainy Sundays," she said.

Lex expected her to look at him, but she didn't. He dressed and opened the door to the balcony. He took a seat in the chair next to the coffee table. The whisky bottle again caught his eye. The golden liquid barely covered the bottom, and he cursed himself for not leaving enough for a decent drink. He could have done with some Dutch courage before telling Linda his decision. He took the plunge.

"I'm going to hand you over to the police, but ...."

"You're a bastard," she burst out. "I thought you cared for me."

"I do. Just hear me out."

It caught him by surprise when she suddenly jumped out of bed and ran out onto the balcony. Through the open door, Lex saw her climbing over the railing. She put her bare feet on the ledge and held on with both hands.

Lex rushed to the door.

"I'd rather die than be locked up again." Her cheeks were wet, and Lex gathered it wasn't only from the rain.

"For Christ's sake, Linda, don't be so melodramatic. I doubt you'll go to prison."

She ignored him and pulled her left hand off the railing.

Horrified, Lex stepped towards her. He looked at her, then downward, and then towards her again. She put her hand back on the railing, and Lex detected misgiving in her expression.

"Take my hand," Lex said, reaching out for her. She lifted her left hand again, and as she reached for him, her right hand lost its grasp on the wet railing. It all went very fast. Lex rushed forward to grab hold of her as she tilted backwards.

Although the effect of his vertigo and hangover didn't help, he miraculously managed to grab hold of her left hand with his right. She dangled at the end of his arm, and Lex felt her wet hand slipping out of his grasp.

"Grab onto the ledge!" he shouted. The move gave him the split second he needed to catch hold of the shoulder of her bathrobe with his left hand. Using the last of his energy, Lex pulled her up and dragged her over the railing. They fell backwards, and she landed on top of him.

Gasping for breath, they lay on the balcony floor, and he felt a tremor running through her body. Ignoring the pain in his right arm, Lex held her tight.

"You're safe now, but we need to stop this madness."

Linda didn't respond and sobbed.

"I don't know much, but I do know that I have strong feelings for you."

"And me for you," she whispered.

"I would like us to have a fresh start together, here in Amsterdam or somewhere else. But that can only happen if there are no lies between us and if we get out of this mess. And that means going to the police. We both have some explaining to do, and you have to come clean about your involvement."

"Then I'll go to prison."

"Perhaps, but aren't you tired of living a life of deceit?"

"I'm mostly scared."

"Whatever happens, I'll be there for you. I'll back your claim that you killed Jan Berger in self-defence, and as for the money you stole, it's not like you robbed the National Bank."

"Will I have to testify against Allard Kuipers and his associates?"

"Why worry about that now?" Lex let go of her, got to his feet, and pulled her up. He guided her into the hotel room and onto the bed. Lex laid down next to her, and she took his hand. Like the first time they met, he drowned in her big, innocent, emerald eyes.

"I'm going to trust you and do whatever you suggest," she said.

"All will come well," he replied and kissed her.

21

LEX AND LINDA lay in silence on the bed listening to the rain against the window.

"Okay, I'm ready," Linda said as she let go of his hand and rolled off the bed.

Lex looked at his watch. "You may think I'm a total mindless idiot."

"What?"

"There's something I'd like to do before we go to the cops."

"Is that constantly on your mind?" Linda said with a flirtatious smile as she sat back down on the bed beside him.

"I have no idea what you're referring to," he said, laughing, "but I'm thinking about this afternoon's World Cup final."

"Great minds think alike," she said dryly.

"So you wouldn't mind if we watch it before going to the police? It's the most important game ever, and the entire city, country, and world will be watching," Lex said, sounding like an insurance salesman.

"Alright, you've convinced me," she said with a snicker. "Men in tight shorts pushing a ball around doesn't do it for me, and I doubt I'll be able to concentrate on a stupid football game, knowing I might be locked up tonight. But knowing how much it means to you, I'll come for your sake."

"You're such a good sport."

"Are we going to your pub on the Rembrandtplein?"

"I would love to take you there, but we'd better not risk it. With Laurel and Hardy looking for us, the place is most likely under surveillance.

"You lost me there. Why should two dead comedians be looking for us?"

"Laurel and Hardy are the official nicknames for my two old colleagues, Wouter Schenk and Roy Holst, at the Leidseplein police station. You'll know why when you see them together."

"I'm confused. You've just convinced me we should go to the police, and now you're telling me we should avoid your local pub because they might look for us there."

"It's because my old colleagues hate my guts and would love to have me cooped up in a detention cell while they watch the game upstairs. I'll prefer for us to stay free till after the game."

"I see. What do you suggest?"

"Let's watch the game at the Half Moon Lounge downstairs."

"Okay, but on one condition."

"Tell me."

"You treat me to lunch there before the game."

BEING A bar and restaurant catering to an international audience in an American hotel chain, the Half Moon Lounge did the minimum to advertise that Holland would be playing West Germany in the World Cup final in a couple of hours. Lex couldn't care less as long as they showed the game. With its thick blue carpet, heavy teak furniture, and conservative decorative style, the old-school lounge had limited its football decor to some West German and Dutch flags.

"No need to go over the top," Lex mumbled as he counted twelve of each.

"What?" Linda said.

"Just talking to myself."

A middle-aged waiter approached. "Good day, sir madam." He gave Linda the elevator eyes. Lex couldn't blame him, as her red sheath dress clung to her body, enhancing her bust and petite frame. *She must be tired of men looking her up and down with a lustful gaze,* Lex thought.

"Can we have some lunch?" Lex asked.

"Have you booked a table?"

"We're guests at the hotel. Room 702," Lex said as he looked around the half-full lounge.

"That's not entirely true, as we've just checked out," Linda said.

"No problem. Would you like to sit outside?" Lex looked out of the open door and onto the covered terrace with a view towards one of the city's many canals.

"Looks tempting, but we would prefer a seat inside and near the television. There's a game on in a couple of hours."

"Is that so, sir?" the waiter said with a cheesy grin. He guided them to a small round table at the far end of the room.

"That's at least fifteen metres from the television. Do you have something nearer? How about that one there?" Lex asked and pointed.

"I'm afraid that table is reserved, sir."

"Never mind. This one will have to do."

"Very well, sir. What would you like to drink?"

THIRTY MINUTES to kick-off, and the tournament's closing ceremony was in full flow at the Olympiastadion in Munich. Lex felt the butterflies, and it didn't help to calm his nerves that a noisy and champagne drinking German party of two women and two men now occupied the reserved table nearer to the television.

"Do they have to behave like a German victory is a foregone conclusion?" he said to Linda as he nodded in their general direction.

"Calm down, Lex. They are just enjoying themselves on a rainy afternoon in Amsterdam."

"Not for the first time, and we'd better also win this one," he mumbled.

While the two teams lined up and the marching band played the two national anthems, Lex fetched a pint and a glass of white wine at the bar. He returned to see Rob Rensenbrink and Johan Cruijff standing in the centre circle with the ball, waiting for the English referee Jack Taylor to blow the whistle for the kick-off. Lex put the drinks on the table and sat down.

"What's he waiting for?" he said nervously.

"According to the commentator, someone removed the corner flags after the closing ceremony and forgot to put them back."

"So much for German efficiency," Lex scoffed, loud enough for the German party to hear. Linda and everyone else ignored his remark.

"Come on, Holland," Lex barked as Johan Cruijff finally got the game underway. The Dutch defence pushed the ball around before returning it to Johan Cruijff. From the halfway line and with a burst of energy, he darted towards the German penalty area and then into it, where a clumsy Uli Hoeneß tripped him up.

"Penalty," Lex shouted, and fortunately, the man in black agreed.

"Go away, Beckenbauer," Lex said as the German captain protested in the face of the referee. Lex could hardly watch as Johan Neeskens stepped up to execute it. Straight down the middle, and no chance for the German goalkeeper Sepp Maier, who dived to the left. Lex jumped to his feet and did a celebration jig, mainly for the benefit of the German party. The brilliant Dutch team had taken the lead within two minutes, and before any German player had even touched the ball.

For the next twenty-five minutes, the Dutch should have taken advantage of a shell-shocked West German team. But they didn't, and were punished when Bernd Hölzenbein waltzed into the Dutch penalty area with the ball at his feet. He conveniently fell over when challenged by a defender.

"What a dive. Someone give him an Oscar," Lex exclaimed. The replay showed he had a point, but Jack Taylor was determined to make history by being the first referee to award two penalties in a World Cup final. Paul Breitner took responsibility for the kick and scored to the left of Jan Jongbloed, who hardly moved.

The roar made Lex realise that at least half of the customers in the Half Moon Lounge were Germans, or at least supported his sworn adversaries.

"I'm now regretting that we didn't take our chance to watch the game at Café Monico," Lex said to Linda, as the German party made sure to let him know that they had not overlooked his previous insults.

"Too late now. But why so negative, Lex? It's only one apiece, and there's plenty of time to score another goal," Linda said.

"Or to concede one," Lex replied, insisting on being defeatist.

He knew that when a West German team had the bit between their teeth, it was only a matter of time before they punished you. And so it proved when Gerd Müller, a couple of minutes before half-time, turned on a plate and, with a relatively tame shot, navigated the ball between the legs of a defender, and past Jan

Jongbloed, who, as with the first West German goal, hardly moved.

"Of all the players, why did it have to be that little twat?" Lex sighed as he looked to the ceiling in despair. Linda reached across the table and put a hand on his arm.

"Poor you. I now realise how much a silly football game means to you."

"More than you know, baby. More than you know."

"I don't know much about football, but to me, it seems the Dutch team, after they scored that early goal, buggered about in an attempt to humiliate the Germans for the crimes of the Second World War," Linda said. Lex looked at her in astonishment. *Where did that come from*? he thought. It was a good point, and the colour mounted in his face, as he felt that the observation was equally meant for him.

To end the first forty-five minutes on an even sourer note for the Dutch team, the referee booked Johan Cruijff for contempt as they walked off. While the players were enjoying their half-time tea, some probably more than others, Lex visited the men's room and then bought another round of drinks. Seeing the outrageous prices, Lex couldn't help thinking about bartender Bart at Café de Monico, God bless him, having halved the already reasonable prices. Leaning against the bar, waiting for the drinks, Lex studied Linda stretching her suntanned legs at the open door to the terrace.

You miserable sod, he said to himself. *The Dutch may lose, and the prices be inflated, but what does it matter when you're here with the girl of your dreams.*

Lex put the drinks on the table and walked over to embrace Linda.

"What's that sudden affection for?" Linda asked.

"Because you're the most beautiful woman in the room, and I love you. And because this afternoon, you're mine."

The players and the referee returned to the pitch, and Lex and Linda returned to their seats. West Germany kicked off, and it didn't take long before the second-half descended into a dog fight, which seemed to suit West Germany better than the Dutch. Lex wanted desperately to support the team, but as the Dutch failed to create any clear-cut chances, despite having most of the possession, he found it increasingly hard to concentrate on the proceedings unfolding on the relatively small screen in the distance. It didn't help much that heads, arms or hands often obstructed his view whenever the German party reacted to events on the pitch, such as when Gerd Müller thought he had scored another goal, only to be denied it by the linesman flagging for offside. Or when Hölzenbein tried another dive in the Dutch penalty area. This time, however, referee Jack Taylor's whistle remained silent.

Not long after, the game ended, and the West German party poopers were world champions.

"That's it, we're leaving," Lex said, ignoring the victorious Germans celebrating around them. "I'd rather see Laurel and Hardy than Franz Beckenbauer holding the trophy above his head," Lex said and paid up. He guided Linda out of the Half Moon Lounge and to the reception.

"Can we have our bags, please," Lex said to a young man behind the counter.

"Sorry about the result," the receptionist offered, as he handed them their bags.

"No need to apologise, young man. It's hardly your fault that our brilliant team chose this holy Sunday to inflict a national trauma for years to come," Lex said.

"Sometimes you're so dramatic," Linda said.

"You wait and see, baby."

They exited the Hilton and walked towards his scooter. Fortunately, the rain had stopped.

"Let's go make our confessions."

"Convince me again it's a good idea," Linda said.

"Stop it. You know it makes sense, unless you want to keep living a life looking over your shoulder. Is there any need to go over it again?"

"Will you wait for me?" Linda asked, looking worried.

"Happy to repeat what I've said several times. You have my full support, and I'll wait for you till the end of days."

"Hopefully, it won't take that long," Linda said with faraway eyes.

"You're only twenty-three."

"Twenty-four."

"Still young."

"Can I ask you something that might make it more bearable?"

"Anything."

"You said you'd like for us to have a fresh start together, here in Amsterdam or somewhere else. Can we make it somewhere else?"

"Have you got somewhere in mind?"

"Why not make it Paris? You're half-French, and you speak the lingo."

"I would love to live with you in Paris, but it's not much fun on the breadline unless you're Henry Miller."

"But you can set up shop as a private detective, and I can pursue my dream of becoming a model."

"You may have something there, and it's made me think. My only uncle lives in Paris, and as it happens, he owns a real estate agency. Perhaps he can offer us a good deal on a rental?"

"For the first time, I feel the urgency to get this mess cleaned up and my life back on track," Linda said, as she climbed onto Lex's scooter. She put her arms around him and rested her head against his back as he pulled away from the Hilton Hotel and headed towards the police station at Leidseplein.

PARIS
1975

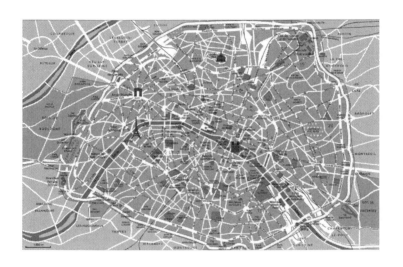

22

LEX PULLED the French windows open and pushed aside the shutters. The morning spring sunlight streamed into his small office. He leaned against the iron railing and looked down into the old cobbled street. To make it nearly Parisian picture-perfect, a red Citroën 2CV passed below, and his gaze followed the car as it drove up Rue Norvins towards Place du Tertre.

He pinched himself to make sure it wasn't a dream that he had been living in the heart of Montmartre for the last couple of months. In a way, he'd come home, as his late mother was born in the Marais, and as a kid, because of his father's work, he'd lived in Montparnasse until the family moved, when he was eleven, to Amsterdam.

Lex jumped when the phone behind him rang. He'd almost forgotten it was there, as the bells of the Sacré-Cœur, only about three hundred metres away, chimed more frequently. He turned away from the window, walked to the desk and lifted the receiver.

"Private Detective Lex Spijker. How can I help?"

Lang zal hij leven

Lang zal hij leven

Lang zal hij leven in de gloria

In de gloria

In de gloria

"Roos!?"

"Happy birthday, young man."

"Thanks. I didn't know you had such a beautiful voice. Edith Piaf got nothing on you."

"Stop teasing me."

"I mean it."

"How is it to be thirty? Tell me. It's so long ago, I can hardly remember myself."

"You're not even fifty," Lex protested.

"I didn't call to discuss my advanced age," she said, laughing.

"How is Amsterdam?"

"Same old same old, but I want to hear about Paris. What are you doing on your big day? Tell me all about it."

"I plan to have lunch at my local, followed by a stroll on the Champs-Élysées, and this evening my uncle has invited me to a fancy restaurant."

"You sound happy," she said. Roos had worked as his part-time secretary for about a year, while Lex operated as a private detective in Amsterdam. After some gangsters roughed her up and threatened to kill her pug dog by dropping it from a second-floor window during a case the previous year, she'd seemed relieved when he'd told her about setting up shop in Paris.

"How is your apartment?"

"Compared to Rembrandtplein, it's like a palace."

"Most apartments would be. If you pardon my French, that was a real dump."

"It's not fair to compare the two. My apartment here is double the size, in any direction, if you know what I mean. And as you can imagine, the ceilings are covered with beautiful stucco. And guess what?"

"You tell me."

"There's a decent-sized bathroom with a bathtub. You know, one of those classic ones on cast iron legs."

"Marvellous. That will be put to good use when Lure joins you in a few days."

"You mean Linda."

"Did I say Lure?"

"That's what I heard."

"Sorry, old habits die hard."

"No, problem. I often think of her as Lure myself."

"You must be looking forward to her arrival?" she said.

"You bet. I'll pick her up at the Gare du Nord on Saturday."

"I know."

"You talked to her?"

"I visited her last week."

"How was she?"

"She looked well, and her beauty has gone up a notch. You would think prison life should have the opposite effect, but not on Linda."

"Did she mention me?" Lex said with anticipation.

"I got sick of hearing your name. If I didn't know better, I would think she was in love with you," Roos said with a chuckle. "You're a lucky man, Alexander."

"Don't I know it."

LEX RETURNED home from his afternoon stroll on the Avenue des Champs-Élysées in time for a nap and a refreshing half hour in the bathtub, accompanied by a glass of white wine.

He dressed in black trousers, a white shirt with a thin black tie, a pair of Dr Martens, a black leather jacket, and a pork pie hat. He studied himself in the hallway mirror and nodded with approval. While the outfit had occasionally made him seem overdressed in Amsterdam, there wasn't much chance of that happening in the city of Laurent, Lagerfeld and Laroche.

The spring evening was dry and mild, and he decided to walk the two kilometres to the restaurant on Rue du Faubourg Saint-Denis. *Was it Hemingway who wrote if you're tired of walking in Paris, you're tired of life?* Lex thought. The scenery and atmosphere change with each new street and every corner you turn. And if your legs are up to it, you can walk forever without the risk of crossing your tracks. And if you, for some reason, want to stay hidden or anonymous, Paris is your town. To locate a 'missing' person in Paris must be a nightmare, although, as a private detective, with more time than money, he would welcome any paying client hiring him to do just that.

Lex passed the massive arch of Porte Saint-Denis, and knowing his uncle was a stickler for punctuality, he arrived early at the restaurant. He waited in front of the red facade that, with its upscale appearance, seemed oddly out of place. He lit a cigarette and studied the busy street. Compared to many other parts of Paris, the Faubourg St. Denis neighbourhood seemed shabby and run down. It made him feel at home, but he wasn't sure about his uncle. Maybe he was prejudiced, but from the look of it, men who wore suits and shirts tailored at Cifonelli and hand-sewn shoes from Aubercy seemed as rare in Rue du Faubourg Saint-Denis as rocking horse droppings. Perhaps his uncle would compromise for the sake of the restaurant? He didn't have to wait long for the confirmation.

"Happy birthday, Alexander."

"Good evening, Jules. How are you?" They shook hands.

"Hope you don't mind me luring you to, let's say, this 'interesting and colourful' part of town on your birthday, but the restaurant will make up for it. I'm confident you'll find the art nouveau decor magnificent and the food excellent."

Jules held the door, and Lex followed him into the restaurant. A stained glass ceiling hovered about four metres above their heads, and white table cloths covered the numerous tables in the big room. Nearly all of them were occupied. A youthful-looking man in a traditional French waiter's costume approached.

"Monsieur Lévy, how are you today?"

"Top of the world, Étienne. Especially as I'm here with my nephew."

"Welcome, monsieur."

"And Madame Lévy?"

"She is in Israel attending to a family matter."

Lex hoped Jules wouldn't reveal it was his birthday, as he envisioned the restaurant's lights being dimmed while Étienne or some other waiter approached their table with the traditional dessert decorated with festive fireworks and the entire restaurant singing for him. His false modesty could do without the attention.

"My nephew is thirty today, so you'd better be on your toes," Jules said.

"Congratulations, monsieur. Table twenty-four is ready for you."

They followed the waiter over the tiled floor to the back of the restaurant. He pulled out the table for one of them to access a seat on the red upholstered bench that ran along the entire wall. Lex caught a glimpse of himself in the big mirror and realised he was still wearing his pork pie hat. He hung it on a hat stand nearby.

"You go in, Lex, so you can enjoy the mise-en-scène," Jules said.

Lex nodded politely to a young couple at the neighbouring table as he slid into the seat. He noted, with some satisfaction, that they'd reached the coffee part of their dinner. You could say many positive things about the French tradition of eating shoulder to shoulder with strangers, but Lex couldn't think of any this evening. The table to the right was empty, and he hoped it would remain so.

The waiter pushed the table back in place, and Jules lowered himself onto the seat opposite. He removed his heavy framed specs, fogged up the thick lenses with his breath, and cleaned them with the white napkin. He could be mistaken for Serge Gainsbourg with his thick, dark, curly hair, hooked nose, and big ears, although it was doubtful anyone would catch the French singer wearing a tie, silk or otherwise.

"Edith Piaf used to dine at this table with her lover, Marcel Cerdan, the champion boxer," Jules said.

"I feel honoured."

"I had the pleasure of seeing her here a few times back in the day, and it's strange to think she was no older than I am now when she died."

"Early forties?" Lex suggested.

"That's kind of you, but I'll be forty-eight this year."

The waiter interrupted with the wine card and menus and asked if they wanted an aperitif. Jules flipped the wine card open.

"It's your birthday, and you're my guest tonight. Relax and let me be in charge. Can you live with that?"

"I'm sure I can get used to it."

"Let's have a bottle of Chateau Siran 1953 Margaux and a big bottle of Perrier."

"Very well, Monsieur Lévy."

"And you can take the menus, Étienne. We'll have the *escargots*, followed by the *chateaubriand*." The waiter bowed respectfully and retreated with the wine card and the menus.

"How is your apartment on Rue Norvins?" Jules asked. He took a particular interest in Lex's accommodation, as his company Agence Immo Lévy had generously set him up in the beautiful two-bedroom apartment a stone's throw from the Basilique du Sacré-Coeur.

"I love it—compared to my old apartment in Amsterdam, it's like a palace."

The waiter returned with the wine and the sparkling water. Skilfully, he uncorked the bottle and presented the cork to Jules, who studied it meticulously before putting it to his nostrils. He nodded, and the waiter poured enough of the ruby liquid into his glass to cover the bottom. Jules lifted it, swirled it, stuck his nose into the large glass and breathed deeply. He sipped, swished the wine around in his mouth, swallowed, and with a blissful expression, he murmured, "Phenomenal."

The food deserved the same adjective, and the conversation flowed as smoothly as the excellent wine. Uncle Jules had a way of looking at his companions that made them want to spill all their little secrets. Maybe it was the short-sighted squint below his bushy eyebrows, magnified by the thick lenses. Perhaps it was his calm, authoritative, all-embracing manner. Before Lex had chewed the last piece of his tender steak, he'd told Jules all about his reasons for relocating from Amsterdam, how he'd met Linda, her imminent release from prison, and her coming to Paris to live with him. Before her imprisonment the previous August, they'd only spent a few days and nights in each other's company, and the prospect of a life together filled Lex with apprehension. Her natural beauty had overwhelmed him and made him irrationally intoxicated with her. He'd visited her about ten times in the prison south of Amsterdam before moving to Paris, and having not seen her for a few months, he was longing for her arrival at the end of the week.

"By the sound of it, you'll soon need more space," Jules said with a grin.

"I doubt we can afford it, even with another generous settlement from you," Lex replied.

"Nonsense! Your business will be up and running in no time."

"I still haven't received my licence."

"Don't let the French bureaucracy stop you. I never do."

"It doesn't make it easy to attract customers."

"I might need your help on a matter."

"What?" Lex said eagerly.

"It's quite trivial, but I will pay for your services if you agree to take it on."

"I wouldn't charge my favourite uncle."

"The one and only, you may add."

"Especially that one."

"I insist on paying you."

"Some francs going into my meagre coffers would be nice, but more importantly, it would be nice to do something purposively."

"That's what I thought. I feel we're about to be interrupted, so I'll enlighten you over coffee and cognac."

As soon as he said it, the lights dimmed, and Lex knew what was in store. The waiter approached with a dessert decorated with a couple of sparklers, and a chorus of *Joyeux Anniversaire* rang out all around them. Maddeningly self-conscious, the colour mounting in his face, he felt like hiding under the table. Instead, he managed a polite smile, while nodding appreciatively to the outpouring of congratulations from around the restaurant.

The waiter placed a sparkling *Dame Blanche* in front of Lex. Fortunately, the sparklers burned out quickly, and the lights came back on.

"Let's have half a bottle of Chateau d'Yquem 1963, Étienne," Jules said when his dessert arrived.

"Certainly, Monsieur Lévy."

"You may think a Sauternes is an unusual choice with ice cream, but it's a match made in heaven," Jules said to Lex, who was sure his uncle didn't expect him to have any meaningful opinion on the subject of Sauternes and that he said it merely for his own benefit.

The waiter brought the bottle, and after going through the wine presentation ritual for the third time, Jules lifted his glass, and they clinked. Silence descended upon them for the first time that evening as they enjoyed their desserts and sweet wine. Lex promised himself to make Sauternes part of his ice cream experience on more occasions in the future.

"Time for your present," Jules said. He produced a small, square package from a pocket in his jacket and pushed it across the table. With a "you shouldn't have", Lex tore off the paper and opened the box to reveal a pair of zebra striped, silver cufflinks.

"They're beautiful, Uncle Jules."

"And they come with a nice story." Jules leaned forward to catch Lex's eye. "My sister gave the cufflinks to me when I turned thirty. I'm sure your mother would appreciate me passing them on to you now that you're thirty."

Lex's eyes teared up at the thought of how his late mother would have enjoyed this evening with her son and brother. Both Lex's parents would have. Shortly before she died, she told him how close she was to her younger brother, a bond strengthened by them being the only two Lévy family members to have survived the holocaust.

"My tailor in Rue Marbeuf expects a visit from you one of these days. I've instructed him to measure you for a couple of shirts."

"It's too much, Uncle," Lex protested.

"Nonsense. What good are cufflinks without formal shirts? And it's a small token of my gratitude to have my favourite nephew on my doorstep in Paris."

"The one and only, you may add," Lex said, repeating his words from earlier in the evening.

"Especially that one," Jules laughed, repeating Lex's.

"You wanted to tell me something about a small matter."

"Let's order some coffee and cognac first."

"Sounds good," Lex said as he offered his uncle a cigarette.

"Let's keep the cigarettes for later. I think the occasion calls for a cigar." Jules lifted a black leather cigar holder from his inside pocket, removed the lid, and offered Lex the choice of two cigars. He pulled one out, and fortunately, it didn't take a cigar aficionado to read the name Romeo y Julieta Churchills on the band.

With a lit cigar in one hand and a vintage cognac in the other, Lex was eager to hear what Jules wanted him to investigate. Jules must have sensed it as he said, "The matter you could look into is, as I mentioned, rather trivial, but it does require you to be discreet."

"Of course."

He paused as he sipped his cognac and drew some smoke from his cigar. Lex waited him out.

"I have a client that I suspect of subletting one of my apartments. It's, obviously, illegal, but my real fear is that it's being used for some criminal activity."

"Like what?"

"The neighbours are complaining that there's constant coming and going. It could be a private sex club or casino."

"What does the client say?"

"That he has a large family and many friends."

"As the agency that rents him the apartment, can't you gain access to see if there's anything illegal going on?"

"According to French law, I have no such right. So unless he invites me in, my hands are tied. "

"Is it a big apartment?"

"About three hundred square metres."

"Where is it?"

"On Avenue Foch near the Arc de Triomphe "

"Fancy part of town."

"As well as respectable. But if the tenant uses the place for criminal activities, it doesn't matter where it is, if it's rented through my agency."

"What do you want me to do?"

"I could, if I had nothing better to do, perch myself outside the property, but it will be more efficient to hire you as a private detective. I leave it to your professional discretion to establish if there is indeed any funny business going on."

"Leave it with me. What's my deadline?"

"It's not urgent. If you come to lunch with your fiancée at Place des Vosges on Sunday, you can update me. The kids and I would love to see you both." Jules signalled to the waiter, and while they waited for the bill, he asked, "How do you get around Paris?"

"I walk and use public transport," Lex replied.

"It might be handy for you to have some wheels. Gigi probably has to stay in Tel Aviv for a while, and —"

"How is her mother?" Lex interrupted.

"I'm afraid she's not long for this world."

"Sorry to hear it."

"I gave my wife a new car when she turned forty in March, and it's not much good parked in the street. If I leave the key at the office, you're welcome to pick it up opposite our apartment sometime next week."

"That's kind of you. Much appreciated."

"My pleasure. Or Gigi's, I should say."

"I need to know the brand and the colour."

"Didn't I say? It's a three-door red Renault 5TS Sedan with a canvas sunroof. You can't miss it."

"Nice small car for city traffic."

"Especially if you're unaccustomed to driving in Paris. I don't intend to make you nervous, but Gigi will crucify you if you return it with any damage," Jules said with a snigger, "and one more thing—smoking in the car is a non-starter. Not even with the sunroof open."

"Aye, aye, sir," Lex said and lit a cigarette.

23

LEX PARKED in front of the Gare du Nord, purchased a parking meter ticket and tossed it on top of the dashboard. He looked at his watch—another thirty minutes to Linda's scheduled arrival. The prospect of seeing her again woke him at dawn, and he'd counted the minutes since. Lex hadn't seen her for a few months, with no intimate contact for more than ten. As much as he longed to hear her deep and resonant voice and to caress her beautiful body, he'd awaited the day of her arrival with equal measures of excitement and dread. He felt like a schoolboy on a first date.

Lex entered the station and checked the platform number on the giant display—the *Étoile du Nord* arrived at platform four at 12.05, which gave him another twenty-five minutes to kill. He bought a newspaper and headed for the counter at a *tabac* with a view of the platform. He ordered coffee and considered asking for a shot of Calvados to calm his nerves, but thought better of it. Linda could most likely do without the smell and taste of alcohol. About to light a cigarette, he thought better of that too, as she could probably also do without the smell and taste of tobacco.

He did his best to read the paper, while regularly lifting his head to gaze towards the platform and checking the time on the white clock above the main exit. He turned to the sports section; Paris Saint-Germain had drawn 2-2 at Marseille in the first leg of the quarter-finals in the Coupe de France the previous evening. According to the match report, Marseille had managed to squander a two-goal lead in the last thirty minutes, allowing the local club favourites to reach the semi-final in the return leg the following Tuesday. He made a mental note to catch the game in a café somewhere and hoped to persuade Linda to join him. His mind drifted back to the previous July when they'd watched the World Cup final between Holland and West Germany at the Hilton Hotel in Amsterdam. It was the last afternoon they'd spent together before she'd turned herself over to the police. He'd appreciated having Linda hold his hand during the tense affair and comfort him when the brilliant team in orange had lost. After all, he was half Dutch, and the loss to West Germany had been a personal and national trauma.

Lex looked up from the paper and saw the *Étoile du Nord's* massive grey locomotive blocking the view of the platform. He folded the paper and navigated his way through the crowd. In the great confusion of people, Lex didn't spot her at first, but then noticed her in the distance. She stood out in her tight black outfit, and he recognised the familiar red and white plaid handbag that hung from her shoulder. Linda was struggling with two big suitcases, and he rushed towards her. She looked up when he was about ten metres from her, and seeing him, she froze. Her long, lean legs were slightly apart, and her hands clasped in front of her. For a moment, they stared at each other, and like that June Sunday morning when her persistent ringing of his doorbell had dragged him from his couch, her beauty stunned him—she still looked like a clone of Raquel Welch and Jacqueline Bisset, with a dose of Jane Seymour thrown in for good measure. The smile on her face outshone the sun in the sky—and the stars at night.

"So what," she said, "ain't you going to embrace your fiancée?"

Lex opened his arms, and she threw herself into them with a force that knocked the pork pie hat off his head. Lex squeezed her tight as he whispered: "Welcome to Paris, baby." Their lips met, and he felt her tongue on his. Lex heard a wolf whistle, and somebody poked his shoulder. Annoyed, he let go of Linda's mouth, turned his head and saw a fresh-faced youngster handing him his hat.

"You look well," Linda said, holding him at arm's length, "and the traces of red lipstick suit you, sir," she laughed happily. With her thumb, she removed the smear from his lips.

"That may be," he replied, "but you look gorgeous." Her long hair seemed darker than he remembered—and longer.

"Nothing like a few months in the pokey to get the best out of you. I can recommend it," Linda said with a gloomy expression.

"Thanks, but no thanks. Now that you're here, I'd prefer to stay out of the nick." Lex seized her hand and squeezed it. "Let's head for home. I can't wait to show you our apartment." Her emerald eyes became moist. "What's the matter?" he asked.

"Thanks for saying 'our' apartment. I'm glad you feel that way. I feared our separation might have changed your mind and that you might have run off with some chic Frenchwoman."

He held her face in his hands and kissed her lightly on the nose. "You can't imagine how happy I am that you're here, and I won't find any Frenchwoman as chic as you." Lex picked up the suitcases and guided her towards the exit.

"Have you won the lottery?" she said when he stopped at the red Renault parked by the curb.

"The car belongs to my aunt, and I've borrowed it while she's visiting her sick mother in Tel Aviv."

"Not bad to have a supportive uncle and aunt in Paris."

"You'll meet him and his kids tomorrow. I hope you don't mind that I've accepted an invitation for Sunday lunch?"

"Not at all, as long as it's nobody but us today. We have a bit of catching up to do," she said with a sultry expression.

Lex unlocked the car, squeezed one suitcase into the boot, and the other onto the back seat. He opened the sunroof to get the most out of the mild and bright spring day.

As expected on a Saturday lunchtime, the traffic on the Boulevard de Magenta was moderate. Linda gazed around in delight as they passed the trees along the boulevard, their vivid green leaves glowing in the sunshine, the crowded café terraces, the industrious Parisians and the relaxed tourists.

"It's your first time in Paris, isn't it?" Somehow they'd never talked about it.

"And I love it already. I can understand the enthusiasm in your letters."

"Oh, so you did receive them."

"I'm sorry I didn't reply to any of them. I wanted to, but I'm useless at putting words on paper, and I'm sure you can appreciate there wasn't much to tell. Even growing up in Diemen held more excitement."

"I understand."

"I did send you a birthday card."

"Still to arrive."

"And I called you on Monday."

"I was out most of the day."

"I didn't bring you a present, but I know what I want to give you."

"Yer, and…?"

"You'll know soon enough, and you must come with me to buy it."

"I'm intrigued. When can we go?" They both laughed.

"Are you hungry?"

"I ate a sandwich on the train."

"I've cheese, bread and wine at home."

"Sounds like heaven."

Lex turned left at Rue Doudeauville, and the heavily loaded car reacted to the street's incline. He managed to shift the manual transmission into a lower gear with some difficulty. "Sorry about that; I'm a little out of practice." She ignored it by asking him for a cigarette. "I've promised my uncle we won't smoke in the car."

"I can wait."

"We'll be home in five minutes."

LEX DREW the curtains, and the bright afternoon light streamed into the bedroom. He opened the window and felt a mild breeze against his naked body. He jumped back into bed, where Linda lay on her side with one hand under her head. He kissed one of her erect nipples.

"That's the best fuck I've had in almost a year," she said

"Me too. The best and the first."

They giggled like naughty teenagers as he lifted two cigarettes from a packet on the bedside table, lit them, and handed her one. He placed the ashtray between them, and they smoked for a while in silence.

"How's your business going?"

"To be honest, I haven't got much going."

"Now that we're in this together, I want you to know that you don't have to worry as I do have some savings."

It surprised Lex to hear her say she had money, as he believed she was skint.

"That's sweet of you, but I'm alright for the moment. I did a bit of work for my uncle."

"Something you can talk about?"

"I could, but I rather wait until I've presented the results of my investigation to Jules tomorrow. Right now, I'd prefer to pay my beautiful fiancée some attention." Lex removed the ashtray and pulled Linda back down to the bed.

THEY ATE dinner at a small local restaurant. Linda surprised him when she, in decent French, asked the waitress for the ladies' restroom.

"I'm impressed," Lex said when she returned to the table. You told me you didn't speak any French?"

"That's some time ago, dummy," she laughed, "but I'm glad you're impressed. For the past few months, I've been self-studying the lingo. God knows I had the time."

Lex reached across the table and took her hand. After his pregnant fiancée was killed in a car accident with him behind the wheel a few years back, sitting across from this beautiful woman reminded him that God had given him a second chance for a happy relationship. *Don't fuck this one up*, Lex told himself.

He thought of his life in Amsterdam over the past few years, when he'd lived in a small, rundown apartment on the Rembrandtplein and worked as a private detective after quitting the police force. It was a period in his life when he had used any excuse to feed the demons—too much booze, self-pity, and too many nights sleeping fully dressed on the couch. It had culminated in his irrational intoxication with the girl across the table landing him in some nasty business and wreaking havoc on his mental state and physical well-being.

With the move to Paris and turning thirty, it was time to limit hungover Sunday mornings, self-pity, and behaving like an irresponsible bachelor.

He felt Linda's warm hand on his arm.

"Ground Control to Major Tom."

"Sorry, I got lost on a trip down memory lane."

"Would you care to enlighten me?"

"Maybe later. Would you mind if we strolled past the Sacré-Cœur?" At that moment, Lex could think of no better way to show his gratitude than to light a few candles.

"Lead the way."

24

LEX STUCK to the grand boulevards and avenues: Bagtignolles, Courcelles, Wagram, Champs-Élysées, and the Place de la Concorde. With Linda accustomed to the low gabled houses, narrow streets and canals of Amsterdam, he wanted Paris' grandeur to impress her. Like the day before, she looked around delightedly at the scenery.

"I'm overwhelmed, and I can't believe how busy it is on a Sunday," she said.

"You'd better get used to it—Paris never sleeps," Lex said, thinking it wasn't entirely true, as there were times and places at night where the emptiness and the silence were equally overwhelming.

Lex followed the road into the north side of Places des Vosges, where he to his surprise was offered the choice of several available parking spaces along the park's tall iron fence. His uncle lived opposite, in a majestic building of red bricks over vaulted arcades.

They exited the car, Lex with a bottle of wine in one hand and a Manila envelope in the other. Linda carried a container of Hollandse Drops brought from Amsterdam, which would come in in handy for the youngsters.

"Please remind me—what are the names of your cousins?"

"Jean-Luc and Ami. He's eighteen, and she's thirteen." They crossed the street, and Linda rotated 360 degrees.

"Amazing, how all the facades are built to the same design," she exclaimed. "I wonder what the style is called?"

"I'm sure my uncle will happily tell you all about it." They entered the arcade and headed for number 28. Lex pressed the buzzer, and the concierge let them in.

"*Monsieur-dame*," he said from behind a small counter. He looked like a student with a weekend job.

"Jules Lévy on the third floor is expecting us." He nodded, and his eyes gobbled up Linda as they headed for the broad marble staircase. Lex couldn't blame him—she looked stunning in her tight, black bell-bottoms, black turtleneck, and ankle boots.

As they reached the first floor, a door was opened higher up.

The concierge must have announced their arrival.

"Hold the drops for a second," Linda said, "I need to adjust your tie."

They climbed to the third floor—the right-hand door of the tall, brown, carved, wooden double doors was ajar. There was no nameplate to interfere with the beautiful Rococo design. Lex knocked.

"*Entrée*," Jules shouted from somewhere inside, and Lex pushed the door open for Linda to enter. He followed right behind her, and Jules walked towards them across a hallway big enough to contain their whole living room at Montmartre. Before Lex could introduce Linda, Jules said, "I'm delighted, Mademoiselle." He held her shoulders and stretched to kiss her cheeks.

"Thank you for inviting me."

"Nonsense," Jules said in perfect English. "I should thank you for making time on only your second day in Paris. I'm sure you two love birds have plenty to catch up on," he said, offering a titter.

"Nice to see you, Uncle," Lex said as he admired Jules's crisp white shirt and light blue silk tie. They shook hands.

"How's the car?"

"Still in one piece. It drives like a dream and carried us straight to your door."

"Did you order the shirts?"

"I plan to do it tomorrow or Tuesday."

Lex handed him the bottle of wine, and he looked at the label.

"Chablis Premier Cru 1969. I'm impressed."

"Don't look at me," Lex laughed. "The guy at Nicolas was most helpful."

"We have some traditional Dutch liquorice for Jean-Luc and Ami," Linda said.

"They'll love that."

"Are the kids here?" Lex asked.

"They'll join us shortly."

Jules led them into the living room. As on Lex's last visit, the grand room's modern and chic contemporary style, with the exquisite white, Rococo stucco ceilings dazzled him. Lex passed one of three low white couches placed in a horseshoe as he headed for one of the tall French windows. He looked down into the square and the park. A group of middle-aged men were playing *pétanque*, and nearly all of the benches seemed occupied in the mild spring weather. He turned to have a better look at the decor.

"It's a fantastic room, Uncle."

"Gigi redecorated the room a couple of years ago to make it more contemporary. It's more her style than mine, but I've grown used to it."

"How big is it, if you don't mind me asking?" Linda said.

"About 80 square metres."

"I meant the entire apartment."

"Eight rooms spread over 290 square metres."

"Have you lived here for many years?"

"It's a long story."

"I'd love to hear it," Linda said with enthusiasm.

"First, we need a drink. What can I offer you?"

"Some dry white wine would be nice."

"As it happens, I have one that will knock you off your feet, so you'd better take a seat," Jules said. "And what can I get you, Lex? A whisky?"

"You can knock me off my feet too," Lex said, chuckling.

"Wine it is. You make yourselves at home, and I'll be right back."

They sat on the sofa facing the tall windows.

"He seems to be a nice man," Linda said.

"He's my favourite uncle, for sure."

"How many do you have?"

"One."

"You're a strange guy, Lex," she said, "and I think I'm in love with you." She put a hand on his knee, and they kissed. They heard someone enter behind them, and Lex let go of Linda's full lips. He looked over his shoulder to see Ami entering the room. A white polo dress with a red belt covered her lean young body. They both stood as she walked towards them. Lex didn't see much of Jules in her, but plenty of Gigi.

"*Bonjour*, I'm Ami." She ran one hand through her dark, shoulder-length perm and offered the other to Linda.

"I'm Linda; nice to meet you, Ami. I'm sorry, but my French is poor."

"I speak a little English," Ami said. "*Bonjour*, Lex." He sensed she was unsure how to greet a cousin she hadn't often seen. He solved her dilemma by hugging her. She excused herself to fetch her brother, and Lex and Linda returned to their seats on the sofa. Linda was about to speak when Jules returned with a tray. He lowered it onto the glass surface, lifted the wine bottle and filled three glasses. He handed them one each.

"*Santé, mes amis.*" They clinked the crystal and drank.

"Delicious," Linda said. "What is it?"

"It's a Chateau de Chasseloir Muscadet Sevre et Maine Sur Lie from 1961. A fantastic year, in my humble opinion," Jules said, pleased that she'd asked.

"You were telling us about the apartment," Linda said.

"My wife's parents bought the apartment in 1933. During the war, a high ranking Nazi lived here while they lived in exile with relatives in Switzerland. After the war, they returned, and when I married Gigi in 1953, we moved in with them. After a couple of years, my company was making a decent profit, and we decided to buy our own place. But when my parents-in-law decided to relocate to Israel, we took over this apartment instead."

"I'm sorry to hear your mother-in-law is sick," Linda said.

"Thanks. It's especially tough on Gigi, as her father died only a couple of years ago."

Lex wanted to say something appropriate, but a chubby little woman with a Mediterranean complexion appeared at the door before he had the chance. She dried her hands on a striped apron and announced that lunch was ready.

"*Obrigado*, Mariana. And please ask the kids to join us." Jules walked to a double door and pushed it open. They followed him into the dining room. Coming from the living room with its modern decor, it was like going back in time. The mahogany table in the centre of the room set for five might have accommodated another ten. A large chrome-plated chandelier with white coloured glass hovered over the table. The chairs, without armrests, were upholstered in a burgundy colour that matched the textile wallpaper and the draperies. Lex was no expert on styles, but this one had Art Deco written all over it.

"That's what I call a dining room," Lex exclaimed spontaneously as Ami and Jean-Luc walked into the room. The son was taller than his dad, but had inherited his thick, dark, curly hair, hooked nose, and big ears. Linda's beauty stopped him in his tracks as he walked towards them. He swiftly regained his composure as he did *la bise*, then turned to Lex, extending his hand. He grabbed it, pulled Jean-Luc close and hugged him.

"How are you, young man?"

"Can't complain, Alexander."

"Lex and Linda, you sit here," Jules said, pointing to the chairs that faced the windows. Ami took a seat opposite Lex and Jean-Luc opposite Linda.

Jules fetched a bottle of red wine from a mahogany buffet and filled their glasses.

"Can I have red wine, dad?" Jean-Luc asked.

"Of course, son." Jules half-filled his glass, returned the bottle and sat at the end of the table.

The lunch was lovely. Mariana served a classic quiche Lorraine, a mixed salad with walnuts and lemon Dijon vinaigrette, followed by a platter of French cheeses, and to make it complete, a *tarte au citron*. Jules filled their glasses with great wine, and Linda reminded Lex he had to drive later. In English, French and Dutch, the conversation flowed as freely as the wine, and both Ami and Jean-Luc contributed, with the confidence of being allowed to speak their minds. Lex wished he'd possessed the same confidence level when in his teens. *We've come a long way. Not least from the student unrest of May '68, which continued to influence French society, and the new generation that had emerged from the movement,* he thought. Lex doubted that it had succeeded as a political revolution, but it did as a social one.

After the dessert, Jean-Luc excused himself to take his girlfriend to the movies.

"What movie?" Lex asked.

"*The Towering Inferno* with Paul Newman and Steve McQueen."

"I read about that. It's about a fire in a skyscraper threatening to destroy the tower and everyone in it," Lex said.

"That sounds horrific, and I doubt it's any good," Jules said.

"It won three Oscars at the Academy Awards last month," Linda said.

"How well informed you all are," Jules said. "I rest my case. Have fun, son."

They were mulling over coffee and cigarettes when Jules said, "Have you ever done any modelling, Linda?" "Do tell me if you feel it's none of my business," he added as she hesitated.

"It did cross my mind a few years ago," she answered, "but I've never acted upon it."

"I happen to know one of the art directors at *Vogue*. I think you have potential, and it would make me happy to introduce you."

"We've yet to talk about our future together in Paris, but I'll keep it in mind," she said, as the tip of her finger caressed the almost invisible scar under her chin.

Her answers and hesitation surprised Lex, as he recalled her telling him about how a failed career in modelling had led her to work as a call girl and how she'd encouraged him to relocate to Paris for her to pursue her dream of becoming a model. To Lex, it was her main objective in life and why, in all honesty, she'd come to live with him in the city of light.

"I understand. I want to help in any way to make your new life in Paris as successful as possible."

"You're already doing that, Uncle," Lex said, "and I doubt I can return all the favours."

"You can do me the favour of telling me what you've discovered about my client."

"I have a few photos I'd like to show you."

"Let's go to my office. I'm sure Linda can entertain herself for half an hour."

"Take your time. I'll have a chat with Ami. I'm sure we have plenty to talk about," Linda said.

"Let's have drinks afterwards," Jules said and guided Lex to his office. Like the other rooms in the large apartment, the decor was meant to impress. With its deep colours and exuberant details, the Baroque style was striking, and the flamboyance of the room would have made President Valéry Giscard d'Estaing feel right at home. Were it not for the red IBM Selectric typewriter on the antique office desk, they could have returned to the 17th century. A circular conference table of solid wood occupied the centre of the room. Jules pulled out a couple of chairs, and they sat down.

"Okay, let me hear what you've discovered."

"I staked out the address on Friday from around six until midnight. As far as I could judge, there was the normal activity of people coming home from work and shopping for the first couple of hours. Then nothing much happened until ten. Then around fifteen people, mostly middle-aged men in suits, arrived over the next hour. I can't be sure they visited the apartment you rent out, but it fits with the complaints you've had from the neighbours. I took a few photos of the people coming and going. You might recognise some of them." Lex took a small stack of black and white photos from the envelope and placed them in front of his uncle. Jules flipped through them and stopped at one showing a middle-aged, well-groomed man in an expensive suit.

"A familiar face," Jules said.

"Who is he?"

"I'm surprised you don't know him. It's Killian Lamarre—a middle-aged entrepreneur and philanthropist whose suntanned and well-groomed face smiles at you from many a Parisian newspaper kiosk."

"He arrived just after ten and left shortly before midnight," Lex said.

"He could be visiting friends in the building. Anyhow, I'll get the proprietor involved."

"You're not the owner?"

"My agency rents it out for someone, and therefore we're responsible if one of our clients sublets the apartment. Regardless of what's going on in the apartment, subletting is a criminal offence."

"Anything else I can do?"

"I'll take it from here and let you know how it pans out. You've done well, and I'm sure I can use your services another time." Jules got up and took a small envelope from the work desk and handed it to Lex.

"I hope two thousand francs will cover your time and expenses?"

"Much too generous, Uncle."

"Nonsense. Now let's have drinks and snacks."

They entered the living room and saw Linda and Ami talking on the couch. Ami jumped up and walked enthusiastically towards her father. She grabbed both of his hands.

"Dad, will it be alright for Linda to take me shopping after school on Tuesday? She wants to buy me a new dress for the summer."

"That's awfully kind of her, and I don't see any reason you shouldn't go," Jules said tenderly. "As long as you do your homework after supper." He said it casually, and Lex sensed it was more for the benefit of him and Linda. Jules was immensely proud of his daughter and most likely knew she needed no reminding. Ami returned to her room, and Lex sat beside Linda and squeezed her hand gently.

"What can I get you?" Jules said and headed for the drinks cabinet.

25

THE FOLLOWING week Lex and Linda prioritised each other, and as they only spent about half the time in bed, Lex had plenty of opportunity to introduce Linda to Paris. They strolled around town hand in hand and dined out in the evening like newlyweds. Lex was the happiest he'd been for a long time, and Linda seemed in equally high spirits.

Monday, Linda escorted Lex to a hat shop to buy the promised birthday present—a beautiful Panama straw hat.

"Suits you, sir," she said lovingly. "No offence, Lex, but a bit of competition for that pork pie hat will do no harm." Afterwards, they visited his uncle's tailor to measure Lex for the two shirts promised on his birthday. Linda also persuaded him to let the tailor measure him for a single-breasted jacket. He let her choose a superfine Merino wool fabric with a classic pinstripe in light blue. "That will go nicely with your new hat," she said, "and it will be a joy to see you in something else other than your black leather jacket."

Her enthusiasm rubbed off on him, and he warmed to the idea of becoming trendier and more like a Parisian gentleman.

Tuesday afternoon, Linda picked up Ami from school to take her shopping for the promised summer dress.

In the evening, Lex and Linda found a café on Place de Clichy for a light supper, and afterwards watched Paris Saint-Germain's return leg in the Coupe de France's quarter-final. Having drawn at Marseille in the first game, Lex favoured his new local team to reach the semi-final.

"It brings mixed emotions to watch football with you, Lex," Linda said.

"Indeed, the Dutch should have beaten West Germany," he said, knowing she wasn't referring to the result of the FIFA World Cup final they'd watched together the previous summer.

"I can't believe it's less than a year ago. It seems more like a lifetime," Linda said and took his hand. "Now I'm grateful that you persuaded me to turn myself over to the police."

"Thank God we'll have none of that after tonight's game."

Not to spoil the good mood, Paris Saint-Germain scored twice to reach the semi-final. As they walked back after the game, arm in arm, Linda told Lex about her afternoon with Ami.

"We had a great time, and I bought her a beautiful dress and a pair of shoes. You should have seen the joy on her face. When you consider she comes from a wealthy family, it was heartening to see how happy a few new possessions made her.

"She is indeed a lovely girl. No wonder Jules is so proud of her," Lex remarked. He observed a shadow passing over Linda's face. "What happened? You look like someone walked over your grave."

"I hope not. Ami told me a secret about her best friend, and although I promised not to tell anyone, it's nagging at me."

"I promise not to tell anyone."

"Ami asked me if I was a Catholic and if I was confirmed. I told her I grew up as a Protestant, and although confirmed, that I was not a practising Christian. As I'd already guessed, she told me that the family are not practising Jews, but she did regret missing out on her *bat mitzvah*. Then suddenly, she said to me that her best friend claimed she was being abused at her sacrament preparation classes. Coming totally out of the blue, it took me aback, so I asked her to explain. Ami said that her friend Angeline told her that the priest—these are the words she used—asked her 'to be nice to him' and that God would reward her for it."

"I don't like the sound of that," Lex exclaimed.

"Nor do I. I asked if her friend had told her the name of the priest."

"And?"

"He's called Father Blanchet."

"And did she mention the church?"

"It's the Sacré-Cœur."

"Of all the Catholic churches in Paris."

"I wish we could do something to help the poor girl."

"I don't see what we can do, but let me keep it in mind."

LINDA AND LEX saw a few posters in the metro advertising the spring-summer collection at Galerie Lafayette. After Wednesday breakfast, they walked to the department store in the 9th arrondissement. Spending time in big department stores usually made Lex brake out in a rash, but he forgot time and place watching Linda do the catwalk just for him. *She's a natural,* Lex thought, and promised himself to be supportive should she decide to let Jules introduce her to his contact in haute couture.

Afterwards they jumped on the metro to eat lunch at Café de Flore—*rillettes au pain Poilâne*, and a bottle of Beaujolais Saint-Amour. It was a memorable few hours in the famous establishment on Boulevard Saint-Germain, even without Jean-Paul Sartre and Simone de Beauvoir at their usual table.

In the afternoon, they strolled in the nearby Luxembourg Gardens to watch the kids and a few adults pushing little sailboats round the Grand Bassin duck pond.

"I can see you would like to rent a boat, Captain," Linda laughed.

"Is it that obvious?"

"I don't mind if you do."

"Let's come back another day. I'm tired and think we should head home.

"I keep forgetting you're way past thirty," Linda said as she pulled his chain.

Lex and Linda returned to Montmartre on the metro, and as they walked up the hill, Linda realised that she too was exhausted.

"Can I suggest a nap?" she said.

"I'm all for it," Lex replied.

A SENSUAL dream woke Lex after an hour and a half, and his erection didn't go unnoticed.

"Hello there. What are we to do with that?" Linda asked, now wide awake beside him.

"You tell me." She turned her back to him, pulled down her knickers, and directed him inside. A bit of late afternoon sex was a nice bonus after a beautiful day.

Afterwards, Linda soaked in the bathtub for half an hour while Lex did a workout, pushing the vacuum cleaner around the apartment.

"I need your help, Lex," Linda shouted over the noise from the motor. He switched it off.

"Which of my new dresses shall I wear?"

"Take the blue one with the polka dots," Lex suggested. Linda slipped it on and added a light blue cardigan over it. She studied herself in the mirror in the hallway.

"Do I look all right?" she asked.

"You look wonderful tonight."

Lex watched her put on her make-up and brush her long black hair.

"Let's have dinner at Le Consulat," Lex suggested. "It's about time I introduced you to *le patron*, Alain."

"Lead the way."

THE NEXT day, Thursday, Lex drove Linda for an intake session at the Berlitz language school near the Opéra. She told him she could make her own way, but he insisted.

"I have a fine ear for languages, and I'll speak perfect French in no time," she told him in the car.

"It's great to see you so confident."

"That's because you believe in me and treat me with respect."

"I think it's called love."

"I know," she said with a smile. She leaned over to kiss him, then got out of the car and slammed the door shut.

"See you at four," he shouted, but she didn't hear. Lex watched her black dress blowing in the wind as she crossed the street.

He put the little red car into gear and headed for Les Halles. He'd promised himself to visit the building site of a new multidisciplinary cultural centre with a planned opening in a couple of years. The former French President, Georges Pompidou, had initiated the project, but would not see its completion, as he had died in office the previous year. Seeing the big frame with pipes located on the outside and escalators in glass tubes to transport people towards the sky, Lex understood why it was the talk of the town. With its futuristic architecture, he also understood why some critics claimed that Paris was creating a monster. Among the grand old buildings, Centre Pompidou did seem as out of place as a submarine in a bathtub.

On his way back to the Opéra to pick up Linda, heavy rain was slowing the traffic, and Lex arrived ten minutes late. He expected to see her waiting at the spot where he'd dropped her off, soaked and disgruntled. But she wasn't, and he followed the traffic flow and circled the Palais Garnier once more. Still no Linda, and he pulled up to the curb to wait. A car behind rewarded him with an aggressive hoot. *It serves you right for riding on my bumper*, he thought. A couple of minutes later, someone knocked on the passenger seat window. Lex turned, expecting to see Linda, but instead saw an exasperated gendarme gesturing for him to rejoin the traffic. Lex held up a hand and pulled away at the first opening. He circled the opera house once more, and as he passed the pick-up spot, he checked his watch—twenty-five minutes past the agreed time.

By now, he was teed off, and a bit worried. Perhaps the intake had taken longer than anticipated, or maybe Linda had decided not to wait for him in the rain. Having had enough of driving in circles, he decided to head home.

LEX CALLED his uncle.

"Can you tell me anything about Ami's friend Angeline?"

"Why are you interested in her?"

"If you tell me what you know about the girl and her family, I'll tell you why."

"She's twelve years old, and I think you can safely say she's a pretty girl. She is, as far as I know, an A grade student. She lives in Montmartre, not far from you, with her parents and a younger brother."

"Why is she in Ami's class?"

"Because they used to live in a small apartment not far from Places des Vosges. They relocated to Montmartre two years ago and decided not to move Angeline to another school. I know it made both Angeline and Ami happy, as they're terrific friends."

"Do you know the family?"

"We don't exactly move in the same circles, but her father Albert is a plumber with his own little business, and he sometimes works for me."

"Did you have anything to do with the move?"

"You guessed it."

"What's their surname."

"It's Pernet. Albert and Marie Pernet. They are a good Catholic family and happy to live within earshot of the bells of Sacré-Cœur."

"The reason I'm asking is that—."

"I'm sorry, Lex, my other line is trying to get through, and I have to run. Please give me a call tonight."

"Okay, Uncle." Lex replaced the receiver, lit a cigarette, and studied the notepad in front of him. With nothing to do workwise, he made a spontaneous decision. Lex took a telephone directory from the drawer and flipped through it until he found the number for the Sacré-Cœur secretariat. Lex dialled it and told a woman with a pleasant and welcoming voice that he planned to marry a Catholic woman and needed some guidance as to the process. A friend of his recommended talking to Father Blanchet. The woman informed Lex that he would need counsel on the Rite of Christian Initiation of Adults and granted him an audience with the Father the following day at ten.

AT SEVEN, Linda had not yet returned, and Lex was pacing the floor. All kinds of nightmare scenarios played in his mind. Lex opened the window of his office, leaned out and stared up and down the street. He lit a cigarette and told himself to relax. Linda was a big girl, enjoying her freedom in a city with plenty to keep anyone distracted for a few hours. But he'd passed the point where he could calm himself and paced the floor some more. Although it didn't make much sense to walk the streets, Lex grabbed his leather jacket and pork pie hat, flew down the stairs and nearly knocked Linda over as he pushed the door open. She smiled happily, and her beauty overwhelmed him, as it always did when they had been apart for some time.

"Thank God you're home," he exclaimed, unable to keep the torment out of his voice.

"What's the matter?" Linda said. "You're all flustered."

"Forget it."

"Don't tell me you're upset because I toured the town on my own for a few hours?"

"Can we talk about it upstairs?"

"Sure." She followed him up the stairs with her hands full of bags. He deliberately did not offer his assistance, as he wanted to punish her. Lex slammed the door to the apartment shut after her and followed her into the living room.

"My feet are killing me," she said, dumping the bags on the floor and herself onto the couch. Lex remained standing as he said, "I was sick with worry."

"I don't see why?"

"Because it's more than four hours since I was supposed to pick you up."

"You're the one who insisted on driving me. I told you not to bother and that I would find my way home."

"But how can that take four hours?" he demanded.

"You're being unreasonable. I don't have to account for every minute to you. I'm your girlfriend, not your daughter."

"But why did you agree to meet at four?" he said, sounding like an abandoned child.

"Excuse me, I was there at four, but you were not. When the rain came on, I sought shelter in a café. I honestly believed you'd lost track of time. When the rain stopped, I decided to explore the city. It's sweet of you to show me around, but it's tedious; you have to be in control all the time." Her face darkened.

"I imagined all kinds of misfortunes."

"Such as?"

"What do I know? An accident or a mugging."

"That's ridiculous."

Lex knew deep down that he was acting unreasonably, but his pride prevented him from backing down.

"I've bought some nice bread and cheese so that we can eat in for a change," she said and turned to look at him. He avoided her eye. "If you can snap out of it, you can show me you still love me by pouring me a glass of wine," she said with a timid smile. It broke the evil spell, and he walked over to her and pulled her up from the couch.

"I'm sorry, baby. Forgive me for acting like an idiot" He held her tight. She shifted her head, and they kissed.

"Pour me that glass of wine, and I'll forgive you."

26

LEX FELT in high spirits on this glorious spring morning in the city of light. The previous evening's crisis had resolved itself before getting out of hand, so he'd left home with a sense of blissful harmony. And for him to go somewhere with a professional purpose added to the positive feeling. Lex walked along the Sacré-Cœur's white travertine stone wall until he reached the facade's only side door. He stopped to stamp out his cigarette on the cobbles. Lex counted the fifteen steps as he mounted the concrete staircase. He leaned against the low stone wall to look into the trench that separated the basement from the street. Lex pressed the single buzzer, and as no one came to the door, he did it again. Still no response. He looked at his watch—right on time. He pushed it once more, and now with a little more conviction. Having made an appointment, Lex was reluctant to join the hustle and bustle of tourists at the main entrance. He had made it halfway down the stairs when the door creaked open. He stopped and turned, and a middle-aged nun in a grey tunic appeared at the door. Her dark, prying eyes stared out at him from under her black veil.

"I'm Monsieur Filip Clou," he said, using his middle name and the French word for his surname. Not much of an alias, but it would have to do.

"I have an appointment with Father Horace Robert Blanchet." A light dawned on her, and a timid smile played on her lips.

"Come in, Monsieur Clou; the Father awaits you."

"Thank you, Sister."

He took off his Panama hat and walked through the big wooden door, which the nun closed with a bang. Lex followed her down a staircase to the basement and along a dimly lit corridor.

"Please wait here, monsieur." She stopped and knocked softly on a door.

"Enter," a strong male voice said from inside. The nun opened the door and invited him to go in. He did, and she followed right behind.

A spacious and bright English basement opened up in front of him. A wide window with a view of the trench wall let in a surprising amount of daylight. It was a sparsely furnished room with a work desk, a full bookcase, and a couple of armchairs. Beside the desk stood a man in a full collar shirt and a black cassock. He was a mild-looking, round-cheeked man of medium height and well-padded underneath his robe.

The nun didn't announce him, and before Lex could introduce himself, the priest said, "Monsieur Clou, I presume?"

He walked towards Lex with a smile and a light tread and extended his hand. It was small but firm. "I'm Father Blanchet," he said in a cheerful voice. He was at least fifty years old, although something in his demeanour made him appear younger. He had thick dark brown hair with a parting, a retreating hairline, and a nose and ears that looked too small for his round face.

"Take a seat," he said and pointed to one of the armchairs. With a "Thank you, sister Coline," he dismissed the nun. She bowed, backed out of the room, and closed the door. Lex sat down, and as Father Blanchet lowered himself into the opposite armchair, he noticed that his feet belonged to a much taller man. He offered Lex another smile. It came with a certain boyish charm, which gave him an instant attraction, but it didn't reach his blue eyes.

"Can I offer you coffee or tea?"

"No thanks, I recently drank my morning coffee."

"Did you have to travel far?"

"I live a stone's throw away in Rue Norvins," Lex immediately regretted giving the actual name of his street.

"What number?"

"Twenty-one," he lied.

"I ask because I know a family at number thirteen," he said with another smile, and tapped his cleft chin with his finger. Was he implying that he knew Lex had lied about the number? "Why did you specifically ask to see me?" he said.

"A friend of a friend recommended I talk to you."

"Someone I know?"

"A family called Pernet."

"Ah, Albert and Marie Pernet. They're devout people."

"I don't know much about them. I do know they have a daughter."

"And a son. He's ten, and the daughter is twelve. The girl attends my preparation classes for solemn communion," he said, seemingly unaffected.

"That's nice," Lex said in a neutral voice.

"She's an endearing girl and eager to learn," he added.

I bet she is, Lex thought.

"I understand you're here for my advice on the process of the Rite of Christian Initiation of Adults."

"That's right. I'm engaged to a Catholic girl, and we want to marry."

"Bless you, but it's no longer obligatory for a Non-Catholic to convert when it comes to an interdenominational marriage."

"But my fiancée wants to be married in a Catholic church."

"That does raise several issues."

"I thought so, and that's why I'm here."

"Obviously," he said, as if he didn't really believe it to be the case.

"What will I have to do?"

"First, I need to know the condition of your faith. Let's pray before we start."

"I'm not a praying man," Lex said nervously. "What do you want me to do?"

"It's simple—all you have to do is fold your hands. Feel free to close your eyes, but do keep your ears open," Father Blanchet said with a snigger. Lex did all three, as suggested.

"Loving Heavenly Father, we come to you asking for your blessing and guidance in the matters at hand. Show us how to conduct our conversation with joy, enthusiasm, and honesty. Amen."

"Amen," Lex offered, although he doubted honesty applied to the matters at hand.

"Please tell me about yourself," the Father said.

"I was born in 1945 in the Netherlands."

"Your French is excellent."

"I lived in Paris as a child, and I'm half French."

"That explains your surname," he said, assuming it was on Lex's father's side.

"Are you a practising Christian?"

"I'm afraid not."

"Are you baptised?"

"My father was raised as a Catholic, and my mother was Jewish, and although neither of them practised their faith, my father insisted I should be."

"Bless him. It will make the Rite of Initiation much easier."

"I'm glad to hear it."

"Were you married before?"

"No."

"You see how God guides matters in the right direction?"

"If you say so."

"Are your parents still alive?"

"They died in a plane crash five years ago."

"I'm sorry to hear it," he said as he made the sign of the cross.

"They were on the Swissair flight blown up in mid-air by the Palestinian terror group PFLP."

"I remember it—an act of pure evil. Do you have any siblings?"

"I'm an only child."

"What do you do professionally?"

"I'm a financial adviser."

"Who do you work for?"

"I'm a self-employed consultant."

"Please tell me about the woman you want to marry. Have you known each other for long?" Lex told him about the dreamed-up Catholic girl in his life. To make it more believable, he used Linda as the template. "So, you see, we haven't known each other for that long."

"God has blessed you with a beautiful and fine woman," Father Blanchet said. "What's her name? I might know her."

"I doubt it, but it's Linda Vogel."

"German or Dutch?"

"German," Lex lied.

"How old is she?"

"She's twenty-four."

"I'd like to meet her. Does she attend mass at our church?" Lex hadn't thought about that part of his story and paused before saying she didn't.

"Where does she attend mass?"

In search of a satisfying answer, he again hesitated. "My fiancée only moved here from Berlin seven days ago and is yet to find a congregation."

"She is welcome in our church. Why don't you ask her to come and see me?"

"Her French is patchy."

"No problem, my German is excellent."

"Isn't this about me and what I have to do?"

"Indeed. But you're here because you've decided to marry a practising Catholic. I'm sure you can appreciate that it's about both of you?"

"Of course, but I would like to hear about the procedure."

"I will come to that," he said with a smile and without a hint of irritation in his voice. "The good news is that you qualify as a Candidate. Being baptised makes you committed to Jesus Christ."

"I feel so much better," Lex said, somehow more cynically than he intended. Father Blanchet ignored it.

"The bad news is that because you're not a member of any Christian community, the Period of the Catechumenate, as it's called, is longer."

"How long?" Lex said impatiently, in an attempt to stay in character.

"It depends on how you grow in faith, what questions you encounter along the way, and how God leads you on the journey."

"I see. If you're to guide me on this journey, would it be impertinent if I asked you some personal questions?"

"Not at all. Fire away." That boyish smile again.

"Have you been a priest for long?"

"More than twenty years. To please my earthly father, I first trained as a lawyer, but I knew God had envisioned another path for my life from an early age."

"Like a calling?"

"It has to be. Otherwise, I don't think any priest can do his work with total candour."

"And you like to work with the young?"

"I wonder why you say that?"

"Because you give preparation classes for solemn communion."

"To have contact with children is a natural part of all priests' vocation. But you're right; I like young people, and I've worked in Catholic campus ministry for many years. But I felt called to work with even younger age groups. I've dedicated much of my time to some of our youngest believers over the last ten years. It's a true blessing."

"Amen to that," Lex said. "Let the little children come to me and all that."

"That sounded rather cynical, Monsieur Clou."

"I assure you it wasn't my intention. I have the utmost respect for what the church does for the community."

"My many years in ministry have, in all humility, given me a decent understanding of human nature. To judge from our conversation, limited as it may be, I'd say you're a mistrusting person."

"You may be right. Will this harm how God leads me on my journey?"

"Perhaps, but I'm not sure how willing you are to embark on the journey in the first place."

"Why would you say that?"

"Because only total commitment will do. I think you are being less than honest about why you're doing this. Do you know that honesty is the first chapter in the book of wisdom?"

"Is it?"

"It's also the first moral character I look for in a man."

"Why are you telling me this?"

"Because I'm afraid I can't help or advise a person that's not completely honest or committed. The best I can do at the moment is to pray for you. I suggest you contact me again when you've ready." He raised himself onto his big feet, and Lex reluctantly followed. Lex extended a hand, but the Father didn't take it. As he turned to leave, the door opened, and Sister Coline appeared in the opening. Lex wondered if she had been listening at the door.

"May the rest of your day be blessed, Monsieur Clou; the *bonne sœur* will see you out."

27

"WELL DONE, Lex. That went well," he said to himself facetiously, as the nun slammed the door shut. He put his Panama hat on and descended the stairs to the pavement. He tilted his head and scanned the beautiful blue sky above the Sacré-Cœur, which gave him more belief in a God almighty than his conversation with the Catholic priest. Lex didn't know what to make of Father Blanchet, but he knew the charming boyish smile, cold blue eyes, and sanctimonious manner gave him the creeps.

As Lex passed Café le Consulat *le patron* spotted him from the door. Alain was a small, lean man with an impressive black moustache, bushy eyebrows and bald as a coot—almost like a character in a Tintin album.

"You look in desperate need of a coffee and a Calvados," Alain said, stepping out onto the terrace.

"Does it show that badly?"

"Take a seat, my friend," he said and pulled out a chair.

"Make it a double espresso, please."

"And a double Calvados?"

"Better make it a single; I have work to do." Lex lit a cigarette and watched the crowd, primarily tourists, walking to and from Place du Tertre. Within a couple of minutes, Alain returned with the coffee and Calvados.

"Where is your delightful girlfriend?"

Lex looked at his watch. "She's attending her first lesson in French."

"She's not wasting her time."

"She's young and eager, and I encourage her. You don't get far without a decent level of French in Paris."

"*C'est vrai*. I do think the younger generation have improved their English."

"No offence, but it doesn't amount to much," Lex said. Alain shrugged his shoulders.

"Our Ministre d'État wants to introduce more English words into our vocabulary."

"In what way?" Lex asked.

"Replace *la fin de semaine* with the word 'weekend', *d'accord* with 'okay', and *enterprise* with 'business'. That sort of thing."

"*Santé* to that," Lex said and lifted the small glass of Calvados to his nose. The divine aroma of fermented apples filled his nostrils, and taking a sip of the golden liquid did nothing to ruin the experience. After having laced his instant coffee with whisky for a few years, Lex would be the first to admit that it could not compete with espresso with Calvados on the side—especially when enjoyed on the terrace of a café in the heart of Montmartre.

LINDA SHOUTED, "Honey, I'm home."

Lex met her in the doorway to the office. As he'd expected, she looked gorgeous in her new blue dress with white dots. She wore a matching ribbon in her long dark hair, and he felt a strong physical desire for her. He held her in his arms and kissed her while his hands caressed her firm buttocks.

"That's what I call a welcome, sir. Did you miss me?"

"More than you know. I had a strange morning, and I'll tell you later. How did it go?"

"Better than I expected. The French teacher is young, handsome, and extremely talented, as you can imagine," she said with a cheesy grin.

A pang of jealousy gripped him, and it must have shown as she added, "and did I mention she's a nice person?" They both laughed, but Lex knew he would have to address whatever brought on the feelings of mistrust and insecurity—or their relationship was doomed. Linda's youth and beauty bewitched him, and although, by general standards, she was an extrovert, it would be unfair to call her flirtatious.

"Let's go somewhere for lunch," he said to stop the difficult conversation in his head.

"Sounds good. I could eat a horse."

THEY RETURNED to the apartment around nine, tired after a pleasant afternoon and early evening stroll around the city, and decided on an early night in bed with their books. Linda was reading the recently published *Zen and the Art of Motorcycle Maintenance*, and Lex had picked up a second-hand copy of *Maigret in Montmartre* at a bookstall along the Seine. He'd only turned a couple of pages when the phone rang. Lex jumped out of bed, rushed to the office, and lifted the receiver.

"Can you come for coffee at Place des Vosges tomorrow afternoon?" Uncle Jules said.

"Sure."

"Ami's friend Angeline will also be with us, and perhaps you can enlighten me on why you're taking an interest in her and her family."

"I can do it now if you wish?"

"Let's do it face to face tomorrow."

"Okay. What time?"

"Let's make it three."

Lex replaced the receiver and shouted, "My uncle has invited us to Places des Vosges tomorrow afternoon for coffee." But Linda didn't hear; she'd fallen asleep with her face on the book. Slowly, Lex pulled it out from under her chin and switched off her reading light. She moaned and turned over without waking. He intended to turn a few more pages in George Simenon's page-turner, but his eyes refused to stay open. When a yawn backed it up, he switched off the light, snuggled up to Linda, and before anyone could say Jack Robinson, he drifted off.

"WHEN YOUR uncle said coffee, did he mean drinks?" Linda said from the bathtub. Lex watched her firm breasts in the mirror as he shaved. They floated like islands in the soapy water, and her erect nipples didn't escape his attention.

"Why? Does it matter?"

"If we're having drinks, let's take the metro or the bus."

"I'm sure we're just having coffee."

"Perhaps, but with your uncle being the perfect host, he'll insist we stay for drinks."

"I'll take it easy."

"That's what you said last Sunday."

"Did I?"

"You were way over the limit."

"All the same, we made it home alive."

"Let's leave the car today," she pleaded.

"Okay. We'll walk and have lunch somewhere along the way," Lex suggested.

"You're full of good ideas," Linda said. "When you've finished, will you do me a favour?"

"It depends."

"Will you scrub my back?" Her right arm appeared from under the water, and her hand offered him a sponge. Lex finished shaving in no time.

THE SKY was murky and overcast, and the temperature had dropped at least five degrees. Lex was glad he was wearing his leather jacket and old hat instead of his new jacket and Panama. He watched Linda walking in front of him. She looked spectacular in her red sheath dress with black leggings and ankle boots.

"Although you look incredibly hot in that outfit, I hope you're warm enough?"

"If I feel cold, there's an excuse to buy a shawl." He caught up with her and grabbed her hand. They walked along the Boulevard Magenta, and as they passed the Gare du Nord on the left, Linda said, "I can't believe it's a week since I arrived. I'm so glad that, I'm here for more than a holiday. Can you believe I told myself that my presence would tire you within a few days?"

"That's ridiculous, and why should I get tired of you and not you of me?"

"Because it's your patch."

"Not anymore, and I'm eager to live happily ever after with you on our patch," Lex stressed.

"I've considered your uncle's offer to introduce me to his contact at *Vogue*."

"I'm not surprised. I seem to remember you suggested we live in Paris for you to pursue your dream of becoming a model."

"Did I?"

"Never mind. Do I need to ask what you've decided?"

"It might be the break I need, and I'm not getting any younger," she said with a chuckle.

"Thank God, or I'd have to call your parents and ask them to come and take you back to the nursery."

"Might be awkward as they've disowned me." Her face turned gloomy.

"I didn't mean to upset you."

"I can't explain it, but I felt a pang of remorse for the first time in a long time when you mentioned them. Perhaps it's because I'm here with you and feel my life is on the right track. I thought that my parents' bourgeois lifestyle in suburban hell embarrassed me, but maybe it was my own life?"

"Would you like to have contact with them again?"

"Only if I can show them that I've made something of my life."

"Don't you think they've forgiven you for running off, that they miss you and love you regardless of what you've done or achieved?"

"Perhaps, but I'm not yet ready to take that chance."

"If you wait too long, you might regret it. I was your age when my parents died."

"What good is that to me?" she said. "For all I know, they might already be dead."

"Forget it," Lex said. "Let's talk about you."

"I thought we were?"

"You know what I mean. I only want you to be happy."

"I'm sorry if I sounded annoyed."

"If you want to pursue a career as a model, you will have my full support. I'm sure I can get used to seeing my sweetheart on the cover of glossy magazines, in centrefolds, and on the catwalk."

"No pressure," Linda laughed, "but let's not jump ahead of ourselves. Why don't we take one step at a time?"

"You're right," Lex said, "and the next step is to a café for lunch."

FOR SOME reason, Lex expected a shy and immature girl with little confidence. At first sight, nothing appeared further from the truth. Angeline Pernet was, for a twelve-year-old, tall and well developed with an appealing olive complexion. She kept her dark hair at shoulder-length and parted by a light blue headband that matched her dress. Her smile radiated genuine warmth, and her eyes sparkled when she spoke. Her beauty showed itself as pure and non-sexual, and her attraction came from an engaging and confident personality. However hard it was to believe her being a victim of sexual abuse, no doubt the expression of pure and utter perfection she conveyed would be difficult to resist for some sexual predators. She spoke decent English, which gave her an immediate bond with Linda.

After they'd enjoyed a French version of what the English call 'high tea', the girls withdrew to Ami's room, and Jules suggested the three of them take a stroll in the nearby Jardin des Plantes and then, as Linda had predicted, return for drinks.

"But before we go, could you please tell me about your interest in Angeline Pernet?"

"It came about because of something Ami told Linda on Tuesday when they went shopping. You'd better tell it, Linda," Lex said. In a muted voice, Linda repeated what she'd already told Lex.

"Although I'm shocked that anyone could abuse such a sweet girl, I wish I could say I'm surprised," Jules said.

"What do you mean?" Linda asked.

"There are constant rumours of the sexual abuse of minors in the Catholic Church. Unfortunately, nobody seems to be doing much about it."

"Why not?" Linda asked.

"They're scared. The Catholic Church is mighty and powerful in France," Jules said.

"Like everywhere else," Lex added.

"Are your questions about the girl indicating you're looking into the matter, Lex?"

"Yes and no. Out of curiosity, I checked out Father Blanchet."

"In what way?"

"I went to see him yesterday under the pretext that I, as a Protestant, planned to marry a Catholic woman and needed some guidance. Father Blanchet is a well-groomed, middle-aged man—charming with a boyish smile. He did manage to give me the creeps with his cold blue eyes and self-righteous manner. I'd call him a smooth operator, and he told me how much he enjoyed working with the youngsters.

"But because a Catholic priest made your skin crawl, and is fond of children, doesn't mean he's a paedophile," Jules said.

"I know. And because Angeline confides in Ami that the same Catholic priest abuses her, doesn't mean it's true either," Lex said.

"But it could well be," Linda said.

"Are you going to follow it up, Lex?" Jules asked.

"I've yet to decide what to do, if anything."

"I guess that one way to protect Angeline from the abuse would be to stop her from attending classes, but that will require her parents' consent and an explanation," Jules speculated.

"Removing Angeline from the equation wouldn't prevent the priest from abusing others. If there's a case to answer, I've no illusions about her being the only victim and him being the sole rotten apple in the basket and that any inquiry might open a Pandora's box."

"I trust your judgement, Lex. If you decide there's enough evidence to prove something is not kosher, I, as the father of a young girl and being deeply concerned for her friend, would encourage you to look into the matter, with your time and expenses covered by me." "That's kind of you, Uncle, but ..."

"It's not up for discussion, Lex."

"Okay."

"Whatever you decide, I hardly need to tell you to be careful," Jules said, "and now let me show you the Jardin des Plantes."

28

LEX POURED the rest of the golden liquid into Linda's champagne flute and returned the empty bottle to the wine cooler. It was their third bottle, and he messed up his attempt to wrap the white napkin around the neck of the bottle in his inebriated state. He watched it submerge into the icy water.

"Oh, fuck!"

"Why don't we?" Linda said, emptying her glass in one gulp. "I have to agree with anyone who claims that champagne is a leg opener." She had Lex's undivided attention, and suddenly it became paramount to return to their love-nest as quickly as possible

"Alain, *l'addition s'il vous plaît*," Lex called.

Five minutes later, they were staggering arm in arm along the cobblestones on the dimly lit Rue Norvins, occasionally stopping for a kiss and a fumble.

With the door to their stairwell in sight, Lex let go of Linda to get the key from his side pocket. He couldn't find it. He tried the other one.

"I've lost the key."

"You gave it to me, remember?" Linda said, dangling it in front of him. She strolled past him towards the front door, inserted the key in the lock and swung the door open. Lex was about to follow when a male voice from behind said, "Can I trouble you for a light, sir?" Startled, he turned to see a man step out of the shadows. *Where the hell did he come from?* Lex thought. He couldn't make out the man's face in the dark, and he didn't care.

Lex pulled out his lighter from a side pocket, expecting the man to present a cigarette. Lex flicked it on and leaned towards him. That was as far as he got before the man head-butted him, sending the Panama hat flying and Lex to the pavement. Luckily the hat and his forehead took the main impact. Lex tried immediately to get back up and made it halfway before the man's fist connected powerfully with his jaw, sending him crashing back down. Lex tasted blood.

The thug, apparently, didn't want him standing. Lex would have loved to defy him, but his surroundings had become hazy. Did he hear Linda scream? Lex couldn't be sure, as the impact of the man's leather shoe landing in his solar plexus distracted him. Lex gasped for air, and as he rolled into a foetal position, he grabbed the man's leg. When he tried to kick Lex with his other foot, he rolled onto his back with all his strength, catching the man off balance. He tilted over and landed on his back beside Lex.

"*Salopard!*" he cursed. He attempted to stamp on Lex's head with the sole of his boot, and missed by an inch as Lex rolled away from him.

By now, Lex wanted to kick his sorry ass. However, he was aware that if they went head to head, he would be the one getting it kicked.

The man was bigger and stronger, and Lex suspected he was used to inflicting pain on his fellow human beings. Lex also doubted that he'd consumed a few bottles of champagne as a warm-up. The sensible move was to escape while still *compos mentis*. Lex reckoned that if the man had wished to do severe damage, he would have used a knuckleduster, a knife or a pistol.

Mirroring each other's movements, they raised themselves from the ground and stood about three metres apart, face to face.

"Why did you do that, *fils de pute*?" Lex shouted in anger. The man gazed at him furiously, but kept his thin lips tightly together. Lex glanced past him and towards the closed front door to the staircase. He would have loved to see Linda holding it ajar.

Like a raging bull, the thug charged at Lex, who, catching him on the wrong foot, darted past him and down the street. The pain in Lex's head as he ran helped sober him up. He looked over his shoulder and saw the man in pursuit. Lex reached the crossroads and turned the corner, and after about a hundred metres, he looked back, expecting to see the man rounding the corner. He didn't, and Lex stopped for a breather. Perhaps he'd given up or decided to wait for him to return home. Or maybe he'd achieved what he wanted. Linda must have decided to get behind the locked door to the staircase, and he was pleased that she hadn't intervened. He recalled how she once, when cornered, had produced a Baby Browning from her handbag. At the time, it had saved them, and a pistol tonight might have stopped the thug from using him as a punch-bag. But he didn't like it then and wouldn't now— introducing firearms always upped the stakes.

Lex walked the long way round to return home. At a decent pace, he made it up the curved Rue Lepic. Lex pondered how quiet the narrow and sloping streets of Montmartre were on a late Sunday evening, only to hear footsteps coming towards him from around the bend. He crossed the street, walked between two parked cars, and onto the pavement. A middle-aged woman appeared, and as she walked past, he said a relieved, "*Bonsoir*, madame." She ignored him.

Lex followed the left bend into Rue Norvins, and with caution, he approached number thirteen. A black and white Peugeot 504 police car was parked behind his Renault 5 in front of the building. He looked for the Panama hat but couldn't see it. Lex pressed the intercom, and before long, he heard a window open somewhere above. He stepped into the street between the cars and looked up. Linda's worried face stared down at him.

"I'm so happy to see you alive and kicking," she exclaimed.

"So am I."

"I'll let you in."

He heard the buzzer, pushed the door open, and mounted the stairs. Linda met him halfway.

"Ouch!" he said when she hugged him. "I'm sore where the bastard kicked me." She let go and kissed him.

"Ouch!" He said again. "He split my lip when he hit me."

"I'm sorry, honey. I should have seen you're all bruised."

"There's a police car parked in front of the house," Lex said, forgetting she'd looked into the street half a minute ago.

"I know, and a young policeman is waiting upstairs."

"You called the cops?"

"I'd just unlocked the door when I heard a voice asking for a light. It was a bit creepy as I thought we were alone."

"He must have been waiting for us inside the opposite gate in the dark."

"I turned to see you were getting attacked —it freaked me out, and I called out to stop him. I wanted to jump on his back, but I doubted it would have helped. Instead, I called the police from our apartment."

"You did the right thing," Lex admitted.

She held his hand to support him upstairs. Lex spotted his Panama on the hook beside the pork pie hat in the hallway. Linda followed his gaze. "The policeman found it in the street."

They entered the living room. Whatever idea Lex had of what a French police brigadier looked like, the man standing in the middle of the room wasn't it. He was remarkably tall and willowy thin, with black curly hair and chestnut-brown skin. With his impressive black moustache, Lex might as well have been meeting the American basketball star Julies Erving at a costume party, dressed in a French police uniform.

The brigadier was holding a traditional police kepi in his left hand and a mug of coffee in his right. He squeezed the hat under his arm, shifted the cup to his left hand, and extended the right towards Lex, who noticed his long fingers.

"I'm Brigadier Jean-François Diagne." He had a firm handshake and a friendly face. "Your wife kindly offered me coffee."

"Please take a seat," Lex said.

"Would you like coffee, Lex?" Linda asked.

"I'd prefer a glass of water and some aspirin."

The brigadier lowered the mug to the coffee table and himself into a chair. He sat lopsidedly to make room for his long legs and placed his enormous feet in between the chair and the coffee table. He put the kepi on his lap and adjusted the pistol holster in his belt. Lex sat on the couch opposite him.

"Thanks for rescuing my Panama hat," Lex said to break the silence. "It's brand new."

"I found it in the street when I arrived, Monsieur Spijker, and I guessed it might belong to you."

"Do call me Lex."

"Only if you call me Jean-François." His smile was warm and genuine. "Your wife told me someone attacked you in the street, and I guess the bruise on your face proves it," he said instinctively, as his long fingers stroked the five-o'clock shadow on his chin. Linda handed Lex a glass of water and a couple of aspirins. She slid in beside him.

"We're not married," Lex said, as he popped the pills into his mouth and downed them in one swallow.

"Oh, I thought ...."

"Linda is my fiancée." Lex put the glass on the table, leaned back and yawned. "I apologise, but it's been a long day, and I don't recommend mixing champagne with a beating."

"You were drunk?"

"Let's call it inebriated."

"Did you start the fight?"

"I understood that, and it's absurd," Linda said, infuriated. Lex put a hand on her arm.

"The brigadier is only doing his job, Linda."

"I'd just arrived on duty when your fiancée called. I'm one of the few officers who speak decent English, so...." He interrupted himself in English by asking if Linda preferred him to speak English. She told him to continue in French, as she couldn't add to what she'd already told him.

"*Bien, alors.* Your fiancée sounded distressed, so I decided to pay a visit."

"Would you normally do that?" Lex asked. The brigadier looked puzzled. "I mean, come rushing because someone reports two men fighting in the street?"

"It depends on how busy we are, and it helps if the caller sounds like a beautiful lady in distress," he said with a smile towards Linda. She smiled back, but Lex doubted she fully understood what he had said. "And when I heard your name, it sounded familiar. I found your application for a private detective licence and read that you're a former policeman from Amsterdam. I don't like it when old colleagues get beaten up in my arrondissement," he said with a grin.

"You're too kind."

"I'd like to hear your version of events," the brigadier said, as he fetched a small notepad and pen from his side pocket.

"We dined at Restaurant le Consulat, and when we were drinking our coffee, Alain, *le patron*, offered us a bottle of champagne on the house to welcome Linda to Paris. We ordered two more bottles before heading for home."

"What time was this?" Jean-François asked.

"Around eleven, I guess."

"Go on."

"We arrived home, and Linda walked on ahead of me to unlock the door. That's when a male voice from behind asked for a light." Lex recounted the chain of events.

"Can you describe the guy?"

"I didn't see him properly."

"I find that hard to believe coming from a former cop."

"Perhaps, but the poor light and too much champagne blurred my vision," Lex protested, "but he would fit right in as a nightclub bouncer."

"Did you sense he was waiting for you?"

"Isn't it obvious?"

"It raises one important question."

"And that is?" Lex said, as he struggled to keep focus and his eyes open.

"Why?"

29

"HOW DO you feel?" Linda said from the edge of the bed, as she offered Lex two aspirins and a glass of water. He gulped them down and wiped his mouth with the back of his hand.

"I feel okay considering the amount of champagne we drank and that some hoodlum used my head as a punch-bag."

"You seem quite relaxed about the whole incident."

"No one got seriously hurt."

"I wish I felt the same."

"That's unlike you to feel so downhearted."

"I lay awake half the night."

"There must be something else troubling you," Lex said, as she confirmed it by caressing the scar under her chin with the tip of her index finger.

"I know we've agreed to have no more secrets between us, but I'm afraid I have one more to tell you." Lex didn't like the sound of it, but kept quiet.

"I doubt last night's incident is related to what I'm about to tell you, but I'm sure you will be angry and upset with me."

Here it comes, he thought. My jealousy is justified.

"I still have most of the 250,000 guilders."

"What! Where?" he exclaimed and sat up straight.

"It's under the bed—sewn into the lining of the suitcases."

"Don't tell me you transported all that money across two borders," he said incredulously. "You're incredible. Two days after an early release from prison for good behaviour, you've engaged in illegal cross-border, blood-money trafficking."

"You make it sound like I committed another murder?"

"So Allard Kuipers told the truth at the trial when he said he and his associates didn't take back the money."

"I'm afraid so, but luckily no one believed him."

Lex didn't know what to say to her. Part of him was thinking of how the money would ease the constant worry of making ends meet. But he also knew the obvious, that they still had no intention of letting her walk away with their money. Lex did agree with her however that it was unlikely yesterday's incident was related, as it didn't seem to be Mr Kuiper's style to send a lone thug.

"I've told no one about my new life in Paris," she said rather aimlessly.

"That's no guarantee. Considering the efforts I put into finding and freeing you, I'm sure that the possibility of us having teamed up after your release is the first avenue Mr Kuipers will explore. You may be difficult to locate, but it shouldn't be too hard to put an address to my name."

"Can you forgive me?"

"For not telling me before now, or for keeping it?"

"Both."

"Of course, but I wish you hadn't. It means we'll still keep having to look over our shoulders."

"I kept it for us, and you must admit it's nice to have something for a rainy day."

"I think we have more than that. The amount is equivalent to around half a million French francs," Lex said, performing a quick currency exchange in his head. "I doubt the average yearly income in France is much more than 20,000 francs," he added, to put it into perspective.

"I've no intention of being lavish, but I've not come to Paris to be skimpy either."

"Sorry to bring it up, but when you suggested we relocate to Paris, I said that the city was not much fun on the breadline, and you replied that we'd be alright with me as a private detective, and you as a model. What changed?"

LEX TURNED the corner, and Brigadier Jean-François Diagne greeted him from the doorway into the Commissariat central on Rue de Clignancourt. His kepi nearly touched the top of the door frame. He looked as fresh as a daisy and not like someone who'd worked the night shift. It was Monday afternoon and precisely fourteen hours since Lex, overtaken by fatigue, had asked the brigadier if they could postpone the 'interrogation' to the police station the next day. As a former cop, Lex explained, he had always wanted to see a French Commissariat from the inside.

He followed Jean-François up the stairs to the second floor. He hadn't set foot inside a police station since his 'confession' to a couple of former colleagues at HQ on the Leidseplein in Amsterdam the previous July. They wanted Lex charged with accessory to murder, assault, and theft. For various reasons, his former colleagues at the station hated his guts. But it wouldn't stick, and in the end, they let him off with a night in a detention cell and a slap on the wrist.

"Big operation you have here," Lex remarked.

"The arrondissement covers more than six thousand square kilometres and is the second-most densely populated of the twenty."

"How do you rate crime-wise?"

"Are you asking me if it's normal that upright citizens are assaulted on a Sunday evening as they walk home from their local café?" he asked.

"I sincerely apologise if I've added to the statistics. I won't let it happen again."

"Much appreciated." He held the door open, and Lex followed him along a corridor. With a hand to his kepi, he greeted a passing uniformed colleague.

"Let's go in here," he said and pointed to an open door on the left. Lex stepped into a small, windowless interview room. Jean-François switched on the neon light. "Take a seat," he said and pointed to one of three chairs around a table in the centre of the room.

"Is this an interrogation?" Lex laughed.

"Why so nervous? Relax! We're merely having a friendly chat."

"I had an unpleasant experience the last time someone demanded I take a seat in an interview room."

"I'm not demanding anything. Do you want coffee?"

"Please."

"I must warn you—it's pretty dire."

"I doubt it's worse than the coffee we drank at the station in Amsterdam."

"Let it come to the test. Milk? Sugar?"

"Unless I can have it spiked with whisky, black will do."

The brigadier returned with two plastic mugs and handed one to Lex, who took a sip. It wouldn't win any prizes, but it was hot.

"Can I smoke?"

"That's what the ashtray is for."

Lex took a packet of Gauloises Brunes *sans filtre* and a lighter from his side pocket. He held it up, but the brigadier declined. Lex fished out a cigarette, lit it, and inhaled deeply.

Jean-François sat, removed his kepi, and put it on the neighbouring chair. He did his best to fit his long legs under the table. *The world's not made for tall people,* Lex thought, as he pulled his legs of average length towards himself to create more room.

"Out of interest, would you mind telling me what you're working on at the moment?"

Lex hesitated.

"It's just between you and me."

"You can hardly call it an investigation, but I've been making a few inquiries into the alleged abuse of a young girl by a priest at the Sacré-Cœur." Lex told him how it all came about.

"Does the girl have a name?"

"It's Angeline Pernet, and she's twelve years old. She comes from a respectable Catholic family."

"So she's attending classes for solemn communion?"

"Oh, you know about that?"

"I'm a Catholic."

The brigadier is full of surprises, Lex thought.

"You look like I told you pigs will fly."

Lex felt the colour mounting in his face.

"I was born a Muslim in Senegal, but my adoptive parents brought me up as a Catholic."

"I didn't mean to offend you."

"No offence taken—I'm used to it. Anyhow, let's not get side-tracked. What do you mean by a few inquiries?"

"To start somewhere, I decided to check out the priest. His name is Horace Robert Blanchet. Friday, I met him at the Sacré-Cœur.

"Perhaps not the smartest idea to confront him with the accusations."

"I'm not as green as a cabbage," Lex said. "I met him under the pretext I'd proposed to a Catholic woman and therefore needed advice on the process of the Rite of... what was it now?"

"The Rite of Christian Initiation of Adults."

"I told him I lived on Rue Norvins, number 21, and he informed me he knew a family at number 13. It might be a coincidence, but I doubt it."

"It might be true—Montmartre is in many ways a small world. Did you use your real name?"

"I said my name was Filip Clou. It's my middle name and the French translation of my surname."

"How creative," he said and rolled his eyes.

"I wanted to keep it as simple as possible."

"What happened next?"

"He gave me a lecture in honesty—something about the first chapter in the book of wisdom."

"The Wisdom of Solomon."

"I'll take your word for it. As Father Blanchet mistrusted my motives, he couldn't advise me. All he could do was pray for me and ask me to return when I felt ready."

"I don't think you realise how powerful the Catholic church is here. We often hear rumours about abuse, but it's not something anyone feels like acting upon with any real intent."

"There's no justice for the sacred. It's frustrating that we cannot protect the ones that need it the most," Lex said.

"You think I like to turn the other cheek? But if I don't, it will be professional suicide. I'm only twenty-seven, and I don't want my career in the police to end just yet. I have to take enough crap for my skin colour, and I'm not prepared to be holier than Pope Paul."

"I don't blame you, but I won't necessarily turn the other cheek as you put it."

"I wouldn't expect you to, but I doubt you need me to remind you to tread carefully."

"I'd like to hear more about the rumours?"

"Forget it. You may be a former cop, but I hardly know you."

Lex drank some coffee. It was cold by now, and not even a Johnnie Walker rescue mission would have made it remotely drinkable. He lit another cigarette to compensate.

"I feel you want to help," Lex said.

"I just want to do my job."

"I think there's more to it than that."

"And that is?"

"I feel we have a bond."

"Uh-huh."

"Would you be available for dinner?" Lex said, without knowing from where that came. He didn't usually invite someone he'd met a couple of times to dinner. *Nothing ventured, nothing gained*, he thought.

"Is that a bribe?" the brigadier laughed.

"Call it what you like."

"When did you have in mind?"

"How about tomorrow evening? Or are you on duty?"

"Tomorrow, I'm not."

"Feel free to bring your wife and children if you like."

"Not married and no kids, but I'll bring my partner."

"Great. Let's make it seven at Rue Norvins."

THE PHONE rang.

"Please take it, Linda," Lex shouted.

"Got it!" she replied from the living room. He heard her bare feet through the open bathroom door as she crossed the hallway and then her voice from the office.

Lex finished his business, dried his hands, and returned to the bedroom. Linda was still on the phone. He put on a shirt and a tie—something he did without much enthusiasm at least once on most days—but this one was special. After visiting the Commissariat central, he'd picked up the two silk shirts and his single-breasted jacket from his uncle's tailor.

He had a difficult choice—the white or the blue shirt? Lex held them up against the light blue jacket. He chose the white one, put it on, buttoned it up, and tucked it into his slim-fit trousers. He took a skinny blue tie from the rack and used the bathroom mirror to tie it in an Oriental knot. Apart from the bruise on his chin, Bryan Ferry had nothing on him.

Lex returned to the bedroom, pulled out the side table drawer, and picked up a box. He opened it and took out the pair of diagonal striped silver cufflinks his uncle had given him for his birthday.

"Do you need help?" Linda said as she entered the bedroom. Lex handed her the cufflinks, and she fixed them skilfully into the cuffs. She fetched the jacket from the hanger and helped him put it on. Lex turned towards her.

"You look like a million, my Lordship." She bobbed a curtsy.

"And you look foxy, my Lady." He bobbed it back.

"Wait till you see me in my fineries," she giggled.

"What is making you so happy?" Lex asked.

"I had a nice chat with your uncle."

"I wondered who was keeping you on the phone for that long."

"Anyhow, he gave me some great news. I'm to meet a *directeur artistique* from *Vogue* for lunch tomorrow."

"That's wonderful," Lex said, unable to hide a faint pang of jealousy. It made him ashamed, and he hoped Linda didn't notice.

"As soon as I've put on my face, we can leave," she said.

30

LEX WOKE late with a hangover and in a sombre mood. To get loaded again so soon after the Sunday evening champagne bonanza was a terrible idea. But as Monday evening progressed, the heated words between him and Linda had increased, and so did the drinks.

He had no great desire to recall last night's events, but the empty place beside him in the bed brought it back with painful clarity. The evening began pleasantly enough with dinner at Restaurant Au Chien Qui Fume in Les Halles. As expected, Linda was preoccupied with her lunch the next day with the *Vogue* art director and the opportunities it might hold.

Lex did his best to control his jealousy, but the more Linda talked about a potential career as a model, the harder it became. Eventually, he said something along the lines of how the fashion business was full of vultures and that he would hate to see her once again being exploited. It shamed him to admit that he had mentioned how she'd ended up with a high-class call girl agency last time she'd pursued a modelling career.

It was immature and unfair, and she exploded in anger. She demanded to know why Lex claimed she had his full support when he didn't show it. A fair question on an evening where her enthusiasm and happiness made her beauty shine extra brightly—and where his spirits should be high from being part of it.

She stood, threw her napkin on the table, and knocked over her wine glass. Before leaving, Linda specified that she did not expect Lex to wake her later, as she needed her beauty sleep to look her best for the art director the next day.

Lex sank into the dark pool of misery and self-pity that opened up in front of him. He hit the nearest bar, and for a few hours, he let Johnnie Walker do the talking, so he could focus on getting hammered and feeling sorry for himself.

Lex returned home at around 2 a.m. and as he crawled into the dark bedroom, he saw the contour of Linda's back in the bed. He had no idea if she was awake as he slid in between the sheets, staying near the edge to avoid any physical contact. The booze he'd consumed gave him an uneasy sleep, but he was out for the count when daylight came and didn't register Linda getting up.

Lex rolled out of bed and walked into the living room with the open plan kitchen. Linda wasn't there, and he returned to the hallway. He opened the door to his office, crossed the floor and pulled the French windows open. Lex pushed the shutters and squinted in the morning spring sunlight. He leaned against the iron railing to look up and down the old cobbled street in the hope of catching a glimpse of Linda.

Lex turned and saw a note on his desk. It read, *My dear Lex. The bedroom smelled like a distillery when I woke, so I let you sleep (it off). As you know, I have a busy day—lunch with the art director (dare I mention it again), and afterwards, my French lesson. I'll shop on my way home and cook for our guests this evening. It's fish, so buy some decent white wine. I'll let you be in charge of the dessert. Your despicable behaviour last night is not forgotten, and we need to have a SERIOUS talk. For the sake of the policeman(!) and his partner, let us agree to a 'ceasefire' this evening. Kisses, Linda. Didn't she tell me she wasn't good at putting words on paper?* he thought.

He found the note encouraging, although some of it made him cringe. The out of control jealousy horrified him, and he couldn't explain it. Admittedly, his resentment was never far away, but he was usually able to shrug it off. Lex found it hard to believe that Linda's youth and beauty were enough to stir such strong feelings in him. She might be a few years younger than him and a total knockout, but in all modesty, he was still in his prime, and with his square jaw, warm brown eyes, Roman nose, and thick dark hair kept short at the back and long in the front, he often made women turn their heads. Linda wasn't flirtatious or indifferent and gave plentifully of her affection. All the same, he often felt inadequate, like an impostor, a hustler, that didn't deserve to have a beautiful and bright fiancée.

It wasn't rocket science that the fear of losing her fuelled his jealousy, nor that it might eventually drive her away. It wasn't straightforward what to do about it, but putting his cards on the table would be a good start, or getting professional help or sharing it with a friend.

"Time to grow up, Lex," he told himself. But first, he needed a cold shower and a pot of hot black coffee.

LINDA RETURNED a few minutes past five. It pleased him to see her smile, and, to be on his best behaviour, he immediately asked about her lunch with the art director.

"He was an absolute peach," she said, "and they want to do a photoshoot with me on Thursday."

"Congratulations, I'm so happy for you. I think that calls for champagne."

"I hate to spoil the party, Lex, but I'll prefer a cup of tea and a hot bath."

"Fine," Lex said, disappointed not to be celebrating with the champagne he'd bought for the occasion. "You get in the tub, and I'll bring you a nice cup of tea."

"Thanks, darling. How much time before the guests arrive?"

He looked at his watch. "A couple of hours."

"Plenty of time. I'm counting on you to peel the potatoes and make the salad?"

"No problem. What are we having?"

"Mediterranean-style sole fillets baked in a buttery lime sauce."

"Yummy."

"Did you buy some dessert?"

"I made it myself, and you're in for a treat."

"What is it?"

"My famous chocolate mousse."

"You are a good boy," she said as they walked into the living room. She looked towards the kitchen and spotted a bouquet of white roses.

"What is this? Are they for me?"

"I'm so sorry for acting like a jerk last night."

"Flowers will get you anywhere," she laughed.

They embraced and kissed passionately. Lust overwhelmed Lex. He stroked Linda's back, lifted her dress, and put his hands on her buttocks.

"I thought you were making me a cup of tea?" she said and pushed him away.

"You're right. Tea and tub, and no rub," he said, to back down with as much grace as possible.

THE DOORBELL rang at seven.

"I do like punctual people," Lex remarked to Linda as he pressed the buzzer. "You realise this is the first time we've entertained together?"

Lex opened the front door to the stairwell and heard steps ascending. He saw the back of Jean-François' afro, and as he rounded the bannister, his perfect smile beneath his groomed moustache. He wore a long, colourful, loose-fitting garment and had a bottle of red wine tucked under his arm. Behind him walked a pleasant looking, round-cheeked man in his mid-thirties. He had wavy ginger hair and wore a camel-coloured sports coat with an open-collared white shirt that swelled around the curve of a comfortable belly.

He carried a bunch of red roses. Beside the tall, thin Jean-François, he appeared even broader and shorter.

"Monsieur Brigadier, I hardly recognised you without your uniform." Lex said with a laugh to hide his surprise that his partner was a man.

"When I disguise myself as a civilian, I prefer my *boubou*," he replied.

Lex shook his hand and stepped aside.

"Let me introduce my partner Joseph de la Fontaine," he said ceremoniously.

"My friends call me Jos." His hand was firm and warm.

"I'm Alexander Filip Spijker, and my friends call me Lex." He invited them into the hallway, and Jean-François handed him the bottle of red wine.

Linda appeared from the living room looking gorgeous in a burgundy cocktail dress with an embroidered lace bodice.

"Good evening, beautiful lady," Jos said. Linda offered her hand, and he kissed it symbolically before presenting her with the red roses.

"They are beautiful. Ain't I a lucky girl; this is the second time today a handsome fellow has presented me with flowers. Look, Lex, how they match my dress."

"I'm delighted to meet you under more joyful circumstances," Jean-François said. He bowed down to *faire la bise*.

"I find you handsome in a black uniform, brigadier, but I prefer you in that colourful shirt."

"You are too kind," Jean-François said.

"It speaks to the African in him," Jos said with a snigger.

"I may be French, but I'm proud to have my roots in Africa."

"That's also why I love you," Jos said.

Lex sensed they'd had the exchange before. Perhaps it was their party piece?

"Come and take a seat." Lex gestured towards the couch. "Let me get you a drink. What's your poison?"

LINDA REMOVED their plates after the main dish.

"You're a great cook," Jos said. He lit a cigarette.

"Not only a pretty face," Linda said with a smirk.

Lex refilled their wine glasses.

"Nice Chablis, Lex."

"Thanks. We bought a bottle for my uncle recently. He's a connoisseur and seemed impressed."

"So is Jos, and he has an impressive collection of wine at his place," Jean-François said.

"So you don't live together?" Linda said.

"We've discussed it," Jos said, "and I'd like to."

"It's a bit complicated," Jean-François said.

"I don't mean to pry, but it must be hard to be gay in the police," Lex said.

"If it were official, I wouldn't be," Jean-François said.

"That's in the police, not gay," Jos stressed.

"I guess it's easier for you as a newspaperman?" Linda asked.

"Sure. It's not talked about, but I believe it's common knowledge at the firm that I play for the other team and that I'm in a steady relationship."

"If my colleagues at the station knew I preferred my partner to be male, my presence would make them feel uncomfortable," Jean-François stressed.

"Now you mention the station, perhaps we can continue our talk from yesterday," Lex said, "and perhaps, for the benefit of Linda and Jos, I should recap."

"I'd prefer not to get our partners involved. Let's keep it as professional as possible. Me as the brigadier and you as the private detective."

"Don't mind us," Linda and Jos said in one voice. "I'm sure we have more exciting things to talk about," Jos added.

"We'll move into my office," Lex said.

"Let's have your homemade chocolate mousse first," Linda said.

LEX INVITED Jean-François to sit down. He turned the chair away from the desk to make room for his legs. Lex heard a car passing on the wet cobbles in the street below through the open window.

"What do you think of Jos?" Jean-François pursed his lips with anticipation.

"A nice man and very engaging. For a journalist and editor, he talks remarkably little about himself."

"That's what I think, but he has come through some rough times."

"How's that?"

"He had a gambling problem—blackjack and poker. When he was busted for the third time, he admitted his addiction and accepted that he needed to get treatment."

"I don't understand. Busted for what?"

"For playing illegally. Casinos are, since 1920, banned in Paris."

"So it's all underground?"

"You won't believe how many private clubs there are in Paris, and most slip under the radar. The majority deal in gambling, sex and drugs. Some in all three."

"Interesting."

"Talking about private clubs brings me neatly to the information I've, after some consideration, decided to share with you. I made some enquiries and have some information about a possible link to your Father Blanchet."

"Facts or rumours?"

"A little of both."

"Uh-huh."

"A few months ago, the police received an anonymous tip-off about the whereabouts of Ramírez Sánchez, and ...."

"Carlos the Jackal," Lex cried.

"So you know about him?"

"I know some. He's the terrorist that took part in a couple of failed grenade attacks in January on El Al aeroplanes at Orly Airport. The hostage situation involved hundreds of riot police and your Interior

Minister. It all ended in a gunfight at the airport, but the Jackal managed to escape."

"You're well informed."

"My parents died on the Swissair flight blown up in mid-air by the Palestinian terror group PFLP, and I'm somehow drawn to terror attacks involving aeroplanes."

"I'm sorry to hear that."

"I wonder what the Jackal has to do with sexual abuse?"

"I'll come to that if you let me."

"You mind if I relieve myself before we continue?" Lex asked.

"As long as you don't do it here," Jean-François said with a snigger. "While you do that, I'll see if Linda and Jos have left us any of your Chablis. Would you like a refill?"

"Please."

When Lex returned to the office, Jean-François was standing by the window. There were two glasses of white wine on the desk. They sat down.

"*Santé,*" Lex said and lifted his glass.

"To friendship." Jean-François clinked his glass against Lex's, and they drank.

"Did they miss us?" Lex asked and lit a cigarette.

"They hardly noticed me. I think your fiancée is making Jos spill all his secrets."

"She has that effect on some men. I know from experience."

"Where was I?" Jean-François said as he stroked his moustache.

"You were telling me about the Jackal," Lex said.

"Correction. You're the one talking about him, while I try to get to why I mentioned the terrorist in the first place."

"Please do. I'm keen to make a connection."

"When the police raided the address, given by the anonymous informer, late one night in the hope of catching the Jackal in his PJs, they didn't find him or anything else related to terrorism. Officially nothing came of it, but if you listen to the rumours, which I don't, they stumbled upon a group of middle-aged men, all pillars of society, in the company of girls on the younger side, if you know what I mean."

"A private sex club offering the clientele sex with teenage girls? Do any of the dirty old men caught with their boxer shorts around their ankles have names?"

"Middle-aged men was the expression I used, and I never said they were caught with their, as you put it, boxer shorts around their ankles."

"You know what I mean."

"Sure, but it's all speculation."

"I asked if any of them had a name?"

"Not officially, but does the name Killian Lamarre mean anything to you?"

There's a surprise, Lex thought. He opened the top drawer of his desk and took out a copy of the black and white photo of the middle-aged entrepreneur and philanthropist he'd taken. He handed it to Jean-François.

"That's him, alright. When and where?"

"He's coming out of an address on Avenue Foch, and I took the photo just before midnight last Friday on a job for my uncle, an estate agent, who suspects a client of subletting an apartment at the address."

"What do you know about Killian Lamarre?" Jean-François asked.

"Not much. The case is closed as far as I'm concerned, so I haven't taken it any further."

"He's been every mother's dream of a son-in-law for the last thirty years."

"Isn't he married?"

"He's on his fourth marriage, and they are getting younger and younger."

"Apparently not young enough," Lex said with a shiver. "It's all fascinating, but I still don't see what that has to do with Father Blanchet."

"The whole thing is rather far-fetched, and I almost forgot why I told you about it in the first place. Anyhow, the reason is that I stumbled upon an interesting fact about Killian Lamarre that links him to your priest. He recently funded a major restoration of the grand pipe organ of the Sacré-Cœur. And guess what—Father Blanchet sits on the church's Restoration Committee."

"There's a surprise."

"There's no evidence the connection is dodgy."

"Perhaps not, but it does make you wonder."

"Sure."

"Reporting information about the Jackal's hideout was a clever ploy to get the address raided," Lex speculated aloud.

"Indeed."

"You don't happen to have an address for the place?"

"Unfortunately not."

"Could it be on Avenue Foch?"

"Who knows?"

"Can you find out where it is?"

"Perhaps, but I'm not going to. As a policeman, I find the lack of resources to stop any potential abuse frustrating, but I'm a tiny cog in a huge piece of machinery. A tiny black wheel, you may add."

"But I'm not, and I wouldn't mind talking to Killian Lamarre," Lex said.

"About what? As I mentioned, it's all rumours, and it's no secret he likes beautiful girls and that he likes them young."

"Let's say it's because I have nothing better to do with my time."

"I'm not going to stop you from contacting him."

"If I pretend to be a journalist writing a piece about him as a successful entrepreneur for a Dutch newspaper, I doubt he'll be able to resist giving me an interview."

"Probably not."

"You think I can use Jos as a reference?"

"Why don't you ask him? At the very least, he can give you some background and journalistic advice."

"Okay."

"Unless there's a new development, my hands are tied. But if there's any truth in the rumours, I'd like to help as much as possible."

"I appreciate it, brigadier," Lex said and lifted his empty glass. "Let's rejoin the party."

31

AN UNPLEASANT ringing sound interrupted his dream. Lex opened his eyes and realised it was the doorbell. He turned his head to look at Linda beside him. She didn't react. He stumbled out of bed and slipped on his boxer shorts and a T-shirt. Before he reached the front door, the bell chimed again. He pressed the buzzer and heard it buzzing three floors down. Immediately someone knocked on the door, and he pulled it open. A postman in full uniform greeted him with a finger to the brim of his cap.

"The postman always rings twice," Lex muttered.

"Pardon, monsieur, I didn't hear."

"Good morning."

"No offence, but it's past eleven," the postman said, opening the flap of a brown leather shoulder bag. He fished out a letter and handed it to Lex. To his delight, he spotted the logo of the *préfecture de police*, and in his eagerness to see the contents, he was about to close the door when the postman held out a notepad and asked for a signature. Lex pretended to sign with his finger.

"I recommend you use a pen, monsieur," the postman said as he produced a blue Bic pen from his breast pocket. Lex scribbled a signature. The postman withdrew the notepad, and Lex returned the pen.

"*Bonne journée*. What's left of it," the man said with a straight face. Lex shut the door and hurried into the office. He fetched a paperknife from the top drawer, opened the envelope and pulled out the letter. As Lex unfolded it, a red plastic folder the size of a passport dropped onto the floor. He bent to pick it up, and as he got up, the back of his head banged against the underside of the open drawer.

"Ouch! Goddammit!" he cried.

"What's going on? Are you alright?" Linda called from the bedroom. He'd managed to wake her.

"I'll survive." He flipped the folder open. "My private detective licence has arrived."

"Wonderful. Let me see," Linda said with suitable enthusiasm.

She was sitting at the end of the bed when he entered. He handed the folder to her, and she opened it.

"Nice photo, but why didn't you use a recent one?" she said.

"It's from when I applied three months ago," he protested.

"I'm teasing you." She studied the document. "What does it give you licence to do?"

"To set up shop, advertise my services, and charge for it."

"It seems we're getting our shit together," she said happily.

She pulled him onto the bed beside her. They embraced and tilted backwards. Lex kissed her ear and whispered, "Have you forgiven me for acting like a spoiled child?" Lex felt her warm cheek against his as he waited for her to say something. Eventually, she murmured, "Forgiven, perhaps, but not forgotten."

"Do you want to talk about it?"

"Not now. Please, not now. Whatever's happened, make love to me."

And he did; not just sex, although there was a bit of that too.

LEX WATCHED Linda disappear down the stairs before he closed the door. He marched to the office and pulled the French windows open. Leaning against the iron railing, he looked down into the street to see her exiting the front door. She stopped to check something in her handbag before rushing down Rue Norvins. Lex glanced at his watch—she had twenty minutes to get to her French lesson at the Place de l'Opéra. The clatter of her heels on the cobbles bounced off the walls in the quiet street. Lex hoped she would turn so he could give her a wave, but she didn't, as she disappeared round the corner to Rue Girardon.

It was Linda's tenth day in Paris, but it seemed much longer, and he'd already found it hard to imagine a life without her. He recalled his secretary

Roos scolding him for his irrational intoxication with the *femme fatale*. Back then, she'd been right, but as he'd learned the many facets of Linda's character, the intoxication had become less irrational. Her youthful and easy-going manner and her lust for life were addictive.

The phone rang to stop his philosophising.

"Private detective Lex Spijker," he said pompously —looking at his official licence beside the telephone.

"Editor Joseph de la Fontaine from *Le Figaro*."

"Oh, it's you, Jos."

"Thank you for a great time last night."

"A pleasure to meet you."

"I think I've fallen for your girlfriend," he said. "She's a beautiful and clever girl with a fascinating story."

"I guess that's some compliment from a newspaper hack."

"You're probably busy," he said, "so I'll cut to the chase."

Lex was no such thing, but felt no need to tell Jos otherwise.

"I have a direct number for Killian Lamarre. Have you got a pen?" Lex wrote it down.

"Out of interest, I asked the librarian in our text archive to collect articles related to Mr Lamarre."

"Anything to incriminate him?"

"Afraid not—the positive spin we give him, you would think he'd hired us as his PR firm."

"Perhaps he's a major advertiser?"

"I have no idea, and it's not something I care much about—that side of our business often seems to get in the way of the truth."

"Have you interviewed him?"

"Not personally, but as a former business editor of a major French newspaper, he knows my name."

"He'll most likely ask me where I got the direct number from. Can I, as we discussed last night, refer to you?"

"Sure. You're an acquaintance from the Dutch *NRC Handelsblad*. What's your name again?" he asked.

"Jan Blokker."

"And what's your angle, Jan?"

"We're doing a series on influential international entrepreneurs."

"That should get his attention."

"Do you have time for a few questions?"

"Fire away."

"Negative press on Killian Lamarre is, apparently, hard to come by, but you would think that the young girl thing might raise some eyebrows?"

"Sure, but it's not something Mr Lamarre or his cronies try to hide. I mean, he's in his late fifties, and whenever he's spotted at a social event, at least one girl that's young enough to be his daughter accompanies him. It's like a badge of honour."

"Not only a pompous arse, but also a dirty old man."

"Perhaps, but people just seem to treat it as an oddity. The actor Alain Delon is a good example—in a recent quote, he said something along the lines of, 'I like beautiful young women. Who doesn't? But Killian likes them so young it's almost criminal.'"

"Is it a surprise he knows Alain Delon?"

"Not at all. Lamarre may be a pompous arse and a dirty old man, as you put it, but he's also a wealthy one. Somehow, wealth is a magnet for celebrities and people from the corridors of power. As you can imagine, his so-called friendships are never without you-scratch-my-back-and-I'll-scratch-yours."

"And how do Delon and Lamarre scratch each other?"

"Lamarre has a stake in the actor's beauty product line."

"If they're business partners, why did Alain Delon say what he did?"

"I'm sure Alain Delon meant it as a tongue-in-cheek remark and that the middle-aged entrepreneur takes any reference to his relationship with beautiful young women as a compliment. But to us normal people, if you know what I mean, it indicates something not a hundred per cent kosher."

"Does Lamarre have any children?"

"A son from his first marriage and two teenage daughters from his second. He has blended the daughters' names to name his company Sanna Invest.

"Let me guess. The girls are called Sandra and Anna?"

"Not even close," Jos laughed. "It's Sandrine and Lyna."

"How cute."

"With his reputation, it's indeed a sweet story."

"I wonder how his teenage daughters like their daddy's sexual association with girls their age."

"It's all rumours, and I'm sure Killian Lamarre and anyone associated with him will say it's malicious gossip. And French law does not include a fixed age of consent."

"But you can still be prosecuted for sex with minors."

"Sure, but your proof must be solid. Killian Lamarre has friends in high places and the best lawyers money can buy."

"Does he have many friends in the press?"

"Undoubtedly, but he ain't a friend of mine. I will run the story with pleasure if you bring me proof he's a paedophile."

They ended the call, and Lex headed to the kitchen to make himself a coffee. He put the kettle on the stove, and while the water was boiling, he wondered if it was really worth contacting Killian Lamarre. The rumours did place him in a private sex club that offered the clientele sex with girls in late childhood and early adolescence. And what about his connection to the potential abuser Father Blanchet? And what was he doing at the Avenue Foch address on Friday evening? *Somebody needs to rattle the bars of Lamarre's cage, and it might as well be me*, Lex thought.

He made the coffee and returned to the office. He sat down, drank some, lit a cigarette, inhaled deeply, exhaled, lifted the receiver, and dialled the number to Killian Lamarre. Lex let it ring three times, and was about to give up when someone answered.

"Yes? What?" a deep and impatient voice growled.

"Is this Killian Lamarre?"

"It depends."

"My name is Jan Blokker, and I'm a journalist with a Dutch financial newspaper."

"What paper?"

"*NRC Handelsblad.*"

"Never heard of it."

"It's relatively young, but it has become the major business newspaper in Holland and Belgium."

"How did you get my direct number. I'm not listed."

"A friend of mine at *Le Figaro* gave it to me."

"Does this friend of yours have a name?"

"Joseph de la Fontaine. He's the…."

"I know who he is," he interrupted, "and he's not on my Christmas card list."

"My newspaper is doing a series on major and successful entrepreneurs from the nine-member countries in the European Common Market, but if….?"

"I'm all ears," he cut Lex short again. He sounded slightly less dismissive. *Flattery will get you anywhere,* Lex thought.

"You're the first one in the series, and I wondered if you were available for an interview?"

"Over the phone?"

"I'd like to interview you in person."

"Are you calling from Holland?"

Lex decided it wasn't worth lying. "I'm already in Paris."

"I'm afraid I'll be out of town for a few days."

"When are you back?"

"Why don't you come to my private residence in Rueil Malmaison on Saturday?"

"What time?"

"Come at three."

"And your address?" Lamarre told him, and Lex wrote it down.

"*A bientôt*," Lamarre said and ended the call.

From the bottom drawer of the desk, Lex fetched a blue Michelin map book of Paris and Banlieue to get an idea of the location of Killian Lamarre's private residence. The commune of Rueil Malmaison was west of the Bois de Boulogne.

Through the open window, Lex heard a distant clock strike two. He felt his blood sugar running low and realised he'd had sex for breakfast and nothing for lunch. He grabbed his jacket and the Panama hat and headed for Restaurant Le Consulat.

HE PUSHED open the door to Le Consulat, and it surprised him to see nearly all of the tables occupied, including his favourite one in the far corner. The German language could be heard from most of them. Lex stopped, indecisive, as Alain came towards him.

"Is Paris invaded again?"

"You could be excused for that notion. However, this group are here as tourists; they're fairly well-behaved and usually pay before leaving. So no complaints from me."

"And neither from me if you can find me a seat away from this crowd."

"There's one for you in the back room, but you'll have to share the table with a Catholic priest." Lex walked towards the adjacent room, and another surprise halted him in the doorway. Of all the priests in Paris, it was Father Blanchet. The back of his black cassock was turned to the door. Lex decided to go somewhere else, but before making his escape, the priest spotted him in the big mirror. He turned and said, "Well, isn't that Monsieur Clou?" He winked and flashed a grin.

"You have a good memory, Father."

"Do join me." He pointed to the opposite chair.

"That's kind of you, Father, but I'd hate to disturb your peace."

"Good luck with that," he said, putting on the charming boyish smile Lex had seen before and which made the priest instantly attractive. *He would make a great used car salesman*, Lex thought, hanging his hat on a nearby hook. He squeezed himself into the seat.

Alain approached.

"I see you've met Father Blanchet. Allow me to introduce Monsieur Lex Spijker. If you need a private detective, he's your man," Alain said. Lex felt his face go red.

"It's a pleasure, Monsieur Spijker," Father Blanchet said, not missing a beat.

"What can I get you, Lex?"

"A *croque madame* and a beer," Lex said, "and perhaps something for you, Father?" he added, to counter the feeling of embarrassment.

"*Merci.* I'll have another glass of Beaujolais." They sat for a moment in awkward silence, and Lex did his best not to make eye contact.

"I think you owe me an explanation." Lex's mind raced to come up with an alternative version of his previous story. The truth would be the most straightforward explanation. Still, he had to consider what damage it could do to his investigation and, more importantly, the harm it could do to Angeline Pernet.

"I apologize for spinning you a line last time we met," Lex said to gain time.

"You're an awful actor, Monsieur Spijker. I knew within a few minutes that you weren't telling the truth about your reason for consulting me."

"You implied as much."

"Let me tell you why...." He paused to let Alain serve them. With a *bon appetite*, his focus shifted to the German tourists.

"*Santé,*" Lex said and raised his glass of beer. The Father lifted his wine, and they both drank. The smell of the food hit Lex's nostrils.

"You'd better eat before you start drooling," Father Blanchet said. He occasionally sipped his wine whilst watching Lex devour the *croque*. Lex emptied his glass of beer and set fire to a cigarette. He felt human again. "You wanted to tell me why I came to see you the other day, Father."

"I'd like to give you my theory."

"So why did I?"

"I get you don't respect the priesthood all that much and that you don't like me. But you mustn't take me for a fool, Monsieur Spijker. As soon as you mentioned Angeline Pernet the other day, I suspected the real reason for your visit."

"And that was? "

"You wanted to see if I was a monster."

"That's ridiculous. Why should I want to do that?"

"Because Angeline Pernet is a naughty girl, telling tales of inappropriate behaviour on my part."

"Sexual abuse of a minor is the expression you're looking for, Father," Lex offered.

"It's malicious gossip from people who are against the Catholic church."

"To me, Angeline Pernet seems a nice Catholic girl."

"I meant, in general," he said, annoyed.

"There's no smoke without fire," Lex proclaimed.

"Spare me the clichés." Father Blanchet's smile had lost most of its boyish charm and all of its attraction. The white dog collar enhanced the red rash that had formed on his neck.

"I wonder why you reacted to a girl's frustrated fantasies about her priest, if you call yourself a professional private detective."

"So you think Angeline Pernet is attracted to you?"

"I get it all the time. The devout young girls can't help it, and you won't believe how flirtatious they are. I seem to evoke something in these girls, and it's not my fault they harbour romantic ideas about me."

Lex found it hard to listen to his deluded rambling. He did not doubt that many people, not least those with some religious conviction, took to his smooth voice, youngish demeanour, blue eyes and slick dark brown hair. His fatherly manner undoubtedly appealed to some young girls, but the big feet, pot belly, small hands, and nose and ears out of proportion in a face with a cleft chin, hardly made him a James Dean or a Casanova.

"Not that you'll know, young man, but living in celibacy comes with certain challenges and temptations, but the Lord makes the burden bearable. I'm not perfect, but I've dedicated my life to serving God and my community. What have you dedicated yourself to, Monsieur Spijker?" Without waiting for a response, he continued, "I detest any rumours of abuse that implicates the church I represent or me."

"Do you know Killian Lamarre?" Lex asked.

"Of course. He's the best-known entrepreneur in France."

"I meant personally."

"That's a strange question. To my knowledge, he's not a religious man."

"I know that he recently funded a major restoration of the grand pipe organ of the Sacré-Cœur. I also know that you both sit on the church's Restoration Committee."

"So what? He didn't personally attend any of our meetings, and I've never met him." The red rash that had first appeared on his neck had now spread to his cheeks. When he lifted the glass of wine to his lips, his hand trembled. *I've hit a nerve*, Lex thought.

"It's a bit rich when you accuse me of telling tales," Lex said.

"What is it that you're accusing me of?"

"I'm not accusing you of anything, but I sense you might be keeping a few skeletons in the cupboard."

"That's ridiculous," he said for the second time. "Let me warn you about spreading unfounded rumours and false accusations, Monsieur Spijker. It could get you in all kinds of trouble."

"Is that a threat?"

"Not at all. I'm merely telling you that your conduct may have consequences."

"Perhaps you arranged to have me beaten up to warn me off?"

"I have no idea what you mean. I'm a man of God, not a thug."

"Amen to that."

"I'm afraid I have to go, but I've enjoyed our little chat," the priest said. "As I told you the other day, I shall pray for you." He touched the golden cross on his chest and raised himself from the table. Lex followed the back of the black cassock as the priest strolled out of the room.

32

SLEEPING ON top of almost a quarter-million guilders, sewn into the lining of the two suitcases pushed under their bed, kept Lex awake, so after breakfast and before a planned trip to the Cimetière du Père-Lachaise, he had a safe installed in his office. They transferred 237,000 guilders to the safe, took almost 3,000 guilders to the local bank, exchanging it for around 5,000 francs and opened a bank account for Linda. With Lex's own bank account in free fall, Linda insisted they deposit some of the money into it. Lex didn't argue, although he knew that it would niggle him every time he spent any of it.

LEX AND LINDA exited onto the Philippe Auguste metro station platform, and hand in hand, they followed the *sortie* signs to the Cimetière du Père-Lachaise. He'd visited the famous cemetery once before on a school outing in 1955. He only remembered it because the family had overslept on the excursion day, and his mother had driven him to the cemetery to join the class. He didn't remember much about the trip or the graves they came to see. Later in life, he read that the cemetery was the final resting place for celebrities like Edith Piaf, Oscar Wilde, Frédéric Chopin, Marcel Proust and Honoré de Balzac.

As Lex and Linda came up from the metro, it began raining cats and dogs, and they raced for shelter at a nearby café. They stood at the *comptoir* and ordered coffee and Calvados. Lex lit two cigarettes, and Linda helped herself to one from between his lips. She looked spectacular in her tight, black bell-bottoms, a shirt in psychedelic colours, and chunky heel sandals. The shirt deviated from her usual style, and he teased her for dressing up for a dead rock star, whose grave was the main reason Linda had suggested a visit to the cemetery. Lex didn't know much about him, but Linda informed him that Jim Morrison of the Doors had moved from Los Angeles to Paris in March 1971. On the eve of 3 July, he had gone to the movies with his girlfriend, returned home to their apartment in Le Marais, listened to records, fell ill and died of heart failure in the bathtub. He was twenty-seven years old. In the presence of his girlfriend and the band's manager, who'd flown in from California, Jim Morrison was laid to rest four days later.

Linda asked for the *toilette*, and Lex asked for the bill. As he waited for the waiter to bring it, a man about Lex's height stepped right up to him. In a dark jacket, black tie on a crisp white shirt, the man could have been an undertaker, a member of the Jehovah's Witnesses, or a secret agent. Judging by his clean-shaven face, he was around forty, but it was hard to tell as a black fedora covered the top of his head and sunglasses covered his eyes.

"Can I help you?" Lex asked, surprised by having his private space invaded by a stranger.

"No, but perhaps I can help you with some advice."

"I doubt it."

"Your woman is very sexy, and if she were my girlfriend, I wouldn't let her stray any more than necessary."

"I'm not sure I know what you mean."

"Oh, yes, you do." The man turned and walked out of the café. If it weren't for Linda expecting to find him at the *comptoir* and the waiter collecting his money, Lex would have pursued him into the street.

"Are you okay, Lex? You look ruffled," Linda said as she returned from the toilet.

"Must be the price of the coffee and Calvados," he blabbed, not wanting to worry her.

They left the café, and to their delight the heavy rain had become a drizzle. As Lex and Linda strolled along the Boulevard de Ménilmontant to the cemetery's main entrance, he couldn't help scouting for the fedora man.

They entered the cemetery through an imposing and massive gate of sandstone and iron. Linda headed straight to a sign with visitor information.

"Please translate for me, Lex," Linda said.

Lex read, "The cemetery, opened in 1804, is named after Père François de la Chaise, a confessor to Louis XIV. He lived from 1624 to 1709. Napoleon

Bonaparte established the cemetery with the declaration, 'Every citizen has the right to be buried regardless of race or religion.'"

"And he isn't even buried here," Linda said.

"You'll have to do with Edith Piaf, Oscar Wilde, Frédéric Chopin, Marcel Proust and Honoré de Balzac."

"And Jim Morrison."

"Where's the grave of your famous rock star?"

"How should I know? It's my first visit, but there must be someone to ask." As soon as she said it, a sexton came out of a small lodge on the right.

"Are you looking for the grave of Jim Morrison?" he asked.

"Is it that obvious?" Lex said.

"Yes and no. You, monsieur, look like an Edith Piaf kind of man, but you, madame, look like a groupie," he said as he scanned Linda from top to bottom. "Don't be offended, mademoiselle; I meant it as a compliment."

Lex looked at Linda, ready to translate, but her smile told him she understood.

"Are there any signs we can follow?" Lex asked.

"I'm afraid not. It's a public cemetery, not a tourist attraction."

"Perhaps you can point us in the right direction?" Lex said.

"I can do better." The sexton brought out a piece of paper from behind his back. It showed a primitive map of the cemetery with the famous graves marked.

"Jim Morrison's grave is in Division 6," he said and pointed with a nicotine-stained finger.

"How much?"

"Ten francs, monsieur."

That's a bit steep, Lex thought, but he supposed that everyone needed to make a living, even if was on the back of the dead. Lex handed him a ten franc note, and Linda took the piece of paper.

"Lead the way, my beautiful groupie."

While they walked along the narrow lanes and avenues, Linda told Lex about Jim Morrison and his rock group.

"I had a chance to see him perform in Amsterdam in 1968. I'd just turned eighteen when I saw the Doors in concert. A band called Jefferson Airplane kicked off the evening, and at the end of their show, Jim Morrison suddenly appeared from behind the stage. He was visibly drunk or stoned and danced like a madman. He tried to take the microphone from the singer Grace Slick, who pushed him away. Someone helped him off the stage, which was the last we saw of him. I later learned he ended up in hospital."

"No wonder he died young," Lex said. "His bandmates must have been furious."

"They seemed surprisingly relaxed about it and asked us if we minded a concert without Jim Morrison. Hardly the real thing, although their keyboardist, Ray Manzarek, did a decent job of the singing."

"At least you attended the gig." They strolled in silence along the cobblestone paved lanes with low trees cutting through a mixture of densely packed gravestones, crypts and small mausoleums—many elaborately decorated. They met no one, and the place was, in its tranquillity, an extraordinary sanctuary in the city that never sleeps. *But don't let me wake up here at midnight*, Lex thought.

"I'm sure it's here," Linda said, studying the map.

Lex approached an enclosure and spotted a rectangular concrete frame surrounding dark soil with a few withered flowers and plants. It looked more like an abandoned flowerbed than a grave. To say it appeared shabby and neglected was an understatement. It wasn't helped much by a small, almost pathetic headstone with 'Douglas Morrison, James' and '1943-1971' handwritten on it. Lex called Linda over.

"Not what I expected for a famous rock star," Lex remarked.

"Probably what he wanted."

"Still makes me feel sad for the guy. If I die in the tub tonight, I hope you'll make a little more effort with my grave than his girlfriend did."

"Why so morbid?" Linda said with a hollow laugh.

"Beats me," Lex said as he scanned the crammed graves and tombstones.

"I doubt this will lift your spirits, but Jim Morrison's girlfriend died of an overdose in America about a year ago."

"What is this? A Greek tragedy?"

It started to rain again, and they sought cover under a tree. Linda studied the map. "Chopin's grave is right over there," she said. Lex gazed in the direction she pointed, and out of the corner of his eye, he caught the top of a black fedora before it disappeared behind a mausoleum. His mind could have been playing tricks on him. "Just because you're paranoid doesn't mean no one is following you," he whispered.

"Are you talking to yourself or me?" Linda asked.

As she didn't know about the incident at the café, Lex felt no immediate desire to enlighten her, but it didn't prevent him from speculating. What if Father Blanchet and Killian Lamarre shared their mutual interest as part of the same paedophile ring? What if the priest kept the entrepreneur in the loop? Perhaps Killian Lamarre had arranged a nice little beating to warn him against taking an interest. Maybe, after Lamarre was informed about his chance rendezvous with the priest at Le Consulat yesterday afternoon, he'd put a tail on them. With unlimited resources at his disposal, Lex sensed that intimidation and extortion were second nature to Lamarre. Perhaps not a healthy idea to 'interview' Killian Lamarre in his remote residence without an entourage. It struck Lex that he'd mentioned the possibility of being accompanied by a photographer and that Jean-François Diagne would look great with a camera around his neck. Lex decided to give him a call later.

A warm hand on his neck brought him back to the present.

"You seem more preoccupied today than usual, Lex," Linda said. "Is anything the matter?"

"I'm sorry. That damn abuse thing is constantly on my mind. Did I tell you I met Father Blanchet yesterday?"

"Only twice, but let's not talk about it right now."

"If you wish."

"Let's enjoy the moment together in this special place. Right here, and right now. I hope you feel the same way."

"I do, baby, but I'm easily distracted. You must be patient; I'm only a man."

"Although I pity you, I wouldn't have it any other way," she said with a disarming smile. The rain had stopped, so Lex suggested they let Jim Morrison rest in peace and check in on Frédéric Chopin, Oscar Wilde, and Edith Piaf.

LEX LIFTED the receiver and dialled the number Jean-François Diagne gave him for the Commissariat central. After being transferred a couple of times, he learned the brigadier wasn't in. Lex left a message for him to return the call.

Half an hour later, he did, and Lex told him about the planned interview with Killian Lamarre, his accidental encounter with Father Blanchet, and the incident with the fedora man at the Cimetière du Père-Lachaise.

"I think Killian Lamarre may be behind it," Lex said.

"It's probably true, but I don't see what I can do to help."

"I'm having second thoughts about going alone to see Killian Lamarre, and I'd like to bring you along as the photographer."

"You are kidding me. I know as much about photography as I know about giving birth. And, as you can imagine, that doesn't amount to much."

"You just have to pretend."

"But I don't have a camera."

"I do."

"What if I told you I'm on duty on Saturday."

"Are you?"

"No, but…."

"It's a couple of hours on Saturday afternoon," Lex interrupted. "You'll be doing me a great favour. Don't you want to break up the paedophile ring?"

"Hold it, Lex. It's all speculation."

"Perhaps, but the whole affair is riddled with hints, and I don't like it."

"I'm not a great fan of this undercover business. If, as you claim, Killian Lamarre is the puppeteer, he knows who you are, so why pretend to be someone else?"

"I doubt his highness would grant me an audience if I told him I was a private detective."

"But if what you're telling me is true, he already knows your real motive."

"That's why I'd like you to come along—if it gets nasty."

"I still struggle to see what good a meeting will do?"

"I'd like to check him out and perhaps rattle his cage." The line went silent.

"Are you there, Jean-François?"

"Still here."

"So, what's your decision?"

"Okay, I'll come with you, but don't make me regret it."

"You're a star. Can you come to Rue Norvins at two? That'll allow me to show you which buttons to press before driving to Rueil Malmaison. And one more thing."

"What's that?"

"Remember to dress like a photographer," Lex said.

"Don't push your luck," Jean-François killed the call.

33

THE BEDROOM lay in darkness, and the usual dread Lex felt with a new day on the horizon was immediately challenged by Linda's cheerful humming from the kitchen. She had plenty to be upbeat about with the afternoon's photoshoot. He got out of bed, opened the shutters, and squinted in the low sunlight that made the Sacré Coeur dome, with a cloudless azure blue sky as a background, shine with a sacred gleam.

He planned to spend the day in the office creating an advert for his services, now that he'd finally received his licence, then placing it in the local Montmartre paper and *Le Figaro*. With the prospect of Linda's career taking flight, it was time for him to follow suit and get his one-man-band detective bureau formally established.

Linda entered the bedroom with a tray of fresh coffee, juice and a toasted baguette with butter and brie.

"Room service, monsieur," she said and lowered the tray onto the bed. As she bent over, he admired her bosom, supported by a white lace negligée. He was happy to report it was of the see-through kind.

"That looks appetising, baby," he said with a lustful grin, "and so does the breakfast."

"Would you like me as a starter or as dessert?" She flung herself down on the bed between him and the tray.

"You make my life so sweet, so let's make it as dessert," he said, not to spoil the platitudinous exchange.

"It's your choice. To judge from the swelling in your boxer shorts, I doubt you'll linger over your baguette this morning."

"I'll pour the coffee," he offered, slightly embarrassed, as his pulse raced in anticipation of this attractive woman, once again, sharing her beautiful body with him.

"Would you mind if my hair was shoulder-length or shorter?"

"I love your long hair, so don't do it for my sake."

"The stylist at *Vogue* may have other ideas."

"A sin to cut it if you want my opinion."

"It's no use looking like a flower power child if the magazine wants something more trendy. Anyhow, it's out of my hands, and I'd go a long way to get this gig. It means a lot to me. But I do appreciate you like me the way I am."

"I can't get enough of you, baby, and I doubt *Vogue* can do much to make me love you less."

To change the subject, Lex told her he was considering buying a TV.

"Don't do it for my sake," she said, echoing his response to the discussion on changing her hairstyle. "I would prefer a record player or a radio."

"Luckily, it's your birthday soon," Lex said as he rolled off the bed. "Finished?" She nodded, and he carried the tray to the kitchen. He was ready for the dessert.

IT TOOK Lex a couple of hours in the office to place an advert in *Le Parisien* and *Le Figaro*. Before Linda left for *Vogue*, she told him not to expect her for dinner and that he was free to make whatever arrangements he wanted. Lex did his best to sound casual as he asked about her plans. She did her best to stay patient, informing him she planned to enjoy the city. Lex wanted to tell her that he preferred to know her whereabouts at all times because of the potential threats, but he knew she would brush it off and say he was using it as an excuse to be in control.

After Linda left, he called his uncle's office. Luckily Jules was in with no plans for the evening. Lex invited him to have dinner in a small restaurant in the Marais. His parents had taken him to the place on a visit to Paris in the mid-sixties, and it didn't surprise Lex that they'd also taken Jules.

Lex ate lunch at home while he turned a few pages of the second-hand copy of *Maigret in Montmartre* he'd begun a few days ago. The couple of glasses of red wine he drank with the sandwich made him sleepy, so he crawled onto the couch for an afternoon nap.

Lex didn't know how long he had been sleeping before the phone in the office woke him. He rolled off the couch and stumbled through the hallway into the office as if he was punch-drunk. He cleared his throat and answered, "Private detective Lex Spijker at your service."

"Did you say Len Spider? I'm trying to reach the journalist Jan Blokker."

"I hear you," Lex said, baffled, "but you've dialled the wrong number."

Someone, probably Killian Lamarre, had put two and two together and now shared the sum with him. Another day, another warning. Tomorrow's interview at Lamarre's private residence should be interesting, and Lex was happy he'd persuaded Jean-François Diagne to join him for the ride.

LEX WALKED to the restaurant in the Marais, and as he had underestimated the distance, he arrived ten minutes late. He opened the door to the restaurant and spotted Jules seated on the left. The square room, with half of the eight tables occupied, was, as far as he recalled, unchanged.

"However much it pleases me that you've begun to dress like a real Parisian, I'm sorry to see you've also adopted the habit of being late," he said. As always, Jules was flawlessly dressed in an azure jacket over a white shirt with a red silk tie.

"*Mon excuse,*" Lex said as he tipped his Panama hat to show off the cufflinks Jules gave him for his birthday.

"How's the shirt?"

"Like a dream," Lex said as he pretended to straighten his tie.

"Classy pinstripe jacket. Is that also from Rue Marbeuf?"

"Indeed." Lex hung the Panama on a nearby hat stand, pulled out a chair, and sat down.

The waiter approached from behind a counter at the back. He held a black tablet with the menu written in chalk. He explained that the *terrine de lapin* and the Provencal braised lamb shanks with green lentils were their specialities. They followed his recommendations. Lex nervously asked for the wine list in the knowledge that his uncle, the connoisseur and wine snob, was keeping a watchful eye on him. To Lex's relief, *le patron* recommended a Bourgueil 1970 for the starter and a Crozes-Hermitage 1965 for the main course. Jules nodded enthusiastically.

Apart from praising the wine and the food, Jules didn't say much while they ate.

"You're unusually quiet tonight," Lex remarked after another attempt to engage him in conversation.

"Unfortunately, Gigi's mother's condition took a turn for the worse this afternoon. I'm afraid she's not long for this world."

"I'm sorry to hear it, and maybe I shouldn't have dragged you out this evening?"

"Nonsense. I'm happy you called, and, as always, I enjoy your company. I needed something to take my mind off things."

"And if Gigi calls while you're here with me?"

"What can I do? I may be Jewish, but I'm not a rabbi or Jesus," he said with a bashful smile. "Ami is at home, and she has the number of the restaurant."

"You don't mind her being alone at home in the evening?"

"I can hear you're not a father. She's thirteen and independent for her age. And she's not alone. Angeline Pernet is sleeping over."

"I hate to ask you this, but now that you mention Angeline, can I talk to her?"

"Why? I don't see what good it will do?"

Lex explained the latest development in the 'investigation' and that it might be advantageous for Jean-François Diagne to get a first-hand impression of the girl.

"Has it become official police business?"

"Not yet, but my police contact is taking a keen interest," Lex said, knowing it was an exaggeration.

"In that case, it might be a good idea, and I'll see what I can arrange. Will Sunday afternoon work?"

"That's ideal. I'm interviewing Killian Lamarre tomorrow."

"In what sense do you mean interview?"

"In the journalistic one, as a correspondent from a Dutch newspaper. Brigadier Diagne will join me as my photographer."

"I trust your judgement, Lex, but I don't think it will achieve much."

He told Jules about the incident at the Père-Lachaise.

"And you think Killian Lamarre is behind it?"

"Father Blanchet has kept him informed all along, and as far as I can judge, Killian Lamarre doesn't suffer fools gladly. Given his status and resources, he'll do anything to prevent even the faintest rumours from surfacing that can damage his reputation. With his, let's say, alternative lifestyle, I guess he spends a few bob on lawyers and private investigators to suppress and intimidate anyone challenging his lifestyle."

The waiter interrupted to remove their plates and ask if they wanted dessert and coffee. Lex had a sweet tooth but followed suit when Jules settled for a double espresso.

"By the way, any news about your subletting client on Avenue Foch?" Lex asked.

"To be honest, I've been too busy to set anything in motion. I'll let you know."

"Okay."

The meal ended on a happy note when Jules told a joke about the Rebbe miracle stories.

"Three Jews are bragging about their teachers' miraculous abilities. The first Jew tells his friend that his rebbe is so powerful that once when he was out walking, a lake stood in his path. He waved his handkerchief, and the lake was now on the right and on the left, but not in the middle. To this, the second Jew retorted, 'That's nothing. My rebbe is even more powerful. He was out walking once, and there was a huge mountain in his path. He waved his handkerchief, and there was the mountain on the right and the left, but no mountain in the middle.' 'Ha! That's nothing,' said the third Jew. 'My rebbe is the most powerful. He was walking once on Shabbos when it's forbidden to handle money. In his path was a wallet crammed full of cash. He waved his handkerchief, and it was Shabbos on the right, Shabbos on the left, but not Shabbos in the middle.'"

LEX RETURNED to Rue Norvins at midnight. Quietly he let himself in so as not to wake Linda, took his shoes off in the hallway, and slid across the wooden floor towards the bedroom. His effort to make as little noise as possible was rewarded with a splinter in his right big toe, and he bit his knuckles to choke back a cry of pain. He pushed the door open and tiptoed hurriedly through the bedroom to the bathroom, closed the door and turned on the light. Seated on the toilet, he pulled off his sock to see the damage. Luckily, the splinter had aspired to be a log, and he removed it quickly with the help of his fingernails. He pulled off his other sock, stood, lifted the toilet seat, pissed, washed his hands, brushed his teeth, splashed cold water onto his face, dried himself and undressed.

Lex switched the light off, opened the door slowly, crossed the floor to the bed, and slid between the sheets. He reached out, expecting his hand to connect with some part of Linda's warm body, but all it touched was an empty duvet. He sat up and switched on the bedside lamp—no Linda.

Should he be worried? Perhaps not, but she had left almost twelve hours ago. Her photoshoot was at two, and afterwards, she might have spent the afternoon and some of the evening enjoying what Paris offered. He wasn't proud to admit it, but his worries about what had happened to her included visions of her having the time of her life with some fancy and stuck-up creative *Vogue* director. It made his blood boil, and Lex hated him already. His immediate notion was to pour himself a generous whisky, and wait up for her return, so he could 'interrogate' her.

What's the matter with you, Lex? he thought. *Why does she ignite such jealousy in you?* A feeling he would have denied existed in him before she arrived less than two weeks ago. She wasn't especially flirtatious and did her best to show she wanted to be with him. *Do yourself a favour*, he told himself, *turn off the light and go to sleep.* He managed the first part to perfection, but sleep was somehow more difficult to come by. He drifted in and out, and at some stage, he sensed Linda sliding into bed beside him. He felt her hand on his abdomen but pretended to be asleep. He wanted to punish her for staying out half the night without him.

34

LEX STROLLED through the neighbourhood to clear his head. Montmartre in the early morning, before the daily influx of tourists, is like an abandoned movie set, frozen in time. Had Henri de Toulouse-Lautrec passed him in the street on his child-sized legs and adult-sized torso, the post-impressionist painter would have looked less out of place than Lex.

He bought a newspaper and headed for a café on Place du Tertre. As he entered, two men in working clothes, seated at the *comptoir*, turned their heads, and he nodded politely. They ignored him and returned to their coffee and hard-boiled eggs. Lex took a seat near the window, and one of the men shouted, "*Gaston, un client!*" Lex heard footsteps ascending the stairs from the basement, and a bald head with bushy eyebrows appeared, followed by the rest of a stout middle-aged man.

"Pardon, monsieur, but my useless son is late again, so I have to take care of all the preparations before the Saturday rush. And the toilets don't clean themselves, you know," he said, panting. Lex presented a sympathetic face. "What will it be?"

"Can I have a *café au lait*?" The order didn't do anything for his sad face, and unless Lex told him he'd won the lottery, he doubted anything would.

He bought Lex the coffee and descended the stairs to the basement with heavy feet. The coffee was hot but milkier than Lex preferred. He lit a cigarette and flipped through the paper without paying attention. His mind was preoccupied with the alleged deceit around him—the deception of his lover, Father Blanchet, Killian Lamarre—and not least, of himself. Lex had no proof that Linda had cheated on him, that Father Blanchet had abused Angeline Pernet, or that Killian Lamarre was involved. He was acting purely on suspicion and gossip. *Time to wake up and smell the roses*, Lex thought. As for Linda, he decided to tell her about his feelings of jealousy and inadequacy.

While he'd been in his own little world, the two workmen had left, and a young man, who must be the son the owner had been bitching about previously, now stood behind the counter. Lex finished his cigarette and coffee, then paid up, and left the café with urgency in his step, eager to return home.

WITH HIS long legs stuffed under the small car's dashboard and his knees near his chest, Jean-François looked far from comfortable.

"Are you alright there?" Lex asked, concerned. To see the policeman cramped up in the passenger seat did little to ease his conscience for dragging him along to a dubious and phoney photo assignment on his day off.

"Don't worry about me. I can blame you for many things, but I doubt my height is one of them. Apart from that, I'm used to it—my police car is not much bigger."

They passed La Défense with its chrome and glass skyscrapers standing shoulder to shoulder.

"For a guy from Amsterdam, it's an incredible sight," Lex commented. "So that's what money looks like these days?"

"As far as I know, it's the largest purpose-built business district in Europe, and the way the area is booming, it's hard to believe that the economic crisis halted nearly all construction a couple of years ago."

"Does Killian Lamarre have offices there?"

"I have no idea, but why don't you ask him in half an hour?"

Perhaps because Lex was meeting the tycoon undercover, he felt butterflies flapping their wings. He needed a cigarette to calm his nerves, but stopped himself from lighting up in time to honour his promise not to smoke in the car.

"I wish you'd found me a proper camera. This one makes me look like a bloody day tripper."

"I doubt you'll get a chance to take his portrait, as he'll have kicked us out before we get to that part."

"You don't listen, Lex; it's not what I said."

"What are you saying?"

"Never mind, just get us there."

Ten minutes later, they turned into a hamlet called Hameau de la Jonchere, stopping by a barrier across the entrance. A man in uniform came out from a small porter's lodge and approached the car. Lex rolled down the side window.

"We're here to see Killian Lamarre by appointment," he roared. "Journalist Jan Blokker and his photographer." The guard nodded, headed for the barrier, and leaned on the end. It swung open, and Lex drove through the gate into the promised land of large mansions hidden behind high fences to keep the ugly world at a safe distance.

"The rich are well prepared for the next revolution."

"I didn't know you were a socialist," Jean-François said, keeping a straight face.

A hundred metres along the narrow road with well-groomed trees on both sides, a sign told Lex to turn right to get to Avenue Saunte-Bathilde. As he followed the curve, they saw a modernistic building leaning against a hill. It was a mix of glass, concrete, bricks and dark wood distributed in perfect harmony on three levels with a few balconies thrown in.

"Nice clean style," Lex said as he hit the brakes.

"It's called Bauhaus," Jean-François informed him as he lifted the Canon camera from his lap to his eye and clicked.

"The emphasis is on the form and the materials, and every element is intended to serve a purpose," he added.

"Thanks for the lecture, professor. No disrespect, but how does a policeman know so much about architecture?"

"It's a long story, which I might tell you one day."

Lex put the car into gear and rolled up the driveway. "Killian Lamarre lives dangerously leaving his gate open."

"Perhaps, but the surveillance cameras will keep him well informed about anyone unable to resist the temptation to enter uninvited."

An Aston Martin DB5 was parked in front of one of two garage doors. "Hope the car doesn't come with a licence to kill," Lex said.

"Double-o-seven?"

"Correct, and if he says 'my name is Lamarre, Killian Lamarre', I'll kill him."

Lex parked the car in front of the other garage door. Next to the British luxury grand tourer, the Renault 5 seemed to be trespassing—apart from the concept of four tyres and an engine, the two cars didn't have much in common.

Side by side, if not shoulder to shoulder, considering Jean-François's height, they walked up the garden path. It was paved with white marble tiles and ended with four steps that took them onto a vast terrace paved in the same stone. They headed towards the wooden front door surrounded by a glass facade with a timber frame. Lex was about to ring the bell when the door opened.

A middle-aged man with grey shoulder-length hair, a receding hairline, and a clean-shaved, tanned face appeared in the doorway. Below a significant snout, an ironic smile played on his thin lips. From several press clippings, and the photo he'd taken, Lex knew the man was Killian Lamarre, but the fact that he was wearing a grey jogging suit confused Lex's perception of him as a dandy. *Maybe he has one of those days when the rich and famous go out of their way to show that you don't need to go out of your way when you're rich and famous*, Lex thought. Did Lamarre want to be photographed in that attire? Or perhaps he already knew there would be no photo and no article?

"Mr Lamarre, I presume?" Lex said with a slight hesitation.

"And you must be Mr Blokker?" He had warm eyes and a crafty smile.

"Call me Jan," Lex said and extended a hand. Lamarre's handshake was limp and his palm moist. *Perhaps I'm not the only one feeling nervous*, Lex thought.

"This is my photographer, Philippe." Jean-François extended a hand, but Killian Lamarre ignored it.

"We don't need a photographer. If you leave an address, I'll tell my PR department to send you a few portraits."

"The article will be more authentic if we take photos in situ," Lex protested.

"I said no photos. We won't need you today, Philippe, but you're welcome to wait in the kitchen with my bodyguard if you so wish." He stepped aside and pointed into the house. Lex caught the eye of Jean-François, who did a bit of eye-rolling as he shrugged and said, "You'll know where to find me if you change your mind." He entered through the door, and his afro nearly grazed the header.

With Jean-Francois gone to keep an eye on the tycoon's bodyguard, if not the other way round, Killian Lamarre suggested that they conduct the interview on the terrace as it was a pleasant spring afternoon. Under a first floor balcony was a chrome and glass coffee table surrounded by a couple of white sofas. They sat down, and Lamarre asked what Lex wanted to drink. He asked for a beer.

"Dimitri, bring us a couple of beers and some peanuts," he shouted through the open door. There was no reply, and it seemed he didn't expect one. Lex took a notepad from the side pocket of his jacket and an Olympus voice recorder from another. "Do you mind if I …?"

"I'd prefer not to be recorded—your notes will have to do," Lamarre insisted. Lex sensed he was used to getting it his own way without any fuss.

"You don't make it easy for me, Mr Lamarre." Lex heard footsteps from behind and saw an arm with a dark jacket sleeve put a tray on the table. He looked up to make eye contact with the owner. Lex thought it could be the man he'd seen at the Père Lachaise café a couple of days ago and who'd warned him against letting Linda stray more than necessary. Without the fedora and sunglasses, Lex wasn't sure.

"Thank you, Dimitri; you can leave it there." The man bowed and made himself scarce before Lex managed to get a decent look at him.

"Tell me about your paper."

"The *NRC Handelsblad* was published for the first time in 1970 after a merger between two other newspapers. It's the major business newspaper in Holland and Belgium."

"What's the circulation?"

"It's around half a million copies," Lex said without knowing. He took a sip of beer to disguise the discomfort of making it up.

"I'm impressed. Who's your editor-in-chief?"

"He's called André Spoor." At least he'd done that bit of research. "I doubt you would know him," Lex added, as he sensed Lamarre trying to catch him out. "I'm supposed to interview you, not the other way around, so do you ...."

"Steady on, young man. I think you owe it to me to say why I'm of interest to your paper."

"I told you over the phone."

"Tell me again."

Lex fished out a packet of cigarettes and a lighter from an inner pocket.

"Would you mind not polluting the fresh air?"

"You don't like smokers?"

"That's not it, but I gave it up about five years ago, and I now do my best to keep my home a smoke-free zone. Not least for my girls."

"How many children do you have, Mr Lamarre?"

"A son from my first marriage and two daughters from my second." Lex detected pride in his voice as he said it.

"And your company Sanna Invest is named after your daughters."

"I'm surprised you know that."

"Isn't it common knowledge?"

"I don't know, but you'll, in all likelihood, use it in your article."

"If you don't object?"

"After that, no more about my family."

"Okay," Lex said and sipped his beer.

"You were about to tell me why I'm of interest to your readers."

"Right! As a consequence of coming out of recession and the oil crisis, the *NRC* will run a series on major business tycoons within the European Common Market and what effect the crisis has had on their business."

"As you can see, I've landed on my feet," he said.

"What is it that you do, Mr Lamarre?"

"How long have you got?"

"If you were to describe it in a few sentences?"

"I invest. If there's a project or business venture I find promising, I throw money at it. Obviously, with a healthy commission."

"But you also give money to projects without expecting anything in return."

"Is that a question? You sound like you're thinking of something specific."

"You recently funded a major restoration of the grand pipe organ of the Sacré-Cœur."

"How do you know about that?" It's not common knowledge, but yes, I'm the benefactor."

"Does the name Father Blanchet ring a bell?"

"Should it? I'm not a religious man."

"That's what the Holy Father told me, but I know you both sat on the church's Restoration Committee."

"So what? I can't see the importance."

"Do you know that Father Blanchet is a child sex abuser?" Lex said, deciding to go all out.

"You've lost me there, Mr Blokker."

"There's a rumour placing you in a private sex club offering the clientele sex with young girls ."

"That's malicious gossip made up by envious people. I like beautiful young women, but I'd never play around with anyone underage. For Christ's sake, I'm the father of two teenage girls."

"There's also a rumour that Father Blanchet uses his position in the church to supply girls."

"Can you prove any of this?" he asked, and without waiting for an answer, he added, "and you can drop the bullshit. You may be Dutch, but you're not a journalist."

"I'm Jan Blokker from the *NRC Handelsblad.*"

"Please, don't insult my intelligence. You're on my patch, and if you think you can come here and make wild accusations, I have news for you, Mr Spijker."

"Is that a threat?"

"Not at all. It's a fact of life. Your life and the life of that cute little girlfriend of yours."

"She has nothing to do with it."

"Although she's a bit old for me, she can give me a rub-down anytime," he said, smacking his lips. "That's if she's not too busy elsewhere?"

"What's that supposed to mean?"

"There's a rumour you're not the only man giving it to her."

Lex felt his face redden and his fingers tightened around the beer glass.

"You look uncomfortable, Mr Spijker. Did I hit a nerve?"

"I have no idea what you're talking about."

"Did you know your fiancée was dining with a man last night? Although the couple left arm in arm, I'm sure it's all very innocent."

"Have you been spying on her? On us?" Lex said as he got up. His knee struck the table and knocked over the beer glass. He watched it roll over the edge and smash against the tiles.

"What are you going to do? Beat me up? I'd advise you not to go down that route. You may have your phoney photographer to back you up, but I'm afraid you're outnumbered."

Lex heard someone approaching from behind and spun round, stepping on the broken glass.

"Dimitri, will you escort the gentleman and his friend to their car before they get hurt. Although they're no longer welcome, we don't want them to come to any harm, do we now?" Killian Lamarre said, his voice thick with contempt.

Jean-François came out of the house with the bodyguard on his tail. Lex didn't pay much attention to the man, he felt he'd seen his ugly bald head before, but wouldn't bet on it. Like the guy who attacked him the previous Sunday, he belonged to the stereotype of husky individuals in cheap suits that seem in their element at a nightclub entrance.

"Are you alright, Jan?" Jean-François asked.

"I'm fine, Philippe, but I guess we're about to leave."

"Excuse me for not getting up, but I don't intend to waste any more energy on you, Mr Spijker."

"I'm warning you to leave my fiancée and me alone."

"And I'm warning you to stay out of my affairs."

With Dimitri as a shadow, they retreated down the white marble steps and the garden path. Halfway down, he stopped and watched them as they reached the car.

"Let me drive while you calm down," Jean-François said and swung the door open to the driver's seat. Lex walked around the car, opened the door, and slid into the passenger seat. Jean-François pushed the seat way back to make room for his legs, then reversed adeptly out of the driveway. Neither of them talked as they headed towards Paris.

35

LINDA'S SCREAM catapulted Lex out of bed faster than a bat out of hell. He rushed through the hallway and into the kitchen. She was sitting on the kitchen table, her legs and feet dangling in terror.

"What happened, baby?"

"A rat ran over my feet," she stuttered.

"You gave me a shock. I assumed you were in serious distress."

"I am. I hate rats, and it's as big as a cat." Lex put his hands under her arms to help her down, but she resisted.

"You must guarantee it's gone." He opened the cupboard under the kitchen sink to humour her and hoped it wouldn't jump out at him.

"You see, it's gone."

"I can still smell it."

"Nonsense. All I can smell is fresh coffee and croissants."

"I wanted to surprise you with Sunday breakfast in bed. Instead, a big, fat rat surprised me."

"What's the occasion?" Lex asked and helped her down.

"It's Sunday, the sun is up, and life is generous."

"And I love you, and you love me," Lex supplied.

"That as well. And I wanted to buy the newspaper," Linda said. She pointed towards the dining table.

"Why? Do we have fish today?"

"If you flick through it, I'm sure you'll spot my sudden interest in the news."

The article wasn't hard to find. On page nine, a tantalising Linda posed in a black and white photo with the Eiffel Tower as a backdrop and under it was the heading: *From prison to pomp and pride.* The sub-heading read: *Linda Vogel has thrown off the shackles to start a new life as a Vogue model.*

"Wow, what a surprise—a full page in *Le Figaro.*" Lex noticed the byline read 'Joseph de la Fontaine.'

"Jos insisted on writing an article about me for the Sunday edition. He interviewed me on Friday evening over dinner, and I wanted to surprise you," she said, beaming with pride and happiness. Lex felt relieved that Killian Lamarre's spy had seen her dining with Jean-François' boyfriend. *No threat there,* he thought.

"Aren't you proud of me?" she asked, when he didn't respond.

"I am, but you don't need an article in the newspaper to make me proud of you."

"I'm aware of that, but it won't hurt. What will it take for you to share my joy with less restraint?"

"I doubt it's a sound idea to advertise your whereabouts with an article in the biggest ...." Lex hesitated, realising that the advert for his own services was also in the Sunday edition. He flipped to the *publicité* section and immediately spotted the advert. He pointed to it.

"If I'd known there was an article about you in the Sunday edition, I would have waited to place the advert for my services."

"I might say the same," she said. "Anyhow, why so paranoid? What are the chances that anyone would make the connection?"

"Allard Kuipers will, if he sees it," Lex pointed out.

"Perhaps, but he's in a Dutch prison, and I know from experience that their library doesn't subscribe to *Le Figaro*."

"The gang is, or was, dealing in trafficking. Don't you think they have contacts in Paris and France? Criminals also read newspapers, you know."

"Right now, I don't give a damn about your concerns. I'll enjoy my fifteen minutes of fame, and you can join me or fuck off." Linda slammed her palm on the kitchen table.

The exchange offered another déjà vu moment, and right there, Lex asked himself why he was bothering to discuss any concerns with her. It only angered her and created a void between them. He was the private detective, and it was his priority to keep them both away from harmful situations. And although Linda wasn't making it easy, Lex had to accept her *laissez-faire* attitude as part of her DNA. She was a spirited 24-year-old woman who wanted to get the most out of a second chance. If he didn't like the ride, he could, as she put it, fuck off. More than anything, Lex wanted to rebuild his life with her in their magnificent new city. Instead of laying his concerns on her, he needed someone to watch their backs, and Lex knew the right man for the job. A guy called Alwin Smit, or Big Al, to his friends.

In an hour of need, a friend had referred Lex to him. He recalled the friend saying that Alwin Smit was as big as a house, as strong as an ox, and as bright as Muhammed Ali. Lex soon discovered that the description of the former boxing champion was accurate. He had also learned that the gentle giant suffered from bibliophilism, and that his library contained enough first editions to make collectors of rare books pay attention. He lived in Amsterdam, and Lex hoped to convince him that he needed a paid holiday in Paris. Lex decided to give him a call later.

"Let's have breakfast, and I'll translate the article for you," Lex said, hoping to relieve the tension.

"Would you? I can spell my way through, but it's a treat and a new experience if you could read to me—especially something about myself."

WITH A late breakfast, they skipped lunch. Linda wanted a walk in Parc Monceau, but Lex had an appointment with Jean-François at three in his uncle's apartment to talk to Angeline Pernet. And before going, he wanted to get hold of Big Al, so Linda decided to do homework for her next French lesson instead.

Lex closed the door to the office, sat at the desk, and looked up Big Al's phone number in his address book. He dialled, and after a couple of rings, he heard Alwin Smit's familiar high-pitched voice.

"The master of the house," he said, followed by the distinctive chuckle Lex knew so well and which had endeared him to the big man from the first time they'd met.

"It's your old friend Lex."

"Of all the people to disturb me on a sacred Sunday afternoon, what are the odds?"

"Luckily, you were in."

"Some men wash their cars on Sunday afternoon, and some dust their library," he said with another chuckle.

"How are you?"

"I keep my feet on the ground and my head above water. How about yourself?"

"I'm in Paris."

"Have you won the lottery?" he said. "No offence, but as far as I can remember, you didn't have enough for a tram ticket last time I saw you."

"I've lived here since March. You remember Lure?"

"Of course. A neat little operation. Pity you killed the big guy."

"Not my finest hour."

"It was you or him. Anyway, we saved the girl. I wonder what happened to her?"

"She's now called Linda and has lived here with me for the last couple of weeks."

"So, in the end, you won your precious first prize."

"Was it that obvious?"

"No shit, Sherlock."

"Uh-huh."

"Do you still work as a private detective?"

"That's why I call you Watson."

"Please don't."

"What?"

"Call me Watson."

"How about a trip to Paris, all expenses paid?"

"It depends, but feel free to convince me."

Lex told him about the investigation into the alleged sexual abuse, the threats from the French tycoon , and Linda still being in possession of nearly all the money she stole from the gang.

"Stupid move, although I guess they'll have a hard time tracking her down."

"Yes, until this morning when she surprised me with an article about herself in the newspaper."

"Not the best way to keep a low profile."

"That's what I told her, but she just gets upset with me."

"It's too late now, anyway."

"Indeed, and that's why I would like to use your services as soon as possible. That's if you are available?"

"I might be. As it happens, I just finished a job for Tom de Wit a couple of days ago."

"Good old Tom. I haven't spoken to him in ages. How is he?"

"As far as I know, he's fine. He plans to retire by the end of the year, which is making a few people in his milieu nervous. Occasionally he needs my help to calm them down, if you take my drift."

"And you could calm me down with a visit to Paris."

"What do you want me to do?"

"First of all, I'd like to show Killian Lamarre and his footmen, by your presence, that we won't be intimidated. Secondly, I predict it might soon get ugly. Thirdly, it would surprise me if we don't soon get a confrontation regarding the stolen money. So ..."

"You've convinced me."

"Would you like me to book a train ticket?"

"I'll drive, but get me a room at a hotel near your place."

"Consider it done. When can you be here?"

"Will Tuesday afternoon do?"

"Perfect."

"Give me your address."

IT SURPRISED Lex to see Jean-François in his uniform, and it must have shown on his face.

"What's the matter? You must be used to seeing a black policeman by now?"

"It's not that," Lex protested, "but I assumed you wanted to keep your involvement undercover?"

"After the humiliation yesterday, there's no more of that on my part. I also think it's time to make it official police business."

"Can you do that? Won't you get into trouble?"

"I'll take my chance. Anyhow, let's first talk to Angeline Pernet."

They entered the arcade and headed for number 28. Lex pressed the buzzer, and the concierge let them in.

"Monsieur Brigadier," said a young man, sitting behind a small counter. Lex recognised him from two weeks ago. He jumped to his feet, and it looked as if he was about to salute.

"We're here to visit Jules Lévy."

"Third floor," he said as he stood to attention.

He didn't seem to recognise Lex, and he wasn't surprised. On their first visit, Linda was the one who'd sucked up all his attention.

As they climbed the stairs, Jean-François said, "How did you like Jos' article about Linda?"

"Most entertaining and amusing—he's a fine writer."

"Nice publicity, wouldn't you say?"

"Indeed, and Linda's over the moon. It will get her career as a model off to a flying start." As Jean-François didn't know about the stolen money, Lex couldn't tell him that advertising Linda's whereabouts might be risky. They reached the third floor.

"Beautiful Rococo design," the brigadier said as Lex knocked on the tall brown carved wooden double door. Within a few seconds, the door opened, and Jean-Luc appeared. "Nice to see you again, Alexander. My father is out but will be back any minute. I'm about to leave for the cinema with some friends." They stepped into the vast hallway. Lex introduced Jean-François to Jean-Luc.

"What's showing?" the policeman asked as he took off his kepi.

"Pardon, monsieur, but I don't understand."

"What movie?"

"It's the new Peter Sellers movie."

"Ah, the *Return of the Pink Panther*."

"You've seen it, monsieur?"

"Of course. I am a French policeman, after all. Hopefully not as incompetent as Inspector Clouseau."

"I guess you know why we're here," Lex said.

"To talk to my sister's friend."

"And do you know what about?" Jean-François added.

"I have a general idea, but I'm staying out of it," Jean-Luc said as he showed them into the living room.

"Better that way," Jean-François said.

"I'll get my sister."

They remained standing. Within a minute, Ami entered with her brother. She hugged Lex and offered Jean-François a hand. She wore a beautiful yellow polo dress with a red belt. *Perhaps the one she bought with Linda the other day*, Lex thought.

"Angeline hasn't arrived yet." She checked her wristwatch. "It's unlike her to be late."

"We'll give her another fifteen minutes," Lex said.

"Take a seat. Can I get you a drink?" Ami said.

"Please. Can I have a coke?" Lex asked.

"Me too," Jean François said.

"I'll say goodbye," Jean-Luc said.

"Enjoy the movie," Lex said, as his cousin nodded and left the room.

They sat down, and while waiting for the drinks, they heard the front door open and close. Jules rushed into the room, and they rose.

"Sorry I wasn't here to welcome you, but I had a showing," Jules said, holding up a folder. He was, as usual, impeccably dressed in a grey suit with a white shirt and a light blue silk tie.

"This is Brigadier Jean-François Diagne, and he is taking a keen interest in the case."

"I'm Jules Lévy, and I'm afraid my daughter started all this."

"She did right to talk about it," Jean-François assured him.

"I didn't expect my nephew to get the police involved. At least not at this stage."

"A twist of fate," Lex protested.

Ami entered, holding a tray with the refreshments.

"Hello, daughter," Jules said. "It delights me to see you taking good care of our guests."

"What will you have, papa?"

"I'll have a glass of white wine. There's a Puligny-Montrachet open in the fridge." It surprised Lex that his uncle didn't mention the year. Most people say there's a bottle of white wine open, but Lex realised that when it came to wine, his uncle was not only a geek, but also a snob.

Nursing their drinks, Jules asked about the 'investigation'. Lex told him about the unexpected encounter with Father Blanchet and their visit to Killian Lamarre's residence.

"It sounds like you are treading on a few toes and need to be careful," Jules said.

Lex contemplated informing him about his friend from Amsterdam, but the sight of Jean-François in uniform reminded him there was no need to complicate matters. "I just hope it doesn't endanger Angeline Pernet," Lex said as he looked at his watch. "I wonder where the girl is?"

"It wouldn't surprise me if she got cold feet. It's a big ask for a young girl to talk about being abused. And it doesn't help to be Catholic, believe you me," Jean-François said.

"Are you Catholic?" Jules asked, but before Jean-François could answer, the phone rang.

"Ami, can you take it in the office?" Jules shouted. "It's hopefully your friend." They heard her running along the corridor, the ringing stop, and Ami's blurred voice. Suddenly she was standing at the door to the living room. "It's mum."

"Excuse me," Jules said and rushed out. Lex heard the door close.

"My aunt is attending to her sick mother in Tel Aviv," Lex explained to Jean-François.

"I know. You told me that's why you're driving her car."

Lex heaved himself to his feet and walked to the window. He watched a group of middle-aged men as they played *pétanque* in the park across the street. *Plus ça change*, he thought. Come back next Sunday. Or in a year. Or in ten or a hundred years. Someone will still be throwing balls.

Lex spun around as he heard the office door open and Jules and his daughter talking. Jules entered the living room. He looked pale.

"Are you alright, Uncle?" Lex asked, concerned.

"My mother-in-law died about an hour ago."

They both offered their sincere condolences. Lex didn't act heartbroken, as he hardly knew the old lady.

"She had been ill for some time," Jules said, more to himself than anyone else. "I hope you don't mind, Brigadier Diagne, but I would like a word with my nephew in private." Lex followed his uncle into the office.

"The kids and I will join Gigi and the family in Tel Aviv for the funeral."

"Please give my love and condolences to Gigi."

"Will do, thanks. As you know, the burial should take place as soon as possible, and we'll have to observe a period of intense mourning with the family for seven days after the funeral, so we'll be away for at least ten days. I'm worried about the girl, and I'd appreciate it if you could keep me informed." Jules scribbled a number on a sealed envelope and handed it to Lex.

"What's this, Uncle?"

"A small retainer to make sure you're not out of funds."

"That's kind of you, but it's not necessary."

"Nonsense. It's one way I can show my support."

"Is there anything I can do while you're away?"

"That's sweet of you, Lex, but my excellent staff will take care of matters while I'm away. And Mariana will look after the apartment."

"Before you go, a client of mine gave me a couple of tickets for the European Cup Final at Parc des Princes on Wednesday. I was going to take my son, but obviously, that's not happening. Can I give you the tickets?"

"By all means. Thank you," Lex said, as he did his best, under the circumstances, to suppress his excitement. "We'll leave you in peace," Lex said as they rejoined the brigadier.

Jules, uncharacteristically, hugged Lex, shook Jean-François' hand, and they left him and the kids to their grief.

36

LEX RETURNED to Rue Norvins late in the afternoon.

"I'm home, baby," he shouted, waking Linda from her slumber on the couch.

"How did it go?" she asked drowsily.

"A dreadful afternoon. The girl didn't turn up, and Gigi called from Tel Aviv to say that her mother had died."

"So sorry to hear it. How are you?"

"I'm okay. I feel for the family, but I hardly knew the old lady. I could do with a pick me up."

"What do you have in mind?"

"My cousin mentioned watching the *Return of the Pink Panther*. How about a trip to the cinema?"

"With him?"

"Just you and me. We can find a cosy bistro somewhere for a snack after the movie."

"Sounds like fun. Count me in."

They caught an undubbed version of the movie in a cinema on the Champs-Élysées. They'd never watched a movie together, and Lex enjoyed both the film and being physically close to Linda for a couple of hours. That she every so often leaned over to kiss him and to put her beautiful, long fingers on his groin didn't hamper the overall experience. They behaved like teenagers on a first date.

Afterwards, Lex and Linda ate *steak-frites* and shared a bottle of Beaujolais at Café Weekend on Rue Washington. Linda talked about her upbringing in Diemen, a suburb of Amsterdam, and how she hated her parents' bourgeois lifestyle. She'd talked about it before, but never in such detail and never without bitterness. Tonight she spoke about it with level-headedness and a new self-belief. She spoke of her year in prison and how self-pity had made her cry herself to sleep most nights for the first couple of months. It took a visit from Lex's former secretary to change her outlook. The middle-aged Roos reminded her she was still young and that her time in prison would wipe her slate clean and give her a second chance. She also mentioned that Linda had the love and support of a man waiting for her in Paris.

Lex and Linda had such a happy, relaxed and intimate time together, that he scarcely looked over his shoulder to see if anyone was following them when they walked home arm in arm.

LEX WAS singing in the shower when Jean-François called. Linda took a message to call him back at the Commissariat central immediately. Lex cut his songbook short and, within fifteen minutes, returned the call.

"What's up, brigadier?"

"Angeline Pernet's father has reported her missing."

"Why am I not surprised?"

"Perhaps, because it was predictable."

"Allow me to think aloud," Lex said. "The poor girl goes to her Solemn Communion Sunday class at Sacré-Cœur. She's a bit too vocal about her appointment with a private detective and a police officer later in the day, so she's prevented from attending. How does that sound?"

"You couldn't make it up."

"So what happens now?"

"I am on my way to talk to her parents."

"Can I join you?"

"I'm not sure it's a good idea."

"Look, I feel responsible, and …."

"Alright, but you let me do the talking."

"Scouts honour. Will you pick me up?"

"No need. You can walk to the apartment in a couple of minutes—the address is Rue Chappe 23. Meet me there in thirty minutes."

"Aye aye, captain."

"It's brigadier."

While Linda made coffee, Lex told her about the disappearance of Angeline Pernet.

"You must be careful, Lex. These people have no shame and will not accept anyone or anything that prevents them from enjoying their perverted world."

"Don't worry; I've taken my precautions."

"Like what?" she asked.

"I called Big Al yesterday, and he arrives tomorrow."

"Nice of you to tell me."

"I didn't want to worry you."

"I wish you would stop treating me like a little girl."

"I try not to."

"Well, try harder."

"I hope you don't object to me calling him."

"Why should I? I can't say I know him, as I've only seen him once when heavily drugged. But if it weren't for him, I wouldn't be here with you."

"I apologise for not telling you yesterday, but we had such a wonderful evening. I'd like to explain my reason for inviting Big Al to Paris, but as I'm meeting Jean-François at the Pernet residence in fifteen minutes, I'll do it later. I guess we'll go and see Father Blanchet afterwards, so don't expect me home for a few hours."

"Don't worry about me; I'm a big girl." She pursed her beautiful mouth in a self-justified smirk.

"I love you too," Lex said and kissed her goodbye.

The rain came on as Lex walked down Rue Gabrielle, and as he crossed the street with too much pace in his stride, he slipped on the wet cobblestones. He landed on his back, and his pork pie hat fell off and rolled towards a mature couple who watched him as he did his best to make a fool of himself. The man picked it up and came to his aid.

"Are you hurt, sir?" he said in French with a strong American accent.

"Only my pride," Lex said, as the man helped him to his feet and handed him the hat. Lex dusted himself down, thanked him, and wished the couple a pleasant day. Lex put his hat back on and continued down the street at a more sedated pace.

A car hooted from behind. Lex turned and saw Jean-François in his black and white Peugeot 504 police car. He rolled down the window as Lex walked alongside the vehicle.

"Rue Chappe is the next street on the right, where the stairs descend. I'll be with you shortly after I've parked the car."

Lex walked to the corner and looked down the picturesque staircase that made up the first part of Rue Chappe. Number 23 was on the right, in an attractive building with a white facade, tall windows with French balconies, black iron railings and white shutters. It was a decent place to live for a plumber, and Lex knew his uncle's agency had given the family a generous deal when they relocated from the Marais.

Jean-François joined him, and they descended to the paved landing to reach the front door.

"It's on the first floor," Jean-François said as he pressed the buzzer on the right. Someone let them in, and Lex followed the brigadier through the door and up the steps. To his annoyance, Father Blanchet was waiting for them at the door. *What the hell is a potential suspect in the girl's appearance doing here?* Lex thought.

"You look surprised to see me here, Monsieur Spijker,"

"I'm just wondering what the fox is doing in the henhouse," Lex sneered.

"The family asked for my presence in their hour of need. As you're not a man of faith, I don't expect you to understand."

"I am, Father," Jean-François pointed out, "and I understand why a devout family finds comfort in your presence. I also know that you, in all likelihood, are one of the last people to have seen the young girl yesterday, and that you're not above suspicion for having something to do with her not returning home from class."

"I can assure you there's been no impropriety on my part," he said, indignant at even being considered a possible object of suspicion.

"I could spell it out, but I'm not sure it's a good idea in the presence of Monsieur and Madame Pernet. What do you think, Father Blanchet?"

"That it's a sacrilege to mention spiteful, malicious, and unfounded gossip to the poor people."

"Spare me the sanctimonious crap," Lex said. Jean-François put a hand on his arm.

"I don't see why Mr Spijker's presence is necessary," Father Blanchet said.

"He's here because I invited him. I'll ask the questions, and he'll be as discreet as possible."

"Okay, you'd better come in," the priest said. They followed him into the hallway. It was small and dark, but light enough for Lex to see dandruff on the back of the Father's black cassock. He opened a door on the right and ushered them in. In the centre of a spacious living room stood Albert and Marie Pernet. He was visibly older than his wife, and with his somewhat stout appearance, big nose and bushy eyebrows, Lex doubted he had contributed much to his daughter's beauty. He was at least four inches shorter than Lex, but seemed tall beside his petite wife. Her dark hair, drawn back in a bun, displayed a face with pleasant and even features. She had a clear likeness to her daughter.

"I'm Brigadier Jean-François Diagne from the Commissariat central, and this is Monsieur Lex Spijker. He met your daughter at the home of Jules Lévy, who is his uncle. He specialises in missing persons as a private detective, so I reasoned it would do no harm to bring him along." It was news to Lex that he specialised in missing persons, but it sounded feasible.

"We have the utmost sympathy for your circumstances, and we're fully dedicated in our pursuit to bring your daughter home."

"Thank you, brigadier," a teary-eyed Marie Pernet said.

"How are you holding up, madame?" Jean-François asked.

"I'm sick with worry, but it helps to have the Father here." The priest rewarded her remark with a consoling smile.

"Can we offer you coffee?"

"Don't go to any trouble, madame," the brigadier said.

"It's no trouble at all. I need to occupy myself, and I'd prefer it if you talked to my husband." She offered a perfunctory bow and exited the room.

"Won't you sit down?" Monsieur Pernet said. They arranged themselves around the coffee table—Jean-Francois and Lex on the couch, and the Father and Albert Pernet next to each other in a couple of *bergères*.

To a fly on the wall, we must look like a strange party, Lex thought. A youngish man, in need of a haircut, in a white shirt with a slim black tie and a leather jacket. A lean black man with remarkably long legs in a police uniform. A middle-aged Catholic priest with massive feet and small hands in a well-padded black cassock and a stout man in dirty blue overalls.

Lex looked around the spacious room, which, apart from the seating arrangements, was furnished with an armoire, a buffet, and a display cabinet—all mahogany and resting on a navy blue wall-to-wall carpet. Apart from a faded and framed colour print of the Virgin Mary, and a crucifix, the walls were bare.

"Don't think me uncaring, but I hope it won't take all afternoon. I have my own company, and I need to get back to my workshop," Albert Pernet said—perhaps also to explain why he was wearing overalls.

"Where is that?" Jean-François asked.

"Rue des Minimes in Le Marais."

"Did you expect your daughter home straight after class?" Jean-François said, in the knowledge that he and Lex had made an appointment with her yesterday afternoon. He pulled out a notepad and a pen from the breast pocket of his uniform.

"We only expected her home around nine last night as she was going to her friend Ami Lévy's house for afternoon tea and supper," Albert Pernet said.

"Does she usually come home on time?"

"My daughter is very conscientious."

"When did you last see her yesterday?"

"We attended mass at seven with Angeline and her younger brother, Raphaël," Albert Pernet said.

"At the Sacré-Cœur?"

"The early morning mass is held in the Chapel of the Virgin Mary at the far end of the Basilica," Father Blanchet supplied.

"Do continue," Jean-François said, ignoring the priest.

"We came home for breakfast around half past eight, before Angeline returned to the church for her eleven o'clock class with Father Blanchet."

An awkward silence descended upon their little party, thankfully broken by Madame Pernet's arrival with the coffee.

"What time did the class end?" Jean-François asked Father Blanchet as Marie Pernet served the coffee.

"Precisely at one."

"Did she seem any different than usual? In any distress or ...."

"Not that I noticed. Angeline is a quiet girl."

"You didn't give her any special attention after the class?"

"What's that supposed to mean?"

"Answer the question."

"She left immediately after class."

"Alone?"

"There were another six girls in the class, and to my knowledge, they all left at the same time."

"We need to talk to the other girls. Please supply us with a list of their names and addresses, Father Blanchet," Jean-François said.

"I doubt they can tell you much. Angeline Pernet keeps herself to herself."

"Just supply the list."

"Shall I have someone bring it to the Commissariat central?"

"No need. I'll come with you afterwards."

Jean-François turned his attention to Monsieur and Madame Pernet. He sipped his coffee and looked at his notes, saying, "You called the Commissaire central at ten to eleven. When did you call the Lévys?"

"We waited for her return until around ten before we called," Albert Pernet said.

"No one replied," Marie Pernet said.

"My aunt's mother died yesterday, and my uncle and his kids flew to Tel Aviv last night," Lex explained.

"My sincere condolences, Monsieur Spijker," Father Blanchet said as he crossed himself.

"And ours. We don't know the family well, but my husband sometimes works for Monsieur Lévy, and our daughter is best friends with Ami. You are all in our prayers," Marie Pernet said.

"Thank you," Lex muttered.

"I'm sorry to ask, Monsieur Pernet, but if your daughter is such a conscientious girl, can you explain why you waited an hour before calling?" Jean-François said.

"What do you want me to say, brigadier? I'm not sure I care much for your tone of voice."

"I wanted to call earlier," Madame Pernet said, barely audibly, "but my husband insisted we wait."

"Never mind. Do you have a recent photo of Angeline?" Jean-François asked.

Marie Pernet slid off the chair, walked to the buffet, and pulled out a drawer. She handed Jean-Francois a small black and white photo. "It's two weeks old. Angeline turns thirteen in July, so we've applied for a passport."

"Can we see her room?"

"If you feel it will help," said Albert Pernet.

"She shares it with her brother," Marie Pernet supplied.

"That can't be easy for a young girl," Lex said.

"She never complains," Albert Pernet said.

"The children have a special bond," Marie Pernet explained.

Lex drained the cup of lukewarm coffee and hopped to his feet, eager to get out of the room stuffed with unspoken tension.

"Before we break up, I'd like to pray for Angeline and her safe return," the Father said.

"Count me out," Lex said. Even if he was a praying man, he couldn't stomach it. Lex expected Jean-François, a Catholic, to stay for the prayer.

"We'll have a look at Angeline's room, and when you've prayed, we'll come with you, Father, to get the list," Jean-François said.

37

THE DOME of the Sacré-Cœur was visible from the Pernet apartment, and they could have walked the distance in a couple of minutes. Jean-François insisted they drove, thereby taking the long way round, which gave them ample time to grill Father Blanchet in the confined space of the car. The priest sat in the passenger seat, and Lex sat behind him, close enough to make him feel his breath. Lex recalled a scene from *The Godfather,* where a man in the passenger seat is garrotted to death by someone seated behind him. As his last act, the victim kicks a shoe through the windscreen. He wondered if Father Blanchet had seen the movie and if the scene made him, as it did Lex, feel ill at ease whenever someone breathed down his neck from behind.

"Now, Father, why don't you tell us what happened yesterday?" Jean-François said.

"I've already told you. The class ended at around one, and all the girls left at the same time."

"And did you give Angeline any special attention?" Lex remarked.

"Not more than I give any of the other girls."

"And how much is that?"

"I strongly reject your insinuations of anything inappropriate on my part."

"So Angeline left with the others?" Jean-François said.

"I said, all the girls."

"Can anyone back it up?"

"Sister Coline can. She let the group out."

Jean-François approached the square in front of the Sacré-Cœur.

"Use the entrance on Rue du Cardinal Guibert," Father Blanchet said nervously. Lex guessed he was keen to attract as little attention as possible when exiting a police car.

Jean-François pulled up to the curb and stopped. Father Blanchet jumped out, and pulling up his cassock, he hurried up the concrete staircase. Lex expected him to produce a key, but instead, he pressed the buzzer. As the door creaked open, they joined him on the landing. A middle-aged nun in a grey tunic appeared at the door.

"Oh, it's you, Father Blanchet. Have you forgotten your key?" She sounded annoyed at being called away from her chores.

"Not this time. But as the brigadier would like to speak to you, I thought I might as well summon you to the door."

"Rightly so, Father."

"Monsieur Brigadier and Monsieur Clou," she greeted them.

"Sister Coline," Lex said and took off his hat.

"Do come in. How can I help?"

The Sister seemed friendlier than at his last visit.

"Sister," Father Blanchet said, "Please tell the brigadier that you let Angeline Pernet out yesterday with the other girls."

"That poor girl. I've prayed for her all morning."

"So you know about her disappearance?" Lex said.

"Father Blanchet told me before leaving, and after the parents called. I can't imagine..."

"Please confirm to the brigadier that you let all the girls out at the same time yesterday after class," Father Blanchet interrupted. The Sister hesitated, and Lex thought she was in two minds about her loyalty to Father Blanchet and the church or giving an honest response.

"I'm so sorry, Father, but I can't say with certainty when Angeline Pernet left yesterday. I'm afraid Father Simon distracted me."

"Let me understand this correctly. You didn't see any of the girls leave?" Jean-François said.

"That's right. Father Simon needed me for some urgent business, and I assured myself the girls could let themselves out."

"So you don't need a key?" Lex asked.

"Only from the outside." She turned the knob to demonstrate, and the door opened.

Father Blanchet stepped forward and slammed it closed again. "I'm sorry *la bonne sœur* didn't do her duty to see the girls out, but that doesn't mean they didn't leave together."

"Never mind. The girls will tell us what happened. Just let us have the list with their names and addresses. If you hear anything of significance, I expect you to contact the Commissariat central immediately."

"Of course, Monsieur Brigadier. Let me get you the list," Father Blanchet said as he headed for the stairs with some urgency. *By now, he'll be glad to see the back of us,* Lex thought.

Before parting, they agreed to visit Killian Lamarre at his Paris office the next day before lunch. To put maximum pressure on the tycoon, they decided not to make an appointment in advance, taking the chance that he might not be there.

Lex wanted to ask Jean-François if he might make another inquiry into the location of the private sex club they had previously discussed. Before he could do so, the brigadier rushed off in his car to have the Angeline photo distributed and contact the girls on the list.

LEX RETURNED home to ask Linda to join him for lunch at Le Consulat, but she wasn't there. He looked in vain for a note, as he couldn't recall if she'd told him about any appointments. Perhaps she was attending another French lesson? Or a photo session at *Vogue*? Or maybe she'd decided to go for a walk? Or …?

Lex only speculated to calm his anxiety whenever he didn't know her whereabouts. He excused it by thinking about the potential threat to her safety, but he knew that his possessiveness, or to put it kindly, overprotective nature, had a lot to do with it. The prospect of lunch at the café no longer seemed attractive. He opened the fridge, and he was pleased to see a few eggs and a block of Emmental cheese.

"How's the omelette, babe? It's good, a little cheesy, though. Yeah, they usually have better jokes," he quipped to himself. No-one laughed. Not even the house rat.

THE PUBLIC library at Place Jules Joffrin was as rundown as a trotter in the Grand National and as quiet as the Gare du Nord in the rush hour. Lex didn't care, as he wasn't there to absorb himself in the great philosophers, but to dig out potential critical press coverage on Killian Lamarre. The middle-aged librarian became overly helpful when he asked her for information about the tycoon, especially press with a critical view of his philandering.

"If you want my opinion," she said, "he's a freak, with too much money and time on his hands."

"When not using them to fondle young girls," Lex offered. She asked him to take a seat while she dug up material from the archive.

Within ten minutes, she had returned with a few issues of *Le Canard Enchaîné* (*The Chained Duck*). She pointed out the pages that might be of interest to him. Lex didn't know the publication, but she explained it was a weekly satirical newspaper featuring investigative journalism and leaks from sources inside the world of politics and business, combined with jokes and cartoons.

"As you can imagine, with Lamarre's bohemian and alternative lifestyle, they do not always see eye to eye."

Lex flipped to the pages she'd pointed out. A cartoon depicted Lamarre as a naughty headmaster at a girls' school and another cartoon as a scoutmaster for a group of girl scouts in short skirts. A satirical article mentioned how his teenage daughters' girlfriends were in the running to be the next Mrs Lamarre, as his present and fourth wife, at the age of twenty-six, was getting on a bit. Apart from a father's quote that he'd forbidden his daughter from visiting the Lamarre girls and another from a former housemaid that not all the girls came to the Lamarre residence to visit his daughters, the article didn't give concrete proof of anything suspicious going on. Next, Lex saw an article that ridiculed Lamarre for his promiscuous lifestyle and publicly defending a Cardinal, a member of the Académie Française, after he scandalised the church by carelessly dying in the arms of a young prostitute. That the Cardinal had also been carrying a large sum of money, added extra spice. The church claimed that he had brought the money to put up bail for the prostitute's lover. However, the press and the general public remained somewhat cynical concerning the Cardinal's altruism.

Lex stayed another half an hour before returning the material. He thanked the librarian for her assistance.

"My pleasure. Whatever it's for, I hope you make the most of it," she said, with a piercing stare over the rim of her glasses.

"I shall do my best, madame."

LEX ASCENDED the stairs and heard music booming from the apartment. He took off his shoes, jacket and hat as he entered. He stopped in the doorway to the living room, and watched as Linda, stripped down to her underwear, swayed her beautiful body to the rhythm. The sweet smell of marijuana hung in the air, and through the speakers Lex heard the enticing voice of a male singer singing, "Come on baby, light my fire, try to set the night on fire."

Lex waltzed up behind her, put his hands on her hips, and synchronised his movement with hers. His sudden presence behind her didn't seem to frighten her, and he massaged his crotch against her posterior. Lex kissed her neck as they swayed to the music. After a while, Linda freed herself and swung round. Her mascara was smudged, and he wondered if she had been crying. He kept his hands on her hips, but she grabbed his left hand and pulled him towards the couch.

"Make love to me, Lex," she said into his ear, overpowering the music and the words of the singer, "The men don't know, but the little girls understand."

KILLIAN LAMARRE'S office was on a side street of the Avenue des Champs-Élysées, with a view of the Grand Palais and a giant banner that announced the exhibition 'French painting 1774-1830, the Age of Revolution'. A substantial queue waited for the museum to open at ten.

It delighted Lex to see the Aston Martin DB5 parked in front of the office building.

Competing with the Beaux-Arts architecture of the Grand Palais, Lamarre's classic building didn't impress much.

"I didn't know he could be this discreet," Lex said and pointed to the inconspicuous gold nameplate with 'Sanna Invest' engraved on it. Jean-François pressed the golden button above it. Within ten seconds, someone had buzzed them in. Lex followed the tall brigadier up a few stairs and through a glass door. A young man behind a reception desk made of chrome and glass looked up.

"We would like to talk to Killian Lamarre." Jean-François said.

"Do you have an appointment?"

"I'm sure you know that we do not. As you may have noticed, we're the police."

"I did wonder when I saw your uniform, brigadier."

"I'm sure Mr Lamarre doesn't pay you to be cheeky, young man," Lex remarked, ignoring the fact that they were about the same age.

"You'd be surprised what he pays me to do," he retorted.

"Would you care to expand?" Lex challenged him.

"Never mind. I'll let Mr Lamarre know the police are here to see him." He pressed a button on the intercom system. "Didn't I tell you, Kevin, that I didn't want to be disturbed?" the voice of Killian Lamarre barked.

"I'm sorry, boss, but it's the police, and they insist on talking to you." Silence followed. "Boss?"

"Send them in."

Kevin pointed to a door on the right, and before they made it that far it opened, and Killian Lamarre's grey mane appeared in the doorway. He wore a light blue suit, the jacket and the four top buttons of his yellow silk shirt were unbuttoned to show off his hairy chest.

"Oh, it's Foottit and Chocolat." Lex didn't know what he referred to, but had no doubt it was a racial slur, which was confirmed when Lamarre added, "where's your camera, Chocolat?"

"The name is Brigadier Diagne," Jean-François said, keeping his cool. To him, it was probably a typical day as a black policeman.

"Nice location for an office," Lex said, "if you can get it."

"No problem when you're the landlord. I own a few properties in the area."

"Does that include the Grand Palais?" Lex said with scorn.

"Not yet."

"Shall we conduct our business out here, or ...?" Jean-François asked.

"Come in, if you must. I'll give you five minutes," Killian Lamarre said and turned on his heels, "and close the door behind you."

His office could have housed a tennis court, and the size of his desk would have given a snooker table an inferiority complex. He jogged around it and climbed onto an oversized swivel armchair. He tilted it backwards and put his feet on the desk so they could admire his hand-sewn shoes. A couple of club chairs in front of the desk remained empty, as he didn't invite them to sit down.

"As you look busy, I'll cut to the chase," Jean-François said. "Have you heard of a girl called Angeline Pernet?"

"Should I?" Killian Lamarre said without hesitation.

"I'm sure Father Blanchet keeps you well informed," Lex said.

"Now, why would you say that?"

Jean-François's facial expression made it clear that he would have preferred Lex to keep his mouth shut.

"The girl didn't return home on Sunday after attending sacrament preparation class with Father Blanchet. We've talked to most of the other girls in the class, and none of them knows if she ever left the church."

"What's that to do with me? Why don't you ask the priest?"

"We did, and he told us to talk to you," Lex lied. Jean-François rewarded him with a disapproving look, and Lex knew he'd gone too far.

"*Quelle connerie.* I don't have to listen to this bullshit." Lamarre reached over and pressed a button on the intercom system.

"Kevin, my meeting with Foottit and Chocolat is over, and you can show them the door."

"I'll be right in, boss." Within five seconds, the door opened, and Kevin charged in, eager to do his master's bidding. Jean-François held up a hand to stop him.

"If you prefer, we can continue the interview at the Commissariat central on Rue de Clignancourt."

"That's great. I'd love a chat with my old friend Major Saint Martin about how one of his subordinate officers and his mate, a detective of ill repute, is harassing a private citizen. I'm sure he'll find the story about a tall, black brigadier as an undercover photographer, of interest. I might even suggest to my friend that he should consider making the same brigadier walk the beat and revoke a certain private detective's licence. Now get out before I ask Kevin to call security."

The receptionist held the door open as he motioned to them to get out, like a couple of unruly children.

"Hold it. I'm not sure if you want your employee to hear this, but we have talked to a few girls that claim you came on to them," Jean-François said.

"What girls?"

"Angeline Pernet's classmates at the church."

Killian Lamarre dragged his feet off the table, but he didn't get up. "Kevin, you'd better return to reception." The young man trotted out and closed the door.

"Yesterday, we interviewed some of the girls that attended class with Angeline Pernet. We heard a few stories of interest." Jean-François took a seat, and Lex followed his example, sliding into the neighbouring chair. Lamarre leaned forward. "Let me hear the latest fabrications."

"First of all, they told us that a middle-aged man with grey shoulder-length hair accompanied the Father on several occasions."

"There are plenty of middle-aged men with grey shoulder-length hair in this city."

"Perhaps, but only a few have their face constantly published in the media. We showed the girls a few photos."

"So what? That doesn't prove anything. You've already established that I'd funded a major restoration and that I sat on the church's Restoration Committee. As did Father Blanchet."

"The man in question chatted up a couple of the girls and claimed he would make their dreams come true. A few of Angeline Pernet's classmates told us that she was one of them."

"I think that's called grooming," Lex contributed.

"Who'd take teenage girls full of oestrogen seriously? Let them repeat their lies in court."

"The girls might be afraid that whatever happened to Angeline Pernet could happen to them, but it would be foolish to underestimate their courage and desire to see their friend return home safely," Jean-François said.

"Home safely from what?"

"Didn't I say? She's been missing since Sunday."

"That's terrible. I'm a father myself, and I can imagine the dread her parents must be feeling," Killian Lamarre said as he choked back tears. *A magnificent performance from a skilled sociopath*, Lex thought, *and wealthy enough to be seen as merely eccentric.* But he didn't fool Lex with his cold and manipulative behaviour, and he would love to have seen him taste some of his own emotional abuse. Lex felt the anger take hold of him and knew he'd better leave before doing or saying something he might later regret. He rose to his feet and hurried out of the office.

38

HIS MASSIVE frame blocked out the light from the staircase. It reminded Lex of when they first met almost a year ago on a staircase on Rembrandtplein in Amsterdam. Alwin Smit's muscular arms and chest stretched his dark green polo shirt to the limit. He'd stopped colouring his grey hair brown and had let it grow long enough to cover his ears. He'd also shaved off his horseshoe-shaped moustache, which made his flattened nose, a testament to a career in amateur boxing, more prominent. He offered Lex a hand the size of a 14-ounce ribeye steak. Lex shook it, relieved he came as a friend.

"Welcome to Paris, Big Al. I hope your trip was okay?"

"The drive from Amsterdam went smoothly, but it was a bitch to find your love nest."

The big man followed him into the apartment, and while he freshened up, Lex made coffee.

"That's what I call a bathroom," Big Al said, as he joined Lex in the living room. "This apartment is some upgrade compared to your place at Rembrandtplein."

"I can't argue with that."

"You must have won the lottery."

"My uncle is a real estate agent, and he let us have it on the cheap." Lex offered Al a seat on the couch as he doubted the big man would fit into the armchair.

"You still drink it black?"

"Sure."

Lex poured the coffee and sat down.

"It's nice to see you, but do remind me why I'm here?" Al said.

Lex repeated why he'd asked him to come to Paris, filling him in on Angeline Pernet's disappearance and the confrontation with Killian Lamarre at his office. Lex also told him about his Paris life with Linda and the prospect of her modelling career.

"Where's your lovely lady, by the way?"

"As far as I know, she is attending a French lesson."

"Can I suggest that until we've eliminated the threat, you inform each other about where you are and when?"

"I keep telling her, but she's a great believer in personal freedom. Perhaps you can convince her."

"No can do. Since my divorce twenty years ago, I've enjoyed the freedom of not having to convince anyone of anything. Especially women."

"Unless you apply some pain."

"That's professional—and a little pain never hurt anyone," he said with the chuckle Lex had come to expect.

"I doubt Allard Kuipers would have agreed about that after you'd broken a few of his fingers."

"Please don't remind me, or you'll make me weep."

Lex looked at his watch. "Let's get you checked in, so that we can have a drink before our dinner appointment with Linda."

"Okay."

"Give me five minutes to get ready."

Lex adjusted his silk tie, put on his new light blue pinstripe jacket and grabbed his Panama hat from a hook in the hallway.

"I see the Parisian style is growing on you," Al said.

"Blame it on my uncle and Linda."

"All it takes is a rich uncle and a beautiful woman to give you a touch of class."

Lex descended the stairs behind Al, making them more or less the same height. Al held the front door for Lex, and they entered the street. Instinctively, Lex scouted for any unwanted attention, before a dark blue Volvo Amazon station wagon parked behind the Renault 5 caught his attention. He recognised the car from their mission the previous year.

"I see you still have the same wheels."

"Eight years old and the best car I've ever owned."

"It takes me back to an early, misty summer morning at the Amsterdam harbour."

"Sweet memories of a successful mission."

"I can't tell you how happy it makes me that you're here."

"No need—your wagging tail shows it. Let's hope I can live up to your expectations one more time."

"I'm full of confidence in you."

"That's what worries me," he said and unlocked the door to the passenger seat. The last time Lex had sat in it, they were also on their way to a hotel—the Amsterdam Hilton—to get a room for Linda, who'd been lying on the back seat, too doped up to sit up straight.

They met light traffic as Lex directed Al through the narrow and crooked streets to the hotel on Rue des Trois Frères, two hundred metres in a beeline from the apartment. As they reached the Hôtel du Commerce, a Ford Escort pulled out in front of them, offering somewhere to park. Lex watched with fascination as Big Al manoeuvred the station wagon into a space most drivers would have abandoned.

"Like a glove." He killed the engine, pushed the door open, and squeezed his massive frame out. Lex followed his example, as Al fetched a duffle back and a peacoat from the boot. They entered the hotel.

"Checking in," Lex said.

"Welcome to the Hôtel du Commerce. Can I have your name, monsieur?"

"It's Alwin Smit," Lex said. The receptionist checked the register.

"You're booked for five nights, Monsieur Smit. He put a registration card on the counter. "Name, address and *le numéro de passeport, s'il vous plaît.*"

He looked surprised when Lex stepped aside and Big Al approached the small counter.

"Do you have a pen?" Al asked in English, while his right hand made a fluttering motion. The receptionist handed Al a pen, and he filled in the required information.

"You remember your passport number. I'm impressed," Lex said.

"It's only seven digits."

"I can't even remember my phone number," Lex said. Al handed over the card, and the receptionist exchanged it for a key.

"It's room 402 on the fourth floor. The lift is on your right."

Lex pressed the button, and nothing happened. He did it again.

"I think it's already here," Al said and pulled the door open. A telephone booth seemed spacious in comparison.

"Not my size. I'll take the stairs," Al said.

"And I'll take your bag."

When the lift reached the fourth floor, Al pulled the door open.

"Welcome to the top," he said, with no hint that he'd climbed four flights of stairs. *For a man on the wrong side of fifty, he's in perfect shape*, Lex thought.

Al unlocked the door to a spacious room with a small desk, a chair, an armoire and a washbasin in the corner. Lex put the bag on the king-size bed.

"Hope it's not a problem that you have to share the toilet and the shower."

"As long as I don't have to share it simultaneously."

"You're welcome to use our bathroom."

"Thanks. It could be a challenge in the middle of the night, but I'll keep it in mind. Which reminds me —do you have an extra key to the apartment? It might come in handy, and I promise not to barge in unless it's essential."

"If you remind me next time we're at Rue Norvins, I'll give you our spare keys." Lex checked his watch. "We're meeting Linda for dinner at seven, so let's go for that drink."

HAD IT been located in Amsterdam, Le Tagada Bar would have qualified as a brown café. To emphasise it was neither, Lex ordered a Pernod Ricard.

"What's your poison?" Lex asked.

"The same. Last time I drank pastis was after I'd boxed the French amateur champion in Lyon in 1951."

"Who won?"

"I floored him in round four. We reconciled over some pastis afterwards and remained in contact until lung cancer knocked him out for good about ten years ago."

"That's a bummer," Lex said and lit a cigarette. "Now that you mention sport, my uncle gave me two tickets for the European Cup Final at Parc des Princes tomorrow evening." Lex said it casually with the knowledge that Big Al wasn't a great fan of the beautiful game and would probably prefer to spend a couple of hours in the company of a good book. Lex didn't reveal the teams for the same reason, and Al didn't ask.

"I recall you persuaded me to watch Holland against Brazil at your local pub last year. Before that match, I believed only sissies played football, but the way those twenty-two youngsters in tight shorts inflicted pain on each other demanded respect. The number of knee-high tackles impressed me, and I'll consider joining you if you can guarantee the same level of brutality and entertainment."

"It's between an English and a German team, so no love is lost between them. And that also goes for their fans. The English supporters are especially famous, or infamous if you wish, for their hooliganism, so with a little luck there ...."

"Stop! I've heard enough of your sales pitch. I'll come to your football game."

"Cheers." Lex held up his class, and they clinked.

Big Al excused himself and headed to the toilet at the back. While he did his business, Lex caught a glimpse of himself in the opposite mirror. The two-day shadow and the bags under his eyes didn't favour his pretty-boy face. In the reflection in the mirror, Lex saw a man wearing a fedora gazing through the window with hands cupped around his eyes. Lex couldn't make out his face, but his tired mind decided it was Killian Lamarre's lackey, Dimitri. Lex lurched to his feet, darted for the door, and as he pulled it open, two men entered, blocking his way. Lex pushed past them and into the street. He scanned up and down, but the fedora man had disappeared.

"What happened to you?" Big Al said from the café door.

"One of Killian Lamarre's men was peering through the window. Or so I thought."

"How am I expected to watch your back if you rush off like that?"

"As you see, the guy's not here. Perhaps it was my imagination. Let's go back in."

They returned to their seats, and Lex ordered another round of pastis. They sat in silence until Lex asked Al, "How's business?"

"In what way?"

"Helping people get out of trouble."

"I've more or less retired. I'm too old to put myself in the line of fire."

"How old are you, if I may ask?"

"I turned fifty in February."

"Really? You don't look a day over forty."

"That's because I colour my hair grey," he said, laughing.

"Too young to retire, too old to hire," Lex suggested.

"But not too old to do something else." Al took out his wallet and handed Lex a business card. It read, 'Alwin Smit, Rare books & First editions.' "It's big business."

"You should know. I guess you've spent considerable amounts stocking your home library," Lex said.

"For a few years, I've wanted to turn my hobby into my job."

"Good for you, Al." The gentle giant with the flattened snout wouldn't go unnoticed in the antiquarian community.

"Let's drink up. We have dinner with Linda in five minutes."

"Sounds good. I've eaten nothing apart from breakfast and lunch all day," Al said.

They ascended the stairs to the Place du Tertre, and as they strolled along the street towards the restaurant, Linda approached from the opposite direction. She waved and smiled, and in her new blue dress with polka dots, she looked as alluring as ever. Lex embraced her and introduced Big Al.

"Delighted to meet you again," Al said.

"And I'm delighted to get a chance to thank you personally for saving my life, Alwin. I'm afraid I was too drugged to remember much about it." Linda reached up and kissed him on the cheek. Her red lipstick made a mark.

"Glad to be of service, and I believe you might need it again."

"I'm not so sure. Lex tends to exaggerate our troubles."

"If you allow me to use a cliché, a trouble shared is a trouble halved."

"Maybe so, but ...."

"Let's talk about it over dinner," Lex interrupted. The tantalising aroma of garlic from the restaurant was making his stomach grumble. He put his arm around Linda and escorted her towards the entrance.

HIGH ON delicious food, tasty wine and stimulating conversation, they bade Big Al good night and watched him float towards the Place du Tertre. He had a light stride for a big man, and Lex imagined him, in his heyday, as a boxing champion dancing around his opponents.

"Alwin is a real gentleman," Linda said, "and good fun."

"He's a cornucopia of interesting stories, but I'm not sure you should have asked him to tell you how Allard Kuipers managed to get his fingers broken."

"After what that man did to me, I feel no sympathy, but it did make a chill run down my spine."

Lex unlocked the door to the stairwell and held it open for Linda to enter. She walked up the stairs in front of him, giving him ample time and opportunity to admire her posterior.

"Your phone is ringing," Linda said.

"You mean our phone."

"Shall we argue about whose telephone it is after you've answered it?"

"If you move out of the way, I'll give it my best shot." He flew up the stairs, fumbled with the key, unlocked the door, and another ring greeted him. He switched on the light, dashed into the office, and lifted the handset.

"Private detective Lex Spijker," he panted, only to hear a click. "Damn, too late." He walked around the desk, replaced the handset, and dumped his tired body into the office chair. He lit a cigarette, inhaled deeply, and as he ashed it, he noticed a filter butt in the ashtray among his own unfiltered cigarette ends. He lifted it and read the brand.

"Who was it?" Linda appeared at the door.

"I arrived too late."

"Typical."

"Did you smoke a Marlboro cigarette in my office today?"

"No, dad, I didn't."

"Well, someone did."

"If there's no trace of lipstick, perhaps it was the Marlboro man?" she said with a grin. "Pity I wasn't here; I would love to meet a bona fide cowboy." Did she blush, or did he imagine it?

"It's no joke," Lex said, disgruntled.

"Why so serious?"

"Because someone visited my office today without my knowledge."

"Or mine," Linda added. "Is anything missing?"

"Too early to tell," Lex said, as he gazed towards the safe in the corner, "and we'd better check the rest of the apartment."

"Good idea. I'm right behind you."

39

LEX POURED Al a second cup of coffee.

"If not for that stupid Marlboro filter butt," Lex said and lit up a Gauloises.

"It does sound strange, unless whoever paid you a visit left it there as a message," Big Al said, helping himself to another croissant.

"Or unless Linda has a secret lover who smokes Marlboro," Lex said with an uneasy laugh.

"I think we can rule that one out."

"Why do you say that?"

"The way she looks at you with her big, beautiful eyes ought to convince you that you're her man."

"Perhaps you're right." Big Al lowered his coffee mug and looked straight at Lex. "Don't tell me you're jealous?"

"Can I be honest with you?"

"I should think so, and I hope you have been all along?"

"Sometimes I feel in my gut that I'm not good enough for her and that she's looking elsewhere for fulfilment."

"Do you have any proof that she has deceived you?"

"No, and I'm not even sure I can pinpoint what makes me feel the way I do."

"I doubt it can be easy to date such a beautiful young lady, and from the first time you talked about her, I did feel she'd cast an unhealthy spell on you. But here you are, living together. As your friend and an older man, I would like to reassure you that you have no reason to feel inferior. You're a handsome guy and, although occasionally a bit immature, a decent chap. Why not enjoy the moment? There are no guarantees of love and happiness in this life," Al proclaimed, "and sorry if I sound like a homespun philosopher."

"You don't, and I'll take your advice to heart."

"Where is she, by the way?"

"She had an appointment at *Vogue*, and the plan is to meet her for lunch at one. Can you entertain yourself while I give my contact at the police a call?"

"No problem," he said and pulled out a thin paperback from the inside pocket of his peacoat that hung over the back of the chair.

"What are you reading?"

"One of my favourite Henry Miller books." He held it up to show the cover. It read *Quiet days in Clichy*.

"Isn't that pornography?"

"I can tell you haven't read it. You really should; especially now you live in Montmartre. Can I read a passage to you?"

"Go ahead."

Al read aloud: "I remember the first day I entered the Café Wepler, in the year 1928, with my wife in tow; I remember the shock I experienced when I saw a whore fall dead drunk across one of the little tables on the terrace and nobody ran to her assistance. I was amazed by the indifference of the French; I still am, despite all the good qualities in them which I since have come to know."

"Fascinating. Brasserie Wepler is still there on the corner of Place de Clichy," Lex said.

"I know, and I'll like to invite you and Linda there for dinner. Any plans for this evening?"

"It's football night," Lex said.

"How did I forget? Tomorrow?"

"Perfect. Let me check with Linda."

"Sure. Now go make your call so that we can hit the town."

Lex called Jean-François's direct number at the Commissariat central, and after a couple of rings, the brigadier answered. He had one foot out the door and told Lex he had no news about Angeline Pernet.

"Is there anything I can do?"

"Thanks, but no thanks. You'd better leave it up to us professionals. We're doing all we can to find the girl."

"I'm sure."

"Any developments on your side?"

"None that I can think of."

"I'll have to run, Lex. I'll keep you posted."

LEX AND AL took their seats ten minutes before kick-off. The red plastic seat was not made for a person the size of Al, but he managed to squeeze in by sharing some of Lex's space. The guy seated behind Al didn't look too happy, but Lex was content. They had a clear view of both halves of the pitch, with the English supporters at one end and the Germans at the other, trying to drown each other out. A great spectacle, and the pre-match excitement took hold of Lex who loved the atmosphere in a stadium packed with expectant fans a few minutes before kick-off. Without his team, Ajax, in the final, as in 1971, '72 and '73, a "Come on Leeds!" burst out of Lex when the two teams emerged from the tunnel. His outburst made two young men, in their early teens with Beatle haircuts, turn and look at him. Apart from one wearing the white colour of Leeds United, and the other the red of Bayern Munich, they looked identical. Lex locked eyes with the one in the white shirt and gave him the thumbs up. The young man smiled shyly before returning his attention to the proceedings on the pitch.

The two teams lined up for the national anthems and the opportunity for the officials, the players and the managers to shake the hand of the recently elected French president Valéry Giscard d'Estaing. Undoubtedly, a great honour.

The French referee, who seemed to be the smallest man on the pitch, blew the whistle, and Bayern Munich got the game underway. Leeds dominated the early stages, and it seemed only a matter of time before the first goal. A clear handball inside the box by the

German captain Beckenbauer somehow escaped the referee's attention, and he confidently waved away any protests. Minutes later, the same German defender smashed into the English attacker Clarke inside the penalty area. Apart from Beckerbauer and the referee, everyone else saw a clear penalty. Again the referee waved away the protests from the Leeds players. The first-half ended with Bayern Munich running down the clock.

"I hope you are not too bored," Lex said to Big Al.

"Bored? Are you kidding? I don't know how you do it, but unexpected things happen whenever I watch football with you."

"And there's another half to come."

"The first match we watched together had knee-high tackles flying all over the place, and this one is clearly fixed," Al mused.

"Perhaps the referee's best mate is the German captain?"

"Or someone presented him with a nice, fat envelope before the match."

"And a couple of high-class hookers," Lex suggested.

"Let's see how the referee honours his commitment in the second-half."

"Bring it on," Lex said.

To the bemusement of the British players and the thousands of Leeds fans who had crossed the channel, it only took twenty minutes of the second half for the referee to honour whatever agreement he had made with the German captain. The Leeds midfielder

Johnny Giles sent a free-kick into the crowded penalty area, and when the ball broke loose, his mate in midfield, Peter Lorimer, smashed the ball into the net for the game's first goal.

The referee blew his whistle, pointed to the centre, and the Leeds players, fans and so-called neutrals celebrated wildly.

"Don't get carried away," Big Al bellowed to drown out the pandemonium. "Their captain is having words with the referee."

"What's there to talk about?"

"A nice fat envelope."

"And a couple of hookers."

After consultation with his linesman, who'd kept his flag down, the referee disallowed the goal for offside.

"Surprise, surprise," Al mocked.

The injustice was hard to take; many Leeds fans could not contain their feelings of frustration, and missiles rained down from behind the goal.

With twenty minutes left to play and the referee still adamant that he would not let any decision go the way of the English team, Bayern Munich counter-attacked and the midfielder Franz Rofthwith scored. Predictably the violence escalated, and the Leeds fans used anything they could get their hands on as missiles. Lex saw a few plastic seats ripped from their moorings and launched like flying saucers.

"Now it gets interesting," Big Al said, as he pointed to a group that were climbing the wall onto the pitch. Confronted by French gendarmes, fighting broke out.

It didn't stop the game, and ten minutes from time, the German team launched another counter-attack, and the ball ended at the feet of the attacker, Gerd Müller. He duly put the ball in the back of the net. Bayern's fans celebrated a certain victory, while supporters of Leeds turned the violence up a notch at the opposite end.

"I'm afraid your brother will win this one," Lex said to the twin in the white shirt.

"What are the chances that my brother would be supporting Bayern."

"I can say the same about you, Jens," the other twin said.

"Mind your own business, Christian."

"Where are you from?" Lex asked, to stop their banter from escalating.

"Copenhagen."

"You speak decent French young man. Do you live here?"

"Our father works here," the brother said and pointed to a man on the right, who sent Lex a friendly nod.

"We attend the English School of Paris, and I'm dreading going in tomorrow. They're all Manchester United fans," Jens stressed.

"Well, at least they're not all Bayern Munich fans," Lex said. Jens smiled, and Christian didn't. "No disrespect to you, young man," he added, "and well done for winning the cup for the second time in two years."

Lex and Al stayed in their seats to watch the police as they escorted the referee from the pitch and for the French president, as he presented the colossal silver cup with the big ears to the winners. The German team embarked on the traditional lap of honour.

"Surely they don't plan to run past the end with the English supporters?" Al said. But they did and were rewarded with a bombardment of missiles.

"It's a sad day for football," Lex said.

"Perhaps, but it's entertaining and does add some spice to the game."

"Like adding curry powder to *coq au vin*," Lex moaned.

"You look like there was a death in the family."

"But there was, remember? That's why my uncle gave us the tickets."

"He gave them to you. I'm here because you asked me along."

"I've seen enough; let's get out of here."

"Lead the way."

Coming out of the stadium, they walked into utter mayhem as the Leeds supporters transferred their frustration from the stadium into the surrounding streets. The French gendarmes did their best to contain the violence, but Lex doubted they'd expected that a football match could turn into something reminiscent of the civil unrest in May '68. With Big Al by his side, Lex felt unruffled, confident that any hooligan, however high on frustration, alcohol and adrenalin, would think twice before engaging with the gentle giant.

As they strolled along the boulevard in the direction of the metro station at Place de Porte de Saint-Cloud, they had a stroke of luck. A taxi had just offloaded a party, and Lex rushed over, hoping it was available for hire.

"*Embarquez-vous, messieurs*," said the chauffeur. And they did—Lex in the front, while Big Al occupied most of the back seat.

"Take us to Montmartre, my good man," Lex said, his spirits boosted by the thought of avoiding a ride on the metro full of intoxicated football fans.

LEX WATCHED the taxi disappear up Rue des Trois Frères and suggested a nightcap at Le Tagada Bar. Big Al declined, with the excuse that he was dead beat and had an appointment with his Henry Miller novel. Lex bade him good night and avoided the temptation to go for a drink without him. Ten minutes later, he ascended the stairs to the apartment, hoping Linda was still up. He unlocked the front door and entered the apartment, pleased to see the living room lights on.

"It's me, baby," he said and walked in. Linda was sitting on the couch in the company of two men. A man of medium height with thick brown hair under a cap and a dull complexion stood by the window facing the door. His right hand held a pistol with a silencer. His mate, with a sunny disposition and a blond crew cut, who was sitting beside Linda on the couch, stood as Lex entered.

"*Welkom thuis, heer Spijker*. I bring greetings from Amsterdam." He switched to English, perhaps for the benefit of his mate. Lex looked at Linda, her face bruised.

"Are you okay, baby?"

"I'll live," she said defiantly, "but I think you'll have to show our uninvited guests how to treat a lady with respect in her own home."

"I'd prefer to show them the door," Lex said.

"You can as soon as you've given us what we came for," Blondie said.

"And that is?"

"Money, Mr. Spijker. 250,000 guilders of it."

"Do I look like a millionaire?"

"You look like a bum, but Linda Lovelace here looks like a million."

"It's Miss Vogel to you, mate," Lex said.

"Enough small talk," Blondie said. "Let's get down to business."

"You can hire me for 150 guilders plus 40 guilders to cover expenses."

Blondie took a step towards Lex and raised his right hand. Lex expected to be hit, but Blondie merely pointed his index finger at him.

"Now shut up, or I'll ask my French friend to make you. All you need to do is follow my instructions. Is that understood?"

"If you insist."

"As you might have guessed, we're here on behalf of Allard Kuipers, as he's prevented from travelling. But I don't have to tell you that, as you've made sure her majesty's government are supplying him with board and lodging. The lies you both told at the trial and his time in prison haven't made him less eager to retrieve the money. Or to see you punished. He has specifically permitted me to twist a few fingers if you don't cooperate. To return the favour, if you know what I mean."

Lex did, and he recalled how big Al had persuaded Mr Kuipers to tell them what happened to Linda after he and his associates had abducted her. The middle and index fingers were enough to make him talk. Allard Kuipers' screams still made Lex shiver, and he would never let Linda experience anything like it.

"Your girlfriend told us, before you joined the party, that you're keeping the money in the safe in your office and that you're the only one with the combination."

"I'm not sure I can remember it."

Blondie struck Lex across the face with the back of his hand.

"What the fuck did you do that for?" Lex hissed, as he wiped the blood from his lower lip.

"To make you understand the situation you're in."

"If we have the money and give it to you, will you promise to leave us alone?" Lex said.

"Perhaps. But as you're not in a position to negotiate, you'll have to take your chance," Blondie stressed.

Lex regretted he'd turned down Al's offer to escort him home after the match. Lex doubted he'd be able to do much held at gunpoint, but his presence would have introduced an element of uncertainty.

"How did you find us?" Lex asked to gain time.

"Thanks to our French connection." He gestured towards the man with the pistol.

"Does the frog speak?" Lex said.

"Tell them," Blondie said, careful not to use the man's name.

In French, he told Lex how he couldn't believe his luck when he saw an article about Linda and an advert for Lex's services—all in the same Sunday edition of *Le Figaro*.

"Enough talk; it's time to check out the contents of your safe. "Follow me. My French friend is right behind you to ensure you don't get any funny ideas." Blondie stepped past Lex. He could do with some deodorant, Lex thought. Linda raised herself from the couch and joined Lex, and he squeezed her clammy hand.

The party relocated to the office. Blondie took a seat in the office chair, and the guy with the pistol leaned against the door frame with his back to the hallway.

"Open it," Blondie demanded.

Lex's problem was not giving up the money, but it worried him that it might not be enough and that they would feel compelled to inflict some harm on behalf of Allard Kuipers.

"Okay, but I need ...."

"I'm all out of patience, Mr Spijker," Blondie interrupted. "Shut up and get on with it."

Lex knelt in front of the safe, entered the code and pulled the door open. Around 240,000 guilders stared him in the face.

"Now, move over to the corner. The both of you. I'll take over from here." They watched Blondie retrieve the money from the safe and stack the bundles on the desk. His lips moved as he counted the notes. Lex doubted he was an accountant, but you didn't have to be to add up the around twenty-four bundles, each containing one hundred 100-guilder notes .

"We have a problem," Blondie said. "We're almost 11,000 guilders short. How will you make up the difference?"

"We can't," Linda said.

"You can have 11,000 guilders' worth of pain. Say you pay 2,500 for every finger we break, and then I'll give you a thousand discount. Two fingers each— that's fair."

"You're a sick bastard," Linda said.

"Perhaps, but your boyfriend inspired this finger breaking business. Perhaps you have another suggestion about how to make up for the missing money," Blondie said and put a hand on Linda's bottom.

"Get your hand off, creep," she shouted and pushed his hand away. He grabbed her wrist and twisted her arm.

"Stop! You're hurting me."

Lex forgot all about the man with the pistol as he planted a fist on Blondie's chin; he stumbled backwards, hit the desk, and slid to the floor. Lex expected the guy by the door to reward him with a bullet. He closed his eyes and waited for it.

40

LEX HEARD a thump instead of a bang. He opened his eyes to see the guy with the pistol drop to the floor. *Two down and none to go*, Lex thought.

Big Al stood by the door with a baton in one hand and a pistol in the other.

"Take his pistol, Lex." He stepped over the unconscious man and picked it up from the floor.

"What took you so long?" Lex said with a euphoric sense of relief. Lex pointed the pistol in Blondie's direction. He lay on the floor with a perplexed expression on his suntanned face and held a hand to his chin.

"I'm disappointed in you, Lex, for not inviting me to the party. I believed us to be friends," Big Al said, chuckling. "Luckily, I could gate-crash using the key you gave me."

"Where the fuck did you come from, big man?" Blondie cursed.

"Mind your language in front of a lady, mister."

"She ain't no lady, so you can go fuck yourself."

"Cover me, Lex," Big Al said as he stepped into the room. He stuffed the pistol in his waistband and raised the baton. Blondie held up a hand to ward off the expected blow. But Al didn't hit him; instead, he grabbed the man's arm and pulled him up like a toddler picking up a doll.

"I suggest you keep quiet, or I'll give you a taste of my baton. You can ask your friend how that feels when he comes round."

As if on cue, the man on the floor moaned, shifted his body, and opened his eyes. He removed his cap and put a hand to his head. He looked at it as if he expected to see blood, but there was none—his woollen cap had prevented his skull from cracking.

"Get up," Big Al ordered. The man struggled to get to his feet, but he eventually made it with the assistance of the door frame.

"Your office seems slightly crowded, so let's relocate to the living room," Al suggested.

And so they did. Al ordered the two gangsters to sit on the couch and keep their hands on their knees. He squeezed himself into a chair opposite as he held them at gunpoint. Linda and Lex stood by the window.

"I have a good idea why you're here, gentlemen," Big Al said, "but I'd like to hear it from either of you."

"I think Blondie is the talker," Lex said.

"Piss off, and I'd prefer you didn't call me Blondie."

"Sure, but what shall we call you?"

"Mister will do."

"Tell us all about it, mister," Al said.

"I've nothing to say to you or the police."

"Who said anything about the police, mister? I'm sure we can find an amicable arrangement to the, shall we call it, misunderstanding," Al said.

"There's no misunderstanding. Linda Lovelace stole from a friend of mine, and we're here to take back what belongs to him. It's not complicated."

"So why didn't you do that and leave?"

"Part of the money is missing, and we were discussing how to resolve the problem when you interrupted our little party."

"As I remember it, you laid on the floor, and your mate had a finger on the trigger."

"A minor glitch."

"How do you want the situation resolved, Lex? It's your call."

"I have an idea, but I'll have to discuss it with Linda behind closed doors."

"Why don't you do that, and I'll prevent these two buffoons from getting any funny ideas."

Linda followed Lex into the office, and he closed the door.

"Let's give it back," Lex said, as he gestured towards the bundles of guilders on the desk.

"What's left of it, you mean?"

"Indeed."

"But it's not their money in the first place."

"Not our problem, and for all we know, it's blood money."

"But it ..."

"Listen, Linda," Lex interrupted. "I'm afraid I'll have to insist. It only brings misery, and we don't need it anymore."

"I do."

"Why? You'll make money from modelling, and I'll soon get a few jobs, now that I've advertised my services."

"It's not like you to show that kind of optimism."

"What option do we have? If we hand them over to the police, we'll have to explain a situation we can't. And it won't solve the problem of having to keep looking over our shoulders."

"Even if we give back the money, what guarantee do we have that Allard Kuipers will not want retribution?"

"There's none, but we'll have to take our chances on that one."

"What's your plan?"

"We send the two clowns packing, obviously without the money, but with the message that we're ready to trade 235,000 guilders for leaving us alone. If the response is positive, we ask Big Al to take care of the handover."

"And they live happily ever after," Linda said acidly.

"Why not? We have every opportunity to make our life together into a fairy tale." Lex replied, "but if you have a better solution to your problem, I'm all ears."

"My problem?"

"You stole the money in the first place, then lied about the gang taking it back. Honestly, I can do without it."

"You do like to spend it."

"Wrong. Like most people, I like the freedom that money gives, but I have qualms every time we spend any of it."

Lex realised the incident had triggered a change in him and that he wanted to accept the things he had no control over and take charge of the things he did. If Linda wasn't with him, Lex was willing to risk her being without him.

"It's my way or the highway," Lex stressed.

"What's that supposed to mean?" Is this an ultimatum?"

"If you like."

"I don't have a say in the matter, do I?"

"That's right. I've already saved your pretty arse once, and if it weren't for Big Al, we would be without the money anyway, and most likely without the use of a few fingers or worse." Lex put a finger to her mouth to stop her from replying and then covered her lips with a kiss. She sidestepped to break the connection, but Lex moved to keep his mouth on hers. The situation was comical, and they let go, laughing.

"Okay, we'll do it your way," she said.

"You won't regret it," Lex said, relieved. "Let's rejoin the party and get this one put to rest."

BIG AL joined Lex and Linda for breakfast at ten. After the previous night's lucky escape, spirits ran high, and the conversation flowed freely. At eleven, Linda got ready for another *Vogue* photoshoot at Avenue Hoche. When she was ready, Big Al offered to drive her. Linda protested, but he wouldn't take no for an answer.

After they'd left, Lex brewed fresh coffee, lit a cigarette and went to the desk in his office. He lifted the receiver and was about to dial Jean-François' number when the doorbell rang.

"That was quick," he said to himself, convinced Big Al had returned. Lex pressed the buzzer and left the front door ajar. He returned to his desk, and within a couple of minutes, someone knocked lightly on the door.

"Do come in."

"Monsieur Clou?" a woman's voice said. The door opened slowly, and a middle-aged nun in a grey tunic stepped into the hallway.

"*Ma bonne sœur Coline.* What a surprise."

"Monsieur Clou? Or do you prefer Monsieur Spijker?" She smiled knowingly at him as she'd done at the previous meeting at the Sacré-Cœur.

"Lex will do. How can I help?"

"I'm here to help you."

"Why don't you take a seat?" Lex said and motioned her towards the chair opposite his desk. "Can I offer you coffee or tea?"

"I'll have some water if it's not too much trouble?"

Lex fetched her a glass of water from the kitchen, walked round his desk and seated himself in the office chair. Somehow, seeing her out of her natural environment made her appear more pious. She lowered the glass and fumbled nervously with the crucifix under her black veil.

"I think you know why I've come to see you?" she said.

"Perhaps, but please enlighten me,"

"You suspect Father Blanchet of sinful behaviour and for being involved in the disappearance of Angeline Pernet."

"Do I?"

"I've known about his devilish behaviour for years, and it makes me sick to my heart. I want it stopped, but no one listens to a grey and insignificant middle-aged nun."

"I do, sister Coline."

"I've prayed the Lord would send a good Samaritan," she said.

"I don't know about that, but I'll do what I can to help."

"Bless you, young man."

"How did you know where to find me?"

"I saw your advert in the local paper."

"And how did you know my real name?"

"I overheard Father Blanchet."

"How convenient."

"But that's not all I heard."

"Why not go to the police?"

"Unfortunately, they don't seem interested, and I don't trust them to do anything."

"I think you're mistaken; the police are eager to find the girl."

"Sure, but there's much more to it, and they had their chance to act."

"I'm not sure I follow, Sister."

"A few months back, I reported a private sex club engaged in the abuse of minors. When I didn't even get past the front desk, I decided to give them a tip-off that was hard to ignore."

"So you claimed to know the whereabouts of Ramírez Sánchez, aka Carlos the Jackal?"

"So you know about that? I'm afraid the club is still there." She let go of the crucifix to drink some water. Lex needed a cigarette, but to light one in her presence didn't seem right.

"How did you find out about the private club in the first place?"

"Does it matter? Isn't it more important what I know about this sordid affair?"

"If you don't mind, I like to know."

"If you insist. A few months ago, a young woman came to see me. I'd known her well when she did her solemn communion with Father Blanchet. She was about to get married, and as she carried an awful secret that she feared would ruin their happiness, she wanted to take someone into her trust."

"And what did she tell you?"

"As I'd expected, she told me about being abused by Father Blanchet. But she also told me something that I didn't know, which shocked me even more. On a couple of occasions, she was driven to a secret location and abused by other men."

"Did she know where?"

"She wasn't sure. A week or so later, I overheard Father Blanchet on the phone saying he'd be at Club Dolores tomorrow."

"Did you follow him?"

"Too risky. I asked my younger brother to do it."

"Did you tell him why?"

"No, and he knew me well enough not to ask. Anyhow, that's how I found out where it was."

"Is it on Avenue Foch?" Lex asked.

"Why would you say that?"

"Just some rumours I've heard."

"The address is 36 Avenue de Clichy."

"Do you know the floor?"

"From my brother's position on the street, he believed that Father Blanchet pressed the bell to the second floor."

"Uh-huh."

"As soon as he gave me the address, I made my first attempt to get the police involved. When I told the Paris Police Prefecture about Father Blanchet and the Club Dolores, and they didn't seem interested, I made up the story about the Jackal's whereabouts."

"A clever ploy that worked, in so far as the Direction de la Surveillance du Territoire raided the place. Unfortunately, as they expected to find a terrorist and not a group of dirty old men, they passed it on to the Préfecture de Police, who apparently again, did nothing," Lex speculated.

"Anyhow, I'm convinced that the girl is being detained at the private club."

"Why is that?"

"I heard Father Blanchet on the telephone, telling someone that necessary steps were being taken to keep the girl from talking. I also heard him saying, 'if you visit tomorrow night, you can see for yourself.'"

Lex wondered if that someone was Killian Lamarre.

"How interesting. But Father Blanchet didn't specifically mention the club?"

"No, but isn't it obvious?"

"Perhaps. What do you expect me to do?"

"I don't expect anything, Mr Spijker, but I hope you can convince the black policeman to instigate a raid. But you must keep my name out of it."

"I'm sure he'll be discreet."

"I need your promise."

"Do you fear for your safety?"

"It's not that. But even with God on my side, I can't afford to make an enemy of the Catholic Church."

"And if I'm not able to convince the police to raid the club?"

"All I can do is pray you'll make the best possible use of the information I've given you."

FROM THE landing, Lex watched the back of Sister Coline as she descended the stairs. Halfway down, he heard the front door open, and as he looked over the bannister, Lex saw the top of Big Al's grey mane. He was halfway up the flight of stairs before the nun appeared in front of him on the landing. Although Sister Coline was a tiny woman, the size of Al only allowed air to squeeze past him. He immediately backtracked, and Lex heard the nun say, "*Merci*," as he opened the door for her.

Al eventually made it to the second floor, and Lex greeted him, leaning against the door jamb.

"I met a nun on the stairs. Did she come from you?"

"You sound surprised?"

"I didn't know you were religious or that they did house calls."

"We mostly discussed earthly matters, and she gave me some vital information."

"Whatever it was, she looked scared."

"Surely from meeting you on the stairs."

"Come in and make yourself at home, and I will tell you all about it. But first, let me make us some coffee." Lex put the kettle on, lit a cigarette, and inhaled greedily.

"Later, I have to go to the Commissariat central in Rue de Clignancourt to talk to my police contact."

"I'll drive you," Al offered.

AT LUNCH, they grabbed two sets of *sandwich camembert beurre* and *demi de bière* at a café opposite Moulin Rouge. It turned out to be a real tourist trap— stale baguette, watery beer, and the bill an insult. At least the waiter had the decency to look bashful when Lex gave him an earful in French.

While he used the toilet, Big Al fetched his dark blue Volvo Amazon station wagon from a nearby side street. Lex entered the square and saw Al parked in front of the café with the motor running. He pulled the door open, slumped into the passenger seat, and before he'd slammed the door shut, Al pulled out and joined the traffic along the Boulevard de Clichy.

Five minutes later, he pulled up outside the Commissariat central in Rue de Clignancourt. Lex told him not to wait as he pushed the door open. Al would have none of it.

"I'll park the car and wait in the café on the corner." A car horn hooted impatiently from behind them; Lex got out, watched Al drive off, and entered the Commissariat.

"It's your lucky day. Not only is he in, but he'll be down in a few minutes," said a grey-haired, middle-aged police officer in full uniform from behind the reception desk. Lex thanked him profusely.

Being back at the police station made him think of his five years in the crime unit at Amsterdam's police headquarters. At first, he'd enjoyed the job as a young sergeant, but soon the high level of corruption in the Dutch police force had got to him, and the reluctance to take bribes made his colleagues suspicious.

"Lex, wake up," Jean-François said from behind him. He turned, and as Lex expected, there was the brigadier looking immaculate in his white shirt, black tie and buttoned up uniform jacket. Lex tilted his head and was drawn to the impressive black moustache that hovered at least twenty centimetres above his point of view.

As on the previous visit, Jean-François led him up the stairs to the second floor, along a corridor, and into a small, windowless interview room. He switched on the light and pointed to one of three chairs round a table in the centre of the room. This time he didn't offer coffee.

"Take a seat."

"How is Jos?"

"As far as I know, he's fine. Can we drop the small talk and cut to the chase? My colleague told me you have information about the missing girl."

"I talked to a source that claimed to know her whereabouts."

"Really? Where? Who?"

"I've promised not to reveal their identity."

"Tell me what you know."

He listened without interruptions while Lex recounted what Sister Coline had told him. He resisted the temptation to gloss over some of the weaker points in her narrative. It was no surprise when Jean-François eventually pounced on the fact that the source hadn't overheard Father Blanchet refer directly to the private club or mention Killian Lamarre by name.

"I'm afraid it all sounds a bit too flimsy to impress my superior," he said, avoiding eye contact.

"But it can't be a coincidence that the source knew the story about the Jackal's whereabouts?"

"I'm not keen to bring that old story to the attention of the top brass. However much I would like to follow the lead, it's not up to me."

"I can't see how the police can afford not to turn every stone."

"It's all politics, and apart from that, something else has come up, which may explain why the girl hasn't returned home."

"What can that possibly be?"

"When we interviewed Albert and Marie Pernet on Monday, I don't know if you noticed how the father seemed somehow detached?"

"I did find his remark about when he could return to work slightly uncaring, but people react differently when they're worried."

"Perhaps. Anyhow, it nagged me, so yesterday, I approached Albert Pernet at his workshop in Rue des Minimes. He admitted having had words with his daughter and that it wasn't the first time."

"What about?"

"Mostly about her doing badly in school. It turns out she played truant on several occasions and wouldn't tell her parents what she was doing when she wasn't at school."

"Even though Angeline is not quite the angel she's made out to be, it all seems normal to me for a young teenage girl. From what I've heard, she's a class A student, and couldn't her sudden lack of interest in her schoolwork be a sign of her being abused?"

"Maybe, but there's more. About a month ago, the girl ran away from home after another row with her father. She travelled by train to an aunt in Nantes, who called the parents almost immediately, against the girl's wishes. The following day Albert Pernet drove there to bring her home. I suggested that it must have worried him that his daughter had run away from home, but he seemed more concerned that it had cost him a whole day off work to get her back home."

"So now it's a case of a girl running away from home?"

"It's a possibility."

"But if it's a sign of rebellion, don't you find it strange she's been gone for four days?"

"Only if she, as last time, was staying with a relative. But I think she's already learned that this was not a good strategy. Now she stays somewhere else."

"Did she take any extra clothes?"

"No, but it was a spur of the moment thing. Same pattern as the first time the girl ran away."

"Listen to yourself. You don't even believe it."

"It doesn't matter what I believe. My hands are tied."

"So you keep telling me."

"Do I?"

"So you'll ignore what I told you?"

"I didn't say that, but it won't be top of the agenda."

"I think we're done," Lex said in disgust. "I'll find my own way out."

"Just one thing before you leave, Lex."

"Uh-huh."

"If you feel inclined to act on the information, who am I to stop you?"

"I hear you."

"Just remember I explicitly told you to leave this one to the police."

"Of course you did."

41

AL WAVED at him from behind the window. Lex pulled the glass door to the café open and walked up to him. He closed his paperback and placed it on the table beside an empty cup of espresso.

"How did it go?" Al asked.

"Not as I expected," Lex said and slumped into a chair. A waiter approached, and he ordered coffee and Calvados. Big Al asked for a glass of milk.

"What's the sour look for?"

"Just that I assumed my brigadier friend would be delighted with the information about Club Dolores."

"Did you say Dolores?

"What about it?"

"I guess it's too obvious to call the club for Lolita."

"You've lost me," Lex said as the waiter served the refreshments.

"The name Dolores appears in the novel *Lolita* written by the Russian-American novelist Vladimir Nabokov. The protagonist, a middle-aged literature professor, is obsessed with a 12-year-old girl, Dolores

Haze, with whom he becomes sexually involved after marrying her mother. Lolita is his private nickname for Dolores. The novel was first published in 1955 by Olympia Press here in Paris. The Henry Miller book I'm reading was also originally published by them." Al pointed to the paperback on the table.

"Is there anything you don't know about books, professor?" Lex said and lit a cigarette.

"Plenty, but I have an affection for avant-garde literary fiction."

"And now you will tell me you have the first edition of Lolita at home?"

"Only the edition in Dutch."

Lex's attention was distracted by a group of schoolgirls in identical navy blue culottes and white tunics chatting as they passed the café. *Each of them is a version of Angeline Pernet and a potential target for a paedophile ring*, Lex thought. It made him more determined, with or without the help of the police, to pay the club a surprise visit. After all, they'd already carried out one successful mission together to save a girl in distress, when raiding a house in the Amsterdam harbour area on an early July morning the previous year.

"Are you up for some action tomorrow evening?"

"As long as it's not another football game," Al said, but Lex saw from his expression that his friend knew what kind of action he meant.

THEY SPOTTED the gentle giant as they approached the busy Place de Clichy. Al had his broad back turned as he looked at the *banc à coquillage* outside the Brasserie Wepler.

"See anything you like?" Lex roared, to drown out the noise from the traffic. Al turned.

"My mouth waters, and my stomach rumbles," he said, "and those oysters right there have my name on them."

Al shook Lex's hand and gave Linda a peck on the cheek.

"Nice shirt and tie, Alwin," she said.

"I bought it this afternoon to look my best for the occasion."

"What occasion?" Lex said, surprised to see him all dressed up.

"I don't know about you, but this is the first time I've invited a *Vogue* fashion model to dine with me," he grinned. To see Linda's face beam put a smile on Lex's. Linda did look like a fashion model in her bright yellow sheath dress with a matching silk neck scarf, highlighted by her long dark hair.

Al held the door, and they entered the brasserie. A waiter directed them to a table in the centre of the large room. The decor of old wood, lots of red leather, and mirrors created a relaxed and authentic atmosphere. Low wooden partitions offered guests a certain intimacy, without taking anything away from the joyous spirit that characterised the place. Big Al whispered something to the waiter, who nodded enthusiastically. Linda lowered herself onto the leather sofa and slid along the table to make room for Lex. Al dropped onto a chair across from them. He scanned the room and smiled happily.

"Did you know that Henry Miller, Toulouse-Lautrec, Picasso and François Truffaut were once counted amongst the regulars of this elegant brasserie? Wouldn't it be wonderful if one of them joined our little party this evening?"

"Difficult for Toulouse-Lautrec," Lex said.

"What do you mean?"

"That he's dead."

"So is Picasso."

"Really?"

"He died a couple of years ago in the south of France."

"I can't believe his death escaped me," Lex said.

"I can," Linda offered. "You're the most absent-minded person I know."

"That's because I'm preoccupied with you, baby."

Fortunately, a waiter brought a bottle of champagne and three flutes, interrupting the futile exchange. Another waiter put a floor standing wine bucket at the end of the table.

"Moët et Chandon Brut Impérial 1970, monsieur," he said and presented the bottle portentously to Big Al. Cradling the bottle like a midwife handling a newborn, the waiter uncorked it with a pop without spilling a drop. He poured some of the golden liquid into Al's glass.

"You can fill our glasses, my good man. I'm sure it's drinkable."

"Let's drink to a fruitful outcome to all our endeavours," Al said. They drank. It tasted a cut above the three bottles of champagne Linda and Lex had devoured at Le Consulat the Sunday evening someone had mugged Lex.

"If either of you don't like seafood or suffer from a shellfish allergy, now is the time for you to object, as I'm going to order the Wepler platter."

"No objection from me," Lex said. They both looked at Linda.

"Gee, I don't know? I've never eaten it before."

"But surely you must have eaten some kind of *fruits de mer* before?" Lex insisted.

"Not that I know of, but if that's what they're having at the neighbouring table, it looks too tempting to care about a little allergy," Linda said.

"I wouldn't say that. My wife once had an anaphylactic reaction, so I know from experience that it can be life-threatening," Al said.

"I didn't know you were married," Linda said.

"Ex-wife."

"That bad?" Lex said.

"Happy to report she survived, and as far as I know, is still going strong."

"Do you have any kids?" Linda asked.

"Nope."

"I think you would be an excellent father."

"Perhaps, but it will probably never come to the test."

Again the waiter came to the rescue to end a slightly awkward conversation. He took the bottle of champagne from the ice bucket and refilled the flutes.

"We'll have the seafood platter," Al said, "and another bottle of bubbles."

"And some Perrier," Lex added.

After the waiter had taken the order, silence descended upon their table while they sipped the champagne. Lex lit a cigarette and offered one to Linda, who declined.

"Lex tells me you collect first editions. No offence, but I find that an unusual hobby for a hired gun and a former boxer."

"It's a long story."

"I'd like to hear it."

"Me too," Lex echoed.

"About fifteen years ago, I acted as a bodyguard for a publisher who'd just published the Russian-American writer Vladimir Nabokov's novel *Lolita* in Dutch. Banned in France and USA at the time, a group of people from the Dutch Bible Belt felt it should also apply to the Netherlands. When that didn't happen, the publisher received several death threats, and after someone gave him a black eye and a broken nose outside his home on his way to work, I escorted him for a while. Anyhow, my point is that he had a *substantial* library, and as there was not much for me to do while he was working in his office, it gave me plenty of time to explore his many literary treasures. As you can imagine, it opened up a wonderful new world for me, and I'm pleased to say I've now built up a collection that, in all modesty, makes most book collectors pay attention.

"Lex tells me you plan to start a business with rare books," Linda said.

"I'm almost there," Al said and presented her with his business card.

"Alwin Smit, Rare books & First editions," she read. "Looks professional."

"God knows I've spent serious money sustaining my hobby, or book addiction if you like, but I now feel experienced enough to reap some benefits from my ...." he paused.

"Investments?" Lex suggested.

"I was about to say knowledge, but that as well. And I'm not getting any younger, and I feel it's time to retire from the bouncer business."

Two waiters approached their table. "*Pardon, messieurs-dame*," said one, as he placed a stand at the centre of the table, while the other slid on the seafood platter. With a "*Bon appétit*", he topped up the champagne flutes.

The colourful selection of oysters, crabs, langoustines, prawns, mussels, clams, cockles and shrimps made Lex's mouth water.

"Do help yourself," Big Al said.

Later, nursing their coffee and cognac, in a by now, sparsely populated restaurant, Linda, who seemed slightly tipsy, said, "Did Lex ever tell you how I got mixed up in that nasty business that got me abducted and eventually sent to prison?"

"I read something in the newspaper, but I didn't talk to Lex after dropping you off at the Hilton."

"About three years ago, fed up with living on the bare minimum in Amsterdam, I tried my luck as a model. It didn't work out, so I joined an agency that provided high-class girls to exclusive customers, and that's how I met the guy from the Dutch Football Association."

"Allard Kuipers," Lex explained, as if they needed reminding.

"We were a group of four girls invited to entertain at a cocktail party at their headquarters in Amsterdam. We were offered booze and cocaine at the party, and Allard Kuipers picked me as his girl for the night. I did what the agency paid me to do, on the couch in his spacious office. Afterwards, he acted as though I'd done him a great favour and insisted on giving me a tip. Like in a gangster movie, he had a safe hidden behind a painting. I saw stacks of money in there as he took out a small bundle of notes to give me."

"So, you decided to steal it?" Al said.

"That was later, when I met a small-time hustler called Jan Berger with grandiose behaviour and an inflated opinion of himself. He bragged about how he could open any lock or safe, so I challenged him to open the one in Allard Kuipers' office. I promised him half the contents for his efforts, but I made the mistake of keeping all of it."

"I think your mistake was to steal it in the first place."

"Lex, for Christ's sake, we've been over this a thousand times—let me just tell my story to Alwin."

"Sorry, you're right." Lex took a sip of cognac and lit another cigarette to camouflage his displeasure at being rebuffed—or perhaps the embarrassment of not being able to keep his mouth shut.

"What I didn't know was that Jan Berger had also stolen a bag of cocaine from the safe and was careless enough to get his stupid face caught in the act on their closed-circuit TV. When Allard Kuipers and his gang tracked him down, he handed over the cocaine and told them, as was the truth, that he did not have the money but that he knew who did. By that time, and to get away from him, I'd relocated to an apartment owned by a friend's aunt while she was on a long holiday in Italy. I was convinced he'd never find me, but one day I spotted him as he was sniffing around in my new neighbourhood."

"That's when you got me involved," Lex exclaimed as a waiter approached the table. He asked if they would like the bill, and they realised that it was almost midnight and that the restaurant, apart from two other guests, was empty. Big Al got the hint.

"Let's go for a nightcap somewhere," he suggested. "I'd like to hear the rest of the story."

"Why don't we walk you back to your hotel and have a drink at Le Tagada Bar," Lex suggested.

"I'm game," Linda said. "But before we leave, I need to use the restroom."

"Me too," Lex said.

"You do that while I bail us out," Big Al chirped.

THEY STROLLED along the Boulevard de Clichy in the atmospheric light so characteristic of Paris, and Lex wondered if any of Killian Lamarre's thugs were watching from the shadows. He shrugged it off, not wanting his concerns to ruin a wonderful evening with his beautiful fiancée and their guardian, who'd treated them to a magnificent dinner.

Lex recognised the man behind the *comptoir* at Le Tagada Bar from the last visit, and apparently, it was mutual, as he greeted them warmly. Or maybe he just felt relieved to have customers in the otherwise empty bar.

"I don't know about you, Lex, but as a creature of habit, I'd like to have a pastis."

"Count me in. As you paid for the dinner, this one is on us.

"If you insist."

"What can I get you, Linda?"

"I'll stick with the white grapes."

"Champagne?"

"A glass of dry white wine will do."

Lex ordered at the bar. "Slow night?" he offered to the bartender.

"*Pas de tout, monsieur*, we cater for the night owls on Thursdays and Fridays, so we've just opened."

"Uh-huh."

"Remember, monsieur, you're in the city that never sleeps."

"Isn't that New York?"

"Perhaps, but stick around for a couple of hours, and you'll be amazed how crowded it gets in here." As if on cue, the door opened, and a group of youngsters entered.

The bartender promised to bring the drinks, and Lex returned to the table. With her back turned, Linda didn't see him, and he overheard her saying to Al, "…. and I don't know how to tell him."

"Are you talking about me?" Lex said and put a hand on Linda's shoulder.

"We don't talk about you all the time, Lex," she said with a nervous laugh, "and this was a private conversation between Alwin and me."

Lex felt his colour mounting. Was it because he had overheard a snippet of something he shouldn't have or because he had been told to mind his own business? Probably a combination of the two. To divert from his embarrassment, he suggested, rather cold-heartedly, that Linda tell Al the rest of the story of how she managed to end up in prison for manslaughter. "It will have to wait for a rainy day. I've momentarily lost my enthusiasm for telling the sad tale of my life on such a lovely evening. I wonder what got me started in the first place?"

"Wasn't it because you felt that Al deserved to know the full story, as part of our little rescue operation?" Lex suggested.

"Now I remember—it all came about because I thought of Angeline being kept prisoner somewhere and that made me think of my own story. Anyhow, whatever plans you have, gentlemen, please promise me you'll do whatever you can to help the poor girl return home safely.

"It's a promise," Lex and Al said in unison as the bartender brought the drinks.

42

THE TREES on the Avenue de Clichy with their sturdy, ascending branches and heart-shaped, dark green leaves, looked about as vigorous as Lex felt feeble, after another late night with too much alcohol. With the temperature in the twenties, it was the warmest day of the year so far, and his shirt, under the leather jacket, felt damp against his back. The morning sun made all things bright and beautiful, but his hangover failed to appreciate it fully. He lifted his pork pie hat to wipe the sweat off his forehead with the palm of his hand.

"Are you alright, Lex? You don't look so hot," Al said.

"Not as hot as I feel, you may add."

"Would you like to rest on a bench for a moment?"

"That will not be necessary as long as you slow down. I have no idea how you get all that energy. Surely you must feel slightly jaded after being up drinking most of the night?"

"I'm not letting a few drinks spoil a bright new day in a beautiful city. Moreover, we have work to do."

"Thanks for the encouragement, and it doesn't help much that you're twenty years my senior."

"Nothing beats experience," Al said with a wink. "Just hang on, and it will come to you too."

Lex pulled himself together. Al was right—they did have work to do—valuable work with a deadline that had no sympathy for a hangover.

Number 36 on Avenue de Clichy was located in a stylish six-storey sandstone building. Lex let his gaze travel up the ornamented facade. If Sister Coline was right, somewhere behind the tall windows and the iron balustrades on the second floor, Angeline Pernet was being kept against her will and forced, with other adolescent girls, to engage in sexual acts with middle-aged men from the elite of French society.

Al and Lex crossed the busy street and stopped at the entrance, a double wrought iron glass door with a woman's face, and a festoon carved in stone above.

"At least there's a concierge," Lex said and pointed.

"And?"

"It gives us easy access this evening."

"I appreciate your enthusiasm, but I don't think gaining access is our main concern. It wouldn't take me long to open the door lock with a tension wrench. Or a toothpick, for that matter."

"I don't doubt it, having seen you in action previously, but I meant the access to the apartment."

"I'd love to hear all about it, but I don't think we should linger here too long."

"Let's find a café." They moved away from the building and turned the corner to Rue Gannon, *et voila*, about fifty metres down the street, the traditional red canopy of a café presented itself. *Of all the things Paris has to offer, the density of its cafés takes the prize*, Lex thought.

"Les Quidams?" Big Al said.

"If I'm not mistaken, *quidam* means 'the unknown', in the sense of being unable to name someone."

"John Doe in French?"

"If you like."

A group of noisy Dutch youngsters were occupying the tables just inside the door. *Noisy Dutch tourists are a trial at the best of times*, Lex thought, and as this wasn't, they headed for a table in the back.

"Drinking beer at ten in the morning. What has the world come to?" Al muttered, pretending to be Holy Joe.

"I'm shocked too," Lex said, as he told the *garçon* to bring him an espresso and a Calvados. Both double. Al ordered a *café au lait*. Lex took off his leather jacket, hung it on the back of a chair and dumped his hat on the table.

"Whenever you're ready, I'd like to hear your plan," Al said, as soon as the waiter had served them. Lex sipped at the espresso, downed the Calvados, and lit a cigarette. "It's nothing elaborate. We arrive around nine this evening and ring the bell for the concierge. When she comes to the door, we'll ask her politely, if you know what I mean, to let us in and help us gain access to the apartment."

"How do you know it's a woman?"

"From watching *The Day of the Jackal*."

"Nice to hear you've done some proper research. Have you given it any thought that perhaps the concierge has no idea about what's going on or that she's paid a nice little retainer to keep her mouth shut?"

"Or perhaps she turns a blind eye, and is just waiting for someone to come and fix it?"

"I like your optimism, but say she refuses to talk?"

"I'm confident you'll persuade her to cooperate."

"What if she calls the police while we're in the apartment attempting to rescue the poor girl?"

"Perfect—that will safe us the trouble."

"Okay, you seem to have the plan all worked out, and I guess it isn't any worse than when Napoleon Bonaparte and Adolf Hitler planned to invade Russia in the winter."

"You're too kind."

"On a serious note, I guess it might work, and that we shall find out this evening," Al said. "Will you pay while I powder my nose?"

Lex caught the attention of the waiter and paid up. By now he was feeling as worn out as a pair of old shoes. Perhaps the double Calvados wasn't such a terrific idea. He needed to get back home to catch up on his sleep. A couple of hours should put him right. Big Al returned, and Lex explained the situation.

"I wouldn't mind a recharge. I'm not as young as I look," Al said as he ran a hand through his thick grey mane.

"Okay, let's head home and meet again for lunch at Le Consulat at two."

"WAKE UP, Lex." He forced his eyes open and felt the dampness on his cheeks.

"Are you alright? You were crying in your sleep," Linda said tenderly. She sat on the edge of the bed and looked down at him with her eyes full of compassion. He felt the warmth of her hand as it rested on his shoulder.

"A nightmare," he said, stating the bleeding obvious.

"Would you care to tell me about it?"

"It's a bit hazy and weird, and I'm not sure you'll want to know."

"Now, you have no choice but to tell me."

Lex paused, in an attempt to bring it to the surface. "A lot of confusing stuff happened, but the gist is that we were driving along a riverbank. I assumed that I was in the passenger seat, but when you screamed at me to keep the car on the road, I realised that we were driving Killian Lamarre's Aston Martin with the steering on the right. I grabbed the wheel with both hands, but too late to prevent the car from flying over the embankment and into the water. It didn't take long for the car to become submerged and for the inside to fill up with water. I attempted to open the door on my side, but it wouldn't budge. Nor would the passenger door. I then tried to roll down my window, but the handle broke off, and there was no handle on your side. We were trapped, unable to prevent the water from rising above our heads. The air bubbles rising from your mouth are the last thing I remember."

"Hopefully, it's not an evil omen?"

"Let's not go there. Thank God it was only a nightmare. I hope you don't believe too much in dreams?"

"But I do. I believe dreams are real manifestations of the subconscious—a consequence of our thoughts and actions when we're awake. You could say our subconscious is always awake."

Lex gazed at Linda, realising how little he still knew about her inner life and beliefs. The alarm sounded, and they both jumped. They locked eyes and laughed. "It's my wake up call. I'm going to meet Al for lunch at Le Consulat. I would love you to come with me."

AL WAS waiting for Lex outside the hotel as he rounded the corner to Rue des Trois Frères. In the warm glow from the street lamps, Lex observed the big man wearing dark trousers and a black T-shirt. He carried a backpack over his shoulder. Al greeted Lex with a hand to his black cap, but said nothing. He looked calm, cool and collected, which soothed the butterflies Lex always felt before a mission. Al started walking, and Lex followed.

"Where are you parked?"

"Down there somewhere." Al pointed. "It took me some time to find a free spot yesterday."

"Too many cars in this city," Lex offered.

"And people," Al added.

Lex knew what he meant, although all they could see was a mature couple further down the street.

"What is the population anyway?"

"Almost nine million."

"I prefer Amsterdam with less than a million."

"At this moment, I prefer my life here in Paris."

"Who can blame you? You're half French, you speak the lingo, it's springtime, and you're in love."

They reached the car, and Al unlocked the door to the passenger seat and pulled it open.

"You drive," he said and handed Lex the key. Although surprised, Lex didn't argue. Tonight Al was in charge, and he would follow his lead.

They drove in silence. Big Al studied the busy Parisian streets, and Lex focused on manoeuvring the station wagon through the dense traffic. As they made their way up the Avenue de Clichy, Al told Lex to drive past the entrance to number 36 and turn at the first street on the left.

"Nothing looks out of the ordinary," he said as they passed, and Lex activated the indicator. As the car turned, Lex caught sight of Rue des Dames on the blue street sign. About a hundred metres down the street, a parking spot presented itself. It was tight, and Al jumped out to direct him.

"Perfect," Al said with encouragement through the open side window after patiently helping Lex get the Volvo into position. Lex killed the engine and pushed the door open. He got out.

"I suggest you leave your hat in the car. That pork pie gives you away a mile off," Al said from the other side of the car. Lex took it off, put it on the seat, slammed the door, and locked it.

"Toss the key to me." Lex did, and it disappeared into Al's big right hand. He locked the door to the passenger seat and set his big frame in motion. Lex followed along the narrow street. A Renault van turned the corner and drove at speed towards them, and they stepped in between two parked cars and walked along the pavement. They reached Avenue de Clichy, and Al stopped and looked across the street to the apartment block. The first floor lay in darkness. Light shone through the curtains of four of the seven windows on the second floor. No light came from three of the windows on the third, but they couldn't be sure about the four others as they were covered by black curtains. On the fourth floor, light shone from two of the windows.

"Shall we go?" Lex said.

"Wait until there are people passing the entrance on the pavement from both sides. It makes us look less conspicuous." Good luck with that, Lex thought. Al would look as inconspicuous as a stranded whale in most settings involving average-sized people.

They waited a minute or so until a group of youngsters came from the right and a mature couple from the left.

"Let's go," Al said, and they quickly crossed the street through the steady flow of cars. They let the noisy youngsters pass and approached the double wrought iron glass door in front of the couple. Lex pressed the bell for the concierge and leaned towards a small speaker above it. Within a few seconds, it said, "*Oui?*" Instead of giving a reply, Lex pressed it again. "*Ce qui?*" He pushed the bell for the third time. "*Ca alores!*" a voice from the speaker said. It didn't take long before a middle-aged woman with a headscarf and a tired house dress flung the door open. Al stepped into the doorway and pushed her gently aside. Lex followed and shut the door behind them. Her mouth dropped open, but nothing came. Perhaps it intimidated her that Al, double her size, was towering over her.

"Don't be scared, madame," Lex said. "We're not here to hurt you, but we do need your cooperation in an urgent matter."

"How dare you? It's a respectable establishment," she said as she regained some of her composure. Lex guessed she was, as most concierges were, used to taking a lot of nonsense and therefore would take none from a couple of strangers that forced themselves into her building. "I demand you leave immediately, or I'll call the police."

"We're not here to harm you," Lex repeated, "but we insist on your assistance. Give me a minute to explain. It's not too complicated." Her suspicious eyes darted from Lex to Al before she seemed to decide the best option was to listen.

"There's no need to block the hallway. I suggest we go to your apartment," Lex said, and Al guided her, as gently as possible, but with enough force to make sure she understood who was in charge, towards the open door to her apartment. Lex followed right behind as they entered a room with a small open kitchen, a dining table with a couple of chairs, and a buffet with a telephone and a small television on top. It was on, but the sound was barely audible. Through an open door Lex saw a single bed with a cover and a cupboard . Before the concierge closed the door, Lex noticed a crucifix on the wall.

"Take a seat, madame ...."

"It's Torrence." Reluctantly she lowered herself onto an old wooden chair. Lex pulled its twin out and took a seat opposite her. Al remained on his feet right behind her. "How well do you know the tenants, Madame Torrence?"

"As well as you know anyone after a few months."

"When did you begin as a concierge?"

"In February."

"What happened to your predecessor?"

"She inherited some money and bought a small house down south."

"So you weren't here when the police raided the apartment on the second floor?"

"I'm afraid I don't know what you're talking about."

"You wouldn't, would you now," Lex mumbled.

"What, monsieur?"

"Never mind. Who lives in the apartment?"

"On the second floor?"

"Yes."

"A respectable lawyer and notary."

"You know his name?"

"It's Anatole Dupont."

"And how long has he lived and operated from the apartment?"

"I don't know, but for many years."

"Why is there no nameplate at the entrance?"

"That's what he prefers, and as I understand it, he operates by appointment only. His clients are important people from the establishment."

"Do you let his clients into the building?"

"Sometimes, but mostly they ring the bell to the second floor."

"So you don't always see who comes and goes?"

"A concierge has many duties, monsieur, and I'm not here all the time. Monsieur Dupont receives visitors at all hours and not always as clients. Most Fridays, he entertains in the evening, and tonight is no different."

"Do you know who Killian Lamarre is?"

"*Bien sûr.* Anyone who reads *Paris Match* will know that."

"Did you see him come or go?"

"You mean here?"

"Where else?"

"I haven't."

"Are you sure?"

"I think I would remember, but if I did, I wouldn't find it strange if he was a client of Monsieur Dupont."

"Is he married? Kids?"

"Killian Lamarre?"

"You know very well I mean Anatole Dupont."

"As far as I know, he's a bachelor."

"The girls he likes are too young to marry," Lex said.

"Why would you say that, monsieur?"

"Because we suspect that the respectable Monsieur Dupont also uses his apartment as a private club for paedophiles."

"Is that why you're here?"

"You haven't seen any young girls come and go?"

"Not that I recall. And if I did, I doubt they would be here to see Monsieur Dupont."

"Have you heard about the young girl that's missing?"

"Of course. I'm not deaf or blind. But I don't see what it has to do with Monsieur Dupont."

"We suspect that the girl is being held against her will in his apartment."

"That's ridiculous."

"And that she's being abused."

"I find it hard to believe that Monsieur Dupont has anything to do with her disappearance. It's not that I know him well, but to me, he's always considerate and proper—surely you are mistaken?"

"Perhaps, but we're here to find out."

She moved uneasily on her chair. *Did she know or suspect that some of the activities in the apartment on the second floor were deviant?* Lex wondered.

"As I said, this is a respectable house, and I keep my nose out of matters that are no concern of mine."

"Isn't being nosy part of the concierge job description?"

"That's hardly fair, monsieur. Obviously, as a concierge, you take an interest in what goes on in the building. But that's not the same as being a nosy-parker."

"Do you have a key to the apartment?"

"Of course. I have a spare key to all the apartments. But it's not to be used unless Monsieur Dupont locks himself out or there's an emergency."

"Tonight is an emergency," Lex pointed out.

"I'll only give the key to Monsieur Dupont in person. Why don't you ring his bell? As I told you, he is entertaining tonight."

"We would like to catch him and his guests off guard. You can give us the key, or we'll help ourselves," Lex said and looked towards the buffet.

"It's in a locked drawer," she exclaimed.

"It won't be for long when I ask my friend to open it." The concierge again seemed to consider her options; but only when Al put a hand on her shoulder.

"Okay, I'll give you the key." She brushed off Al's hand with an irritated gesture, rose to her feet, and walked to the cabinet. She took a key from behind the television, unlocked a central drawer, and pulled it out. She looked into it for a moment before taking out the key to the apartment on the second floor.

"I can't prevent you from using the key to gain access to Monsieur Dupont's apartment, but I'll call the police if you do." She threw the key with an attached label onto the table. Al picked it up.

"Please do; that'll save us the trouble." In Dutch, Lex said to Al, "Let's pay Monsieur Dupont and his mates a visit. Hopefully, we'll interrupt them entertaining their young friends."

43

THEY IGNORED the old-fashioned cage lift and mounted the elegant spiral staircase. Al took the lead, and as they reached the first-floor landing, Lex heard voices from downstairs. He couldn't make out what was being said but recognised the voice of Madame Torrence and, to his surprise, of Jean-François Diagne. *No need for the concierge to alert the police*, Lex thought. He wondered what had changed the brigadier's mind about checking out the address on Avenue de Clichy. Al looked at Lex with raised eyebrows.

"I think the cavalry has arrived," Lex said.

"Your friend from the police?" Al asked.

"We'd better see what's going on."

They descended the stairs, turned the corner into the hallway, and saw the back of two men and one woman, all in police uniform, outside the concierge's small apartment. Madame Torrence stood in the doorway, gesturing animatedly. She turned her head in their direction, pointed, and said, "These two men forced me to give them the key to Monsieur Dupont's apartment."

"Good evening, Lex. You look surprised to see me. Let me know if we are spoiling your party?"

"Evening, Jean-François. It was my impression that you and your colleagues weren't interested in putting a stop to a potential sex club for paedophiles."

"That's hardly fair, but I'll let it pass. And besides, we're here now."

"All three of you," Lex said, scoffing.

"What's your problem, Lex? Do I have to ask you to explain why you're here?"

"You know damn well why. I wonder what made you change your mind."

"Something happened this afternoon that convinced my superiors that we'd better check out the address."

"Who already knew the apartment was raided a few months ago."

"As I've already told you, that officially never happened, and I'm not prepared to discuss it again, especially not with an audience."

"Never mind. So what happened?"

"A nun is in a coma at the hospital after a nasty fall down the stairs at the Sacré-Coeur."

"My God," Lex said. "Is it Sister Coline?"

"I'm afraid so."

"How is she?"

"As I said, she's in a coma, and the doctor says her life is hanging in the balance."

"Poor woman, I wish I could have done something to prevent it."

"So you know her?" Jean-François said.

"Did you suspect she was my source?"

"She was a strong candidate."

"Have you arrested Father Blanchet?"

"For what? There's no proof that he or someone else pushed her. But if she's your source, it does seem strange that the day after giving you information about the club and the disappearance of Angeline Pernet, the nun accidentally falls down some stairs that she goes up and down several times a day, year in and year out."

"What's happening now?" Lex asked.

"I have a search warrant for the apartment, and as soon as you stop wasting our time, we'll proceed to do so."

"You're just going to ring the doorbell?"

"What else?"

"The chance of catching the offenders in the act will be seriously reduced without the element of surprise," Lex said.

"I hear you, Lex, but we have to follow procedure."

"But it gives them a chance to cover their fucking arses."

"Steady on, Lex. If we find Angeline Pernet, as your source has claimed, or any other youngsters, it will be hard to explain. Even for Killian Lamarre."

"I guess there's no chance you'll leave it to me and my associate?"

"I don't get you, Lex. Yesterday, you were visibly upset about my passivity, and now you can't wait to see the back of me."

"I'm not sure what I imagined. Perhaps something along the line of storming the place and breaking down the door."

"You've seen too many American movies. We don't do it that way unless it's armed gangsters or a terrorist cell."

"Can I at least come with you?"

"Okay, but you stay in the background."

"And my friend?"

For the first time, Jean-François seem to notice the big man. Apart from being the same height, they were complete opposites: one was as white and broad as the other was black and lean.

"Who are you?" Jean-François asked.

"My name is Alwin Smit. I'm a Dutch citizen, and Lex invited me to Paris last week to assist him. I helped him resolve a case last summer in Amsterdam."

"And you are the size of a 12-tonne lorry and built like, what's the English expression?"

"Like a brick shithouse," Lex suggested.

"I'll take your word for it."

"Alwin deals in rare books," Lex said, as if it would explain why he was about to enter the apartment uninvited.

"Sure, and I'm the party leader of Front National. No offence Monsieur Smit, but you look more like a retired boxer and someone called upon to apply brute force."

"No offence taken. I'm used to people thinking I'm a mean motherfucker, but I assure you I'm as gentle as the breeze that never comes," Al said with a snigger.

"It's all most interesting, but can we have this discussion some other time," Lex interrupted. By now, he was eager to get the show on the road. For all he knew, it could already be too later. Lex wondered if Monsieur Dupont and his mates had managed to squeeze some information out of Sister Coline before she accidentally fell down the stairs.

"Lex and Gilbert, come with me," Jean-François said with sudden determination. "Monsieur Smit and you, Jeanette, stay here to prevent anyone from sneaking out the back door." The female *gardien de la paix* nodded. Lex looked at Big Al, as he imagined he wasn't best pleased at the turn of events, but, as he'd come to expect, Al showed no emotion.

"Let's go," Jean-François said and headed for the staircase. The *gardien de la paix* followed, and Lex followed him. Ascending the stairs, he noticed that the seat of his black uniform trousers were worn and that his black leather shoes, although well-polished, were down-at-the-heel. Perhaps, with the recent economic instability, the national police force had had to cover the costs of their uniforms themselves.

They reached the second floor, and Jean-François pressed the doorbell. Lex heard it ring inside, and they waited for about fifteen seconds for a reaction. As there was none, the brigadier pushed it again. Almost immediately, the door opened, and a middle-aged man wearing a black morning coat, black tie and white gloves appeared in the opening.

"How can I help, sir?" he said with a stiff upper lip.

"Is Monsieur Dupont at home?"

"Monsieur is hosting a dinner party, and unless it's important, I'm sure he would prefer not to be disturbed."

"I can assure you it's important, my good man." After a moment of hesitation, the butler invited them into the vestibule.

"Wait here, and I will see if my master is available," he said and disappeared down the hall. He seemed to glide, his steps barely audible on the parquet flooring. Lex heard a door open and muted conversation that stopped immediately.

"Who's at the door, Oscar?" a voice called out .

"It's the police, sir. They say it's important."

"I'll be right there."

Lex assumed the butler would reappear, but instead, a man almost as tall and lean as the brigadier joined them in the spacious vestibule. Lex didn't need to look twice to see that he had a physical resemblance to the late president Charles de Gaulle—his sleek, dark hair with a side parting and a pyramid moustache. He wore a navy blue double-breasted jacket over a white shirt, open at the neck to accommodate a silk cravat— probably his way of showing a causal attitude to life.

"Monsieur Dupont?" Jean-François said.

"How can I help, brigadier?" He sounded annoyed at being dragged away from his guests.

"I'll cut right to the chase. We've received information that links your apartment to a private sex club."

"Come again. My hearing is not what it used to be, and as French, by the looks of it, is not your first language, I'm sure I misunderstood."

"You heard me alright, and we would like to search your residence."

"Do you happen to have a search warrant, brigadier?"

Jean-François took a piece of paper from his inner pocket, unfolded it and passed it to Monsieur Dupont. He took it like he was handling a dirty nappy and studied it as if it was one before handing it back.

"I'm not sure it will be a wise career move. I'm hosting a dinner for some significant guests, and I'm not without important friends in high places. Your commissioner, for one, is a good friend of mine."

"Is he here this evening? Perhaps you share the same interest in having sex with children?" Lex snapped, no longer able to keep quiet as he'd promised Jean-François.

"And you are?"

"Your fucking nightmare."

"That's enough, Lex," Jean-François said and asked Monsieur Dupont to take them to the dining room, so they could meet his important friends. As they followed the host down a sparsely lit corridor, Jean-François said, "A few months back, the police raided the building. I wonder if you can tell me anything about that?"

Monsieur Dupont stopped and turned towards the policeman. "There's not much to tell. The Direction de la Surveillance du Territoire knocked my door down, claiming that the infamous Ramírez Sánchez was my guest. Absolute cock and bull. If it interests you, I sued the Fifth Republic for violation of privacy."

Monsieur Dupont opened the door, stepped aside and gestured for them to go in. The dining room was big enough to park a bus and sufficiently splendid for Louis the Great to feel at home. Under a magnificent crystal chandelier stood a long dining table upon which a small plane could be landed. Only three of the fourteen chairs were occupied, and it pleased Lex immensely to see Killian Lamarre as one of the occupants. He managed to keep the usual smug grin on his suntanned face, but his dark eyes looked worried. Lex had no idea who the two other middle-aged men were, but he didn't have to wait long to find out.

"For some obscure reason, the police have decided to interrupt our dinner, and for that, I must apologise dear friends," Monsieur Dupont said.

"Stay seated, gentlemen," Jean-François commanded, "and you can join your party again, Monsieur Dupont," he added, pointing to the empty seat across from Killian Lamarre. "I think a round of introductions would be in order."

"I doubt I need to introduce myself," Killian Lamarre said. "Lately, I seem to be mister popular with Foottit et Chocolat." He laughed at his racial insult, which was wearing thin in Lex's humble opinion. Jean-

François ignored him and turned his attention to the man next to him. "I'm not going to pretend I don't know who you are, but please state your name and profession."

"My name is Roman Renoir, and I'm a film director. Don't let our dinner disturb whatever you're here for." Ostentatiously, he grabbed a glass of red wine, lifted it to his lips, emptied it in one gulp, and set it down with force. He wiped his clean-shaven face with the back of his hand before running it through a thick, unruly mane. A jacket hung over the back of his chair, and his shirt showed patches of sweat under his arms.

"And you are?" Jean-François's attention turned to a heavily built, middle-aged man seated opposite the film director. He was in an expensive-looking, grey three-piece suit. His shiny bald head reflected the light from the chandelier.

"I'm surprised you don't know me, brigadier," he said, as he adjusted his silk bowtie with both hands and as his cold eyes studied the policeman over the rim of his spectacles.

"I don't believe we've met, but perhaps your name will ring a bell?"

"My name is Henry de Maupassant, and I'm...."

"Président of the Chambre Criminelle at the Court of Cassation," Jean-François interrupted, finishing his sentence.

"I wonder, your honour, what you're doing in a private club for paedophiles?" Lex said.

"Obviously, as a judge, I've heard of such places, Mr ....?"

"He's a lowlife detective named Lex Spijker," Killian Lamarre offered.

"I can assure you, Monsieur Spijker, that what you claim is a private club is, in fact, the private home of my friend Anatole Dupont. Unless you can back up your accusations, I'd be careful before defaming someone, as it could come back to bite you."

Jean-François put his hand on Lex's arm to stop him from continuing a discussion that was leading nowhere.

"I'll ask you, gentlemen, to stay seated while we check out the apartment," he said.

"Feel free—as I've told you already, there are no criminal activities here to see," Anatole Dupont offered, "and I'll be more than happy to show you around. It's rather a big apartment, and I would hate for you to get lost."

"Unless we find some doors locked, I'm confident we'll manage," Jean-François said. "I'm sure your male servant can help us navigate our way around."

"André is my butler."

"Whatever, but could you please get him in here?"

"André, your assistance is required," Monsieur Dupont called out. Within a few seconds, a door opened. "You called, sir?" André said.

"Can you show the police the apartment's remaining thirteen rooms?"

"Is that my room as well, sir?"

"All rooms, André, unless you want to risk being accused of hiding a group of youngsters."

Jean-François told Lex to 'entertain' the gentlemen seated at the table while he and his colleague checked out the apartment.

The four middle-aged pillars of society had no wish to be entertained by, as Lamarre had put it, a lowlife detective, and ignored his presence. It suited Lex fine, as he preferred to engage as little as possible with what he considered to be dirty old men who believed they were above the law and the petty morals that applied only to other mortals. To prove the point, Killian Lamarre said, "What time are the girls coming?" His remark drew laughter, and Lex longed for the tycoon and his 'friends in high places' to be taken down a peg or two. He no longer believed that Jean-François and his colleague would find Angeline Pernet, or anything linking the apartment to her disappearance or a private sex club. Lex wondered if Sister Coline had got it all wrong, and if so, why she had taken a tumble down the stairs at the Sacré-Cœur after visiting him.

44

THE SEARCH revealed nothing to connect the apartment to the disappearance of Angeline Pernet or a private sex club. Lex did find it odd that there were five guestrooms.

"If you have an apartment with fourteen rooms, there's no law against turning one-third of them into rooms for your guests," Jean-Francois said.

Lex, Big Al, Jean-François and his two colleagues stood by a police car parked on Avenue de Clichy opposite the apartment block.

"I think they were well prepared for a visit," Lex said.

"Unfortunately, we have no way of proving that's the case. I would have liked to speak to Sister Coline myself, but that's not an option with her in a coma," Jean-François said.

"Are you going to put pressure on Father Blanchet?" Lex asked.

"With what? All we have on him is hearsay."

"Perhaps put a tail on him or any other potential suspect."

"We don't have the resources, and you can't put a tail on people just because you suspect them of being involved in some shady business—you need a bit of evidence."

"I should think there's enough evidence to put a tail on Father Blanchet," Lex persisted.

"How can you say that? A girl has told your fiancée that her friend indicated she was being abused. Unfortunately, the girl went missing before we could talk to her. Then we have a nun claiming that Father Blanchet is a sexual predator and that the girl is being held hostage at a private club, and if we visited the address this evening, we would find the girl and a few sexual predators. But we didn't, and we can't talk to the nun, as she's in a coma after falling down some stairs. Have I missed anything?"

"Killian Lamarre and Father Blanchet know each other, and you have some witnesses claiming that the tycoon made inappropriate suggestions."

"They sat on the same church committee, which is legitimate. And the young girls in Angeline Pernet's class only told me that Killian Lamarre chatted them up and promised he could make their dreams come true. Slightly dodgy from a moral point of view, but hardly a criminal act."

"You sound like you're working as their defence lawyer," Lex said, sulking.

"You have a nice evening too, Lex," Jean-François said, "I have some paperwork waiting."

Lex and Big Al watched the police car drive off. According to Lex's watch, the entire failed operation had taken about two hours.

"You're very quiet tonight," Lex said.

"I felt somehow side-lined."

"What do you suggest we do?"

"How about calling it a night?"

"I'm convinced Anatole Dupont and his friends are hiding something."

"I'm with you there, but I doubt they'll admit it unless we break a few fingers."

"What if the club is on the third floor?" Lex asked. They scanned the windows. "What if the group of men first meets for dinner at Anatole Dupont's private apartment on the second floor and then moves upstairs for the entertainment?"

"That would be a neat arrangement," Big Al said.

"I wonder what goes on behind the dark curtains."

"If anything, I doubt we'll ever know."

"If we hadn't already set our minds on the second floor, it would have been a good idea to let the concierge show us the residence ledger."

"I doubt it would have helped us much, and didn't your nun insist it was the second floor?"

"Only it wasn't."

"It might still be. As you said, Anatole Dupont and his friends seemed prepared for a visit."

"Let's revisit Madame Torrence and ask her to show us the ledger. And if we decide it's worth checking out the third floor, we get the key to the apartment."

"Forget the concierge, the ledger, and the key."

"Why? Don't tell me you're about to give up?"

"It's your gig, but why not let the concierge catch up on her beauty sleep and we go directly to the third floor?"

"Wouldn't you prefer it if we had some indication that there might be something illegal going on?"

"Sure, but we had that on the second floor. Yet here we are on the street with empty hands, while Monsieur Dupont and his mates are still sipping their cognacs and smoking their cigars."

"But how do we get in?" As soon as the words passed his lips, Lex knew it was a silly question. Al was a master picklock, and Lex doubted it would take him long, first to open the downstairs door to the building and then pick the lock to the third-floor apartment.

"We might set off an alarm?" Lex said.

"That's a chance we'll have to take," Al said.

"Let's do it," Lex said, feeling energised.

They crossed the street to the entrance of the building. Al slid off the backpack and took out a leather pouch the size of an A5 notebook. He unzipped it and flipped it open, and Lex saw rows of lock-picks and tension wrenches in different shapes and sizes. Al studied the lock and said, "If you cover for me, I'll have this baby picked in no time." Lex positioned himself in front of Al, turned to face the street, and looked at his watch as if to indicate he was waiting for someone. Within a minute, Lex heard a click, turned, and saw the door swing open. They entered quickly, and Al closed the door to the street behind them. As a reflex, Lex reached for the light switch, but Al stopped him in time.

"Let my torch be our guiding light." For the third time that evening, Lex ascended the stairs. They heard classical music coming from the apartment on the first floor, but no sounds from Monsieur Dupont's apartment on the second, and all was quiet as they reached the third-floor landing. Al pointed the torch towards the door, and a small blue sign revealed that the Poseidon Shipping Company operated behind it.

"Hold the torch, Lex, and point it at the door," Al whispered. He knelt, and Lex looked on in fascination as Al's huge hands, like a virtuoso, skilfully operated the tools. The staircase light came on.

"Damn," Lex whispered. Al stayed on his knees, signalled for Lex to kill the torch, and put a finger to his lips. Lex jumped when the lift was set in motion behind them, and he felt the tension as it descended. They heard it reach the ground floor, the opening and closing of doors before it was again set in motion, this time towards them.

Anything but the third floor, Lex thought. To his relief, it stopped on the second, and he heard footsteps exit the lift as the door to Monsieur Dupont's apartment opened. After some muted conversation, the door slammed shut, and within a short while, the light switched off. Lex switched the torch on, and Al continued to pick the lock.

"Done," Al said as he gathered his tools and raised himself from his kneeling position.

"You're a genius," Lex said and handed Al the torch.

"Ready?" Lex nodded, and Al pushed the door open.

Lex felt mixed emotions in the dark hall that greeted them—relieved at avoiding a confrontation and disappointed that the apartment, at first sight, revealed nothing more than what they might have expected on a late Friday evening—a deserted office. They stepped in, and Lex closed the door gently behind them. He saw a reception area with a glass partition in the light from the torch.

"At first sight, it all looks normal, but let's check it out anyway," Al said. He reached into his backpack, produced another torch, switched it on, and handed it to Lex.

The apartment consisted of four rooms used as office space and two for storage. There was a short hallway, with two doors to restrooms at the far end, which ended in a kitchen area with a couple of tables surrounded by chairs.

"So that's it. No sign of anything improper," Al said.

"How many windows facing the street did you count from downstairs?" Lex asked.

"Seven."

"Right, but this apartment only seems to have three."

"Perhaps this floor is divided into two apartments?"

"That may be, but where's the entrance to the second apartment? What if you can only gain access from the apartment downstairs?"

"If there's a staircase, your policeman friend should have found it."

"It must be hidden."

Lex walked to the end wall of the large room and pressed the palm of his left hand against it. He felt a slight indentation. "I think there used to be a door here." He pressed his ear against it. "I can hear the murmur of voices."

"And now you're wondering if there's a connection to the party downstairs."

"And also, what would happen if your broad shoulder connected to the wall. I doubt it will be able to withstand much force."

"Are you seriously suggesting I use my old and fragile body as a wrecking ball?"

"Just an idea."

"Move away, *petit*, and I'll check if it's even possible to break it down." Big Al leaned against the wall and felt it give way to his massive frame. "I have to agree with you that it seems to be a blind door and that it won't take too much force to break down."

"Terrific."

"Hold it there, young man. That doesn't mean I agree with your suggestion. There are a few unanswered questions: What kind of reception will greet me on the other side? Could be some bad guys with weapons?"

"If you'd seen Monsieur Dupont and his mates, I honestly don't think you need to worry. I doubt they feel, in their arrogance, the need for armed protection."

"Okay, I'll give it a go, but you must cover me," Big Al said as he handed the backpack to Lex. "You'll find a pistol in there."

"I don't think ...."

"Don't argue, Lex. I'm the one putting my body on the line."

Lex took the pistol, slid on the backpack, and pointed the torch at the wall.

"As soon as I, hopefully, go through, you follow with the weapon raised," Al said and moved a table and some chairs to make enough space for him to run at the wall.

With a "Here we go," the big man set his perfectly proportioned, hundred-twenty kilos in motion. Like a racehorse, he quickly gained speed, and just before he reached the wall, he adjusted his body to make his shoulder take the impact. To Lex, it looked surreal when he, like a knife cutting through soft butter, disappeared through the plaster, and it surprised him that the resonance from the impact was relatively muted. Lex approached the opening, and then crossed from one side to the other. Lex couldn't believe what he saw in the centre of the windowless room. Nor could he believe their good fortune. Big Al lay on top of a naked man, who lay on top of a collapsed foldable massage table. A few metres away stood a girl with a shocked expression on her young face. Her crossed arms covered her naked chest. Lex felt relieved to see that she was wearing knickers. The operation couldn't have taken more than fifteen seconds, but it felt much longer. Lex stepped past the two men on the floor, took a bathrobe from a hook by the door, and handed it to the girl, who turned her back and put it on.

Big Al raised himself and pulled up the man who was doing his best to cover his groin with his hands.

"Good evening Monsieur Lamarre. I almost didn't recognise you without your clothing."

"Don't get any wrong ideas."

"About what? You're getting a massage from a topless girl, young enough to be your granddaughter. All perfectly normal," Lex mocked.

"Please allow me to cover myself," Lamarre pleaded.

Lex ignored him and turned his attention to the girl. It wasn't Angeline Pernet. "Are you alright?" he asked.

Before she could answer, loud knocking on the door interrupted them.

"What happened? Are you alright, Killian? Please open the door." Al pushed the naked Lamarre down onto a chair in the corner, and Lex pointed the pistol in his general direction. Swiftly Al moved to the door, unlocked it, and jerked it open. With the giant covering the door's opening, Lex couldn't see who it was, but when the person gasped, "Who are you?" he recognised Anatole Dupont's voice. Big Al pulled Monsieur Dupont into the room. He looked dumbfounded when he saw the massive hole in the opposite wall, the collapsed massage table on the floor, and Killian Lamarre slumped naked on a chair in the corner. He was about to speak when Big Al hit him across the face with the back of his hand, sending the tall, lean man to his knees.

"How dare you?" he said, in anger. With minimum effort, Big Al pulled him up. "Stop! You're hurting me."

"You stay right there, or I'll break your fucking neck," Al said. "Hand me the backpack, Lex," he added. Lex did so, and Al opened it and produced another pistol and a length of rope. "Time to show me the rest of the apartment," Big Al hissed as he poked Anatole Dupont in the ribs with the pistol barrel. Lex watched them step into the hallway and heard them walk away.

"Could I have my clothes?" Killian Lamarre pleaded, pointing to a neatly folded pile on a stool near the open door. Lex took a step towards it and, with his free hand, tossed the bundle onto the floor in front of Killian Lamarre, who murmured a "thank you".

"Are you alright?" Lex asked the girl again, while Killian Lamarre hurriedly dressed. She answered with a faint smile, and for what it was worth, Lex told her that the ordeal was over.

"It was nothing but a massage, and I didn't force the girl to do anything she didn't want to do," Killian Lamarre protested.

"Who asked for your twisted opinion? Shut up, or I'll make you," Lex retorted as he waved the pistol. "Do you want to sit down?" he asked the girl and pointed to the stool where Killian Lamarre's clothes had lain a moment ago.

"I'd prefer to stand," the girl said, focusing on the floor to avoid eye contact with him or Killian Lamarre. The silence made Lex feel uncomfortable, but he didn't know what to say. Relieved, he heard footsteps approaching from the hallway. Angeline Pernet appeared in the doorway, wrapped in a white dressing gown.

"You can't believe how happy I am to see you, Angeline," Lex said as she stepped into the room and headed straight to the other girl. "Are you okay, Alice?" she said, and they hugged. Al entered the room and addressed Lex. "Thank God we found the missing girl, but everyone else has gone missing. I guess they made their escape as soon as they heard our less than discreet arrival."

"What have you done to Anatole Dupont?"

"He's slightly tied up," Big Al said. "There's a staircase at the end of the hallway, which leads to the apartment below. Why don't you bring the girls downstairs, find a phone and call your police friend? I'll keep an eye on the two scumbags until the cavalry arrives."

45

"WAKIE-WAKIE, my hero." Feeling Linda's lips on his ear, the enticing tone in her voice and the smell of her perfume gave him a sudden rush of lust. He pulled her down onto the bed and rolled on top of her. She put her warm hands on his buttocks, and he felt her nails on his skin. Linda pushed him off and onto his back. Seeing his erection, she went down on him and feeling her warm mouth and lips around his penis sent him into ecstasy. He caressed her ear lobe with one hand and her bottom with the other. He moved his hand between her legs and slid a finger into her.

"That's a poor substitute for the real McCoy," she said, licking across the head of his penis. She rolled off him and onto her knees, and he slid behind her. He lifted her dress above her hips, and his erection gained a notch with the view of her gorgeous bum. She guided him inside with an arm thrust backwards. She moaned as he rode her, and as she climaxed, he exploded inside her.

Panting, they lay in each other arms, and Lex dozed off again. Subconsciously, he felt Linda roll out of bed and then heard her talking somewhere in the distance, and Lex decided it had to be on the phone.

The next thing he knew was Linda sitting next to him on the bed.

"What's the time?" he asked.

"It's almost eleven."

"Did I dream it, or were you on the phone just now?"

"It was Jean-François. He'll be here for coffee in thirty minutes, so you'd better get ready. If you let me have the bathroom for ten minutes, I'll make the coffee while you freshen up."

"Could you make me an omelette as well?"

"Sure. There is nothing like a bit of exercise to make you hungry."

"I STILL don't condone you and your friend waving pistols around on my patch," Jean-François said.

"Honestly, if we hadn't insisted that Monsieur Dupont and his friends were up to no good, you'd be nowhere nearer knowing the whereabouts of Angeline Pernet, not to mention catching some of the bad guys."

"That's why you both get off with a warning if you promise not to interfere with police business again."

Lex pushed the plate away, sipped his coffee, and lit a cigarette. After being up half the night, he felt human again.

"I'm sure you didn't just come here to lecture me or drink Linda's excellent coffee."

"I wish, but unfortunately, I'm here with some news that won't please you."

"Uh-huh?"

"Killian Lamarre's team of fancy lawyers has him out on bail.

"*Putain!*" Lex cursed, "and how about Anatole Dupont?"

"We had to let him go too. As you can imagine, he knows his way around the law, and we need to work on the evidence to keep him in custody."

"What will it take?" Linda chipped in." From what Lex has told me, Al more or less caught him with Angeline Pernet on his knee."

"And how do they explain the abduction of the girl?" Lex contributed.

"They both claim to have nothing to do with that, and we can't, for now anyway, prove otherwise."

"That's not fair," Linda said, disheartened.

"What about the other girl?" Lex asked.

"She's the daughter of a friend of Monsieur Dupont."

"Her parents must be horrified," Linda said.

"We've only spoken to the father, and he will not press charges. He sounded quite relaxed about it, and I felt he knew about the arrangement."

"That's sick," Linda gasped.

"Welcome to the distorted world of paedophiles," Lex exclaimed.

"Surely Angeline Pernet's statement must count for something?" Linda said.

"Of course, and I was coming to that. We're yet to get it, but I'm interviewing her with a female colleague this afternoon," Jean-François said.

"I want to be there," Lex said.

"Well ...."

"Please don't deny me that."

"Steady on, Lex. If you just let me finish. I was going to say that because you were the one that saved her, Angeline Pernet insists that you are present when we talk to her. I protested, but that's what she wants."

"What time is it?"

Jean-François looked at his watch. "In fifty-five minutes."

THEY WALKED in the Saturday sunshine to the Pernet residence in Rue Chappe. The seriousness of the task at hand kept both of them silent until Jean-François said, "I doubt they'll ask Father Blanchet to attend this time."

"You haven't confronted him?"

"What's the purpose before the girl gives her statement?"

"Quite right, but what if he does a runner? Surely, Killian Lamarre will have informed him about last night."

"We have him under surveillance."

"What about Sister Coline?"

"Still in a coma, but she's stable. We have every reason to believe she'll pull through."

"Thank God."

Lex followed Jean-François down the stairs and across the landing to the front door, where a woman of medium height with shoulder-length blonde hair and in full police uniform was waiting.

"This is *gardien de la paix* Jeanette Benoit."

"We met last night. *Enchanté*," Lex said as they shook hands.

Jean-François pressed the doorbell on the right, and immediately someone buzzed them in.

Albert Pernet, was waiting for them at the door with a gloomy expression as they ascended the stairs to the first floor. He wore the same old pair of dirty blue overalls as last time. Saturday was, apparently, no day for rest, and he must have come directly from work. They shook hands and followed him into the living room. "My wife has taken our son for a walk, and Angeline is in her room. Please take a seat, and I'll get her."

"Before the girl joins us, I'd like to stress that I won't tolerate any interference from you, Lex. Jeanette Benoit is briefed and will conduct this interview," Jean-François said.

"I spoke at some length with the two girls last night, and I escorted Angeline Pernet home," the *gardien de la paix* officer said, "and I feel she trusts me."

"I'll write the girl's statement," Jean-François said.

Albert Pernet returned with his daughter. She wore a white T-shirt with a motive of the Eiffel Tower, blue jeans and white trainers. Her long dark hair hung loose down her back. *It makes her look like the 12-year-old girl that she is*, Lex thought.

"Take a seat," Jeannette Benoit said and patted the empty space beside her on the couch. Angeline slid onto the seat, folded her hands nervously on the table, and focused her gaze on a fruit bowl in the centre to avoid eye contact. As Albert Pernet was about to sit opposite her, she said, "I don't want you to be here, father."

"But why not Angeline?" he pleaded.

"Because you get angry."

"But not with you, my darling."

"I can understand why you want to be by your daughter's side Monsieur Pernet, but in this case, we should respect Angeline's wishes," Jeanette Benoit said.

"I only want what's best for her," he said. "If you need me, I'll be in the kitchen."

As soon as Monsieur Pernet had left, Jeanette Benoit told Angeline Pernet to take her time but to be as specific as she could. "How do you feel?"

"I'm okay," the girl said, biting her lip. "What would you like to know?"

"Why don't you begin when Father Blanchet started giving you extra attention?"

"It was in January, after the second solemn communion class. He asked me to stay behind after class. He told me I was chosen and that God would reward me if I obeyed his commands. He asked me to bend over his desk and pull up my skirt. He didn't touch me, but after a few minutes, I heard him moan. The following Sunday, he asked me to do the same, but this time he touched me," Angeline said, and her shoulders shook with emotion.

"I know it's hard for you, Angeline, but can you be as specific as possible?"

"He put a hand between my legs. Again I heard him moan after a few minutes."

"Did he ever ask you to take off any of your clothes and touch him?" Jeanette Benoit asked.

"Yes, but I'd rather not talk about it right now," she cried. The policewoman put a hand on the girl's arm, and Jean-François handed her a Kleenex.

"Does the poor girl have to spell it out?" Lex exclaimed. "Do we need to hear more to figure out where this is going?"

"Could you tell us what happened last Sunday?" Jeanette Benoit said, ignoring his outburst.

"Again, Father Blanchet asked me to stay behind. When he demanded I remove my underwear, I told him I knew that what he asked of me was a sin against God and that somebody would help me to make it stop. When I began to cry, he said he wouldn't touch me but wanted me to stay for a cup of tea to calm down. He made the tea, I drank it, felt drowsy, and that's the last thing I remember before waking up in the apartment where Monsieur Lex and his friend found me."

"Did you see Father Blanchet there?" Jeannette Benoit asked.

"Once."

"Did he ask you to do anything to him?"

"He only talked to me."

"What did he say?"

"He told me God was angry because I'd revealed our secret and that I would have to stay in the room for a while."

"Did anyone else come to your room?"

"An old man, who said his name was Oscar, came to give me food and take me to the bathroom down the hallway. I was asked to shower twice, and he also brought me clean clothing."

When you are twelve, any middle-aged butler looks old, Lex thought.

"Did he touch you?" Jeanette Benoit asked.

"Yes, but not like that. He was a nice man."

"While you stayed in that room, did anyone ask you to do anything against your will?"

"Not before last night when a tall man came to my room."

"Please describe him."

"Dark hair with a side parting and a small moustache."

"Anatole Dupont," Lex said.

"What did he do to you?"

"He sat on my bed and asked me to take off my clothes and put on a bathrobe. I'd just done that when we heard a boom from somewhere in the apartment. That's when the man left my room."

"Do you know who Killian Lamarre is?"

"Yes, from newspapers and magazines, but I've also seen him at the church and last night in the room with Alice.

"Did he ever touch you?" Jeanette Benoit asked.

"No, he never touched me, but he once told me that I was a nice looking girl."

"Did he promise you anything?"

"No, but Father Blanchet once told me that I would not regret it if I massaged Monsieur Lamarre.

"But you never did?"

"No."

Silence descended on the sombre party, and as if scripted, they heard the front door to the apartment open—then voices from the hallway. Almost immediately, there was a knock on the door.

"Come in," Jean-François said in a firm voice. The door opened, and Albert Pernet appeared in the opening. His face was flushed, and Lex wondered if he'd been keeping an ear to the door.

"My wife has returned with our son, and she's concerned about our daughter," he said.

"Please join us, Madame Pernet," Jean-François called. She appeared at the door, as Jeanette Benoit said, "Thank you ever so much, Angeline. You're being unbelievably brave. Remember, you've done absolutely nothing wrong, and no one blames you for anything." She squeezed the girl's arm gently.

"Can I go now?"

"Thank you, Angeline, you can leave," Jean-François said. She slid out from the couch and walked towards the door. Her mother met her halfway, and they embraced. The girl's body shook with emotion as she finally let go and sobbed. Madame Pernet guided her out of the room. Albert Pernet closed the door, pulled out a chair, and demanded to know what his daughter had revealed about her ordeal. Jean-François told him about Father Blanchet's abuse, how he'd drugged the girl and ensured she couldn't be found to be questioned.

"I find it hard to believe that Father Blanchet is guilty of such despicable and loathsome acts. We trusted him and invited him into our home. He married us, baptised our children, and heard our confessions."

"We have other witnesses to his misdeeds," Lex said.

"The Devil must have led him astray. Can you tell me where my daughter was held captive and who kept her there?"

"I'm afraid that, for the moment, is classified information," Jean-François stressed.

"But you can tell me if anyone else abused my little girl while she was held captive?" Albert Pernet thundered.

"According to her, she was saved just in time last night."

"My daughter has told me about your heroics, Monsieur Spijker. I thank you from the bottom of my heart. May the Lord make His face shine upon you, and be gracious to you."

"I didn't do much. All praise must go to my friend Alwin Smit."

"I thank him as well, but I'm sure you're being too modest."

"We're not going to take any more of your time. We'll keep you informed about any developments,"

Jean-François said, and they all got up. Albert Pernet let them out into the hallway.

"What's going to happen to Father Blanchet?" he said as he opened the door.

"It's too early to say, but he'll have to face up to whatever he has done."

"If you don't mind me saying so, brigadier, that sounds vague," Albert Pernet lamented. "I know what I would like to happen to him."

"And that is?" asked Jean-François.

"Give me five minutes with him, and I will break his neck so that he can burn in hell." The man in his blue overalls pretended to strangle someone, and Lex felt relieved that his hands, strenghtened by hard labour, were not around his neck.

"I understand your anger Monsieur Pernet, but I must warn you not to take the law into your own hands," Jean-François insisted.

"I hear you," Albert Pernet muttered unconvincingly and shut the door behind them.

"I COULD do with a coffee," Lex said to Jean-François as they passed Le Consulat, heading back to Rue Norvins for the brigadier to pick up his car.

"Okay, but it's going to be a quick one."

"I have a few questions I'd like to discuss."

"That sounds more like you're going to give me some suggestions."

Lex found a table in a quiet corner, ordered coffee and Calvados for himself, and coffee for Jean-François.

After Alain, *le patron*, had served them, Lex asked, "When will Father Blanchet be taken into custody?"

"As soon as we have a decent picture of the extent of his abuse, his involvement in the abduction of Angeline Pernet and any other girls, as well as his role in the alleged paedophile ring. Hopefully, Sister Coline will live to tell us what she knows. Adding the testimonials from Angeline Pernet and other girls, we'll have a strong case against him. And it wouldn't surprise me if Killian Lamarre claims he knew nothing and blames it all on the priest.

"Killian Lamarre is a crafty bastard with too much money, hiding behind his connections in high places and too many fancy lawyers in tailor-made suits. I wonder what it will take to end his subversive activities?"

"He's not out of the woods yet, but you're right; it will take some doing to stop him."

"Even when caught red-handed with a 13-year-old, semi-naked girl giving him a so-called massage," Lex said.

"I sense that like Icarus, he'll soon fly too close to the sun," Jean-François said.

46

AFTER BREAKFAST, Lex suggested visiting the recently opened Tour Montparnasse.

"It's the tallest skyscraper in France, and the panoramic view of Paris should be breath-taking. And if you're a good girl, I'll treat you to Sunday lunch at the restaurant on the fifty-sixth floor."

As they were about to leave, the phone rang.

"Please ignore it, Lex," Linda pleaded. He did for another couple of rings, but as it persisted, he told Linda he would have no peace of mind for the remainder of the day if he didn't answer. On reflection, he was glad he did.

"Thank God you're at home," Jean-François said.

"Only just. What's up?"

"I'm calling from the Sacré-Cœur. We need your presence."

"As you know, I'm not a churchgoer," Lex said light-heartedly, "and especially not on Sundays."

"Will you be serious? We have a crisis on our hands."

"Tell me."

"I attended the Sunday mass with a couple of colleagues to pick up Father Blanchet after the service and before his solemn communion class. But Albert Pernet beat us to it and has taken the priest hostage at knifepoint. He is threatening to cut his throat unless the Father confesses his sins. Albert Pernet insists you should hear them as well."

"Okay, I'll be there in about ten minutes."

"Come to the side door, and I'll let you in."

Lex replaced the receiver and looked at Linda, who'd taken a seat in the chair opposite his desk.

"Who was it?" Lex explained the situation to her. She looked only slightly disappointed.

"An act of desperation, but if my daughter was abused, I would be tempted to do the same," Linda said. "You'd better hurry up."

"I'm on my way. Let's visit Tour Montparnasse later today, and I'll treat you to dinner instead."

"Let's wait and see. As you know, it's a special day tomorrow."

"I haven't forgotten," Lex said and kissed her goodbye.

LEX ASCENDED the concrete stairs over the trench separating the basement from the street, and as he was about to press the only buzzer, the heavy wooden door creaked open.

"Come in, Lex. Father Blanchet is being held hostage in the Chapelle Saint Luke," Jean-François said, like someone telling an old friend, "we're in the living room."

"I'm unfamiliar with that specific chapel, so you'd better lead the way."

"Are you trying to be funny?"

"I wouldn't dream of it in this solemn hour."

They entered the nave from a side door and turned left. A small crowd, halted in front of a police cordon, parted to let Lex and Jean-François pass, and a *gardien de la paix* lifted the tape for them to pass under. The Chapel of Saint Luke was the last of three chapels to the left of the choir. At first, the confided space looked empty, but then Lex saw Father Blanchet seated in the corner, to the left of a small altar. He wore a golden chasuble, and Lex couldn't help but notice his relatively large feet sticking out from under the alb. Albert Pernet, in his Sunday best, stood behind him, holding a knife to the Father's throat.

"Glad you could join us, Monsieur Spijker. You saved my daughter the other night and deserve to hear the devil's confession."

"Don't do anything foolish; he's not worth it," Lex said.

"I won't, as long as he confesses to me, you, the brigadier and more importantly before God. Take a seat. I'm sure the Father is eager to lighten his heart." Lex and Jean-François lowered themselves onto a single wooden pew.

"We're ready to hear your confession, Father," Albert Pernet said, easing the pressure of the blade against the man's throat.

"In the name of the Father, and of the Son, and the Holy Spirit," Father Blanchet prayed as he made the sign of the cross, almost touching the knife. "I have sinned against You, whom I should love above all things. I firmly intend, with Your help, to do penance, sin no more, and to ...."

"Okay, that's enough of that; just get on with it," Albert Pernet demanded.

"It's not easy for me," Father Blanchet protested.

"Perhaps it was easier to abuse my little girl? If you don't start talking within ten seconds, you'll have to pay the price," Albert Pernet said, tightening his grip on the knife. Father Blanchet's blue eyes seemed to pop out of his head, and a vein bulged near his temple.

"My faith was not strong enough to fight the temptations of the young and innocent flesh. I admit that I've taken liberties and abused the children God put into my care.

"Be specific, Father. You must confess to how you hurt my daughter."

"I would never harm a child. I love them too much. And I know that they love me. True love can never be faked. And although I've hurt no one, I admit that I've broken my vows of chastity and obedience to the hierarchy of the Catholic Church."

"You're delusional, Father. I'll give you one more chance to say what you did to my daughter, and then you can let us judge if you did more than break your vows," Albert Pernet said. He pressed the knife's blade against the priest's throat with enough force to draw a few drops of blood, which dripped onto the white collar of his chasuble. *Let them be the last drops of blood that flow today*, Lex thought.

"I admit that I asked your daughter to undress and bend over my desk on several occasions and that I touched myself," Father Blanchet bit his lower lip.

"It's called masturbation," Albert Pernet barked without mercy. "Did you touch her or ask that she touch you?"

"Yes," Father Blanchet whispered.

"What's that? Speak up!"

"YES. I did touch your daughter, and she did touch me. But never *concubitus*."

"Take the swine away," Albert Pernet hissed and pushed Father Blanchet off the chair. He stumbled forward and landed on his hands and knees. Instinctively Lex got up from his seat to help the priest to his feet. "Let him be," Albert Pernet shouted. The grotesque sight of a priest in full ornate splendour, crawling on the stone floor like an animal, took them by surprise, and before anyone reacted, he'd crawled past them and out of the chapel. Lex followed after him in time to see him get to his feet, rush under the cordon, past the *gardien de la paix*, and towards a small wooden door on the right.

"Stop him," Lex shouted to no avail, as Father Blanchet disappeared through the door. Jean-François pushed himself past Lex, jumped the cordon with his long legs, and reached the door. He pulled the handle, and flung the door open. Jean-François entered, and Lex followed right behind. To the left of them was a narrow spiral staircase, and from there came the sound of feet rapidly ascending the flight of marble steps.

"He's heading for the dome," Jean-François said, forgetting, as he entered the stairwell, that he measured almost two metres and banging his head against the stone wall above the door.

"God damn it," he cried as he sank to his knees and held a hand to his forehead. "You go, Lex; give me a moment to recover."

Lex rushed up the stairs. Round and round. In the distance from above, he heard a door open and close. He reached a small landing with three doors. After ascending the spiral stone staircase, he was struggling to get his bearings and his breath. He pulled the handle of the one he assumed might lead to the inside gallery just below the dome. The door swung open, and he faced a corridor about ten metres long. On the other side Lex recognised a couple of the arches in the dome. He heard the footsteps of Jean-François ascending below.

"I'm heading to the dome—it's the door on the right," Lex shouted over his shoulder. He made his way along the corridor and onto the narrow gallery that circled the inner dome. Lex scanned the archway openings for the presence of Father Blanchet, but could not see him. He peeked over the concrete railing and down into the nave. His vertigo immediately rewarded him with the sensation of whirling and loss of balance. To shake off the feeling of giddiness, he looked up again. Lex heard footsteps behind him and turned to see Jean-François approaching along the corridor. He moved sideways to make room for the tall brigadier.

"That looks nasty," he said, pointing to a bump on Jean-François' forehead.

But there was no time to discuss any injuries, as Father Blanchet suddenly stepped out from behind a pillar. His cold blue eyes pierced them, but he said nothing.

"It looks like you've nowhere to go, Father," Jean-François said.

"You're wrong," Father Blanchet said as he, with some difficulty crawled over the concrete railing and lowered himself onto the ledge. Slowly he turned to face them. Framed by the arch and in his golden chasuble, it was a sight to behold and, in all likelihood, the first time the Sacré-Cœur had experienced a priest dangling his feet, however big, fifty metres above the pews in the nave. Lex forced himself to look down. A small crowd had gathered in the aisle below—all with their heads tilted back. A couple of policemen were keeping them at a safe distance from being hit by any potential priest falling out of the sky. Lex spotted Albert Pernet in the side aisle with a *gardien de la paix* holding him by the arm. Both had their heads tilted back.

"Don't do anything silly, Father," Jean-François pleaded.

"It's bit late for that, and you should have warned me not to do anything silly many years ago. I realise now that I must make the ultimate sacrifice to atone for my sins against God." Although the priest said the words without sentimentality, Lex noticed a warmth in his blue eyes for the first time, which would quickly prove to be the last.

"Souls fall into hell for sins of the flesh like snowflakes," Father Blanchet shouted as he extended his arms out to the sides and looked up into the dome —or perhaps it was towards heaven. They watched in horror as he, in extreme slow-motion, tipped over into the vast space and dropped like a fallen angel. It took about three seconds for the priest to fall the fifty metres, and before his well-padded body hit the wooden pews with a tumultuous sound. Someone screamed, and Lex saw the area around the body colour red, as blood seeped onto the white marble floor.

"I'll be damned," Lex said.

"Not as much as poor Father Blanchet. May his tormented soul rest in peace," Jean François said, making the sign of the cross.

They walked back along the corridor and descended the spiral staircase with some urgency. Lex pulled open the heavy wooden door to the nave and held it to let Jean-François enter first.

A *gardien de la paix* was holding a crowd, burning with morbid curiosity, at bay. Thankfully the pews blocked any clear view of the scene.

"Let's get the area cordoned off with tape," Jean-François instructed as Lex approached the corpse. The deceased lay face down, and Lex felt grateful to be spared looking into those blue eyes, now colder than ever. Lex turned away and spotted Albert Pernet slumped in a pew on the right, his arms handcuffed behind his back. They locked eyes, and Lex approached.

"I'm shocked, Monsieur Spijker. I may have threatened to cut his throat, but all I wanted was a confession. I regret he chose to take his own life."

"So do I, and unfortunately, he's taken vital information to the grave that could have helped us get to the bottom of this shameful affair."

"I've messed up everything," Albert Pernet said, deflated.

"Don't blame yourself," Lex said with little conviction. He rested a hand on the man's shoulder before returning his attention to the scene. The area was cordoned off, and Lex ducked under the tape and walked over to Jean-François who was standing next to the body.

"Why are none of his colleagues giving him last rites?" Lex said and motioned towards a group of three priests and two nuns lingering at a distance, just on the other side of the tape. They looked visibly shocked, but none seemed about to approach the dead man.

"Because only a living person can receive a sacrament, and Father Blanchet has without a doubt already passed on. You're not the only one to believe that the Catholic Church has a sacrament for the dead, but they never did," Jean-François explained.

"I can't believe he killed himself, as I thought Catholics feared spending eternity in hell if they committed suicide?"

"Maybe that's what he wanted, and perhaps spending eternity in hell is what he meant by the ultimate sacrifice."

"What was it he said?"

"Souls fall into hell for sins of the flesh like snowflakes. If memory serves me right, it's part of the message of Fátima."

"Of what?"

"It's a long story, but it's basically about three children in Fátima, Portugal who, in 1916, were blessed with the presence of the Virgin Mary. She told them to pray the Rosary each day to bring peace to the world and to bring an end to the war. The message emphasises the central truths and devotions of the Catholic faith."

"I'm amazed you know all these things," Lex said.

"You mean as a simple brigadier from Africa?"

"I meant to say 'impressed'."

"Keep digging, but it's common knowledge to most Catholics."

Lex observed two paramedics with an ambulance stretcher approaching down the central aisle. They were accompanied by a small, portly, florid-faced man carrying a Gladstone bag.

"*Bonjour*, doctor Bonheur," Jean-François greeted him. "Awfully kind of you to join us, but I doubt you can tell us much we don't already know."

"If you could certify the cause or issue the death certificate, Brigadier Diagne, there would have been no need to drag me away from my Sunday lunch."

"We'll let you get on with it, doctor, so the paramedics can remove the body, you can return to your lunch, and we can get the scene cleaned up."

Ten minutes later, the deceased was on the stretcher in a bodybag, and the paramedics, accompanied by a couple of *gardien de la paix* to keep the curious crowd out of the way, rolled down the aisle towards the porch.

"I think we're done here," Jean-François said.

"The news of Father Blanchet's confession and death will please Killian Lamarre," Lex said.

"Undoubtedly."

"Now, we might never know his role in recruiting children for the paedophile ring."

"Let's hope Sister Coline pulls through. From what you've told me, she knows a lot about the abuse."

"And without Father Blanchet's testimony, it will be almost impossible to get Killian Lamarre convicted, let alone damage his reputation."

"Perhaps, but I'm not so sure."

47

LEX ENTERED Tabac Lepic and shifted the bag of croissants to his left hand to pick up a copy of *Le Figaro*. He didn't usually buy the newspaper, but today was different, as he expected Father Blanchet's dramatic suicide would be in the news. He opened the broadsheet and saw Killian Lamarre had made it onto the front page. The headline read: *Magnat célèbre impliqué dans un réseau pédophile* and was accompanied by a portrait that did the entrepreneur no favours. Lex doubted that Killian Lamarre, on this occasion, was enjoying the free publicity.

Lex wanted to read the article on the spot, but it would have to wait, so he could get back to celebrate with Linda on her twenty-fifth birthday.

About to pay for the newspaper and a packet of cigarettes, Linda's pretty face suddenly stared out at him from a copy of *Vogue Paris*. He couldn't believe she'd already made it onto the cover. *A morning full of media surprises*, he thought. The man behind the counter noticed Lex transfixed by the photo.

"Pretty isn't she and hot from the press this morning."

"She's my fiancée," Lex blurted out.

"If you say so, monsieur."

"How many copies do you have?"

"The five you see on the counter."

"I'll take them all."

"You can have four. I'll keep one for a regular; otherwise, she'll never speak to me again."

Lex paid, and a "Pass on my best wishes to your fiancée" followed him out into the street.

Putting his best foot forward, he made it back to Rue Norvins within five minutes. He ascended the stairs on the double and unlocked the door.

"Happy birthday, baby," he called out. Linda joined him in the hallway from the bedroom. She was wearing an unbelted blue dress with a fitted bodice and a straight skirt with a cut that accentuated her attractive figure.

"You look lovely, baby, and thanks for wearing the earrings I gave you," Lex said and kissed her, clumsily stepping on her left bare foot.

"Ouch, that hurt."

"I'm so sorry, baby."

"Never mind. Is that the latest issue of *Vogue* you're hiding behind your back by any chance?"

"So you know about that?"

"Of course, but I kept it a secret as I hoped you would spot it at the newsagent."

"As you can see, I did. Congratulations. I'm so proud of you and even told the guy at the counter that the beautiful face on the cover belonged to my fiancée. He asked me to pass on his best wishes, but I'm not sure he believed me, as he said it rather mockingly."

"Any chance you can spare one of your many copies?"

"Of course. But only one," he teased. "I need a copy for myself, one for Al, and one for my uncle."

"It's a bit surreal to see my face on the cover of the *Vogue Paris*."

"The art director must think the world of you."

"What's that supposed to mean?"

"Nothing, only that it's less than two weeks since your first appointment, and there you are on the cover."

"I have no idea what you're implying?"

"Nothing."

"Apparently, he believes my face is pretty enough to sell a few copies. You bought four, so he may be right," Linda said, doing her best to sound cheerful.

"You're not the only one getting your face publicised today," Lex said to change the subject. "Killian Lamarre is on the front page of *Le Figaro*, accompanied by an article claiming he's involved with a paedophile ring."

"About time that creep is confronted with some truths about his so-called 'eccentric behaviour'. What does it say?"

"I haven't read it yet, and it will have to wait until after your birthday breakfast. Big Al should be here any minute."

"Didn't he leave yesterday?"

"I wanted it to be a surprise, and I hope you don't mind that I talked him into staying another day?"

"Not at all. I have a lot of time for Alwin, and it's wonderful to have him here to celebrate my big day."

"You'd better get that," Lex said when the doorbell rang, "and I'll open the champagne and make the coffee."

Lex heard chattering from the hallway and then a "Happy birthday" from Big Al as he entered the room, reminding Lex of the Dutch custom to congratulate everyone present at a birthday event.

"That's the second time I've seen you wearing a tie within a week. You're becoming something of a dandy, Al."

"Just doing my best to look stylish for a classy lady, and rumour has it that you're taking us to some fancy Parisian restaurant for lunch."

"Really? But first, some breakfast," Lex said, putting a pot of coffee and a bottle of champagne on the dining table. He asked Linda to take a seat at the end. Al handed her a present wrapped in brown paper.

"Although it looks slightly boring, I hope you'll appreciate it," he said before sitting down. Eagerly Linda tore the paper off to reveal a copy of Albert Camus' *La Peste*.

"It's a first edition, and I'm sure you'll soon be able to read it." Linda was delighted and embraced the big man.

"I'm impressed. I know you have contacts within the world of rare books, but it was rather short notice," Lex said.

"It's not what you know, but who you know," Big Al said, eliciting a chuckle as Lex filled the flutes with champagne.

"Congratulation on your first birthday in Paris, baby, and making it onto your first cover," Lex said and raised his glass.

"That must be the best birthday present you can imagine. Has it been published? Can I see?" Al said. Linda eagerly got up and fetched the issue from the coffee table. "Fantastic! It must make you so proud. I'll buy a copy later today."

"As it happens, Lex already has a copy for you. He raided the local newsagent while buying the newspaper," Linda said as Lex offered her a croissant.

"Talking about the newspaper, I have another surprise for you, Al." Lex held up the front page with the portrait of Killian Lamarre.

"He made it to the front page again. He doesn't look much prettier than he did on Friday night, but at least in this one, he's not flashing his middle-aged spread. There is no ambiguity about the headline, even in French, but perhaps you could tell me what the article says?"

"I haven't read it yet, but perhaps I could translate it for you?"

"Please do."

"I hope you don't mind, Linda?"

"Go ahead. I'm also curious."

"Joseph de la Fontaine wrote the article, and the headline reads: *Famous tycoon involved with paedophile ring*."

"I like it already," exclaimed Al.

Lex translated, "Killian Lamarre, the well-known middle-aged tycoon, who likes the company of young and beautiful women, was on at least two occasions confronted by the authorities in a private club with girls as young as twelve years old, servicing the clientele of middle-aged men with sexual massages. An undisclosed source has revealed that the police believe that Killian Lamarre is part of a paedophile ring with other members of the French elite. He's linked to Father Horace Robert Blanchet, who, under dramatic circumstances, committed suicide at La Basilique du Sacré Cœur yesterday after confessing to abusing young girls for several years and being part of a paedophile ring. There's a reference to an article on page two."

"Nothing we didn't know already, but it's nice that everyone else does," Al said.

"That's a kick in the old, fat bastard's middle-aged balls," Linda said with glee.

"You want me to translate the article about Father Blanchet's suicide as well?" Lex asked.

"Lex, please, can we now talk about something else on my birthday? I doubt the article can add to the chilling first-hand account you gave me so vividly yesterday afternoon."

"You're right, baby. Let's embrace your special day with love, peace and happiness."

"Hear, hear, brother," Big Al chimed in, helping himself to a *pain au chocolat*.

LEX DROVE the small Renault with Big Al taking up the back seat and Linda in the passenger seat. He'd booked a table at a Michelin star restaurant on Île Saint-Louis. Although it was a bit lavish considering their financial situation, now they'd made a deal with Allard Kuipers and his syndicate to let Big Al return the stolen money, Linda deserved it. Lex forced himself not to think about money and enjoy the day with a beautiful girlfriend and a good friend.

Rounding the Arc de Triomphe reminded Lex, as if he needed it, how lucky he was to be living in one of the world's greatest cities. He looked at Linda beside him and Big Al in the rear mirror. "Thank you both for coming to Paris and making my life so special." Linda put a hand on his knee and turned to look at him. "That's unlike you getting all sentimental," she said.

"It must be his advanced age," Al said as he squeezed Lex's shoulder.

"I love you too," Lex said to the gentle giant.

As they headed down the Avenue des Champs-Élysées, the skies opened. Lex pulled the sunroof shut, and Linda rolled up the window.

The little red car approached the giant Egyptian obelisk in the centre of the Place de la Concorde.

"Wasn't this the site of public executions?" Linda asked.

"Indeed. Louis XVI, Marie Antoinette and Maximilien Robespierre all lost their heads here." Lex said.

"With several thousand others, you may add," Al supplied.

"The reign of terror," Lex said, "and the square was renamed the Place de la Révolution under the French revolution."

"I'm a lucky girl having two knowledgeable and handsome tour guides by my side," Linda said.

Lex hit the two-lane one-way road that ran along the bank of the river Seine. The traffic was, as usual around lunchtime, moderate, with only a few cars in front and behind. He saw the white traffic sign informing him that a left turn towards the Île Saint-Louis was coming up, and as he was about to switch to the inner lane, a car drove up on the inside. It almost touched the side of the Renault.

"Give us some space, mate," Lex said. Annoyed, he turned his head to make eye contact with the driver and to indicate he was getting too close for comfort. About twenty centimetres away, Killian Lamarre's bloodshot eyes stared at him through the window of his Aston Martin. His face was distorted with rage.

"Where the fuck did he come from?" Lex exclaimed.

"Who? What?" Linda said.

"I doubt he liked the publicity in the morning paper," Al said from the back seat.

Killian Lamarre smashed the side of his car against the side of the Renault, and although Lex steered contra, he could not prevent the small car from being pressed against the barrier. The noise was deafening as the side skated along the iron barrier.

My aunt will never forgive me, Lex thought, rather ridiculously under the circumstances.

"He's pushing us into the river," Linda shouted, her hands firmly planted on the dashboard.

"Let go of the gas, and hit the brakes, Lex," Al barked into his right ear from behind.

Lex followed his suggestions, and it worked as far as getting rid of the Aston Martin. But their relief was short-lived when a truck, coming from behind and doing its best to avoid a collision, clipped the left side of the back of the car. The impact flipped the Renault upright, and for a short moment, it lingered as if uncertain which side to fall. Eventually, it decided to tip over the barrier and hit the water upside down.

Lex undid his seat belt and dropped to the ceiling. He pulled the handle but only managed to open the door slightly because of the outside water pressure.

"Roll down the window," Big Al said firmly. Lex did, and the cold water poured in.

"Undo your seat belt, Linda," Lex shouted, but she had been knocked unconscious. Blood dripped onto the ceiling from a wound on the top of her head. Big Al released the belt for her.

"Exit via the window, and I'll push Linda through," Big Al said. "I'll try to squeeze through the sunroof."

The car was still floating but was filling up fast with water as Lex pulled himself through the window. Big Al, trapped upside down on the back seat, pushed Linda's unconscious body to the side window, and Lex pulled her out as the undercarriage let go of the river surface. The vehicle rapidly sank towards the bottom about ten metres down.

Lex had no time to worry about Big Al as he pushed to the surface. Holding on to Linda, he trod water to get his bearings. The embankment wall was about five metres away. He spotted the truck that had hit them parked on the road. It was green with 'Perrier - the water preferred by the sportif' advertised on the side. All Lex would prefer was to be out of the cold water as soon as possible. A man was leaning against the barrier, and to Lex's relief, he lowered a tow row over the side and into the water, which was less than two metres below him. The man was gesticulating wildly, but Lex couldn't make out what he was saying. Lex swam to the rope, and with his free hand, he grasped hold of the loop at the end. Just then, Linda regained consciousness. The bleeding from her head seemed to have stopped.

"Lift your arm so I can tie the rope around you," Lex said.

"Okay."

"Are you able to put your feet against the wall to help the man pull you up?"

"I'll try."

"Ready?" Linda nodded.

"Pull her up," Lex shouted. The man did so, and with Lex pushing as best he could, Linda was up and over the barrier in a flash. The man lowered the rope again, and Lex gripped hold of the iron barrier on his way up, then put a foot on the edge, and the man helped him over.

"Grateful for your help," Lex said.

"Of course. Are you okay, mister?"

"I'm fine, but I'm afraid my friend is still down there."

"I tried my best to avoid you."

"It's not your fault. Did you see what the driver in the Aston Martin did?"

"Total madman."

Linda sat on the curb, holding her head in her hands, her body shaking from shock and cold. A small crowd of drivers caught up in the havoc gathered round them. A woman took off her coat and wrapped it round Linda's shoulder. Linda smiled gratefully, and Lex nodded his appreciation. He heard sirens in the distance, and within a couple of minutes, a fire engine had parked nearby. Two firefighters exited and walked to the barrier to access the scene.

"Is anyone down there?"

"My friend never came up," Lex said.

"Let's get a diver into the soup," the firefighter instructed and moved towards the fire engine. "Chop-chop," he called. A diver in full gear exited from the back and walked swiftly to the barrier. His colleague helped him over the railing, and after a moment standing on the edge, he jumped into the river.

Lex stared into the dark waters that had swallowed his friend and saviour.

"Is Alwin still in the water?" Linda asked and began to weep. She looked dreadful, with dried blood on her face and in her hair. Her beautiful dress was soaked, and one of her high-heeled shoes was missing. Lex lowered himself and hugged her. He heard more sirens in the distance, and about a minute later, a police car and an ambulance joined the scene. A paramedic exited the ambulance, and a brigadier the police car. Lex hoped to see Jean-François, but what were the chances, and it wasn't even his district. Lex stood to wave both men over. The paramedic knelt in front of Linda.

"We need to get you and your girlfriend for a check-up at the Hôpital de l'Hôtel-Dieu. We'll take your statements afterwards," the policeman said.

"I'm not going anywhere until I know about my friend," Lex insisted.

"I understand."

"You should talk to the driver of the Perrier truck. Before he hit us, he saw how an Aston Martin pressed us up against the barrier."

"Did you see the driver?"

"It was Killian Lamarre."

"The tycoon? Why would he try to run your car into the Seine?"

"It's a long story, but it has something to do with an article in *Le Figaro* this morning." The policeman looked puzzled, but the diver reappeared at the surface before Lex could explain. The policeman walked to the barrier and leaned over it to confer with him. He nodded a few times before turning and walking back to Lex and Linda.

"With regret, I have to inform you that your friend didn't make it." Lex expected as much, but hearing it was a shock. He felt dizzy and sat back down on the curb. "Poor, good-hearted Alwin. He didn't deserve such an ending," Linda sobbed beside him.

"Is he still inside the car?" Lex asked.

"He'd made it halfway out of the car's sunroof, but it seems his big frame got trapped between the roof and the river bottom. The diver tried to pull him out, but it won't be possible before lifting the car. If it's any consolation, we believe he was knocked unconscious before he drowned."

"I guess there's not much we can do for him?" Lex said.

"Your friend has passed on, so you'd better think of yourself and go with the ambulance to the hospital. It's only a few hundred metres from here."

48

LEX WIPED away a tear and touched his friend's bare shoulder. It was cold. Dead cold. It had taken the bastard Killian Lamarre and the river to slay the gentle giant. *At least he looks at peace, and as if he's about to send me a chuckle*, Lex thought. Of all Al's little quirks, the straight-faced humour followed by a chuckle was the one Lex would miss the most.

According to the police, Al's tie had got stuck on the handle to the sunroof as he pushed himself through the opening, preventing him from getting clear before the car hit the bottom of the river. Some rotten luck, and Lex blamed himself. If only he hadn't talked Al into staying one more day. If only Al hadn't, uncharacteristically, worn a tie for the occasion. If only ....

Lex signalled he'd seen enough and watched as the mortuary porter dragged the sheet over the dead man. Lex joined Linda, who was waiting for him in a small office down the hallway. She'd passed up the opportunity for a last goodbye saying, "I want to remember Alwin full of life."

Linda was slumped on a chair, looking utterly deflated, and seeing her in the grey sweatsuit, at least two sizes too big, given to her by the police in exchange for her wet dress, brought tears back into Lex's eyes. "I'm so sorry you had to go through this experience on your big day, baby," he said.

"At least I'm alive," she said as her body shook with emotion. Lex lifted her off the chair, and they held each other tight. As Lex was wearing a similar grey sweatsuit, they could have been mistaken for one body with two heads.

"I just want to go home and get drunk," she said in between sobs.

"I don't think alcohol is the medicine the doctor ordered after bumping your head."

"I don't care. It's my birthday, and I can do what I like."

"I rest my case. Jean-François should be here any minute to take us to Rue Norvins." Interviewed by the police at the hospital, Lex had explicitly asked for Brigadier Jean-François to pick them up at the L'institut médico-légal mortuary after their visit to identify Big Al. The brigadier was off duty, but as Lex insisted, and everyone sympathised with his anguish for losing his friend, it was arranged without further argument.

Lex let go of Linda, walked to the window, and looked impatiently into the courtyard in time to see a Peugeot police car drive through the gate. Out stepped

Jean-François in a light blue three-piece suit with wide lapels, flared pants, and a high-rise waistcoat. His white shirt with long pointed collars was open at the neck. *That man looks sharp in any outfit, and in this, he should be at Studio 54 or Club Sept*, Lex thought.

Lex and Linda, arm in arm, met Jean-François on the staircase.

"I'm so sorry for your loss."

"Thanks, and for coming to pick us up."

"The least I can do after what Killian Lamarre did to you. I understand you were on your way to celebrate your birthday, mademoiselle. It now seems pointless to wish you a happy one."

"What? I'm too out of it to understand a word of French," Linda said and put a hand to the plaster covering the wound on her forehead. Jean-François apologised and repeated in English what he'd just said. Linda managed a timid smile and even complimented him on his outfit. The little party reached the car, and the policeman held the door open to the back seat.

"Let me know if you need more legroom," he said.

"I would like to lie down if you don't mind?" Linda said. "I feel like I turned a hundred and not twenty-five."

"Be my guest. I'll get you a blanket from the boot." While he did, Lex opened the passenger seat door and slid in. He heard the back door slam shut, and Jean-François got in and started the engine. He drove the car out of the gate and onto Voie Mazas. Lex turned his head to check on Linda on the back seat. She'd pulled the blanket over her head. "Are you okay, baby?"

" I will be as soon I get home and get a drink," she muttered. They drove on in silence until Lex asked if Killian Lamarre was in custody.

"I'm afraid not, but he soon will be. No number of fancy lawyers can get him out of the pickle he's in after that stunt today."

"What about Jos?"

"What about him?'

"If Killian Lamarre's attack on us has anything to do with the unwanted newspaper publicity, I wonder what he'd like to do to Jos. It's his byline on the article, after all."

"Jos is out of town, so you don't need to worry about him."

"That's a relief. I guess you have nothing to do with Jos getting information about Killian Lamarre's involvement with underaged girls and the paedophile ring?"

"I have no idea what you're talking about."

"You wouldn't, would you now? What will you do to keep us safe until Killian Lamarre is in custody?"

"Give me a break. I didn't plan anything, as I doubt the clown will do anything more after seeing your car hit the water. I guess he'll be keeping a low profile somewhere, horrified that his rage may have caused irreparable damage."

"What are you doing to apprehend him?"

"You mean me personally? I'm doing my utmost to answer your questions and ensure you get home safely."

"I mean in general?"

"What do you want me to answer? We have every disposable officer on the case. I'm so sorry that a madman pushed you into the Seine and for the death of your friend, but you're not the only victim of a crime on this damn Monday."

"If Killian Lamarre hadn't been released on bail, you would have one less crime to worry about, and my friend would still be alive."

"I hope you're not blaming me?"

"Not at all, and I'm sorry for being an ungrateful sod."

"Never mind."

"What about the paedophile ring?"

"Living on borrowed time now that Pandora's box is open. And that's mainly thanks to you."

"And my dead friend."

"Him too. May he rest in peace."

They drove onto Boulevard Périphérique—the ring road surrounding Paris, and not surprisingly, on a late Monday afternoon, the congested traffic was moving at a snail's pace.

"Why don't you make use of the siren?" Lex suggested.

"It's for emergencies and only when I'm wearing my uniform."

"Could you make an exception? Perhaps as a birthday present to Linda?"

"I hear my name mentioned," she said from the back.

"Just trying to convince Jean-François to put on the siren, as a present to you, so we can get home faster."

"I would like that."

"Okay, but don't ever ask me again," Jean-François said and switched on the siren and the emergency light.

The blare of NEE-EU NEE-EU NEE-EU and the flashes of blue light created an immediate effect as the cars in front of them pulled to the side to let them pass. Within five minutes, they had exited the ring road at Porte de Clignancourt, and in the reduced traffic, Jean-François killed the siren and the blue light.

"That was exciting and reminded me of my days as a sergeant in the Amsterdam police."

"I'd love to hear about it, but let's make it another day."

Jean-François turned into Rue Norvins and shifted to second gear to push the car up the hill.

"Linda, we're home."

"Thank God."

"I can't thank you enough, Jean-François," Lex said as he got out of the car and pulled open the door to the back seat.

"Thanks for picking us up and driving us home, Jean-François," Linda said and squeezed his shoulder.

"My pleasure. Keep your door locked tonight, and I'll keep you posted on any developments. Hopefully, it's only a matter of hours before Killian Lamarre is in custody."

LEX DIALED the number his uncle had given him before leaving for Israel. As far as he could remember, Tel Aviv was one hour ahead.

"Jules Lévy speaking."

"Hi, Uncle. It's your favourite nephew."

"The one and only."

"How are you and the family?"

"Under the circumstances, we're fine. The seven days of mourning concludes today, and we're flying home tomorrow evening. I'm happy to hear from you. I've called you a few times, and to be honest, I'd begun to worry."

"A lot has happened since you left, and I hardly know where to begin."

"What about Angeline Pernet?"

"She went missing for a few days, but she's now back with her family and in one piece—at least physically."

"What happened?"

"It's a long story which I'd rather tell you face to face."

"What about Father Blanchet?"

"He committed suicide yesterday."

"I'm shocked. How?"

"He dived from the inside of the dome at the Sacré-Coeur."

'My God."

'Indeed."

"What about Killian Lamarre?"

"This morning, *Le Figaro* published an article about his involvement with a paedophile ring, and at noon he pushed me, Linda and a friend of mine into the Seine."

"Did I hear you right? Are you okay?"

"Linda and I got out of the car in time, but my friend drowned," Lex said and choked up.

"I'm so sorry, Lex. That's awful."

"It was supposed to be a day of celebration as Linda is turning twenty-five today."

"Poor girl. Do pass on our congratulations and tell her she's in our prayers. You both are."

"Thanks. I'm afraid Gigi will crucify me for parking her car upside down at the bottom of the Seine," Lex said.

"When she hears about your narrow escape and the death of your friend, she won't give a toss about the car."

"I'd hoped you would say that."

"If you're available Friday, I'd like to invite you and Linda to dine with us at the restaurant on Rue du Faubourg Saint-Denis."

"That's kind of you, but I'll have to escort my deceased friend back to Amsterdam."

"Of course."

"I haven't told Linda yet. I hope to convince her to come with me, but I doubt she will. If you contact her, I'm sure she'd like to eat with you on Friday. I know she's fond of you and especially Ami."

"I'll call her."

"Thanks, and safe travels."

"You too."

Lex joined Linda in the living room. She was on the couch, sipping a glass of white wine.

"How's the family?"

"They're fine, and send their greetings and love on your birthday. My uncle is shocked to hear what happened."

"And I'm sure your aunt is not best pleased to hear about the car."

"My uncle reassured me that all that matters, also for Gigi, is that we're fine."

"They're so sweet," Linda said.

"Listen, baby , there's something I need to discuss." Lex hesitated.

"I'm listening."

"We have to reconsider our plan about returning the money now that Al is dead."

"Do we need to discuss the matter today?"

"Yes, because I'd like us to escort his coffin back to Amsterdam and attend the funeral. At the same time, we can take the money back and arrange a time for ...."

"Stop right there," Linda interrupted. "I'm not ready to return to Amsterdam, and I want nothing more to do with Allard Kuipers and his associates."

"I get it, but I have to go, and I'd hate to leave you on your own here in Paris."

"Don't worry about me, Lex. You do what you have to do, and I'll eagerly wait for your return."

"My uncle will call you during the week to invite you to dine with the family on Friday, and I'll ask Jean-François to keep an eye on you."

"Okay, but no more planning today. Pour me another drink and put on some music while I slip into something a little sexier than this awful sweatsuit."

Lex did as Linda demanded. It was her birthday, after all.

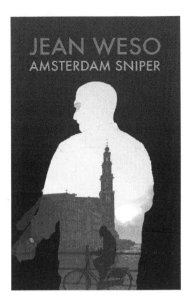

JEAN WESO
AMSTERDAM SNIPER

A RINUS ROMPA NOVEL (BOOK 1)

The December display of Christmas lights and decorations in streets, squares, houses and shops all over Amsterdam is magical. The holiday season is a splendid time to be in the Dutch capital, but every paradise has a snake. In the early hours of the 3rd Sunday of Advent the first victim dies with a bullet to the head. As the police are trying to get their own heads around the hideous crime, there is another killing with the same modus operandi.

A vindictive sniper on a killing spree is the last thing Inspector Rinus Rompa from the Amsterdam Criminal Investigation Department (ACID) needs in his personal struggle to end the year sober and to cope with the expectations from colleagues, a partner with a high sex drive, a sulking ex-wife, and his disappointed teenage kids. With added pressure from the Commissioner, the media and the mayor's office to track down a sniper who won't stop killing, Rompa must dig deep to survive.

A RINUS ROMPA NOVEL (BOOK 2)

The tulips are in bloom and spring is caressing the Netherlands. In Amsterdam, streets, parks and café terraces are packed with locals and tourists getting the most out of some exceptionally mild March weather. Alas, a serial killer has chosen Holy Week and the Easter weekend to terrorise the Dutch capital, upsetting the usual atmosphere of conviviality.

Inspector Rinus Rompa, having only recently returned to the Amsterdam Criminal Investigation Department from a lengthy mental and physical rehabilitation, has, by the skin of his teeth, managed to stay sober for 110 days. His white-knuckled sobriety and fragile state of mind come under severe threat as he embarks on putting a stop to a ruthless and ferocious strangler, while having to deal with mistrust and tension at HQ, an obstinate reporter, and an increasing chaotic private life.

JEAN WESO
AMSTERDAM STALKER

A RINUS ROMPA NOVEL (BOOK 3)

A heat wave has descended upon the Netherlands. In Amsterdam, windows and doors are open around-the-clock to improve ventilation. Unwittingly, this also benefits a violent predator who is sexually assaulting women. The victims describe being attacked in their homes by a man wearing a Jason hockey mask and threatening them with a hunting knife.

On a hot July evening — two weeks into the stalker's reign — Inspector Rinus Rompa is summoned to a brutal double homicide. The stalker leaves a terrifying clue at the crime scene, indicating that he is now targeting couples.

While the Amsterdam Criminal Investigation Department struggle for a breakthrough to stop the stalker from adding to the body count, Rompa has the uneasy feeling that he and his girlfriend are also being targeted. Can he refute the evidence that if the stalker is watching, it is already too late?